C000053370

The Princess's Obligation

The Princess's Obligation

C Tarkington

Carissa Tarkington

Copyright © 2021 by C Tarkington

All rights reserved. No part of this book may be reproduced in any manner
whatsoever without written permission except in the case of brief quotations
embodied in critical articles and reviews.

First Printing, 2021

CONTENTS

1	Chapter 1	1
2	Chapter 2	10
3	Chapter 3	20
4	Chapter 4	32
5	Chapter 5	40
6	Chapter 6	47
7	Chapter 7	56
8	Chapter 8	66
9	Chapter 9	72
10	Chapter 10	83
11	Chapter 11	92
12	Chapter 12	103
13	Chapter 13	111
14	Chapter 14	120
15	Chapter 15	131
16	Chapter 16	139
17	Chapter 17	147
18	Chapter 18	157

19	Chapter 19	167
20	Chapter 20	179
21	Chapter 21	190
22	Chapter 22	202
23	Chapter 23	213
24	Chapter 24	223
25	Chapter 25	235
26	Chapter 26	250
27	Chapter 27	265
28	Chapter 28	278
29	Chapter 29	292

1

Chapter 1

King Maddoc Cadden stretched in bed as the new day's light coming through the window woke him. He turned his head and grimaced. He had not meant to fall asleep in that bed. At least not without dismissing his partner of last night's activities. She was a lovely thing with dark hair and fair skin, but he was not in the mood for any awkward morning conversations with a young handmaiden to the princess.

He carefully got out of bed, making sure to not wake the sleeping woman, and found his clothing he had left on a nearby chair. After dressing, he opened the door of the bedroom and stuck his head out to make sure no one of importance was about. Seeing the hall was empty, he opened the door and walked out into the palace hall. He wasn't sure why he cared if anyone saw him. He was the king of the largest and most powerful kingdom in the land. He could do as he pleased. Still, he had come to pay court to the Parvilian princess on his mother's recommendation, and he didn't want it to get back to the queen mother that he had been anything other than respectful and circumspect.

As he neared his rooms, he thought about the Parvilian princess. She was pretty enough with her blonde hair and blue eyes. She was tall and well-formed. Her kingdom wasn't large, but it was rich. Its army was strong. It would be a good alliance if he were to tie his kingdom to hers. She seemed mostly harmless though he noticed she could be a little catty and rude when she thought no one was paying attention. It did not matter because if he married her, he need only see her for official court business and nightly activities. He wasn't ready to enter into an agreement yet, but she was definitely a strong option for a wife. He would go back to his own kingdom and think it over.

He had time. He wasn't even twenty-three yet. He had been called a king for over ten years, but only officially ruling for two. His mother saw to leading the kingdom as he was taught by tutors and his uncle. Now he was officially the king, though his mother still advised him. In truth, she did most of the ruling of the kingdom along with his uncle. He didn't mind. Her taking care of many of the duties of the royal family left him time to do as he pleased. It gave him more time to drink with friends and bed desirable women.

As he opened the doors to the rooms he had been staying in, he was met by his main servant, Evan. "Ah, your majesty. I suppose you were up early for a morning stroll again." Evan's straight face held the hint of a smile.

"Yes, of course, Evan. I will be traveling today, and I wished to stretch my legs before I spent all day on a horse."

"I just brought your breakfast, and everything is packed and already on the wagon, heading back to Calumbria. Are you sure you do not wish to ride in the royal carriage?"

"I will travel on horseback. It will be much quicker. If I ride hard and stay one night in the forest of Lucidala, I will make it to a nice inn inside the border of our kingdom not long after nightfall the next day." Maddoc walked over to sit on a sofa to partake of his breakfast waiting for him on a low table.

"You will travel through Lucidala?"

"Yes, it will take almost two days off of my travel, much faster route."

"Faster perhaps, but you would do better to take the long road to the south and go around any borders of Lucidala. The carriage will go that way. Forget this plan and travel in the safety of the carriage, your majesty.

You will have to pass through much of this kingdom as well as Lucidala. You don't know who might be lurking about," said Evan with worry.

"I will have five of my royal guard with me including Matthias. Who could stand against a group led by him?"

"The people of Lucidala are very mysterious, your majesty. It is said they have unnatural powers."

"I have ridden in the boundaries of Lucidala before. Not deep into the kingdom, but far enough to reach some habitation. All the villages and people I passed seemed normal enough. They were simple, but there was nothing nefarious about them."

Evan shook his head. "I just worry about you being so vulnerable. When I served your father, he never was out of the royal carriage for long when traveling."

"You did serve my father, Evan, but now you serve me. My father was no doubt a careful man, but it didn't seem to help. He died at the age of only thirty-six of an infection from a cut he received while hunting in the woods." Maddoc picked up a bit of bacon. "I will not live my life in fear. I wish to ride in the open air. I have done so many times. I believe it might even be safer as it does not draw attention as riding in a well-guarded carriage does. You shall take the carriage, and I will be safe and sound in the palace before you are barely in our kingdom's borders."

"As you wish, your majesty," sighed Evan as he walked into the king's bedroom.

Maddoc changed into the clothes Evan laid out for him. He fastened his cloak around his neck as Evan packed up the clothes he had taken off. Maddoc smoothed back his black hair that fell just below his ears. He rubbed his deep blue eyes trying to clear them a little as he was tired, but that was to be expected after last night. He ran his hand over his chin. His face held a hint of stubble. He imagined he might even have a bit of beard by the time he arrived back at his own palace. He glanced in the mirror to make sure his face was clean. The dreary first weeks of fall and being mostly in the palace had made him appear even paler than usual. Seeing that he looked well enough, he turned from the mirror.

After wishing his servant a good journey, he walked from his room towards the front of the palace of Parvilia. He was met in the entryway by Princess Meira who gave him a pretty smile.

"I am sorry to see you go so soon, your majesty. I had hoped you might stay for another week or so." The princess put her hand on his arm as he came close to her.

"I cannot leave my kingdom for long periods, not this close to the harvest. I have been here almost a month altogether." Maddoc moved back a step, and her hand fell off his arm. "You will be journeying to our Winter Festival if the roads are clear. I will see you soon."

Princess Meira nodded. "I shall count the days and hope you will not mind if I write you." She looked up at him through her long lashes.

"I am not opposed to receiving messages from you, Princess Meira."

Princess Meira smiled and held out her hand. "My father is waiting to see you off outside. I wanted to wish you a safe journey."

Maddoc took her hand and kissed it. "Thank you, your highness. Until we meet again."

She took her hand back and gave him a deep curtsey as he walked away from her. He exited the palace as two guards opened the door. The King of Parvilia and several palace guards were awaiting him out on the large landing that rested in front of the palace.

"So, you are leaving us so soon, King Maddoc?" King Brone asked.

"I am. I need to get back to my kingdom. I thank you for your hospitality. I have enjoyed visiting your kingdom and becoming acquainted with you and your daughter."

King Brone nodded. "I do believe my daughter has grown very fond of you over these past weeks. You have spent much time together."

Maddoc took time to choose his words carefully. "She is a pleasant young woman. I look forward to seeing her again."

King Brone sighed slightly. "We will try our best to make it to your annual Winter Festival. If the roads are possible, we will be there. Hopefully, you will be able to further your acquaintance with the princess then."

"If it is to be, I shall look forward to it." Maddoc gave a bow. "I need to be going. Thank you again for your hospitality."

"You are very welcome any time. Tell the queen mother she is welcomed to come as well."

"I am sure she will be happy to see you and your daughter this winter. Good day, King Brone."

The king bowed and Maddoc made his way down the stairs to his large bay stallion being held by one of his own guards. He nodded to the man and mounted his horse smoothly, patting the animal once he was seated. He looked behind him to see a large man in armor, astride his own horse.

"Are we ready to go, Matthias?" asked Maddoc.

"We are when you command, your majesty," replied the large man.

Maddoc looked up at the palace before him where the king now stood with his daughter by his side. Maddoc gave them both a nod before urging his horse forward. Two guards fell into place on his sides with one riding ahead. Matthias rode just behind him with another guard. They made their way through the village, the hooves of their horses clopping on the stone streets. It was early but many villagers were out starting their day. They stood to the sides and watched as Maddoc and his guards rode through.

As they made their way out of the village and into the forest that lay ahead, Maddoc glanced back at Matthias. He knew the large guard would like to have three or four times as many men with them, but Maddoc liked to move swiftly when he traveled. He had never run into any trouble, and if he did, he doubted any man could get the upper hand on Matthias. Maddoc had chosen the head of the royal guards himself. The man was young, but he was skilled and strong.

Maddoc was a decent fighter himself. The road they were traveling on was in good repair. It ran through many lords' of Parvilia lands, and they were well patrolled and regulated. Only a short stretch of the road that ran through the kingdom of Lucidala had any kind of reputation, and he thought it was all nonsense.

Maddoc believed it was all superstition. Lucidala was a secretive kingdom, but they never seemed to cause anyone any harm. Their ruling family kept to themselves, but they never attacked any neighboring kingdoms. A few Lucidala villages even traded with the border villages of

Maddoc's kingdom of Calumbria. As long as the road was passable, he didn't think they would have any problems.

They rode on through the day, stopping periodically for quick rests and to take care of basic needs. The guards weren't very conversational, but it suited Maddoc for the journey. He had much on his mind he wanted to think over. His mother had been pressuring him to think of marrying. He thought back to the conversation they had before he had left on his journey.

"I am glad you are going to Parvilia. I think you will like the palace. It is not as large as ours, but it is comfortable," said his mother, Queen Evalin.

"I am sure it will be fine. Probably a little boring, but that is what most of royal life is."

"Hardly, your majesty." Queen Evalin shook her head, her dark curls bouncing. "I am sure the king and his daughter will entertain you. I understand that Princess Meira is charming and very beautiful. She would make you a proper queen."

"I am not sure I am ready to pick a queen, mother."

"I married your father when he was six months younger than you. He was barely twenty-three when we were blessed with you. I was only twenty."

Maddoc sighed. "I will spend time with the princess and see how I like her, mother. I cannot promise I will come back betrothed, but I will start an acquaintance. They can come to our Winter Festival and maybe things will progress by then."

His mother took his hand and kissed his cheek. "I want to see you well settled. A good queen to help you rule and see to your heirs is important."

"I know, mother. I don't know where our kingdom would be without you." He smiled at her. "I will see to my responsibility of marrying soon."

"And you will see to more of your other responsibilities as well?" Queen Evalin raised her eyebrows at him.

Maddoc gave her a wide smile. "You are so good at ruling, mother. It seems a shame to take away the duties from you."

His mother shook her head again. "You will not charm your way out of your duties, my king. I will not be able to rule forever. You need to see to all of your responsibilities. Your people wish for their king to truly rule over them."

Maddoc was taken out of thoughts by Matthias giving a command to his men to stop. "Your majesty, are you sure you do not wish to take the southern road from here? We could cut through this forest and still connect with the long road."

"Surely you are not frightened by the roads in Lucidala, Matthias? You do not believe in the nonsense people say of the Lucidalan folk?"

"No, your majesty, but it is a kingdom we have very little contact with. I am not familiar with their ways or roads. It would be safer to go south," replied Matthias.

"We shall be fine, Matthias. No one knows we are traveling this way. Any robbers we may come across can easily be overtaken by you and your men. I am not helpless either. We will take a day and a half, maybe two off of our journey going this way. The way ahead looks very well taken care of." Maddoc pointed to the road in front of them.

"Is this your command, my king? Do you wish to take the road through Lucidala?"

"Yes, Matthias. We will travel this way."

"Then may we rest here for a moment? I have two birds with us, and I would like to send one with a note to the Grand Palace to let them know the way we have come," said Matthias.

"Very well. I could use a quick rest and a bite to eat. Have your men dismount." Maddoc moved his horse to the side of the road and hopped down.

They rested for a good half hour, eating a late lunch and stretching their legs. Matthias wrote his message and sent it off with one of their messenger birds. After watering their horses, they all mounted and pressed on. It seemed to Maddoc that the guards and Matthias were moving slower than before. Perhaps they were being extra vigilant, but he thought it was all nonsense. He was anxious to step up their pace so they could make good time while they still had light.

They rode in relative silence as the afternoon wore on. The sun was just going below the trees when Matthias suddenly stopped. "Your majesty, wait a moment."

"What is it?" Maddoc turned to see Matthias moving his horse towards the forest.

"I thought I saw or heard..." Matthias quit talking mid-sentence and stopped his horse in front of the tree line of the woods.

"What is it?" Maddoc asked, but Matthias never had the chance to answer.

A line of men on horseback emerged from the trees. "Surround the king," called Matthias as the two guards on Maddoc's sides came closer to him.

The men on horseback circled around Maddoc and his guards, pushing Matthias closer to Maddoc.

"Hand over your king and no one will get hurt," said a large man who rode forward.

"You will touch our king only over my cold body," snarled Matthias.

"I'd rather it not come to that, so I will give you one more chance," said the man. "Hand over your king, and you and your men can go along."

"Come take him if you think you can." Matthias drew his sword as did the other guards. Maddoc held up his sword as well.

"Take the king alive if you can manage it," barked the man. "Kill the others."

Matthias and the guards rode forward and met the men in battle. Maddoc stayed in the middle of the circle, waiting to fight if it was needed. He watched as Matthias took out three men quickly. The other guards were doing their duty as well, and Maddoc was feeling fairly confident. He even thought they might not be delayed very long until another wave of men came out of the forest.

Maddoc felt his stomach drop and his heart beat faster. There were too many now, even for Matthias. He prepared to fight, all the while wondering if it would be better to run. He lost track of his own guards fighting as three men broke through and came towards him. He met the first one with his sword, managing to battle him and knock the man off his horse. He turned to fight the other when something hit him in his shoulder. It was a hard hit and caused him to slip on his horse.

Something hit him again and this time he fell completely from his horse, hitting his head against the hard road. He sat up slightly, feeling dizzy, his sight dim. He saw a man with a sword coming towards him, and he knew this would be the end. He felt sick at his stomach from his dizzy head. His vision was going dark around the edges, but he sat up further to try and defend himself.

He reached for his sword that was next to him and held it up. Just as the man almost reached him a blinding white light surrounded him, and he wondered if he had been killed. He felt warm and safe within the light. He dropped his sword. The light faded, and Maddoc blinked his eyes, trying to see what he could.

"Sir, are you well? Sir?" asked an urgent voice somewhere over him.

Maddoc looked trying to find the source of the voice, his head spinning and his stomach clenching. He was aware a woman was standing over him. She had lots of wavy golden hair. He tried to focus and found himself staring at the most beautiful pair of eyes he had ever seen. He thought they might have been the color of honey. He felt himself try to smile before darkness overtook him.

2

~

Chapter 2

Anwen Claran picked one of the last roses on a bush close to the bloom, making sure to avoid the thorns. She held the flower in her hand, feeling the soft petals. She looked back at the bush and placed her finger over a bloom that looked half dead. She concentrated for a moment and then sighed as her shoulders sagged.

She supposed at this point she should just stop trying, but so much in her kingdom could be fixed if she could just live into her Gift. She was said to have it, and at times she could use it in ways. Yet she was never able to fully wield her life magic, not in a way that would truly help her kingdom.

"Stop being so hard on yourself," said her companion.

"How did you know?" Anwen asked looking over to her right.

Brennan gave her a small smile. "I have known you almost all your life, Anwen. I know when you are troubled, and I know when you are upset with yourself. You cannot help how your powers have manifested. No one blames you for Lucidala's troubles."

"I think you are wrong, Brennan. I believe my aunt holds me in much blame for our continued troubles. I am sure my mother is disappointed in me as well."

"Your aunt blames everyone for the kingdom's troubles except herself. I can tell you for certain your mother does not fault you for our kingdom's lack of resources. How could she? How could anyone?"

"If I lived into my gift as was prophesied, I could end the famine that stalks our lands," sighed Anwen. "I could heal our crops, and make our livestock healthy and fat. I could save those who suffer from sickness."

"So, you would just spend all your time riding from village to village, keeping everyone's crops healthy, and seeing to anyone with a sniffle? Our kingdom's troubles are bigger than you could fix, even if your powers were fully developed."

Anwen felt the soft petals again and then let the rose drop from her hands. She stared at the beautiful flower on the ground for the moment and then looked back at the barren bush. It was barely fall. The bush should still be full of blooms, but like most things in her kingdom, it failed to thrive.

She felt much like that sad rose bush at the moment. Picked clean much too early in the season. She felt like her promise had never bloomed in full, and now she had been set aside as a sad, barren thing, never to live into what she should be. She was as useless as that half-dead rose bush.

"What can I do to make you smile, Anwen? I haven't seen you in two months, and I should dearly love to see you smile," said Brennan.

"Tell me about your journey. I want to hear all about your betrothed." Anwen took Brennan's arm, and they started walking slowly at the edge of the forest.

"I will tell you my journey was uneventful and dull. I stayed at some very clean inns and met no one interesting in any of them. Bellican is a beautiful kingdom. Their people are hospitable and generous as you can see from the supplies they are sending and will continue to send."

"Thanks to you and the alliance you have made," said Anwen with a grin.

"Thanks to your mother and her charm, you mean. By the time she left, I believe the king was quite smitten with her. I almost think he would have asked for her hand if he thought she would accept."

"Mother always leaves men half in love with her. It is a part of her own Gift, and she is very lovely."

"Yes, she is, and she has passed that loveliness down to her daughter," said Brennan looking at Anwen out of the corner of his eyes.

Anwen laughed. "Hardly, Brennan. You must see how I am nothing but a pale shadow of my mother."

"Don't be ridiculous. You are not a shadow of your mother. You are your own beautiful woman. No one could look at you and not think you are a lovely creature. You know how the young men of our village stare at you."

"I am a princess and presumed next queen of our kingdom. They see nothing but riches and a title," said Anwen waving her hand.

Brennan shook his head and laughed.

Anwen ran her free hand through one side of her long golden hair, moving it behind her shoulder. She wasn't being modest. She was not altogether unhappy with her looks. She had her mother's lovely thick golden hair and her full-lipped smile. Her small nose, which came from her father, was presentable enough. But where her mother was tall, and trim, with just the right curves, Anwen was short and thin. When he was alive, her father called her his little fairy. He said she was so dainty and small, he thought she could fly away with the wind.

"Enough with trying to flatter me. I think well enough about my own looks. Tell me about your betrothed. I want to hear you go on about the beauty of Lady Roxanna. I want you to tell me of your undying love for her."

Brennan stopped walking and looked at Anwen. He opened his mouth but hesitated.

"Go on, Brennan. Do not worry about me. You think just because I have been disappointed in love that I do not wish to hear about another's joys? I wish you to be happy. Reassure me that you love your lady and that I will like her."

"I believe you will like her. She is desperate to meet you, though she is disappointed you will not be her sister," said Brennan looking down. He kicked a pinecone on the ground and looked up at Anwen. "He is a fool, Anwen. I hope you know it."

Anwen chuckled. "He is your brother, Brennan. You cannot speak so of him."

"I can if it is the truth. Any man that would throw you over for any woman, let alone Gwendolyn, must be an idiot."

"My cousin is very beautiful, and some say she will rule instead of me. Your brother has been a friend of hers his whole life. It is no wonder his affections changed."

Brennan walked a few paces away from Anwen and looked at her. "Do not try to excuse what he has done, Anwen," he growled. "He told you he loved you. He made you promises." Brennan walked forward and took her hand. "I know he took liberties with you."

"He took nothing from me, I didn't give willingly," said Anwen with a small smile.

"Only because you loved him and believed he loved you," said Brennan pulling her closer. "I have half a mind to call him out, Anwen. He may be my brother, but it does not change the love I have for you. You have always felt much more like my sister than him my brother."

Anwen leaned down and kissed Brennan's hand. "You cannot do anything to your brother, and you know it. I would not have it. I could not bear your poor parents suffering through it."

"My parents would more than likely understand. Mother cries when she talks about it, and father can barely even look at Lachlan."

"I am sure they will understand in time. Gwendolyn is known as an impressive woman, and she will be a good wife to him. I believe your parents and you will come to care for her in time, especially if she is the queen."

Brennan shook his head. "You are too good, Anwen. In fact, I should be happy you are not marrying Lachlan. There is no way my brute of a brother deserves you." They started walking slowly again. "As far as Gwendolyn being queen, it will never be. Our people will only accept the daughter of Queen Eira. They would never accept someone like Gwendolyn, when their true princess and future ruler is as wonderful as you."

Anwen laughed. "I think you might be biased."

"No, I just see you as you truly are. I see you as most people do. You are a strong, beautiful woman who will serve her kingdom well."

Anwen sighed. "Let us not try to guess the future. Instead, let us talk of the present. Now tell me about your future wife. I would very much like to know all about her."

They walked at the edge of the woods while Brennan told Anwen all about his betrothed. She was happy to hear Brennan say his future wife was not only beautiful but kind and intelligent. He went on quite a bit about the many wonderful things about her, and it made Anwen smile. Even if he was exaggerating the future lady of his home, it showed that Brennan was very in love with Lady Roxanna.

She let her mind wander a bit as he went on and on about his love. She could not deny her heart had been broken this past year. She had always been sure of her love for Lachlan and his for her, but she had been wrong. It shook her to her core. She had determined she would not spend her life pining over a man who did not want her, but it still made her question the things she believed. It reminded her of her shortcomings. It made her doubt her future.

She had been raised the future Queen of Lucidala. She was the only child of the true queen and her king consort. Her father died ten years ago when she had just turned ten. Her mother had never married, though she had plenty of opportunities, leaving Anwen as the only heir to the throne of the Lucidian Palace. It had always been a known thing that Anwen would be the next ruler, but as her mother traveled the land looking for new alliances and supplies for her kingdom, Anwen's Aunt Roslyn seemed to have other plans.

When Queen Eira left over a year ago with her two most trusted lords and a bevy of guards, it was thought that Anwen would rule in her place. Queen Eira had instead said her trusted sister would lead as Anwen was still young and inexperienced. She hoped her daughter would grow more into who she needed to be in the next few years. Anwen was disappointed, but her mother had explained to her she did not want Anwen to have the responsibility of ruling at such a young age.

"You should spend your time being a free young woman a few more years, my dear," she said the night before she left. "Enjoy this time with your young man and your friends. When I return, you will wed, and I will start giving you're the responsibility of the throne little by little."

Now her mother had been gone for almost eighteen months, and Anwen was left alone with the knowledge there would be no wedding. Many of her friends had married and either moved or were too busy with their own wives or husbands. As Anwen listened to the happy chatter of Brennan, she felt a little sadness mix in with her joy for him. He would soon be busy with his lady, and Anwen would not be able to monopolize his time. She was not angry about it. He needed to spend most of his time with his future wife, but she would still feel the loss of his companionship.

Brennan stopped speaking and looked at Anwen. She realized he was waiting for her to say something. "And will you travel to her kingdom for the wedding?"

"Yes, at the start of spring, but she will come here for the winter festivities as long as travel is possible. She is very much looking forward to seeing Lucidala and meeting all the people I care about." He paused for a second. "I hope you will truly like her, Anwen. My greatest wish is that you will be dear friends with Roxanna. "

Anwen nodded. "Then I shall do everything I can to make her feel welcome. I hope she will like me. I would do almost anything to see you happy, Brennan. I am in every way prepared to love your wife as a sister. You and I may never truly be brother and sister as I had hoped, but that does not mean I love you or will love your wife any less."

Brennan looked pleased and opened his mouth to say something when they both turned towards the main road just through the tree line. There were noises that could only be described as men fighting. Anwen looked at Brennan who shook his head at her. She ignored him, dropped his arm, and moved towards the road.

"Anwen, don't," said Brennan as she heard him hurry to catch her.

Anwen did not stop. She ran the rest of the way and stood behind a tree. She poked her head out to see several men fighting. Three already lay on the ground, two not moving. A well-dressed man on a handsome, large horse sat still in the saddle in the center. His sword was out and ready, but he made no move to fight.

"We need to get out of here," whispered Brennan from behind Anwen. "This is none of our concern."

"It looks like those people are attacking that man and his guards." Anwen glanced behind her at Brennan. "We can't just leave them."

"They seem to be doing well enough on their own. Come on before we are seen."

Anwen almost turned to leave with Brennan when more men came out from the forest on the other side. They circled around the group, overwhelming the guards. A few broke through and rode towards the man in the middle. She watched as the man was hit with something thrown at him. He looked like he might recover when another man hit him in the shoulder with the hilt of his sword. The man fell off his horse and hit the ground hard.

Anwen shook Brennan hand off of her arm and automatically moved towards the man on the ground. Brennan yelled something, but it was lost in the buzzing that was sounding in Anwen's mind. She felt the power within her swell as a man moved towards the injured man on the ground, his sword raised. She moved out on the road and raised her hands, letting her power have its way. It moved through her in a rush, erupting in a bright, white light that moved over all of the men in front of her. She felt nothing but warmth and a want to protect the life of the defenseless man on the ground.

The light faded and Anwen felt herself sway for a moment, overcome by the energy the power had taken from her. She felt arms steady her and looked up to see Brennan staring at her with concern.

"Anwen, Anwen," he said urgently, his voice sounding distant.

She shook her head to clear it and took deep breaths. "I am well, Brennan."

He slowly let go of her as Anwen stood straighter. She looked over and saw a few men lay dead on the ground, but the rest had disappeared with their horses. The injured man lay still by his horse, and Anwen moved swiftly over to him, kneeling down.

"Sir, are you well? Sir?" she asked as she reached out to him.

He looked at her, studying her for a moment before he grinned and fell back with his eyes closed. Anwen put her hand on his chest, feeling it rise up and down. She looked over him and could see no wounds or blood. She carefully raised his head and felt a knot forming where he had hit the road.

She looked up at Brennan who was behind her. "He has a head injury. We should get him back to the palace." Brennan didn't move. He only stared down at the man. "Brennan, did you hear me? We need to get this man some help."

"Anwen, do you know who this is? I mean, I think I know, but it can't be, can it?" Brennan looked shocked, and he was rambling.

"What are you going on about?"

"Look at the standard on his shirt. Look at the sword he is carrying."

Anwen examined the man's shirt to see a large red fox surrounded by a golden circle. She traced it with her hand, remembering it was the standard of the royal family of Calumbria. "You think this man is of the Caddens? You think he is connected to the royals of Calumbria?"

"I think he is the royal of Calumbria," said Brennan softly. "Look at his sword. That is a sword of a king." Brennan slowly picked up the man's right hand and tugged his glove off. "He is wearing the fox standard ring on his hand. This has to be King Maddoc of Calumbria, Anwen."

"You think the king of the most powerful kingdom in our land was traveling through Lucidala with only a handful of guards? Why isn't he in the royal carriage or with the rest of the royal guard? If this is truly King Maddoc, why was he out traveling so vulnerable?"

"I don't know the answers to any of your questions, but this has to be the King. Who else would be dressed so or wear the royal ring?"

Anwen looked at the unconscious man as Brennan stood up. He looked very young. She didn't know much about the king, but she knew he had lost his father and come into his crown at a young age. She had heard his mother was seen as the true leader of the kingdom. She also knew his kingdom was not looked on favorably by her people.

Anwen sighed. "We can't just leave him here, Brennan. We must take him to safety and see to his injuries. We can notify his palace of his whereabouts."

"Your aunt will not like you bringing him back to the palace," said Brennan. "He will not be welcomed."

"What do you suggest we do? Should we just leave him here to be taken or die?"

"Where are his guards? Where did you send them?"

Anwen shrugged. "I'm not sure. I just told my power to protect this man. I am not sure what it did with the men who were fighting. Now come help me gently lift him. We can place him on his horse and take him directly to the palace. My aunt may be overseeing the kingdom for my mother, but the palace is still my home. I can bring back whoever I like."

Brennan didn't look like he wanted to help. Anwen straightened up and looked at him. "We cannot leave this man here to die. Our gods demand we treat every life like it is sacred. We must help him. Please, Brennan, I cannot leave him out here like this. My mother would want us to help an injured man no matter who he is. You know she would."

Brennan looked as if he would like to refuse, but he put his hand on Anwen's arm and gave it a light squeeze. He nodded and bent down to pick up the king.

"Be careful, and mind his head," instructed Anwen as she gently held the king's head while Brennan lifted the man and placed him over his shoulder. King Maddoc was a tall, well-built man, but Brennan was strong. Brennan took him over to the king's horse as Anwen held the bridle, keeping the stallion still. She stroked his nose as Brennan positioned the king over the saddle.

They walked slowly together, Anwen making sure the king's head did not bounce too much against his horse as Brennan led the animal.

"Thank you, Brennan," said Anwen as they walked. "I know this is not something you wish to do."

"It is not, but you are correct in this is the right thing to do." Brennan gave a small smile. Besides, who I am to ignore an order from my future queen."

Anwen smiled back at Brennan and fell back to check on the king. She hoped his injuries weren't too serious, and that she could see him out of her kingdom before long. She would like to think her aunt would be understanding of the situation, but she didn't dare believe it.

3

Chapter 3

Maddoc groaned and stretch in the bed he lay. He struggled to open his eyes, his head feeling heavy and sore. His eyes opened slowly, and he looked around trying to figure out where he was. It looked to be a good-sized bedroom. The bed underneath him was large and soft. The furniture that he could see looked fine. A number of candles burned on the table beside him, and he could see a window to his left. It looked like it was dark outside, and he wondered what time it was.

He slowly sat up, his hand going to the back of his head where there was a slight pounding. He groaned feeling an ache in his back and limbs. He tried to focus his mind and think what could have happened. He remembered he was riding with his guards when they were attacked. They had been overwhelmed, and he had fallen from his horse. He truly believed he was going to die as a man had come at him with a sword, but he had not died. There had been a light, and he remembered a woman. Had that been real?

He rubbed his head gently as the door to the bedroom opened and two men walked in with a woman. One man was carrying a tray with food and a cup. The smell of the food made Maddoc realize how hungry he was. The other man held two bottles.

"Oh good, you are awake," said the woman who was walking behind the men. "Please set the tray and bottles on the table next to the bed." The servants did as she asked and looked at the woman. "You may go. I will call you if you are needed for anything else."

The two men both looked at each other. One moved towards her a few steps. "Your highness, shouldn't at least one of us stay?"

The princess smiled. "I think I will be safe with an injured man in my own palace. Leave the door ajar if you like. The Lucidian guards are patrolling the hallways. I am sure if I scream, they could be in here rather quickly. Now go, and see to your duties. I have kept you long enough."

The two men bowed and left the room. Maddoc looked up at the woman as she came closer to him. She had long, wavy golden hair that almost reached her waist. She looked small and delicate. He doubted she would come up to his shoulders. She wore a deep blue gown that showed how diminutive her figure was, though she was not without curves he noticed. She had a very pretty face with full lips and a small nose.

She smiled at him as she approached the bed, and he was immediately drawn to her eyes. He had seen them right before he had blacked out. They were bright light brown, almost golden. He had thought they were the color of honey, but they were richer. They almost seemed to sparkle. He believed they transformed her pretty, dainty face into something beyond beautiful.

"How are you feeling, your majesty?" she asked as she stood by his bedside.

"I am sore, my head hurts, and I am a little confused. Can you tell me where I am?"

"You are in the Lucidian Palace of Lucidala in the village of Awbrey. Your small group was overtaken by some rather rough men. You were injured so I and my companion brought you here to keep you safe."

"And you are?" asked Maddoc as he glanced at the stew and bread on the tray next to him.

"I am Princess Anwen Claran, the daughter of our Queen, Elia Claran," she responded with a small curtsey. "You should eat. You must be hungry. It has been many hours since you fell from your horse."

Maddoc sat up further and grabbed the tray from the table. He started to eat as the princess sat in a chair close to him. "What of my guards? Did any of them survive the attack?"

"I am not sure," she responded as she adjusted her skirt.

"What do you mean you are not sure?"

"When you were attacked, I am afraid my power acted on its own. It sent all of the men attacking you and your guards somewhere. I believe it was to each of their own homes, but I can't be sure. I try to control it, but my power seems to have a mind of its own sometimes."

Maddoc swallowed the stew in his mouth and looked up at the princess in confusion. "Your power?"

"Yes, my Gift is supposed to be life-giving, but all it has really manifested as is lifesaving. I can protect people in need, but as far as healing or giving life, it has never worked out."

Maddoc looked at her as he picked up the warm bread. She must have seen the confusion on his face because she laughed a little.

"I guess you do not know much about Lucidala or my family, your majesty."

"Your kingdom has long been a mystery to my people, and I would say most of the land. You hide away here in secret. How can I know anything about you?"

"I suppose we do not have much contact with you and your people, but we do not hide away as you say," said the princess sounding a little annoyed. "I think it is more correct to say most of your kingdom avoids us because of fear."

Maddoc took a bite of the bread and stared at her while he chewed. After he swallowed, he asked, "So, this Gift you are speaking of. Do all your people have one?"

"Everyone has a gift to share with the world, but no, my people do not share the Gift of our gods anymore. Only the royal family still has it. All the Claran's have some sort of power. My mother's is allure and charm. My aunt's is discernment and a smidgen of mind reading. I believe my cousin is a bit of a clairvoyant though she has never taken time to practice much. Work of any kind isn't really something she enjoys."

"And you are a life-giver?"

The princess sighed. "That was what our clerics defined me as when I was born, but I have never lived into my calling no matter how hard I work. All I am able to do is protect those who are in real danger. When my power saw you in need, it reacted."

Maddoc chewed on a bit more bread, not really sure what to say. This all sounded so unlikely, and he wondered if his head injury had been bad enough to make him hallucinate. The woman in front of him hardly seemed real. Everything about her was almost ethereal. Her hair was far too golden and perfect. Her skin looked much too soft, and her eyes were too beautiful to be real. He had never seen eyes like that on any person.

"You seem confused," said the princess. "I suppose this is a lot to take in for you, and I am sure your head must be hurting. You should finish your supper, and then you can take the medicine our healers have recommended. Once you are rested, we can deal with everything in the morning. We can find a way to get you home."

Maddoc's head was throbbing, and he was very tired. Perhaps if he did as she asked, he would sleep and awake to find himself in an inn or maybe even back in his own palace. This all had to be some strange dream. He took another bite of stew and nodded. Once he was done with his food, the princess took his tray and put it to the side. She measured out some liquid from the bottles and mixed it with some wine.

"Drink this and it will help with the pain. It will make you groggy, but sleep will be the best thing for you. I guarantee your safety. I have guards patrolling the hallways, and no matter how much my aunt blusters, she will not eject you from the palace in the middle of the night."

"Your aunt?" asked Maddoc as she passed him the cup.

"Yes, my mother left her in charge of the day-to-day ruling of the kingdom. My mother is out on a journey. My aunt does not like you being here, but almost anything displeases her. Do not trouble yourself. Drink up, and sleep well."

Maddoc drank from the cup to find the wine sweet and smooth. He took another drink, and then another, emptying the cup quickly. The princess stood up and took it from him. He immediately started feeling tired.

"Sleep well, your majesty." said the princess as Maddoc lay back in the bed.

He tried to thank her, but sleep overtook him. He supposed it didn't really matter. There was no use thanking someone that couldn't be real.

When he next woke up the room was bright with sunlight pouring in from the windows. Maddoc sat up slowly as he opened his eyes. It took him a moment to remember where he was, and he was a little surprised to find himself still in the large unfamiliar bedroom. He had been sure his encounter last night had been a dream, and he was still unsure that all of it was real.

He pushed down the covers to see he was dressed in some comfortable pants and a shirt that was not his own. He looked around for his clothes, but they did not seem to be in the room. As he slowly stood up off the bed, the door to his bedroom opened and an older man stepped in holding a bundle of clothes. Behind him was another man holding a tray of food.

"Your majesty," said the man with a bow. "Princess Anwen has requested that I assist you in dressing. I have brought breakfast as well, but you should eat quickly. Princess Roslyn wishes to speak with you directly."

"Princess Roslyn?" said Maddoc, shaking his head.

"She is ruling the kingdom while our queen is away. She would like to see you directly in the throne room."

Maddoc cocked his head and looked at the man. He wasn't used to being told to do anything. No one told him what to do, except for his mother and uncle. They both knew how well it worked to tell him to do something, but they still tried. Maddoc looked over at the food on the tray that was placed on the table near him. He slowly took some bacon off the tray and looked up at the man who still held his clothes.

"And you are?"

"I am James, your majesty. I oversee the queen's household and was once the head servant to the king. I have come to help you dress, and see to any other needs you might have. Some water will be brought soon for you to clean as you like."

Maddoc nodded as he swallowed his food. "You can leave the clothes there on that chair. Once the water is here you can go and see to your duties. I have no need of assistance."

"Are you sure, your majesty? The princess did ask me to assist you, and I would not like to disappoint her."

"You can tell your princess, I dismissed you with my thanks. Surely, she will not punish you for that?"

"Punish me?" said the older man with a small laugh. "No, your majesty, I will not be punished. I just do not like to disappoint Princess Anwen. She is rather a favorite of mine, of all of us servants actually."

Maddoc looked at the man as he ate a piece of toast. He wondered if all servants in this palace were so familiar. Perhaps this man was bolder due to his position. His own head servant could be very outspoken at times.

"Do you happen to know if my horse was brought in safely?"

"Yes, your majesty. The princess saw to his care herself. She is very fond of horses. He is currently in the palace stables, safe and sound."

Maddoc nodded again. "You mean this Princess Roslyn?"

The man actually laughed at him. "No, your majesty. I am speaking of Princess Anwen, our future queen."

Maddoc huffed, feeling annoyed. "And has a letter been sent to my mother in Calumbria?"

James hesitated. "I cannot say, your majesty. I am sure you will know as soon as you meet with Princess Roslyn who is currently waiting for you in the throne room."

"She can wait a bit while I enjoy my breakfast and take the time to look presentable," said Maddoc a little harsher than he intended. This man hadn't really done anything to him. He had only offered to help him. "I will finish my breakfast and dress directly."

James nodded but didn't say anything further. Once he had seen to the warm water in the washbowl with a clean towel nearby, he bowed and left the room. Maddoc took care of his needs, cleaned up, and dressed. He walked out of the room to be met by two guards who said they would escort him to the throne room. Maddoc nodded and followed the guards down the hall.

As he walked through the palace, he noticed it was a beautiful place full of windows that let in light. There were many handsome portraits on the walls of beautiful women wearing crowns on golden heads, and men wearing long flowing robes. Everything appeared well taken care of, and while it didn't seem to be as large as his own home, it was not unsubstantial.

The guards took him downstairs and stopped at a pair of wooden double doors. One of them knocked twice and the doors opened from the inside. Maddoc took a few steps back as they opened and peered inside. The room was large but mostly empty. He followed the guards inside to find himself walking towards a raised dais. On the dais was a large throne that almost looked like it was made from some strange tree. The top of it had branches carved on it with golden leaves painted. On this throne sat a beautiful woman. He guessed she was a little younger than his mother, but he couldn't really tell. She had blonde hair that was pulled up. Her eyes were a startling green. She wore a golden dress and a long flowing red robe. She held a long golden staff that was decorated with golden leaves down the length of it. On top was a red jewel.

Maddoc stopped once he got close to the dais and looked at the others who stood around this woman. On one side was a younger woman that must have been the lady on the throne's daughter. She was almost an exact copy with long blonde hair and green eyes. She was tall and had a beautiful figure clothed in a red flowing dress. Next to her was a strong-looking man. His light brown hair almost reached his shoulders. His brown eyes were fixed on Maddoc, and there was a small smirk on his full lips. Maddoc instantly didn't like him.

He turned his eyes away from the man to the other side of the dais to find the woman in his supposed dream was very real after all. She was just a petite as he remembered, looking very small next to the regal couple on the other side of the throne. Still, she stood proudly and seemed to radiate strength. Her golden hair was down, and her bright honey-colored eyes twinkled as she gave Maddoc a small grin. He almost smiled back at her but instead turned his eyes on the woman seated on the throne.

"Are you King Maddoc Cadden of Calumbria?" asked the woman.

"I am," replied Maddoc. "Who am I speaking with?"

"I am Princess Roslyn originally of the house of Claran. I have been appointed as overseer of this kingdom until our queen returns." She looked to the couple on her left. "This is my daughter, Princess Gwendolyn, and her betrothed Lachlan Dunne." She smiled at them both as Gwendolyn curtsied and Lachlan bowed." She looked to her left with a frown. "I believe you are already acquainted with my niece, Princess Anwen."

Maddoc bowed as the princess gave a very pretty curtsy. He looked back to Princess Roslyn.

"Why were you passing through Lucidala, King Maddoc?" asked Princess Roslyn.

"I was on my way back to my own kingdom after visiting the kingdom of Parvilia," replied Maddoc.

"I thought you and your people always took the southern route to avoid our borders." Rosalyn moved her cane to her other hand.

"It is much shorter to pass through your kingdom. Your roads seem in good repair, and I know of no harm in Lucidala. It seems I was wrong."

Princess Roslyn gave a small sneer. "Are you suggesting our kingdom was responsible for your troubles on the road?"

"It was on your roads in which I was attacked. Maybe you should have your lands better patrolled for thieves."

"A rather rude thing to say after we have offered you hospitality," said Princess Roslyn with a huff. "What do you suppose would have happened to you had my niece not interfered?"

The way Princess Roslyn said the word interfered made Maddoc believe the lady had wished Princess Anwen had left him to his own fate. "I am not sure, but I am grateful to the princess for seeing to my well-being. I am thankful for the night spent in your palace, but it does not change the fact I was attacked on your roads."

"I do not wish to spend all day arguing with you over the fault of your unfortunate accident. You should head back to your own kingdom. You seem well enough. Your horse can be made ready quickly, and you should leave within the hour." Princess Roslyn paused for a moment. "We will provide you with enough supplies to get you to your own border."

Princess Anwen's head turned towards Princess Roslyn "Aunt, would it not be better to let the king stay here and send out a letter to his palace. They could send a carriage and guards to bring their king back safely."

"I do not wish him here another day. You know the feelings our people have about his kingdom. They have ignored the troubles and misfortunes of their neighbor for many years. He will need to leave today."

Maddoc took a small step back and looked at Princess Roslyn. "We have ignored your misfortunes? I have heard nothing of your troubles. If you have asked for our aide, I am not aware of it."

"But many of your court and family are, King Maddoc, and you have done nothing to help us. You have an old debt to our kingdom, yet your family has long brushed it aside. We live in peace because we must, but there is no love for your kingdom here. You will need to leave as soon as possible," commanded Roslyn.

"Send some guards with him, Aunt," suggested Princess Anwen. "He cannot go out unprotected. No matter what you think of his kingdom, his life is of value, and it should be protected. Our gods demand it."

"We cannot spare any guards at the moment. They are all seeing to the protection of this palace and the needs of our people. The king's safety is not of our concern." Princess Rosalyn gave a soft snort.

Princess Anwen shook her head. "This is not the way of our gods, and it is not what my mother would want."

"Your mother is not here, cousin," snapped Princess Gwendolyn. "My mother is the one in charge, and you should be silent and listen to her."

"I am the future queen of this kingdom, and I will speak my mind," said Princess Anwen as she stared at Princess Gwendolyn.

"Are you so sure in your future position?" smirked Princess Gwendolyn.

Anwen narrowed her eyes at the woman. "I will not see King Maddoc be sent out of my palace unprotected. The value of his life will not be so disregarded by this royal court."

Roslyn turned her head to look at Anwen. "You are overstepping, princess. I have made my decision, and you will abide by it. The king shall leave within the hour on his horse with a few days of supplies. That is the end of it."

"Then I shall go with him and see to his safety myself," said Princess Anwen furiously. She glared at her aunt and walked down the stairs of the dais. She came to stand by Maddoc's side. "I will travel with the king and see that he is safely back in his kingdom."

Maddoc looked down at her. "This is not necessary, Princess. I can ride hard and reach my borders in less than two days. I can find an inn there and alert my palace."

"It is necessary as I will not have you sent from the palace with no protection." Anwen looked up at him with her mouth set in a straight line and her eyes flashing.

He gave her a small lopsided smile as he looked down at her. "You think you can offer me protection?"

"I already have, or have you already forgotten yesterday?" The princess folded her arms and stared at him.

He shook his head as Princess Roslyn spoke. "Anwen, this is ridiculous. You cannot go running off into the kingdom and elsewhere. What would your mother say?"

"She would say I am doing my duty since her sister cannot," shot Princess Anwen.

Roslyn sat back in her chair with a nasty look on her face, but it was Gwendolyn who spoke. "How dare you speak to my mother that way. You are nothing but an insignificant disappointment to your kingdom."

"And you are nothing but a selfish, spoiled, simpleton who thinks she can get through life with nothing but a pretty face and an empty head." Princess Anwen gave a short laugh.

"Enough!" shouted Princess Roslyn. "Anwen, you will not go and that is final. The king will leave within the hour and that is the end of it."

"I will go, aunt, and you cannot stop me. I am free to do as I please."

"I can and will stop you," replied Princess Roslyn.

"How? Do you think the royal guard will really take your commands over mine? Would you like to try and find out?" Princess Anwen walked closer to the dais. "I know you think you are well settled in your position and that your daughter will follow you, but soon my mother, the true queen will be home. When she hears how you have treated a guest on our lands, she will be furious. I doubt she will let you or your spoiled daughter stay in this palace."

"Silence," roared Princess Roslyn. She stood up and looked down at Anwen. "Fine, go with this king if you wish."

"Your highness," said Lachlan disbelievingly. "You cannot mean it. This cannot be wise."

"No, it is not wise, but when has our little princess ever made the right choice for herself or her kingdom. She shall go since she wishes it. Perhaps if she doesn't come back, it will be best for our kingdom."

Gwendolyn gave a little laugh as Lachlan walked forward. "Anwen, you cannot do this."

Anwen gave him a short glare and then turned, grabbing Maddoc's arm. "Come along, your majesty. We need to prepare."

Maddoc stalled for a moment looking at Roslyn. He gave a nasty smile and a half bow. "Thank you for your hospitality, your highness. I will not forget your *kindness.*"

He walked out with the princess. She looked at him as they exited the room. "Go back to the room you were in, and I will send James to you with some clothes so you can prepare."

"I am already dressed, Princess," stated Maddoc.

"You are dressed like a king, and that will not do for our journey," she said as they turned towards the hallway. "I hope you do not mind me saying it, but you seem very naïve for your position. You will have to learn quickly if you want to survive very long as the king of the highest kingdom in our land."

They walked up the stairs together to the second floor. When they got to the top she stopped. "I will go change and meet you downstairs in the entry hall in one hour. Dress in whatever James brings you. I will see to our horses and supplies. Now hurry, your majesty. I want to make good time while the sun is still up."

With that she turned and walked away, making Maddoc wonder how he had just allowed such a little thing to order him so.

4

⌒

Chapter 4

Anwen hurried down to the entryway, hoping she had not kept the king waiting. She had instructed James and several guards to not let the king be alone at any time. She did not want him sneaking away, or her aunt ordering him out of the palace before Anwen could join him. It was clear the poor man had no idea how to see to his own safety.

What had he been thinking, traveling out in the open dressed as he was with only a small guard? Why had he been allowed to do it? She guessed maybe the king's commands were final to his people no matter how foolish they were. She would make sure he was safe this time. She would keep him hidden and see him to his kingdom by traveling off the main roads. It would take some time, but her only goal was to keep him safe.

She wasn't sure why she felt so compelled to protect King Maddoc. He felt like her obligation though she owed him nothing. Still, her power had seen to his protection. It had saved his life, and she would see him safe as much as she could. It was also her duty as a leader of her kingdom and a follower of her gods. Life was precious, and she would treat his as such. There was a small thought in the back of her mind that if she could help the king perhaps, he might help her kingdom.

She had long felt guilty for the problems in Lucidala. For some reason, their crops would not grow as they should. Their livestock would not flourish, and sickness seemed to spread very easily. If Anwen lived into the fullness of her powers she could give life to the crops. She could see the livestock healthy and fat. She would be able to heal those who were sick with just a touch. Instead, she was nothing, but a half-grown princess with half-developed powers.

Others had tried to tell her it wasn't her fault. Her mother had said Anwen had the powers she was meant to have. She had told Anwen she was how the gods made her, and it was enough. Brennan had told her over and over again that she was not to blame for Lucidala's troubles. He had reassured her when the time came, she would be a good and worthy queen.

A time not so long ago, Lachlan had made her believe in herself. He had told her she was beautiful and strong. He had made her feel desirable and powerful, but it had all been a lie. Once he became aware her much more beautiful cousin, Gwendolyn wanted him, his affections changed almost overnight. The past spring, he announced his betrothal to Gwendolyn, acting as if he had never made Anwen any promises. She heard rumors that he said Anwen was nothing but a youthful dalliance.

If her mother had been around, he never would have spoken so. Now Anwen felt like a fool. She tried to put it all out of her mind and not let it affect her, but when she was alone and all was quiet, she would think what an unwanted, stupid girl she really was.

She shook her head. She could not think so at the moment. She could not appear or feel weak. She needed to be strong and confident in dealing with the king. She doubted he would let her order him around so once they were away from her palace. She saw the look on his face when she told him to change clothes. Anwen imagined she would have her hands full as she traveled with the king.

She reached the entry hall to find not King Maddoc waiting for her, but Lachlan. She sighed and shook her head, wanting nothing more than to turn around and wait at the stairs for King Maddoc to appear. She kept walking, knowing she had to get used to seeing Lachlan. He was marrying her cousin, and he would be brought into the family.

She walked into the entry hall and nodded to Lachlan as he moved towards her. He looked as if he would take her hand, but Anwen stepped back and crossed her arms, glaring at him.

"Anwen, this is madness. You must not go," said Lachlan looking down at her.

She kept her eyes on him, thinking about how she once found him so handsome. How his face was at one time her favorite thing to look at now. Now it only made her feel angry and unsettled. "I will go because it is the right thing to do."

He moved a step closer to her. "Do you not see how dangerous this is? You will be alone with this king we know nothing about. He was already attacked once, and we don't know by who. It will probably happen again."

"It could if the proper precautions are not taken. Which is why I must travel with him. I have to see him safely back to Calumbria."

"Why? Why does it have to be you?" asked Lachlan.

"Because my aunt has made it so. She will not allow royal guards to go. I know they will go if I ask it, but I will not let them be censured by her because of me. I will go with the king, and I will see him safe."

"But who will see you safe?" he asked as he looked down at her with a tenderness that made her stomach turn. How dare he look at her like that. She turned away. "Anwen, I cannot bear to think of you in danger. Please, reconsider."

She turned back to him with a slight hiss. "You have no right to think of me at all. You gave up that right when you pledged yourself to Gwendolyn."

He shook his head and moved even closer to her. "You think I can so easily forget what I felt for you," he whispered. "You think I could forget the times we spent together, what we shared?"

She looked up at him, wondering if he was trying to play some kind of trick on her. "How can you speak so to me after what you have said about me? I heard what you have assured my cousin. I was nothing more than some youthful infatuation." She paused and swallowed. "Once you got what you wanted from me, it was enough."

"Anwen," he said in pain. "You must know those were not my words. Your cousin had to say something to save face. She cannot think that I would ever love you over her."

"But you do. You are marrying her, and you will be her husband."

"That does not mean I love her, Anwen. It does not mean my heart does not still belong to you." Lachlan reached out and put his hand on her arm. He tried to bring her closer to him, but she stepped back and shook his arm off.

"I don't know what you are trying to do, Lachlan, but it will not work. If your betrothed or my aunt sent you in here to try to stop me from going, you should know your choice of persuasion is cruel, and it will not work."

"Anwen, please..." started Lachlan, but he was cut off by the sound of someone entering the space.

Anwen turned to see King Maddoc walking into the room wearing a simple shirt and britches. He looked at her and Lachlan with raised eyebrows. "Am I interrupting something? Should I go on outside or leave and come back?"

Anwen glared at Lachlan before turning to the king. "No, your majesty, you are interrupting nothing. I am ready to go." He nodded to her and they walked to the door together.

"Anwen," Lachlan spoke with such tenderness in his voice it made her turn around.

She swallowed and looked at him. "Tell your betrothed and my aunt I will write as soon as I have seen the king safe. Let your brother know I will not be gone long and will be back in time to meet his own betrothed. Goodbye, Lachlan."

She gave a shallow curtsey in her simple dark traveling dress and nodded to the king. They walked out the doors together. Their two horses stood outside the palace, both saddled and ready. Anwen walked up to her large dark mare as a guard came forward. He helped her to mount, and she threw her leg over the saddle, her skirt hiking up a bit to show the tight pants she wore underneath. The king, who stood close by, gave her what she thought was a disapproving look, but she ignored him. If he thought she was going to ride side saddle for days, he was very wrong.

As the king walked over to his own horse, Anwen adjusted her long braid against her shoulder. She reached down and patted her horse before picking up the reins. She looked behind her and saw the king was settled in his saddle. As she was preparing to urger her horse forward, Lachlan walked out of the palace. She glanced at him before snapping her reins causing her horse to move forward. She led the king and his horse out towards the main road.

As she was passing through the gate of the place to enter the village of Awbrey she saw Brennan standing on the side. He stared up at her in dismay. She almost stopped to speak with him but was afraid she would lose her nerve to go on the journey. She steadied herself and looked down at him, giving him a small smile and a nod. He jogged beside her for a moment, looking as if he wanted to say something, but he eventually stopped and waved at her. She held her tears back and put her eyes forward, towards the end of the village and out into the forest of the kingdom.

Once they got to the main road, she turned to the left. As she rode, she looked for the little path to the side she knew existed that would take them deep into the forest. She finally saw it next to two honeysuckle bushes that had long lost their blooms for the season. She turned her horse towards it when she heard the king speak.

"Where are you going?"

"On to this path so we can continue our journey," answered Anwen as she drew up her horse and looked at the king who rode to her side.

"The main road continues this way, and my kingdom is only a day and a half ride from here."

"The main road is too dangerous for you, as you saw before. It will be much safer to take the paths through the forest. Hardly anyone uses them, and you are unlikely to be spotted," explained Anwen.

"How long does this way take to reach Calumbria?"

"We can reach the outermost village in your kingdom in four maybe five days, your majesty," replied Anwen.

"That long?" scoffed King Maddoc. "We will do much better to ride quickly on the main road. If we do not stop much in the night, we can be safe and sound at an inn in my kingdom in a day and a half."

"You want to ride through the darkness on a road on which you have already been attacked? Forgive me, your majesty, but that is simply idiotic. We will take every precaution for your safety and go this way," said Anwen emphatically. "I will have it no other way."

The king's horse paced a bit, moving backward as the king seem to grow angry. "Who are you to tell me what to do?"

"Only the woman who saved your life," said Anwen with a small laugh. "I will not let that action go to waste. I insist we go this way, your majesty. I am not doing so to inconvenience you or usurp your authority. I am doing it to see you safely to your home."

The king took a deep breath and wiped his face with one gloved hand. He seemed to be considering what to say next. "Very well, we shall do this your way as it seems you have the supplies on your own horse, and I would not like to spend the next few days hungry."

The princess gave another small laugh. "Thank you for your cooperation, your majesty," she said sarcastically. "Your magnanimous spirit knows no bounds."

She moved her horse forward, and the king road alongside her on the small path. As they journeyed forward, she could see him glance at her every so often. She finally turned to him. "Is there something you wish to say, your majesty?"

"Some conversation would not be unwelcomed."

"What is it you wish to speak of?" asked Anwen.

"I am sorry if I did interrupt something back there. I know you say I didn't, but I feel as if I did. It seemed you and your cousin's intended were having quite a conversation."

"It was nothing, just as I said," replied Anwen. "He had nothing to say that I wanted to hear."

King Maddoc was quiet for a moment. "It sounded as if he is very fond of you."

Anwen sighed. "If you wish for conversation on this journey, this topic will get you nowhere."

"Pity, I rather like hearing about family drama."

"Then perhaps you could tell me about yours?" snapped Anwen.

"Oh, there is plenty. Would you like to hear about my uncle's displeasure when my mother took over as ruler of the kingdom after my father died? Or do you wish to know about the arguments between my mother, my uncle, and the whole court about who I should take as a bride?"

"Do you have a say in that argument?"

"About whom I take as a bride?" asked the king with amusement. Anwen nodded. The king looked to be in thought for a few seconds. "I suppose I do in a way. I have been given the names of a few young women the court and my mother deem appropriate. As long as I choose from those names, I do have a say."

"Then I hope you find one of those young ladies to your liking, and I doubly hope she likes you. I dare say I even hope you find love."

King Maddoc laughed. "Love? I hardly think love has anything to do with who I pick as my queen."

"You wish to be married to someone for your whole life without loving her?" asked Anwen in disbelief. She shook her head. "That sounds rather sad and unfulfilling, your majesty."

"Did your parents marry because of love, princess?"

"Yes, they did. My father came from his kingdom and courted my mother for six months before she agreed to marry him. They were very much in love." Anwen looked at the king and then down at her horse. "When he died of sickness, my mother almost didn't get over it. She said if it wasn't for me, she was afraid she would not have been able to go on."

"I don't think my parents spent more than five minutes a day together most of the time," said the king quietly. "When my father died, my mother went on as if nothing had happened."

"And that is the life you would like for yourself?" asked Anwen.

King Maddoc shrugged. "I haven't really thought about it. As long as my wife does her duties as queen, and doesn't repulse me so we can produce an heir, I shall be satisfied."

Anwen looked at him, feeling a bit of pity. If this was all he knew of life, marriage, and love, how could she expect him to do any different than those kings who had come before him? "I wish you luck in your endeavor to find a queen, then."

He gave her a small, crooked smile. "What about you, your highness. Are you betrothed?"

"I am not."

"So, no young lord in your kingdom or some foreign prince has caught your eye? Has no one come to pay court to you?"

Anwen looked away for a moment. She thought of Lachlan and how sure she had been she would spend her life with him, very much in love with her husband. She thought of the heartache she had endured the past year. She remembered the pain she felt every time she saw him with her cousin.

"Princess, if I have offended you..." started the king.

She looked up and smiled at him. "No, you have not offended me at all, your majesty. In fact, I think you might be on to something with your ideas of marriage."

He looked at her as though he would like to say more, but instead, he only nodded, and they rode on together in silence as the forest became denser around them.

5

～～

Chapter 5

Maddoc looked over at the princess riding next to him. He wasn't sure what to make of her. He could usually tell almost immediately his feelings about someone, but the princess had him perplexed. She seemed intelligent. She certainly liked to speak her mind. He could tell she was probably kind. She spoke to most people with respect and gentleness. She was harsh with her aunt and cousin, but he could hardly blame her for it especially when she was doing so in defense of him.

At times she seemed very sure of herself. She would order Maddoc around as though he was not the king of the most powerful kingdom in the land. She did not shy away from telling him almost any opinion, and she certainly didn't seem to be trying to merit his favor. He realized most people he met were careful in their words and actions around him. Those outside of his family seemed to be determined to please him. Princess Anwen seemed as if she didn't care what Maddoc thought of her. He believed she said what she said because she believed it. He found it made him trust her even on their short acquaintance.,

He studied her for a while as they rode along. She was very beautiful. Even with her smaller frame and height, he couldn't deny he found her pleasant to look at. She wasn't the usual type that attracted him. He liked tall women with elegant figures. The princess looked so small and dainty that he was afraid she would break if he tried to hold her too tight.

Her hair looked luxurious even woven in its braid. The color of it went well with her skin. She did have a lovely face with her full mouth and clear complexion. Above all, it was her eyes that made Maddoc believe she might be one of the most beautiful creatures he had ever beheld. They were large and framed in dark lashes. The color was one he had been trying to describe in his head since he met her.

Maddoc could not deny he was intrigued with the princess riding by his side. Her beauty, intelligence, and boldness were a combination that made him feel he was not truly angry to be traveling with her. The length of the journey ahead of him did cause annoyance, but her presence almost made up for it. At least he had someone pleasant to look at and entertaining to talk to as a companion.

"Do you need something, your majesty?" asked the princess as she turned to look at him. "I can't help but see you keep looking over this way."

Maddoc tried to keep from coloring, knowing he had been caught staring at her. How silly that he should blush at all. He was a king and could look at whoever he wished whenever he wished it. "You have been quiet for a long time. I was wondering if you had grown tired of my company already."

The princess gave a short chuckle. "I am sure it is not right that I should admit being tired of a king's company, especially one as highly positioned as you."

Maddoc couldn't help but smile at her. "You are a princess and future queen yourself. I am sure you like things your own way. If you are tired of my company after half a day, you may say so. What could I really do to you at this point? I am at your mercy traveling this way."

She truly laughed this time, and Maddoc found he liked the sound of it. "Your presence does not bother me, your majesty, truly."

"Is it the journey then? I am taking you away from your family and friends. You must be sad to be away from your home for at the very least a few weeks."

She sighed. "You see how my family is. Until my mother returns, I do not mind being gone from the palace. Most of my friends have left the area or married. My best friend is to be married this spring. His future wife is coming to Awbrey at the start of winter. I should be back in plenty of time to meet her."

"So, you truly do not have a young man waiting for you in the village?"

She turned away from him, and her eyes lost some of their sparkle. "No." After a moment, she looked up, seeming to try to appear merrier than she felt. "I am young, and I see no reason to rush into any commitments. I have plenty to keep me busy at home, and now I have a nice journey ahead of me into a kingdom I have visited but little."

He nodded as she looked over at the forest on her other side. He had heard more of her conversation in the palace entryway with that man called Lachlan than he probably should have. When he heard them talking, he had paused just outside the entry hall. He had only walked in when the pain in her voice compelled him to move forward. He wasn't sure why, but he did not like her sounding so sad and defeated.

It seemed she had a history with the man, and he had thrown Princess Anwen over for her cousin. He wondered the reasons why. If the man was to be believed, then he was still in love with the princess. Of course, he could have just been trying to keep her from leaving with Maddoc. He could have been sent there by his betrothed's mother. It was a cruel way to trick the princess into staying, but it could have been effective on a weaker mind. Maddoc had a feeling the princess's mind was very strong.

He looked over at the princess to see her still watching the tree line. That was the problem with love if it even really existed. To love someone meant you would experience pain at some point. Everyone left whether by choice, death, or some other reason. If you placed too much care in one person, you were in danger of being lost yourself. His mother and uncle had taught him that marriage was a duty. It was nothing but an arrangement with someone else. Feelings of love or anything else did not need to be a part of it, and in truth, they shouldn't be. Maddoc owed his allegiance to himself and his kingdom. Some stupid notion of the love of woman could never become a distraction.

The princess pulled up her horse, and Maddoc stopped his as well.

"This looks like a good place to rest a moment," she said as she guided her horse slowly towards a patch of brown grass next to a stream.

Maddoc followed her. He dismounted and walked over to help the princess. By the time he got to her side, she had already hopped down. He watched as she pulled up her skirt a bit and adjusted her tight pants underneath. He knew the polite thing to do would be to turn away, but instead, he watched her with interest.

She looked up at him, and her face grew red. "I am sorry if I offend you with my manner of dress and the way I ride my horse, your majesty, but it is such a long journey for side saddle."

Maddoc cocked his head and looked at her. She thought him offended? Why would she being comfortable in the saddle offend him? When he saw her hitch up her skirts and straddle her horse, he had thoughts in his head that definitely did not offend him, though they might her.

"You can rest assure, I am not offended, princess." Maddoc walked back to his horse and took him by the bridle.

"You looked rather scandalized when we began our journey," said the princess leading her own horse towards the stream. "I am sure no ladies or princesses you have come across would ride in such a way."

Maddoc left his horse by the stream to drink and walked back to the clearing. "Perhaps not, but I don't believe you are like other ladies and princess I have met. You do not have the same intentions that they do."

The princess gave him a questioning look as she sat down a bag she had taken off of her horse.

"The young ladies I meet who are high born have only one thought in mind, and that is to be my queen. The other ladies I meet, well, they have only one thought in mind, but it is not something I should speak of with you."

Princess Anwen looked up at him with a small grin. "I am not some blushing maiden, your majesty. I can imagine what other ladies want from you." She handed him an apple and a piece of cheese. "You are right though, my intentions towards you are not like that of other ladies. You can be sure of that."

"I suppose you just want me out of your kingdom and off your hands," laughed Maddoc.

"Mostly," said the princess as she sat down with her own apple. "But I also wish to know you better. You are the king of your kingdom. I hope to be the queen of mine someday. Maybe you and I could repair the relations between our two lands."

Maddoc took a bite of his apple and stared at her, slightly annoyed. "Is this why you agreed to accompany me? To try to win my favor somehow?"

The princess sighed and chewed on her apple. "I would be lying if I said it didn't enter my mind, but no, it is not the main reason I decided to help you on this journey."

"I suppose if it was, it wouldn't be an awful thing. You should look out for the interest of your kingdom. It should be your number one priority."

"It is in many ways. I love Lucidala and all of its people. I want it to prosper once again, and I think having your kingdom as an ally would help, but when I first told my aunt I would accompany you, my kingdom wasn't in my mind at all."

She took another bite of apple as Maddoc ate some of his cheese. He waited for her to go on. When she didn't, he huffed. "Are you going to tell me what was on your mind when you first agreed to help me?"

"Does it really matter, your majesty?" she asked with one eyebrow arched.

He finished his cheese and dusted off his hands. She threw him a waterskin, and he drank deeply from it. "I suppose it doesn't, but I should like to know."

He threw the skin back to her and she caught it. She drank a little from it and said, "Our gods see every life as sacred, even yours." She gave him a teasing smile. "I could not let you be thrown out of my palace without some protection. My mother would not want it to be so." She paused, seeming to hesitate to say what she wanted.

"There is more I take it."

"I feel responsible for you for some reason. The power from my Gift saved you, and I didn't want it to go to waste. I feel like I will not rest until I see you safe within your kingdom."

Maddoc wasn't sure how to respond. She finished her apple and stood up, excusing herself to take a walk and see to her needs. He took the opportunity to relieve himself as well, coming back close to the horses when he was done. As he waited for Princess Anwen he heard a small rustling in the trees to the right of him. Thinking it was either an animal or the princess, he turned his head and ignored it.

The rustling in the forest stopped and all was still and quiet. Maddoc thought to ready his horse when he heard the noise again. He looked up and saw something come flying at him from the corner of his eye. The next thing he knew he was falling towards the ground with the princess in his arms as something flew over them. He hit the ground hard on his back, his arms automatically wrapping around Princess Anwen.

He skidded a bit on his back, his eyes closing as he was jarred. When he opened them, the princess was staring at him with concern.

"Are you well, your majesty?" she asked urgently.

He nodded, his arms still around her. She put her hands on the ground on either side of his head and pushed off, putting some distance between them.

"What happened?" he asked as she looked up and beyond him towards the forest.

She pushed up further, forcing him to release her. She stood up and held out her hand to him. He took it and got up, following her over to a tree where a knife was stuck in the trunk. She looked behind them and ran to her horse. She pulled out a sword and ran towards the forest where the knife had come from.

He watched her for a second before running after her. "Princess, don't." He grabbed his own sword and hurried to catch her in the forest.

He found her just in the tree line looking at the ground. "What are you doing?"

"I'm looking for tracks so I can follow whoever threw that knife."

"And what will you do once you come across them?" asked Maddoc as he reached out and grabbed her arm, turning her towards him.

"Find out who he is, and why he is trying to kill you." Princess Anwen tried to shake his arm off and turn.

"And get yourself killed in the process," hissed Maddoc tightening his hold on her.

"I can take care of myself better than you seem to think, your majesty," she retorted. She pulled harder, and Maddoc let her go.

She walked on, and Maddoc followed her, his eyes darting around. She seemed to spot something as she quickened her pace. She came to a small clearing and bent down.

She let out a loud, frustrated breath. "Whoever it was, rode off from here." She stood up and looked at Maddoc. "We should keep moving. We will need to find somewhere safe to stay tonight. I know of a place, but it is a good way away. We will have to ride hard."

He nodded and followed her out of the forest to their horses. As he walked, he massaged his back, spending a moment marveling at the princess's strength and fierceness.

6

Chapter 6

They rode fast through the dense part of the forest, Anwen continually checking each side of the path they were on for any signs of movement. It seemed someone really was trying to kill the king, and he was obviously not able to take care of himself. She knew now she had made the right choice to escort him on his journey. He probably would have been dead within an hour of leaving her palace.

She would have to remain vigilant during their travels. She had let her guard down when they rested, and she almost didn't hear the footsteps or see the glimmer of the knife in the afternoon sun before it was too late. If only she could have caught the person who threw the knife. She could have questioned him and found out what was truly going on. Now, she had no idea who was trying to kill King Maddoc or for what reason.

She looked over at him to see him watching her. It seemed he spent much of his time looking at her. She wondered why. He didn't look pleased or happy. Perhaps her presence annoyed him. Maybe she was so far outside his idea of beauty that he was marveling in her in inadequacies. More than likely the reason was he didn't trust her. She supposed she could understand his suspicion. They had barely known each other for a day. Their kingdoms had never been friendly. The best they could say about each other was they kept to themselves.

She sighed a little to herself thinking she would have to travel further than she initially thought. She had planned to find a nice inn to leave the king in, but now she was leery to leave him until he was safe and sound in his palace, or at least a trusted lord's home. She knew she would not be able to leave him until she knew he was very protected. She glanced over at him with a half-smile. As strong as he looked, he was actually very vulnerable.

They entered a less dense part of the forest, and Anwen felt she could let her guard down. She slowed her horse a bit to give her a rest and noticed Maddoc pulled up his horse as well. They rode at a slow trot, and for once the king's gaze was somewhere besides on her. Anwen took the opportunity to study the king.

He was tall and well built. It was clear he did not spend all his time lounging around some palace. He must have devoted at least some of his time to riding, and perhaps training with his sword. That gave her some comfort in the event they had to fight or flee. He carried himself like a king. Even though he was in the clothes of a lower lord or commoner, he still did not look like one. His seat in his saddle was perfectly straight. His chin was up and proud. He looked over everything like it belonged to him. She thought he couldn't help it. It was a part of who he was. He had been raised as the next king and recognized as the wearer of the crown at a very young age.

She looked closer at his face, and it struck her just how handsome he was. She had already registered that he was not bad-looking, but now as the setting sun behind them made his black hair shine, she could see just how very attractive he was. His chin was strong, covered by stubble that would soon be a short beard. His nose was just about as perfect as she had ever seen, and his eyes were so deep blue they hardly seemed real. When he smiled it made his eyes crinkle and his nose lift. It surprised her a bit how attractive she really found him.

She had not been able to look at a man with real favor this past year. For a while, she wasn't sure she would ever be able to find a man attractive. When a lord or even a young villager would smile at her, she would be reminded of the betrayal from the one she had trusted completely. She would remember what a foolish woman she really was. She had thought Lachlan loved her. He had told her she was beautiful and charming. He said that he had never met a woman so intelligent or brave. It had all been a lie.

Of course, he had turned to her cousin the minute Gwendolyn showed interest. Anwen could never live up to the grace and beauty of the woman. Where Anwen was short and dainty, Gwendolyn was tall and elegant. Anwen could mix in with a crowd and get lost. Wherever Gwendolyn went, all eyes were on her. Anwen spent her days running around the village or forest. She joined the men on hunts. She ran around with those who were much lower in status than her, having adventures in the forest. Gwendolyn spent her time charming high lords and foreign royalty. Her manners were everything excellent and fine. Anwen thought her rather dull and stupid, but men seem to like that in a woman.

She had thought Lachlan was different. She thought he saw above all of what society wanted and found worth in her. Instead, he had just been biding his time, finding what pleasure he could in her while he played her for a fool. Now, she knew what she really was. She was a broken princess who never lived up to her promise. She was a woman who had been used and cast aside. She wondered who her mother would have to charm and bribe to marry her. No high-born lord or foreign prince would have her without some sort of payment or promise. Anwen had given up any ideas of love for herself. It seemed she was not made for it.

"Do you think we are safe now, princess?" asked the king bringing Anwen out of her thoughts.

"We are safer than we were since the forest is not so dense here. There are not many places someone could hide, but we should still remain vigilant."

"So, where are we headed? Where do you know that is safe for us to rest for the night?"

Anwen looked over at the king. "There is a small, old house some hours away. It is on land that is owned by my family. My great grandfather brought it with him when he married into the royal line. It was once a part of a great estate, but the famine and disease drove the family closer to the main village. The manor burned down years ago, but some of the tenant houses remain. We will stay in one of them my family has made comfortable."

They were quiet for a while as they rode on. King Maddoc eventually turned to Anwen. "How did you know that knife was coming for me?"

"I heard a noise in the forest and looked closely. I saw a person and the glint of the steel. It only took me a moment to realize what was happening. I wasn't being watchful enough, and I almost didn't see it in time. I apologize for having to tackle you so, but it was the only thing I could think to do in the moment."

"There is no need for an apology. You saved my life, yet again, and no damage was done."

"Still, I will try to watch more closely in the future and identify any threats well in advance." Anwen gave a small laugh. "It won't do for me to throw myself at you at every hint of danger."

"Where do you come about your skills? You were able to track in the forest. Where did you learn?"

"My father started taking me hunting as soon as I could sit with him in the saddle. He taught me how to track animals and watch for movement in the forest. After he passed, my mother and a trusted lord took over my training. I am a proficient hunter and can track animals well. Humans are not much different than animals. Watching for them and tracking them is much the same."

The king looked down and was silent.

"You do not approve, I take it," stated Anwen.

The king looked up quickly at her. "Why do you say that?"

"The look upon your face was not one of approval, your majesty. I am afraid I have scandalized you."

"Perhaps you are not as good at reading expressions as you are at hunting, princess," said the king with a small smile. "Or maybe you think I am predisposed to think ill of you. I can assure you, nothing about you has scandalized me or met my disapproval."

"But I am not your idea of what a lady or princess should be, I imagine. I do not sit around the court practicing guarded and careful manners. I do not speak softly or keep my opinions to myself."

"You are not like most ladies or princesses I have met, but I do not mind. You make a much better traveling partner than any of them would. You are much more useful and amusing."

Anwen laughed. "I am a source of amusement for you, am I?" She shook her head and looked forward. She found herself a little angry at his comment. She had saved him twice and agreed to escort him on this little trip to keep him safe. After all, she had done, he found her amusing?

"Now, I am the one who has offended." The king looked over at her, and Anwen turned towards him.

"I am not offended." She took a breath. "I suppose it is better than what I believed you thought of me."

"What do you mean?" asked the king.

"With you looking at me so much, I thought, at first, perhaps my appearance offended you somehow. That maybe you had not seen such an odd-looking woman before and didn't know what to make of me. But after further thought, I believe it is because you do not trust me. Which I do not blame you for."

"You think I do not trust you?"

"How could you? You barely know me," replied Anwen.

"Princess, I find that I do trust you actually. How could I not?" The king chuckled. "You have saved my life twice and agreed to ride along with me on a long journey. Also, you speak your mind freely and give your opinions with no thought to what I might think. While I have not known you long, I do not believe I have to worry about your motives."

She looked at him, not sure how to respond. She found herself falling back on humor. "Then I suppose I must puzzle you with my peculiar looks," she said with a laugh. "That must be why you watch me so."

"Did you ever think that I might just like looking at a beautiful woman?"

Anwen's smile faded from her face, and she felt her face grow warm. "That is a rather cruel tease, your majesty," she said softly.

"I have offended you by openly flirting. I meant no harm by it, princess. I do not plan to try to dishonor you in any way."

Anwen felt her face grow even warmer, knowing her cheeks were bright red. "Your flirting does not offend me, your majesty. It is the way you do it. I would rather you speak truths and not flatter me falsely."

"You do not need to be modest around me, princess. Do not lose your boldness. You can admit to your own beauty. I would not think you would be like other women who would laugh their looks away, while aware of just how lovely they are."

Anwen looked at the king with disbelief. "I am very aware of my own looks, your majesty. There are some very beautiful women in my court. My own mother is known for her great beauty, and you have seen my aunt and cousin. I have always paled in comparison to the rest of the women in my family and court." She swallowed and smiled a little. "I am used to it, and it does not bother me, much."

The king shook his head. "I do not believe it. You are going much too far with your modesty. I am sure plenty of young men have talked to you of your beauty."

"Indeed, they have not," replied Anwen somewhat annoyed. What did the king mean by pressing this? "You do not need to keep on with this, your majesty. I do not spend much time fretting over my appearance."

"Fine, but will you trust that I look at you with no displeasure or ill will?"

"Very well," said Anwen as she turned her eyes to the road.

"Can I ask you something, princess?"

"Obviously, you can, your majesty. You may ask me whatever you like. Whether I answer is another matter."

The king shook his head with a small smile before his face grew serious. "You aunt mentioned that my kingdom had ignored a long owed debt from yours. Do you know what that is about?"

"Of course, I do," said Anwen with some surprise. "Are you telling me that you don't have at least some idea of what she was speaking of?"

The king shook his head. "Will you tell me what she meant?"

Anwen was quiet for a moment as she gathered her thoughts, wondering where to begin. "How much do you know about your kingdom's history?"

King Maddoc shrugged. "The usual things they teach. I know the line of kings. I know we were organized into a kingdom by my ancestors at least a thousand years ago. I can tell you of the main battles we have fought and some principal lords."

"What of the great sickness of over five hundred years ago?"

The king's eyebrows knitted together. "I am not sure what you mean. We have had times of sickness and plagues as any kingdoms has, but I know of none that is talked of more than the others."

Anwen was a little surprised, but she shouldn't have been. If his kingdom had done so much as to ignore the cries of help from Lucidala, it must have suppressed the knowledge of Lucidala's aid to itself.

"Will you tell me what you mean?" asked the king.

Anwen nodded. "Over five hundred years ago, a horrible sickness ravaged your kingdom. It destroyed entire villages and wiped out ancient families. It came closer and closer to your principal village where your Great Palace stands. Your king became panicked, and he traveled around looking for help. He came to Lucidala hearing of our great powers and healers.

"Back then there were plenty with the Gift, not just the royal family. Many of our lords and even some of our commoners had the Gift. The givers of life were still rare and only two resided in the kingdom at the time. One of them was a lord's daughter. She and her father along with several of our healers agreed to travel back with the king to help with the sick.

"The lady worked night and day to cure all she could. She with our healers managed to stymie the sickness in your land. She even saved the life of the king's son. The prince that she saved fell in love with her and asked for her hand. Her father was adamant in his refusal at first, not wanting to leave his daughter in the strange kingdom, especially a daughter with a lifesaving Gift.

"He relented when he realized how much his daughter loved the prince. He agreed to their marriage in exchange for aid to be given to Lucidala when it was needed, and that a daughter or second-born son of the couple eventually settled in Lucidala, hoping that the child would have the gift.

"The lady was married to the prince and eventually became Queen of Calumbria. She had two children. The first was a male who would eventually be the king. The second was a girl. Unfortunately, the queen never recovered from the birth, and she died after the girl was only a year old. Before she died, she made her husband swear that he would uphold the promise he made to her father and our kingdom.

"The king wrote his wife's family and the queen of our kingdom, ensuring he would keep his promise. A few years later Lucidala sent some of our clerics to visit the girl to see what her Gift was. They wrote back that the girl was a life-giver. That was the last my kingdom heard from those clerics. The next news heard was that the king had died in an accident, and until the prince was of age, a council of lords would oversee the kingdom.

"Our queen wrote letter after letter asking about the child that would come to Lucidala when she was of age, but the letters were always unanswered. Eventually, many years later, a letter came announcing the girl had disappeared. Any inquires were met with no action or response.

"Our own sickness and famine came a hundred years later, and our queen at the time wrote to your kingdom asking for aid. Calling the debt that your kingdom owed ours, saying it was doubled because of the missing princess. Calumbria never responded. They ignored us in our time of need and have continued to do so as we suffer from famine and disease.

"As the famine and disease-ravaged our kingdom, less and less were born with the Gift until only my family has had any Gift wielders. We have not had a life-giver born into the land again until I was said to have the Gift, but I have never fully lived into it. Our kingdom has grown quite small, villages being wiped out. Great families have all but disappeared. Every generation, we have written to your kings for help but received none. My mother has written your court at least twice, but nothing has ever been returned. I believe she may plan to plead with you in person if it comes to it. It will hurt her pride, but she is desperate for her people."

King Maddoc was quiet after Anwen finished. The only sound around them was the clop of their horses' hooves on the road, and some birds in the distance. He eventually looked up at her. "Much of that could be folklore, your highness."

"But it isn't, your majesty. We have recorded all of it, and it was not so long ago, really. Even if you don't believe all of it, how could your kingdom just ignore our plight? How could you let our people suffer so?" Anwen felt tears come to her eyes, thinking of the pain of her people.

"I had no idea," he whispered. "I had not heard that you were suffering. I have not heard much of your kingdom at all."

"We have managed to abate the sickness somewhat over the years, but our crops and livestock still struggle. Since our population has dwindled, it is easier to feed the people left. There are some kingdoms that have helped us, but we cannot flourish as we once did. I believe your kingdom does not wish for us to prosper. I think it might want us to disappear altogether."

He looked up at her with a frown. "I do not wish it, and I am the king. When we return to my palace, I will speak to my mother on the subject. We will find out the truth, and I will see what can be done to help your kingdom."

Anwen nodded, but she wasn't very hopeful. The more she got to know the king, the more she wondered how much power he really had in his own kingdom.

7

❧

Chapter 7

The sun slowly went down as they rode on. Maddoc looked every so often in the direction of the princess, but she didn't speak much. His head was much too full for conversation as it was. Could the tale she told be true? He had never heard about a sickness or a life-giver coming to save his kingdom. He worked backward through the line of kings in his head trying to think of the one who would be in her story. He would have been a king who died young, but there had been more than a few. Whether by war, disease, or bad luck, it seemed many of Calumbria's kings did not live long lives.

It had not worried Maddoc much. Besides his father, the past few kings had lived and ruled long. He figured with the increased advances in the treatment of illness and some good luck, he would be another king with a long life, but with the events of the past few days, he was less sure. It did seem as if someone was trying to kill him. The first attack might have been brushed off as a group of bandits looking for ransom of the king. The knife being thrown at him showed it was not just a random, isolated event.

His life was in danger, and he needed to figure out why and by who. He believed if he could get back to the safety of the palace, he would have time and resources to figure it out. His mother and uncle could help him solve the mystery and keep him safe. Until then he would have to be extra cautious and rely on his traveling companion.

He looked over at the princess to see her staring straight ahead. He had tried to not look at her so much since their earlier conversation. He had not meant to make her uncomfortable. He had assumed she was used to men staring at her as most beautiful women were. He could not believe she was serious in the refusal of her beauty. She was surely being modest, playing some game with him.

He wondered what she wanted from him. He had told her he did not worry about her motives, but in his own mind, he questioned them. She had told him she just wanted to keep him safe due to duty and the will of the gods, but he could not believe it. Surely, she didn't think she stood a chance to be his queen. As soon as he thought it, he didn't really believe it could be a possibility. She seemed very attached to her own kingdom, and she would be its queen in time. Perhaps she was just hoping to gain his goodwill and gain access of aid to her kingdom. If that was the case, he wondered how far she would go to gain his help for Lucidala. He knew he should be repulsed at the idea she would trade favors for her kingdom's wellbeing, but he could not help but think time spent with her in more intimate circumstances would not be unpleasant.

He shook his head. That was no way to think of a princess and future queen. She had shown him to be nothing but an honorable woman who had risked her life for his. He felt a little shame in thinking she would act in such a way. He felt even more shame in thinking he would actually be tempted to take advantage of her if she did.

"We are not far, your majesty," said the princess. "We will take this trail up ahead, and then it is just a short ride to the house."

Maddoc nodded and adjusted himself in his saddle. He needed to clear his mind of any improper thoughts of Princess Anwen. She was not some low-level lady or servant he could seduce and then be done with her. She was also not a viable option for a wife. He needed to see her as he should, a future ruler he should respect, but also be cautious of. Her open manners and beautiful looks had thrown him off a bit, but he could not be distracted by her many allurements.

He would continue on this journey with her, and once he was safe and knew who was trying to take his life, he would see to repaying her kingdom in some way. Perhaps with some supplies and medicine. There was no reason Calumbria should not look on Lucidala with a friendly eye. They could become allies. He could see the princess at festivals. He could invite her and her court to his kingdom as he did other foreign rulers. There was no reason why he shouldn't be friends with her. His mother and advisors had said it would be good to make connections with other kingdoms. The princess seemed wise and kind. Her mother sounded like a capable ruler. Perhaps part of his legacy could be bringing Lucidala and Calumbria together.

They turned down the path the princess had spoken of, and after a few minutes exited the forest into open grown-up fields. Maddoc could tell this land was once farmed and used for livestock. He imagined it was quite a sight in its prime. He could see the sun setting just over to his left, and it illuminated the fields in a red light. Up ahead was a small house with a half-broken fence still around it. He assumed that was where they would spend the night, safely hidden.

He followed the princess on her horse up to the house and around it. Behind the home was a covered, large shack that had a place to tie up their horses. A pile of hay lay to one side. Maddoc hopped down off his horse and tied him up. The princess did the same with hers before going over to pick up some of the hay to place near the horses. Maddoc watched her for a moment, before helping her. When they were done, she picked up a large bucket and took it over to a well on the left. She drew up a few small buckets of water to fill her large one. She went to pick it up when Maddoc stopped her.

"Let me, your highness," he said as he picked up the bucket.

She nodded and walked back to the shack. Maddoc placed some water in a trough for each horse while the princess took bags off of her mare. She motioned with her head towards the house, and he took one of the bags from her, following her to the back door of the home.

She stopped near the door and looked down at the ground. Once she spotted something she kneeled down and tipped over a large rock, picking up a key found there. Using it, she unlocked the back door and walked in. Maddoc followed her. He found himself in a simple, clean home. There was one large room with a space for a kitchen, a table to eat at, and a small sitting area with a fireplace.

The princess put her bag down on the table, and he did likewise. She walked over in front of the fireplace and kneeled down in front of it.

"Do you have any flint? Do you know how to start a fire?" asked Maddoc as he walked closer to her.

She gave him a small, annoyed look. "Of course, I know how to start a fire with flint, but I do not need it." She grabbed some logs that were piled up close by and arranged them in the fireplace.

"What do you mean you do not need it?" asked Maddoc as he watched her.

She looked up at him with a sly smile before placing her hand close to logs. She closed her eyes and took a breath. When she opened them, a spark shot towards the logs, and a fire caught. Soon the logs were engulfed in flames, lighting up the room and spreading warmth.

"How..." started Maddoc, not sure how to end his question.

"My Gift has manifested in strange ways. One of them is I can create fire. I think it is because fire is so closely linked with life. I can also manipulate water in some ways, but mostly just in natural sources like rivers or ponds."

"I know you said you had the Gift, but I still had a hard time believing it until I saw what you just did."

"Do you not remember what just happened yesterday?"

"My head was rather foggy from my fall. I thought perhaps I had imagined or dreamed most of it," replied Maddoc.

She smiled as she stood up. "I don't know about you, but I am very hungry." She walked over to the table and opened her bag. "I wish I had thought to hunt a little as we rode, but the incident with the knife threw me off." She pulled out some dried meat, some bread, and a couple of apples. "I will try to get us some fresh meat tomorrow, but this will have to do for now."

She arranged the food on the table and pulled out a wineskin and two cups. She carefully poured some wine into the cups and sat down at one of the small chairs by the table. "Will you join me, your majesty?"

He nodded and sat down across from her. They ate together in relative silence. Maddoc finding the dried meat wasn't too bad, the bread was fresh, and the wine was very good and sweet.

"That wine should help you to sleep." Princess Anwen drained her own cup. "I will see to getting some water for you to clean a bit, though I am afraid it won't be heated unless you do it yourself over the fire."

"I can go fetch the water, princess," said Maddoc.

"No, let me," said the princess as she stood. "I would like to take a short walk and make sure everything is secure."

Maddoc looked up at her, not sure he should let her walk around outside in the dark.

"Come now, your majesty, you must see that I can take care of myself by now. I would say I am much more capable than you."

"You think I am not capable of defending myself?" asked Maddoc, taken aback.

"It looks as if you could hold your own in a fight. I don't know your skills with a sword or any other weapon, but you look strong. You don't seem very aware of your surroundings or the understanding of keeping yourself safe. What possessed you to travel on unfamiliar roads in the open dressed as the king with only five guards?"

"I have traveled that way many times on the southern road with no problems. It was only in your kingdom I was attacked so."

"I checked on the identity of those who attacked you. There were several dead on the road, and I can say for certain they were not of Lucidala. They were not clothed in any particular kingdom's colors, but they were not of my kingdom.

"I am not trying to wound your pride or irritate you, your majesty. I am only speaking the truth. You do not seem to have much knowledge when it comes to traveling safely. I wonder if you would have lasted twenty minutes on the road by yourself."

Maddoc could feel his temper rising along with his embarrassment. Who was this princess from a simple kingdom to judge him?

"Ah, you look angry. Once again, King Maddoc, I am not trying to draw your ire. I imagine you are used to others seeing to your safety, and why would you not be? I imagine your protective force is large and well-trained. Perhaps instead of worrying about your lack of knowledge, I should question why your guards would think it was appropriate for you to travel so unprotected."

He stood up. "My guards do as they are instructed. I was traveling with five of the best fighters in my kingdom, including the captain of my guards. I felt quite safe. I don't appreciate you critiquing my methods."

"And yet, your guards were overwhelmed, and you were almost killed. Then today in the forest, you had no idea someone was stalking you, waiting to kill you with a knife. You may be angry with me for telling you the truth, but you need to hear it if you want to survive. You will have to become wiser to the world around you and your position.

"I will go take my walk now and give you a moment. I do apologize if I caused you any distress, but I will not take back my words. They are only meant to help you."

With that she walked away, Maddoc turning to watch her go. He took the wineskin and poured a bit more into his cup. He picked it up and walked over to the fire, sitting down on an old chair in front of it. He thought over what she had said. He didn't want to admit she had a point, but the more rational part of his mind would not let him dismiss it.

He had never had to think about his own protection much. All his life he had been surrounded by guards. He was taught to fight by his uncle and various tutors. He thought he was more than proficient with a sword, and even somewhat skilled with a bow. He had never run into trouble on the roads before. He hated riding in the carriage, and he liked to travel fast. A small group of very well-trained, strong guards seemed to be the solution to his wants and needs.

Still, it had not helped him the day before. He could easily have died. He would have died had it not been for whatever the princess had done. He could admit to feeling some fear at the moment, though it was overshadowed by pain and adrenaline. He tried to remember what had happened, but besides the start of the fight and him falling off his horse, all he could remember was the safe feeling that surrounding him as he was enveloped in the bright light and the princess's eyes as they looked at him with concern.

He sipped his wine and eventually heard the door open and close. He looked over to see Princess Anwen setting a bucket full of water down on the table. She poured some wine into a cup and brought it over to sit down next to Maddoc by the fire.

"Are you still angry with me?" she asked as she took a drink of wine.

"I don't believe I was very angry with you, to begin with. Your words were not meant to hurt me, though I do believe they were a little harsher than was needed. I am not helpless, princess."

"No, I don't believe you are, but you must see that you have been a little foolish in your actions." She took a large drink. "I do not blame you, or think you are unintelligent. I rather think it is a result of your upbringing. You are used to having your own way, and believing the world revolves around you."

He sat up slightly and thought to argue when she held her hand up. "That came out wrong. I have always been a little too loose with my words." She took another drink. "I suppose our world does revolve around you in a way. Your kingdom is very powerful, and I believe as it prospers so do many other kingdoms. You are an important person and have been treated as such. I just wish they had taught you a little more of self-preservation and self-reliance."

Maddoc thought on her words as he took a drink. "You are right that I have had most of my needs, and even most of my wants, always done to my liking. I wished to ride freely as I could, and I was indulged. Others have told me I was being foolish, at least in a way. Most were not so open with their words except my mother and uncle. My mother has long told me to be more careful and aware. My uncle has said I am spoiled and self-indulged."

"I do not believe you are unkind, though. You might be a little spoiled and soft, but to be honest, I expected our trip to be much more bothersome. You are more helpful than I would have thought of someone in your position. As I said before, you do not seem unintelligent. Perhaps you have been foolish, but who hasn't." She finished her wine. "I have been very foolish myself."

Maddoc sat back as she put her cup down. She reached for her braid and undid the ribbon at the end. Slowly she started to undo her hair as she gazed at the fire. He couldn't help but watch her small hands as they worked, unweaving her hair until it fell loose over her shoulders and down her back. She ran her hands through it as he finished the last of his wine. He knew he was staring, but he couldn't help it. He wondered if her hair was a soft as it looked. He wondered what it would feel like if he ran his hands through it.

She turned and looked at him. "I get a bit of a headache when it is pulled so tight for so long. I couldn't wait to undo it for the night. I hope you don't mind."

"Not at all," said Maddoc somewhat hoarsely.

"We should probably try to sleep. We will want to get going as soon as the sun starts rising. There is a small bedroom through that doorway. The bed isn't too old, so you should be comfortable."

He stood up, but then stopped before he walked away. "It wouldn't be very chivalrous of me to take the bed from you, princess. This is your house after all."

"I can curl up cozily on the sofa here. I am not very large, and I will fit very well. You would hang off the sides and get no sleep." The princess stretched in her chair. "Please take the bed, your majesty. I insist."

He hesitated but nodded. Before going to the room, he found a small bowl and filled it with water from the bucket. After wishing the princess a good night, he walked into the bedroom to find it small but serviceable. He cleaned himself before undoing his shirt and taking off his boots to get comfortable. He found the bed softer than he imagined it would be.

He lay down and realized how very weary he was. His head still ached a bit from his fall, and he felt a day of hard riding all through his body.

He got into a comfortable position and fell asleep. He found himself dreaming of Princess Anwen. They were out in the fields together looking at the sunset. She grabbed his hand and squeezed it causing him to look down at her. She was wearing a simple light blue dress that fit her perfectly. Her golden hair ran down her shoulders in waves. She smiled up at him, her eyes shining in the setting sun.

Maddoc pulled her closer, turning to face her. He wrapped his arms around her, pulling her against him as he bent down towards her. She tilted her head up towards him, her beautiful eyes fluttering closed. He moved one of his hands up her back and ran his fingers through her hair. Their lips met, and Maddoc felt some sort of energy run through his body. It caused an intense longing for her that created an ache within his chest. He groaned and deepened their kiss as her hands went up his chest slowly. He had never wanted any woman so badly.

As they kissed, they both somehow kneeled towards the ground together. They broke apart for only a moment, before hungrily kissing each other again. He slowly laid her back in the thick brown grass, her hair pooling around her. As he gazed down at her she smiled softly up at him. He moved his hand down her leg and started slowly moving her dress up as he leaned down to kiss her. She whispered his name against his lips, and he moaned hers. As his hand reached her thigh, he felt her lips meet his again, causing him to sit up in his bed, wide awake.

He looked around the dark room, breathing heavily. He felt panicked finding that the princess was not really in his arms or even by his side. He almost got up to search for her when he remembered it had only been a dream. He lay back in bed and shook his head. He felt the ache of desire through his body, remembering not only his dream but what the princess had felt like in his arms earlier that day.

He audibly groaned, berating himself for thinking of her in that way. He knew that he was attracted to her, but he had been attracted to many women. He had never dreamed of any of them the way he just had. It had felt so real. He swore he could still feel her lips against his own. His body still felt the warmth of hers. The longing he felt for her was something he had never experienced before. He had felt plenty of desire in the past, but usually, it did not matter what attractive woman met that desire. Now he felt as if no one but Princess Anwen would do.

He lay in the dark trying to still his breathing and dispel his desire. It was all just due to being around her so much. She was a beautiful woman. There was no wonder he had dreamed of her. He had drunk two glasses of strong wine, and his head was still somewhat foggy from his fall. He comforted himself with these thoughts as he started to go back to sleep, half worrying and half hoping he would dream of her again.

8

Chapter 8

The next two days of traveling passed almost without any troubles. King Maddoc was quiet, and Anwen could sense an awkwardness between him. She assumed it was due to the conversation they had in the small house. She should have learned to hold her tongue, but her main goal was not to offend the king. She only wanted to help him realize how unsafe he had been in his travels. She wanted him better prepared for their journey as well as future ones he might take.

She wasn't sure why, but she found she didn't want anything to happen to the king. There was some sort of attachment she felt towards him. She was not sure what it was. She didn't believe it was romantic, no matter how attractive she found him, and she was started to realize just how handsome he really was. She convinced herself it was because he was so very helpless in many ways, and her main instinct was to protect him. She attributed it to her Gift.

Of course, she would want to preserve the life of one so vulnerable. It was her nature, her religion, and the essence that lived inside of her. She may never have lived fully into her Gift, but she was still a life-giver at heart. The king's life was worth something, and she would do all she could to protect it from anyone or anything, even his own foolishness.

They spent the first day of travel in awkward, short conversations. That night they rested well concealed behind a thicket. Although Anwen thought they were as hidden as they could be for the area, she was still uneasy being out in the forest. She told the king there was nothing to worry about, hoping he would sleep well. After dinner, she walked down to a creek that ran nearby and washed up. She even managed to wash a bit of her hair. The ends had gotten quite dirty as she had left it down for the day. Once she was done, she felt fresher, but the upper part of her dress was somewhat damp. She knew some time in front of the fire would help it to dry.

As she rejoined the king, he looked at her oddly. She tried to set him at ease with a small smile as she ran her fingers through her hair by the fire. It only seemed to make him more uncomfortable, so she gave up for the evening. Once she saw him asleep, she kept watch for hours, only letting herself lightly doze with her hand on her sword. Every little noise in the forest would cause her to awaken.

The next day wasn't much better. The king still seemed unsettled around her, and she wasn't sure what to do. She had apologized for being too bold, but she would not take back her words. She had been careful to not say too much to him, but he still seemed uncomfortable and offended. She was growing weary from travel and the lack of sleep.

They traveled on, Anwen wishing she knew a place to spend the night out of the forest, but the only place she knew where they could find shelter was at least a two-day ride. She did manage to find a small alcove in some rock by the river they were near. It would provide more protection than the night before, with only one way to enter and exit. After another quiet dinner, Anwen let herself sleep a little more soundly. She still woke up several times due to animals splashing in the nearby water and a couple of hares who hopped by on the rocks below. She at least found a use for them, killing both hares easily with her bow she had with her, providing them with fresh meat for breakfast.

After breakfast, they traveled on, and Anwen decided to try to break the awkward tension between them. She started by talking about her own kingdom. She mentioned the many villages she had visited and some issues she had been seeing to. She talked of their principal lords. She spoke further of the challenges facing their kingdom, and what her mother was doing to see to Lucidala's future.

"She is visiting every kingdom she thinks will hear her out," said Anwen. "We have already obtained supplies from three different kingdoms. A large caravan of wagons is coming within two weeks from Bellican. It shall have food to help us through the winter as well as medicine. My mother spent almost a month as the king's visitor, though it was probably the alliance my friend Brennan made with their highest lord that sealed the deal. The lord is coming himself this winter to Awbrey, and I am sure he will bring even more supplies for our villages."

The king nodded but did not speak.

"Can you tell me more about your kingdom, your majesty?" asked Anwen, trying to get King Maddoc to say more than two words.

"What would you like to know?"

"What are your villages like? Who are your principal lords? What are the biggest challenges facing Calumbria? Anything really. You can even tell me about your favorite places to travel within your kingdom."

The king didn't look at her. "I haven't really traveled much in my own kingdom. I tend to stay in Quinlan at the palace for the most part. I have been to a few other kingdoms, but none really stand out to me."

Anwen grimaced and sighed a little. "What of the main issues plaguing your kingdom?"

"I'm not really sure," said the king. "I believe all is well for the most part. Any issues a lord has in his lands usually goes to my mother, my uncle, and the king's council. I am usually not troubled by such things."

"You are the king, aren't you?"

"I am." He turned to look at her.

"Shouldn't you be troubled by issues in your kingdom? I understand there are some petty issues that perhaps your council could handle, but shouldn't they at least let you know?" She shook her head. "How do you spend your days, your majesty?"

He made a noise, and Anwen could tell she aggravated him again. She had not meant to do it. She had only wanted to start a conversation with him, but yet again she had gone too far with her words.

"I don't believe my daily schedule is any of your concern, princess," he said haughtily.

"No, it is not. I have said too much once again. I apologize, your majesty. My mouth seems to have a mind of its own. It is one of my many faults."

They were both quiet for a moment, and the king sighed loudly. "I should take more interest in running my kingdom. My mother has been saying it for a while, but every time I try to ask the council or my uncle what I can do, they tell me there is nothing to worry about."

Anwen tried to hold her tongue, but she could not help herself. "You could press further. You could demand to sit in the council's meetings. They are the king's council, and you are the king. They should answer to you. Perhaps you have not tried harder because you really don't want to."

"And why should I? The kingdom is thriving. The people are happy. What do I really need to do?"

"How do you know the kingdom is doing well? How do you know the state of your people's happiness and well-being? It sounds like you know nothing about your kingdom at all besides what goes on in your small circle. What if your uncle or council isn't telling you the full truth?"

"Are you calling my uncle, a prince of the kingdom, a liar?"

"No, I don't know him, but obviously all is not well. You have almost been killed twice. It seems someone is trying their hardest to do away with you. There has to be a reason for it. What if it is due to an uprising in your kingdom or some tiff with another land?" She paused knowing she should stop, but she could not help herself. She was tired and irritable. "What if this threat is coming from your own palace, your own council?"

"Those are dangerous allegations, your highness," snarled the king. "How do I really know it is not your kingdom that is trying to kill me? What if you are leading me to my doom right now?"

The princess laughed. "Do you really think I would have to go to all this trouble to kill you if I wanted you dead? I could have left you to die back in my kingdom. I could have had you killed in my palace. There are a hundred times I could have done away with you on this journey."

"Then perhaps you arranged for my attack back in Awbrey so you could win my goodwill. You think you can take me on some sprawling journey, tell me about your kingdom, and set up attacks to save my life. You try to seduce me with your pretty smiles and subtle ways. You come and sit before me soaking wet. You find ways to touch me and openly flirt with me. You think you can entangle me so thoroughly with you, that I will have no choice but to assist your kingdom or maybe even more."

Anwen pulled up her horse, shocked and angry at his response. He stopped his horse and looked back at her. She held back the tears that were gathering in her eyes. "If that is how you really believe things are, perhaps we should separate ways here, your majesty. I can't imagine a time I have been so offended. I have tried to be open and honest with you. I have tried to keep you safe, and I am exhausted by the effort. If you really do not trust me and think so ill of me, I will leave you on your own. If you keep traveling northeast, you will eventually reach your kingdom's border. Stay close to the river, and you will at least only have to watch your right side. Good luck, King Maddoc."

She turned her horse and rode away, holding back her tears until she had her back to him. Her horse walked on, but Anwen barely registered it. How could he think so of her? He thought she had been trying to seduce him. She wasn't sure where he had gotten the idea. Was she so bold in her actions and words?

She had done nothing to plan to attract the king. Even if she had wanted to do it, she didn't believe it could be done. Surely, he had endured the flirtations of many more beautiful women than she. How could she even begin to tempt him? She was so weary and upset, she didn't even hear him approach until he was next to her.

"Princess, what I said was cruel, and obviously untrue. You have done nothing to show you are untrustworthy. Your words made me angry, but it did not elicit such a response from me."

She kept her head down, hoping her hair was hiding her tears. She did not stop. There was no use in listening to him now. How could they go on after what he had said?

"Please, princess, I want to apologize. I can't imagine what came over me. I do not wish to part this way from you, not after all you have done for me."

She refused to listen to him and kept riding. She was tempted to kick her horse and take off, but she wasn't sure if she could stay on with the way she was feeling. He pulled his horse in front of hers and stopped, making her own horse stop walking. "Will you please listen to me, Anwen?"

She looked up at him as she wiped her face with her hand. He had called her by her name, no titles, or formal words.

He didn't seem to notice. He stared at her for a moment before swallowing so hard she could hear it. "I do not wish to travel on by myself, but if you cannot forgive me, I will understand. Only, let me see you somewhere safe before we part ways. You are obviously tired and upset, and I would hate for you to become careless because of my words and actions. If something were to happen to you, I don't think I could forgive myself."

Anwen closed her eyes, willing her tears to stop. Her head felt so heavy and full. Her body ached for a warm bath and a soft bed. She spoke softly, "There is a lord's manor a few hours up this road. He is very trustworthy and keeps to himself. I believe we can find shelter there for the night. After some rest, I will decide how we shall proceed."

9

⌇

Chapter 9

Maddoc glanced over at Princess Anwen as they rode to see her staring straight ahead. Her eyes looked tired and red. He could still see the streaks of tears down her cheeks. He was the cause of those tears, and he felt like a brute. He wasn't sure what had possessed him to say those things to her. In his defense, it did seem like she was trying to attract him in some way. Why else would she come before him with her dress askew and wet? Why would she smile at him so as she played with her marvelous hair? How else could he explain the charming way in which she tried to draw him into conversations?

Now as he looked at her slumped shoulders and red face, he realized she was just being who she was. He was starting to understand she was a free spirit who spoke her mind as she saw fit. Her dress was wet the other night because she had cleaned her hair and not cared how she came before him. She had no ideas to try to seduce him. She couldn't care less of what he thought of her for the most part. Sure, she didn't like the fact he had basically called her a trollop who would trade favors for her kingdom, but what self-respected high-born woman would?

He wished he could say something to her to make it all better. He wished he could go back and change it all. She had made him angry with her talk of him shirking his responsibilities. She had been right, but he didn't like it pointed out to him. His mother had long said he needed to be more active in the kingdom. He had half tried, but the princess was right, he had not pushed the issue.

The truth was he liked being able to do as he pleased with his time. The benefits that came with being king were much more appealing to him than the responsibilities. He knew this, and it had been pointed out to him before. He hadn't really cared in the past, but when the princess had said it, it had made him angry and embarrassed. He had listened all afternoon as she talked of her love for her kingdom. She was knowledgeable in almost all areas of Lucidala. She knew the villages. She knew what hardships her people faced. She understood what needed to be done, and she had done much herself. She was a true leader to her kingdom.

As he listened to her talk, he realized he was nothing but a man who wore a crown. His power was nonexistent. His influence over his kingdom was nothing. He had let others rule in his place because he couldn't be bothered with it. He had become ashamed listening to her speak. She was everything a true ruler should be, and it showed him just how pathetic he really was.

He closed his eyes and shook his head. This woman whom he had belittled and dismissed was more than he could ever be. She had not tried to seduce him. He doubted she even thought him worthy of being seduced. He had let his own desire for her cloud his mind. He could admit to himself now that he desired her.

He dreamed of her every night. He was hoping he didn't whisper her name out loud in his sleep so she might hear it. He longed for her small touches on his arm. He craved her smiles in his direction. The memory of holding her in his arms after she tackled him made a warm feeling come over his body. He wanted her, but he could not have her. He could not dishonor her in such a way. Besides, he doubted she would want him at all. She certainly did not before, and now she would look at him with nothing but disgust. She might even abandon him tomorrow morning, leaving him to continue on to his palace on his own.

The thought of traveling without her made him feel sad and alone.

Besides the fact he wasn't sure he could make it safely without her, he would miss her company. He did not want to ride on without her by his side, telling stories of her kingdom and flashing small smiles at him. He definitely didn't want her to leave him with the current opinion she held of him. He wanted to find a way to repair what he had broken between them. Just a few days ago he hoped they could become friends, and now he just wished she wouldn't think so ill of him.

"Princess, I want to say again how sorry I am. I am thoroughly ashamed of myself."

"It is no matter, at least not this evening. I do not wish to speak of it. I only want to rest. Tomorrow morning, we will talk more about it." She would not look at him.

"Are we close to our destination?"

"We are. Soon we will turn off this road and ride on for about ten minutes. We will come to a large manor house. The lord inside will keep us safe tonight or for however long we choose to stay."

"You know this lord well?"

"Yes, very well. He lived in Awbrey when I was a child. He helped fill the void of my lost father. When his wife died, he left his duties to his son and moved out to the family country estate. He only keeps a small staff and has practically no company. We can trust him with your identity."

"I believe you. I have full trust in your judgment, princess."

She only took a loud breath and kept staring straight ahead. They rode on mostly in silence to a path off of the one they were on. They came to a large, handsome manor that stood not far from the banks of the river. There weren't many windows lit up, but two torches burned at the entrance, and Maddoc could see a light in the entryway. They rode up to the front door. Maddoc got down from his horse and walked over to the princess. She slid down slowly, landing on her feet. She swayed slightly, and Maddoc reached out to steady her.

"I am fine, your majesty," she said stepping back from him. "I have just ridden too long and not had enough sleep. I wasn't trying to fall into your arms."

He looked at her with a frown. "I didn't think you were," he said softly trying to catch her eye.

She paid him no mind, walking past him to the front door. She pulled the bell cord found there and knocked on the door. After about a minute the door opened, and an elderly, well-dressed servant opened the door. His face was grim until his eyes landed on the princess. His old eyes widened, and a smile spread over his face.

He bowed as low as he could. "Your highness, what an unexpected surprise. I am very glad to see you."

"I am happy to see you as well, Albert. Your lord is home, I take it?"

"Of course, my princess. He rarely leaves the estate these days as you know. Please come in." The man straightened up and looked at Maddoc. "You and your... companion."

She smiled and walked into the entry hall. "Can you have someone see to our horses? I would like our packs brought in as well if it is not too much trouble."

"Of course, it is not, your highness. I will see to it as soon as I alert the master of your presence."

"Albert, who was at the door?" said a voice from the room just beyond them. "Did you manage to get rid of them?"

An old gentleman walked into the room. He was dressed as though he was attending a fancy dinner, though he seemed to have no company. He was tall with white hair that was cut short on his head. Maddoc could tell that he was once very strong and still looked very capable. His light blue eyes were clear, and his face showed he was once a handsome man. He stopped and stared at Princess Anwen as he came into the entry hall.

"Princess Anwen," he said disbelievingly. "Is it really you, my dear girl?"

"It is, Lord Aidan. I am very sorry for giving you no notice of our coming." Anwen stepped forward and held out her hand to the man.

"Think nothing of it, sweet lady." Lord Aidan bent down and kissed her hand. "I am just glad you still want to see me." He straightened up keeping a hold of her hand.

"Of course, I still want to see you. I should have come to visit you sooner, but there has been much to see to."

"You should have forgotten it all and come here." The old man gave a small angry growl. "I can't believe what my worthless grandson has done to you, Anwen. He must be the stupidest boy alive."

"It is no matter now. I only hope he and his future bride will be happy." Anwen looked down for a moment.

"You need not be so strong and magnanimous with me, my dear. Tell it like it is. He is a foolish man who did you very wrong. I wouldn't let him in if he came to my door half dead."

"Yes, you would, and you should. He is still your grandson, and he will see to your legacy. Who knows, with the way things are going he might be a king someday."

"He lost that chance, and you know it. You will be our queen, Anwen. The people will accept no other."

"We will not speak of it tonight. Perhaps we can go into the sitting room, and I can introduce my companion?"

The man looked over at Maddoc as he dropped the princess's hand. He looked back at the princess and nodded.

"I shall see to your horses and bags this moment, your highness," said Albert with a bow.

She nodded at him before letting Lord Aidan escort her through a doorway. Maddoc followed them and entered into a handsome parlor. It was very neat and comfortable though a little out of fashion.

"You look quite done in, dear one," said Lord Aidan as he led Princess Anwen to the sofa. "Let me ring for some food and tea to be brought in before you introduce me to the young man."

Anwen did not argue as she sat down. She looked at Maddoc and pointed to a chair close to the sofa. He sat down as Lord Aidan walked over to pull the cord in the corner. A young woman came into the room promptly, and Lord Aidan gave her instructions. When he was done, he sat in a chair next to Anwen.

"Now, who have you brought to my manor, Anwen?"

"Lord Aidan, let me present to you King Maddoc Cadden, the ruler of Calumbria. King Maddoc, this is Lord Aidan Dunne. He was once the High Lord of Awbrey."

Lord Aidan looked startled for a moment as he studied Maddoc. He turned back to Anwen. "You are telling me this simply dressed young man is the King of Calumbria."

"I am, my lord, and you know I would not lie to you. He was attacked outside of Awbrey, and I happened to be walking by with Brennan. The power from my Gift saved him, though he was injured. My aunt expelled him from the palace as soon as he could stand. I could not let him journey alone to his kingdom. He would not have made it far by himself. He is not used to traveling without guards to protect and guide him. We have taken the path through the forest and by the river. After two nights sleeping on the road, I was hoping to find shelter here for at least one night."

"That is quite a story, my princess," said Lord Aidan as he stared at Maddoc. "And I am not sure how wise it was for you to accompany the king."

"Perhaps not, but what else could I do? My aunt would not allow any of our guards to accompany him. She would not let him stay while I sent a message to his palace. She ordered him away almost immediately."

"Well, you are here now, and there is no reason for you to travel any further. We shall send a message this very night to the palace in Quinlan. The king may stay here until his people come to collect him. Then you and I will travel back to Awbrey together. I wish to visit the village and all of my family."

Maddoc raised his eyebrows at this information. The thought that he could stay here in the manor in safety and comfort should have raised his spirits and it did slightly. He looked over at the princess and knew he would feel the loss of her company. He found he did not want to part with her so soon, especially after their fight. It would take a few days, maybe almost a week for his people to come fetch him. Maybe he could earn her forgiveness by then. Perhaps he could convince her to visit his kingdom with him. If not on his current journey, then for the Winter Festival. She could come and speak with his uncle and his mother about help for Lucidala.

Food and tea came, and Maddoc was very grateful for it. The princess had packed well for them and had killed some wild game as they traveled, but the sandwiches and hot tea were delightful after those hard days and nights on the road. As they ate, Lord Aidan talked to the princess. He asked her how things were in Awbrey, and she filled him in on the state of several families. They spoke of issues in the kingdom until the princess yawned and seem to struggle to keep her eyes open.

"You should go on up and rest, my dear," said Lord Aidan. "Have Sarah bring up some water for you to have a bath. You can take the usual room."

"The letter for the king?" asked the princess as she stood up.

"He and I will see to it as soon as you are upstairs. I am sure he would like you to rest as much as I. Wouldn't you, your majesty?"

"Of course," said Maddoc as he stood up. "You should take care of yourself, princess. You have had a hard few days, and I know you haven't slept well."

She nodded before turning to Lord Aidan. "Thank you so much, my lord. You can't imagine how much you have lifted my spirits and soothed my mind."

He took her hand. "Just seeing your beautiful face has made me very happy, Anwen. Now go upstairs, and we can talk more about your trouble with the king tomorrow."

She smiled as the old man patted her hand with his other one. She turned to leave when Maddoc stepped forward and grabbed her hand. He knew he probably shouldn't, but he felt compelled to wish her good night in the proper way. "Thank you for all you have endured to keep me safe. I could never repay all that you have done for me." He bent down and brought her hand to her lips. He kissed her the soft skin on the back of her hand gently as he looked up at her. "Sleep well, princess."

She took her hand back slowly and stared at him. "I hope you have a full night of good rest, your majesty." She turned and walked from the room.

"Now, your majesty, I will get you some paper and a quill so you can write your letter. Then perhaps you will indulge me with one drink and some conversation before you go on to bed."

"This is your home, and you have shown me great hospitality. I will be happy to have a drink with you, my lord."

Lord Aidan showed Maddoc to a small desk in the corner of the room. Maddoc scratched out a note, explaining his predicament, and where he was located. When he was done, he sealed it and took his royal ring out from under his shirt where it was held there by a chain. He pressed his seal into it and handed it to Lord Aidan. Lord Aidan rang for Albert, who went to see about sending the letter.

Maddoc walked back over to the sofa and sat down. Lord Aidan came over with two drinks. He handed one to Maddoc before sitting down with his own. He took a long drink and looked at the king.

"It sounds like you have had quite an interesting past few days, your majesty."

Maddoc took a sip of his drink and nodded. "I have. Much too interesting for me for the most part. It is not pleasant to have your life threatened twice in four days."

"Twice?" asked Lord Aidan after taking the drink. "Have you had some trouble on the road?"

"The first day we traveled someone threw a knife at me. The princess was able to see it coming and managed to get me out of the way. She tried to track them, but they escaped on horseback."

"Have you had any trouble since then? Have you come across anyone else?"

"None that seem to want to do me harm, and I believe the princess would be well aware of any danger were it about."

"Yes, she has been trained well by her father and me. She is an excellent tracker and hunter." He took a drink. "I hate to think of the danger she has been in these past few days. It seems as if she has had nothing but trouble the past year. She does not deserve it."

Maddoc took another drink. "I wish she had not had to leave the safety of her village to come with me. I told her not to, but she would not hear it. She said it was the right thing to do."

"I am sure she thought it was, but I also think getting out of the village may have been attractive to her. It has not been easy for her, not with the talk and having to see that rascal and her cousin every day."

"You speak of the young man who is betrothed to her cousin?"

"I do. He is my grandson, though I am ashamed to admit it." The lord put down his glass. "Has she told you about her and Lachlan?"

"No, but I overheard them talking back in the palace. It was an accident, and it wasn't much, but I heard enough to get the gist of what was going on. I take it he threw her off for her cousin."

The old man sighed. "He did, and after making her many promises. It was a known thing they would be married. They were as good as betrothed." He sat back and was quiet for a moment. "It is not fair, but her reputation has suffered due to his actions. Not to most people, but to those who like to do damage. The mothers and other young ladies of the court seem to enjoy the princess's misfortunes." He picked up his drink. "Someone out to call the devil out, though I don't know who."

"She was attached to him?"

"She loved him and believe he loved her. You must have seen enough in the princess to know she has an open and passionate heart. My grandson took advantage of it. I worry he will never be shown the mercy of the gods for hurting such a good woman. There is not a better one that has ever breathed, your majesty."

Maddoc only nodded. He wasn't sure what to say.

"This journey she has taken with you will not help matters back home. There will be talk; you know there will be. She is an unattached young woman, and she has been on the road with you for days unchaperoned."

"I haven't done anything to dishonor her," said the king quickly.

The lord smiled a little. "I believe, your majesty, and I know my Anwen. If you tried anything she didn't want, you would have a broken arm at this point. She may be little, but she is a strong and capable fighter. You do not want to test her."

The king chuckled. "I have no doubt of it."

"Still, through no fault of yours or hers, she will face much talk when she gets back. I hope my return to the village will cut some of it. I will make sure my son supports her, though I have no doubt he will. He, like most good people, is fond of the princess."

"I can see where she would inspire much love in her people. She has impressed me with her knowledge and pride in her kingdom. She will be a very capable queen someday."

"She will be a glorious queen, your majesty. I believe she may be the most impressive ruler our kingdom has ever seen as long as she is given the chance. When I said there has never been a better woman alive, I meant it. It is not just talk. Her aunt is beautiful and wise, but she can be cruel. Her mother is kind and alluring, but Anwen is twice as intelligent.

"She has a sense of goodness and fairness like no other I have seen, and she is the bravest person I have ever met." He laughed and shook his head. "Can you imagine a man so foolish to ever give her up after he had won her heart? I plan to have a very long talk with my grandson and find out exactly what he was thinking."

Maddoc finished his drink and thought about what it would be like to win the love of a woman like Anwen. He had never tried to win a woman's heart, and he never planned to, but he had never met anyone like Anwen. Lord Aiden was right in that Maddoc could already tell she loved freely and boldly. Maddoc could tell she was a passionate woman. He wondered what it would be like to have her look at him with favor and even love in her beautiful eyes. He imagined it would be quite an experience to spend a night making love to such a woman.

"Perhaps you could help matters, your majesty?"

"How so, my lord?"

"You will go back to your kingdom owing the princess your life. You could recognize her in some way. I am not sure I would like her to visit your kingdom, but if it was to commend her and give help to Lucidala, it would be worth it."

"I would be honored to have the princess visit my palace. When I return, I will do all I can to see that she is properly recognized and rewarded." He sat back and sighed a little. "Whether she will accept is another matter."

The old man raised his eyebrows. "Have you not gotten on with her on your journey?"

"It's been a mixed experience. The princess does not mince words, and I am not used to being spoken to in such a way. I have said some things I shouldn't have. I have offended in her a way I do not believe she will forgive me."

"But you wish for her forgiveness?" asked Lord Aidan as he watched Maddoc.

Maddoc looked down at his empty glass, wishing he had another drink. "I do wish it. There is not much more I want at this moment than for her to say I am forgiven before we part ways."

"If you truly mean that, then she will forgive you. She is too good to hold a grudge for long if you admit your mistake. Even if you don't, she will not think as badly of you as you believe. Look at how she talks of my grandson. He deserves nothing but her scorn, but she speaks of him with grace and well wishes for his happiness. Can you imagine a better woman, your majesty?"

"No, I cannot not."

"It is getting late, your majesty, and I am weary. I know you must be as well. I will bid you a good night."

Lord Aidan drained his glass and left the room after a bow. Maddoc barely registered he had left as he thought about Princess Anwen. She was an excellent woman. Lord Aidan was right. He had never met a better one. Maddoc finally looked up and realized he was all alone in a strange house. Lord Aidan had not told him whom to ask for a bedroom or given him any instructions.

Unsure of what to do, Maddoc walked into the entryway. He saw a shadow moving on the second floor. Hoping it was a servant who could help him, he walked up the stairs.

10

〰

Chapter 10

After a nice warm bath and another cup of tea, Anwen felt very much refreshed. Some good food, a familiar safe place, and a friendly face had done much to revive her. She sat by the fireplace in her room, running her fingers through her hair to help it dry. It seemed her journey had come to an end.

She should feel relieved that she was finished with this obligation, and a part of her was. After the awful words from the king, she had hardly been able to look at him. Soon he would be out of her life for good, and she could forget the shame and embarrassment he had made her feel. She warmed her hands in front of the fire wondering why she was not happier at the thought of being rid of King Maddoc.

She thought it was because she had hoped to eventually part from him under happier circumstances. She had hoped he would think well of her. Her main goal had been to keep him safe, but she had also wanted to work on her kingdom's relationship with his. Now, he would never want to see her again. He must have thought her a very low woman to think she would stoop to such a thing.

He had tried to apologize, but she attributed that to wanting her continued cooperation in getting him safely to Calumbria. He had been very proper and courtly with her before she retired, but they were in the house of her friend and former lord. He would of course want to make a good impression on Lord Aidan. In less than a week, his people would come collect him, and the king would think of her no more.

She shook her head and stood up. It should not matter to her. She was no worse off than she had been at the start of the journey. She was still the disappointing princess who had failed her kingdom. She was still the woman who had not been worth kept promises. She was damaged and could be easily dismissed. Now she would have to go back to Awbrey and face her aunt and the other gossips. She had ridden off with a single man by herself. She couldn't imagine what was being said about her amongst the viler of the court.

Perhaps when her mother returned, she would send Anwen away. There might be some insignificant kingdom who would like a princess or some older lord who would take her in an attempt to further his line. Her future looked rather bleak, but she would make of it what she could. She was not meant for low spirits or dread. She would face what she must as she always had and try to find joy where she could.

The clock in her room chimed, and she realized how late it had gotten. She wondered if the king had retired yet. She suddenly remembered that Lord Aidan would more than likely not see to the king's needs. He was not used to guests, and in the days he entertained them, his wife always saw to the hospitality of the house. Anwen walked over and pulled the cord in her room to summon a servant. She waited several minutes, but none appeared. Deciding she would see if she could find Sarah or another servant, she slipped on a robe over the nightgown that had been provided for her. She stepped out into the hall and walked towards the stairs.

She heard footsteps coming up the stairs. She hoped it was Sarah or Albert, and she continued to walk towards them. It was not a servant who came to the top, but the king. She felt herself flush as alarm filled her stomach. She stopped walking and turned her redden-faced away.

Maddoc walked towards her slowly. "Good evening, princess. Why are you still awake? I thought you had retired."

"I apologize for my appearance, King Maddoc. I wouldn't dream of appearing in front of you in such a way." She could not look at him.

"Do not trouble yourself. I am not offended, or think you had any wish to see me this evening."

She looked up at him. "I was hoping to find Sarah out on the landing. I pulled the cord in my room, but no one came. I was afraid Lord Aidan would not think to see to finding you a room or having a bath drawn for you. He is a good man, but he is not used to hosting anymore. When he was serving as our high lord, his wife saw to his house and hospitality. He has not been the same since she died. He barely keeps any servants, and I imagine they are all busy or asleep at this point."

"He did retire without telling me where I might find a room. I was hoping to find a servant to direct me." Maddoc paused. "Perhaps you can help me? I believe you have been here plenty of times before."

"I have. I try to visit Lord Aidan when I can. I do not like how all alone he is out here. I have tried to get his grandsons to visit more, but they have been busy seeing to their own futures." She gave him a hint of a smile. "It will not do for me to ramble on as you must be exhausted. You can sleep in the room close to mine. It may not be proper, but I would not like to have you on the other side of the house." She felt herself flush even further, knowing how her words must sound. "I would rather you be close by so I can keep an eye on you."

"You do not trust me," stated Maddoc with defeat sounding in his voice.

She felt a little pity for him. He did seem at least a little sorry for his earlier words. "It is not that, your majesty. I do not think you are looking to cause any mischief. Just after all that has happened, I would like to keep you close in case there is trouble. I said I would see you safely to your people, and I will do it. Now come follow me, your room is just down here."

She turned, and the king hurried to walk next to her. "I am glad to have your help, but I was hoping you would be resting by now. I know you haven't had much sleep the past few nights."

"I already feel much refreshed being in my old friend's home. It seems

I will get plenty of sleep from this point on. I am relieved you will be safely delivered to your kingdom."

"I know you are happy to be done with me, princess. I can't imagine what a burden I have been for you."

She turned and gave him a real smile. "Perhaps you have been a burden, but you have not been without your amusements."

"I suppose you will remember me as the good-for-nothing king who stumbles around unable to take care of himself."

She couldn't help a small laugh. "Not as bad as that."

"It is better than I could hope after my thoughtless and cruel words." They stopped by a door, and the king took her hand. "Princess Anwen, I want to apologize again for what I said. It was wrong and completely ridiculous. You have been nothing but a charming, respectable woman since we left on our journey. I don't know what came over me."

"I suppose you are used to women throwing themselves at you, your majesty. I can almost understand how you might misconstrue my actions."

"No, do not dismiss what I have done. Too many people try to dismiss my wrongs. Just tell me you will try to forgive me and think better of me over time."

She looked down at where he held her hand and nodded. "I will forgive you, and I will not look back on our time with complete displeasure."

He gently pulled her a little closer. "I know you might wish to never lay eyes on me again, but I hope you will come to my kingdom so I can properly recognize you for what you have done. I would like to publicly commend you and see what can be done to help your kingdom."

"I will accept your help for Lucidala if you can manage it, but you do not need to publicly recognize me."

"I do, princess, and I want to. Tell me you will come to Calumbria. You should come to our Winter Festival. I know you would enjoy it, and there will be many people from many different kingdoms attending. You could go almost the whole time and never have to say two words to me."

She couldn't help but smile at him again. "If you officially invite me, and all is well in my kingdom, I would not be opposed to attending."

He gently rubbed her hand, and Anwen we suddenly very aware of how close he was to her. She swallowed trying to think of something to say. She knew she should pull away from him and tell him good night, but something stopped her. She found she did not mind him holding her hand. She looked up at him, and he was looking down at her with a look she could not place. It did not appear he was displeased. He opened his mouth when the sound of footsteps close by made them pull apart.

"Your highness, did you ring the bell? The cook thought she heard it, but I was out in the washroom attending to your dress. I did not mean to keep you waiting," said Sarah as she walked up to them.

"It is no trouble, Sarah. Will you please see that my companion has some warm water for a bath? I know it is getting late, but we have been on the road for days. I know he would appreciate your trouble."

"It is no trouble, your highness. I will see to it directly. Is he in this room?"

"Yes, thank you, Sarah," said Anwen as Sarah curtsied and turned away. She looked at King Maddoc. "I believe you will have all you need now, your majesty. I wish you a good night."

She went to walk past him when he stopped her. "Princess Anwen, perhaps if you feel up to it sometime tomorrow, you might ride around the estate with me. I should like to see the land."

She nodded. "I would be happy to ride with you."

"Good night, princess."

She walked past him and to her room. She went straight to her bed, blowing out candles as she went. She lay down and adjusted her pillow. It took her a while to find a comfortable position as a thousand thoughts ran through her head. Finally, her exhaustion won out, and she fell asleep unsure of most things in her life.

She dreamed of a time when she was young. She was at the edge of the forest with two clerics.

"Now, princess, touch this bud and imagine a fully opened flower. This should be a red rose, so think of a beautiful red rose."

Anwen reached out her small hand and placed it gently on the bud.

She closed her eyes tight and tried to think of a beautiful red rose. She pictured it in her mind and opened her eyes. The bud remained closed.

"Try harder, Princess Anwen. You must really imagine the flower. You have to really want it to open," said the cleric urgently.

She closed her eyes again, keeping her hand on the bud. She thought hard about a red rose and willed the bud to open. She opened her eyes and took her hand off it. It remained closed.

"No, princess, you aren't really trying," said the cleric harshly.

"Dinah, you are scaring the girl," said the other cleric softly.

"She has to learn. She needs to release her Gift," said the cleric called Dinah.

"Perhaps she doesn't really have the gift," observed the other cleric.

"She has it. You know you can feel it within her. She just needs to work harder."

"There should be another, shouldn't there? Aren't life-givers usually born in twos within a few years of each other? Is her cousin not one?"

"No, Princess Gwendolyn barely has any Gift it all, and it is only clairvoyance. Princess Anwen is the only life-giver. I am not sure why the gods only gave us one." Dinah turned to the princess. "You are the only hope for your people, princess, so try again." Dinah pulled the princess hard to another bush.

"I cannot do it," said Anwen sadly. "I am trying as hard as I can, but nothing will happen."

"Well, you are just going to have to try harder or all your people will starve. They will die of sickness, and it will be all your fault."

"What is going on here?" asked Anwen's father as he walked towards Anwen with Lord Aidan following him.

"We are just trying to help the princess live into her gift, your majesty," said the cleric next to Dinah.

"It sounds as if you are speaking unnecessarily harsh to my daughter," said the king furiously. "She is just a child. You cannot pressure her so."

"I do not wish to cause her distress, but she has to live into her gift," said Dinah.

"Come, Anwen. It is time to go home," said her father, holding out his hand.

Anwen hurried to her father's side as Lord Aidan smiled down at her.

"Do not take my daughter from the palace again without my or your queen's permission," said the king as he took Anwen's hand.

They started walking towards the palace when a loud noise made Anwen turn her head. It sounded like a large door being thrown open. It took her a moment to wake and realize the noise was not in her dream but in her actual bedroom.

Her eyes flew open, and she sat up. Two men looked at her from her door. Both held swords. Anwen rolled out of bed, bending down to pick up her sword she had placed under her bed. She straightened up and looked at the men. One stepped forward and smiled at her.

"Now, now, girl, we have no business with you. Why don't you go back to sleep, and pretend as nothing has happened? We will move along and find who we came for."

"I know who you came for, and you will not go near him." Anwen moved closer holding her sword out in front of her.

The man looked at his companion, and they both laughed. He turned and looked at Anwen. "We do not wish to hurt a woman, especially as one who looks as you do. Now, go back to sleep."

She moved closer to them. "You will not go near the king or anyone else in this house."

"Do you really think you can stop us both? What's keeping us from just walking out the door?"

Anwen looked at the door, and it slammed shut. The man closest to it jumped out of the way. They both looked at the door and then her. The man closest to the door turned and tried to open it. He pulled hard, but it would not open. Anwen turned to her dying fire and threw her hand out. The fire roared to life, flooding the room with light.

"Now, you will not leave this room alive if you try to fight me," said Anwen keeping her sword up. "Tell me who sent you and why. If you put down your swords and tell me all you know, I will find a way to let you live."

"We will do away with you and find a way out of this room. We do not like to hurt a woman, but we are very capable," said the man. He nodded at his companion, and they both advanced on Anwen.

She blocked the first man's strike and turned, slashing out at the other man. He moved back, and she turned to meet the sword of the other man. She plunged her sword and almost managed to strike one of the men. She turned quickly to block the other. She spun and rolled away from both the men, closer to her bed. They moved towards her as there was a pounding on her door.

"Princess, is all well in there?" came King Maddoc's voice from the other side.

"Princess?" asked one of the men as he put his sword down for a second. "You are a princess?"

"I am Princess Anwen Claran of Lucidala."

The men exchanged glances. "I imagine your family and kingdom would pay quite a lot to have you back safely."

"You think you can take me alive?" She shook her head.

"Princess Anwen, is all well?" King Maddoc pounded on the door harder.

The two men turned to look at the door, and Anwen saw her chance. She moved forward, slashing out her sword at the man closest to her. She sliced his arm, causing a line of blood to form. He dropped his sword and cried out in pain. Anwen moved forward and kicked his sword away from him.

"Forget trying to keep her alive, Clem. Kill her," snapped the man as he held his arm.

The one called Clem came for her. He struck at her, and Anwen dodged to the right. His sword hit a large vase on a small table, causing it to fall onto the floor and shatter into many pieces.

"Anwen!" yelled the king as she heard a loud noise against the door. It sounded as though he was trying to breakthrough.

The man slashed at her again, and Anwen met his sword. They traded blows back and forth as the other man let his arm go and moved towards her. She could hear the king trying to break through the door as she moved around the room, crossing swords with one man while avoiding the other. The man with the hurt arm got to his sword and picked it up. He walked towards her as the other man had backed her into a corner.

They both looked at her, and she did not back down. She held up her sword, trying to figure out a way to get out of the corner. The men both looked ready to strike, when the door bust open, and King Maddoc stumbled into the room. The two men turned and looked at the king. Anwen stared at King Maddoc, feeling her power churn within her. Those men could do what they would with her, but they would not hurt him.

They both moved towards the king, seeming to forget her in their surprise. King Maddoc looked at them both and then her. She felt the powers from her Gift swell. She didn't want to kill the men. She wanted answers from them, but her powers grew to the point she could not control them. All her Gift wanted was to protect the king. She felt it move through her, and her hands raised. A light erupted from her, and the men were thrown hard against the wall. She heard their bones break and saw blood erupt from their heads.

She dropped her sword and felt herself sway. Her powers within her settled down, leaving her feeling exhausted and weak. She was going to fall. She wished she could make it to the bed, but she knew she could not. Her legs shook as the room became dim around her. She collapsed, but before she could hit the floor, the king moved forward and caught her.

He held her in his arms, staring down at her. "Anwen," he said in dismay.

She reached up towards him, trying to reassure him. She touched his cheek, feeling the short beard that grew there. She tried to speak, but instead, her eyes closed, and the darkness took her.

11

Chapter 11

Maddoc looked down at Anwen in his arms. She was breathing but looked very pale. He moved one hand to her face and brushed her cheek while whispering her name. She didn't stir. He looked over to her bed and picked her up in his arms. She was so light, he barely registered her weight. He took her over to the bed and gently laid her down. As he took her hand, the door opened wider and Lord Aidan walked in the room with his servant, Albert.

He looked over at the dead men on the ground and then to the bed. He gasped and hurried forward. "What happened? Is the princess injured?"

"I'm not sure. I heard voices and noises from my room and came to check on the princess. When I got to her door, I could not open it, but I could hear something was going on inside. I was finally able to force the door open and found two men had cornered the princess, holding up their swords.

"They turned to face me. I believe I was their actual target. She did something with her Gift, I think. There was a bright light, and the men were thrown against the wall. I think she killed them."

"Yes, I think she did," said Lord Aidan looking over at the men. "Is she injured anywhere?"

"Not that I can see. After she used her Gift, she fainted. I caught her, but she hasn't woken up since."

Lord Aidan turned to his servant. "Albert, get the princess some wine and then go to the stables. Get Lenny and Smith to search the estate. We need to make sure no one else is lurking about. Once they are done, they should come here. They can see to the men's bodies after I look over them."

"Yes, my lord," said Albert before turning and leaving.

"Do you know what is wrong with her?" asked Maddoc as he looked down at the princess, still holding her hand.

"She is just exhausted from her use of power. It happens, though it seems this one has done her in worse than most times. I imagine her exhaustion from your travels hasn't helped."

She stirred slightly in the bed, gripping Maddoc's hand. She opened her eyes and tried to sit up.

"No, stay down, princess," said Maddoc softly as he put his free hand on her shoulder.

"Are you well, your majesty?" she asked as she looked up at him.

"I am. I believe it is only because of you." Maddoc pulled her hand up to his lips without thinking. "What of you? Are you alright?"

"I believe so. I am just so tired."

"Then you should rest." Maddoc glanced behind him at the men in the corner. "We should take you to another room. You can sleep in the one I was in. The fire is burning, and it is warm."

She sat up slightly. "What of those two men? Are they both...?"

"I believe so, your highness," said Lord Aidan.

The princess closed her eyes. "I didn't mean to kill them. I was trying to keep them alive."

"You must not feel guilty over this," said Maddoc. "They were trying to hurt you."

She shook her head. "I was not worried about me. Only when they turned towards you could I not control my Gift." She opened her eyes and looked over towards the men. "Now, we shall never know who they are or who sent them."

"I will check over them, Anwen," said Lord Aidan. "I will see what I can find."

"I can help," she said weakly as her hand went up to her head.

"No, you need to rest, my dear." Lord Aidan looked at Maddoc. "Your majesty, you should escort the princess to the other room."

Maddoc nodded. "Princess, do you think you can walk?"

"I can. It is not far." She made to sit up completely, and Maddoc helped her.

She stood up slowly, looking as if she might fall again. Maddoc stayed close to her, putting his arm around her shoulders. She leaned into him, fitting perfectly just under his arm, her head against his chest. He walked with her through the room. She looked at the men as they passed, Maddoc careful to keep her close.

They left the room and turned down the hall towards the bedroom in which Maddoc had been staying.

"You are sure you are well, your majesty?" she asked softly. "You did not injure yourself breaking through the door?"

"No, princess, there is nothing the matter with me. You are sure they did not hurt you in any way?"

She shook her head against him. "They were not able to touch me." She looked up at Maddoc. "Are we for certain it is only those two? There aren't more somewhere on the estate are there?"

"Lord Aidan has two of his men searching the manor."

"You will need to be careful, King Maddoc. Tell Lord Aidan to make sure you are well guarded tonight. I wish I could watch over you, but I don't know how much longer I can keep my eyes open."

"You need to rest, princess. I shall be cautious and aware tonight." They came to the door that was slightly ajar. Maddoc pushed it the rest of the way open.

They walked slowly to the bed. He let her go as he straightened the covers and pillows. Anwen sat on the bed, and Maddoc looked down at her. "I will have the servant bring you some wine when it comes. I am sure it will help settle your nerves so you can sleep."

"I am not sure it will help." She looked down. "Perhaps you might stay with me for a bit until I fall asleep? I would feel better being able to know you are close until the estate is searched."

Maddoc nodded, feeling very much as though he would like to stay near her. After finding her being attacked by two men, he did not like the idea of her being alone. He had felt so frantic and scared when he couldn't open her door. He had imagined so many awful things happening to her with the noises he heard. The door to the bedroom opened, and the servant, Sarah, walked in uncertainly with a glass of wine.

"Thank you, Sarah. You may put it on the table here," said the princess.

The woman hurriedly walked the glass over and placed it down. "Lord Aidan asked for your presence when possible, your majesty." Sarah kept her eyes to the ground and seemed nervous.

"Please tell your lord I will join him as soon as I can."

She nodded and gave a curtsey before hurrying from the room.

"I suppose Lord Aidan told her who you were," said Princess Anwen with a smile. "I had hoped to keep your title a secret from most of the staff, but I guess it slipped out."

"It is no matter," replied Maddoc as he picked up the glass of wine.

She took it from him and took a sip. "You should go see Lord Aidan."

"He will have to wait. I told you I would stay with you until you fell asleep, and I would like to keep my word. I am sure Lord Aidan will understand."

"He might have something important to say to you," said Anwen before taking another drink.

"If it so important, he will come himself. I doubt there is much more important than your well-being, princess."

"I shall be fine, your majesty."

"I told you I would stay. If you wish me to go, then you will finish that wine and go to sleep."

She took a longer drink and went to place the wine glass on the table.

Maddoc took it from her and put it down. She put her feet up on the bed and settled down into it. Maddoc looked behind him, finding a chair close by. He pulled it near the bed and sat down close to the princess. She looked up at him and seemed to be studying him.

"What is it?" he asked quietly.

"I was trying to figure out why my Gift wishes to protect you so badly. I am not sure I have felt such a strong surge of power as I did when those men turned towards you." She moved around a bit in the bed, arranging her hair so it ran down one side of her body. "I really didn't want to kill those men. I wanted to figure out what was going on."

"Perhaps your Gift knows how clueless and helpless I really am," he said with a small laugh. "I think it might feed off of your pity for me."

"I do not pity you, your majesty, not really. I do find I feel a little bit sorry for you, but I am not sure why. You are in the most powerful position in this land, and you must have everything you could ever want. I just wish the people around you had done a better job showing you how to take care of yourself. I wish you weren't so careless with your own safety."

Maddoc sighed a little, thinking she was right. His people had tried to tell him it was dangerous to ride open around the land. He was told to take the usual roads, but he had ignored all advice so he could do as he pleased. It was like that in most areas of his life. His mother had told him to take more responsibility for her kingdom, but he had laughed her off. His uncle had warned him to not be so promiscuous in his personal life, to be more circumspect in his nighttime partners.

He had ignored both of them. By ignoring his mother, he had become an empty king. He had the title and the crown, but no power or responsibility. By ignoring his uncle, he found that he had grown tired of spending nights with many different women. The moments of pleasure were still there, but afterward, he had begun to feel regretful and empty. The women had started to blend together, and he found the brief moments of sated desire did not make up for the vacant feeling he would feel in the mornings and throughout much of the day.

"I have offended you again," said the princess sadly. "I wish I could learn to curb my tongue, but it seems I cannot."

"You have not offended me, princess. You tell the truth. You have told me nothing but truth since we have met. If I am offended by it, it is all my own fault. I cannot ignore my shortcomings forever."

She yawned. "Perhaps I should say something positive about you after I speak so. Maybe it will make the hard truths go down easier if I give you an easy truth to go with it."

Maddoc smiled. "What positive could you say about me?"

"She turned slightly towards him and closed her eyes. "You are intelligent, and can be quite charming." She snuggled deeper into her pillow and seemed to be drifting off. "You are also very handsome."

Maddoc laughed very quietly and watched as she fell asleep. Before he got up to go see Lord Aiden, he bent down and kissed her forehead gently. She made a soft noise in her sleep but did not awaken. He stood up and walked to the door, opening it. Before walking out, he looked at her lying in the bed, wishing he could stay near her and watch her sleep. It was a strange feeling for him. He felt as though he was attached to the princess in some way. It was as if she held some invisible cord that wrapped around some part of him. It was not an unpleasant feeling as if being trapped, but one that made him feel safely tethered and secure.

He took a deep breath and left the room, closing the door behind him. The servant Sarah was standing out in the hall, looking anxious.

"Your name is Sarah isn't it?" asked Maddoc, trying to sound kind.

"Yes, your majesty." Sarah gave a deep curtsey and looked down.

"I know you must be tired, but would you mind watching over the princess for a few minutes just to make sure she is truly asleep. If she awakes and needs anything, I ask you to come find me."

Sarah looked up at him and seem to be trying to suppress a grin. "Of course, your majesty. I do not mind sitting near Princess Anwen."

"Thank you, Sarah, you are very kind."

She gave another curtsey and hurried past him. He watched her carefully open the door to the bedroom and slip in. Feeling better about leaving the princess now that she was not alone, Maddoc walked to the open door and stepped into the room. Lord Aidan was kneeled down with his servant Albert, looking over the dead men. Maddoc moved closer to them and crouched down next to Lord Aidan.

Lord Aidan looked at Maddoc. "How is Princess Anwen?"

"She is sleeping. I am sorry to keep you waiting, but she did not like to be alone until she fell asleep."

Lord Aidan nodded and looked back at the dead men. He held out a slip of paper to Maddoc.

Maddoc took it. "You have found something?"

"Read it."

Maddoc unrolled the paper and read. *I have intercepted another message. The king is in the home of Lord Aidan Dunne on the northeast side of Lucidala.*

Maddoc looked up at the old Lord. "I suppose this means they also intercepted the letter the princess sent from the palace. Maybe even the one my man sent as I first traveled."

"Yes, they seem to have been tracking your whereabouts by your messages," nodded Lord Aidan.

"Have you found anything else?" Maddoc put the paper in his pocket.

"Some containers of substances I doubt are anything good, and a few knives. They came well prepared to kill you in any way possible. It seems they were checking bedrooms and got to the princess before you. My men tell me it looked like they checked the other wing first."

Lord Aidan put his hand on the ground and pushed up to get into a crouching position. Seeing what he was doing, Maddoc stood up and held his hand out to the old man. Lord Aidan took it as his servant helped him to stand.

"This means we cannot stay here much longer," said Maddoc as Lord Aidan stretched his back.

"No, you cannot not. They know you are here and will probably try to strike again."

"You will need to leave as well, my lord," said Maddoc.

"I plan to go to Awbrey as I said I would. I will leave tomorrow as soon as I can pack and send a note to my son. If it makes it, I do not know. I will say nothing about you."

Maddoc nodded and swallowed before speaking. "Will you... will you take the princess with you?"

"Do you honestly think she would agree to go with me and leave you on your own?"

"She might if you requested it of her. She is very fond of you," said Maddoc. He almost wanted her to go with the old man. She wouldn't be safe with Maddoc, but he couldn't imagine traveling on without her.

Lord Aidan chuckled. "She is a loyal little thing, but she seems to feel responsible for you at the moment." Lord Aidan rubbed his chin. "I hope you do not mind me saying it, but you do not seem indifferent to her."

No, he was not indifferent to her. The more he got to know her and thought about her, the more he went from indifferent to the exact opposite. He was starting to find her almost necessary. He could not say that out loud. He shouldn't even admit it to himself. "She has been a good companion on the road. She is extremely helpful, and I do not know the way as she does. I would hate to lose her company."

Lord Aidan examined Maddoc closely. He raised one eyebrow at him. "I suppose if that is all, I could find someone else to go with you. Two of my men know the way to your kingdom, and they are proficient fighters. They would see you safely to your palace, I believe, or at least somewhere friendly in Calumbria."

Everything in Maddoc told him to refuse. He did not want to part from Anwen, but what good would it do to keep her close to him? Nothing could come of any relationship with her. There was also the fact he doubted she even thought of him remotely in that way. "Why don't we let the princess decide for herself in the morning? She would not like us making decisions for her."

Lord Aidan laughed. "No, she would not. You already know her well, it seems." He turned to Albert. "Find the king a room close by and make sure he has all he needs." The old lord turned back to Maddoc. "I will have my people patrol the halls and grounds to keep watch. You will be safe to rest."

"Thank you, my lord. You have done much for me."

"I am doing it for Anwen. She does not want you harmed, so I will make sure no one gets to you. I also want to protect her. She has been through too much in her young life, and she does not deserve any more pain."

Maddoc nodded as Albert walked towards the door. "If you will come with me, your majesty."

"Good night, Lord Aidan. I will see you in the morning."

"Good night, King Maddoc."

Albert took Maddoc to a bedroom a few doors down. The servant kneeled down to build a fire for the king, and Maddoc walked over to help. He handed Albert a couple of logs. "You need not trouble yourself, your majesty."

"I doubt this is your normal work, Albert." Maddoc handed Albert one more log.

"We do not have a large staff here. I pitch in where I can. It does not bother me."

"And it does not bother me to help you," said Maddoc as he dusted off his hands. "I would do it myself, but I am ashamed to admit I can barely start a fire."

Albert smiled as he picked up some flint and a fire striker. He placed some kindling by the logs and hit the metal against the flint. It took a few tries, but the sparks caught, and soon a fire was catching on to the logs.

Albert stood up as did Maddoc. "Do you need anything else, your majesty? A glass of wine to help you sleep?"

"No, I am well, Albert. Go get what rest you can. I thank you for your assistance."

Albert left, and Maddoc walked over to the bed. He turned down the covers and arranged the pillows. He almost got into bed, when he decided he could not sleep without doing one more thing. He walked back to the door and looked out into the hallway to find it deserted. Slipping out the door, he walked quickly and quietly to the bedroom the princess was sleeping in. He slowly opened the door, hoping it wouldn't make a noise. Peering in he saw the bed in the light cast by the fire. Poor Sarah was sound asleep in a chair on one side of the bed.

Maddoc walked closer to the other side and saw Princess Anwen sleeping soundly. She had her hand tucked up under her chin and some of her hair had fallen into her face. Without thinking, Maddoc reached over and gently pulled her stray hair back so it would rest behind her. His fingers grazed her cheek, and he let his touch linger too long on the soft waves of her hair. She stirred, and he took his hand back, hoping not to wake her. She seemed to settle back down as Maddoc watched her.

She was very lovely. Her skin was so perfect it hardly seemed real. Her profile showed her nose had the smallest upturn at the end. Her mouth was small, but her lips were full. They was a slight pout on her face as she slept, that Maddoc found alluring. He started to wonder what her lips would taste like, and how they would feel against his own. He looked at her small outline under the covers. What would it be like to hold her against him, to feel her warm body pressed up against his?

He realized he needed to stop this line of thinking for several reasons. He could not have her in that way. It would be wrong as he could offer her no future with him. She was a woman who deserved a man who could love her and give her security. There were no promises he could ever make her, even if he wanted to. He shook his head. He knew she wanted no promises from him. She could barely stand to be in his presence. Only her goodness and sense of doing what was right had kept her by his side.

In the morning when she was presented with a good solution to her king problem, he was sure she would be satisfied to leave him in the hands of others. She would go back to her home and forget all about him. As he looked at her lovely face, he knew he would never forget her. He looked at her for one more moment, satisfied that she was sleeping well. He walked out of the room quietly and into the hall.

"Is all well, your majesty?" asked Lord Aidan as he walked out of the room where the two men had lay dead. Some servants were moving the bodies out behind him.

"Yes, I only wanted to check on the princess one more time before I settled in for the night. She is still asleep."

Lord Aidan turned to see his men had made it to the stairwell and were walking down carefully. He looked back at Maddoc. "I suppose you wanted to make sure your traveling companion was well enough to journey on with you should she choose it."

Maddoc looked up at the man, unsure of how to respond when Lord Aidan laughed a bit. "Your majesty, you aren't the first person to fall under her spell. I have seen stronger men than you find themselves smitten with the princess."

"I only wished to see if she was truly well, my lord. I have no designs on the princess that are dishonorable. I appreciate what she has done for me, but I know my future, and I know hers."

Lord Aidan was silent for a few too many moments, and it started to make Maddoc nervous. Maddoc bowed and started to walk past the old lord.

"How much do you know about love, your majesty?" asked Lord Aidan making Maddoc turn.

He thought over the question. "Not much, my lord. I do believe I have little to no experience with it."

"As a man who has been lucky enough to experience much love in his life let me tell you a little about it. Love doesn't obey titles or obstacles. It moves around them, paying no mind to what we might think is acceptable and correct. If you remember that and try to act with it and not against it, I think you will find all will turn out well."

"My lord....," began Maddoc but Lord Aidan cut him off.

"I am tired and have a long journey ahead of me. I will say good night, your majesty." He walked down the hall, leaving Maddoc standing in a strange house, unsure of everything he had ever been taught.

12

～

Chapter 12

Anwen could tell by the bright light coming through the window that she had slept later than usual. She sat up in bed and thought over the night before. She had killed two men. She didn't mean to do it, and they had been attacking her. She was sure they would have killed her and King Maddoc, had they been given the chance. She should not feel guilty about it, and she wasn't sure she did. She had an odd feeling about what had happened the night before. She wasn't sure what it was. She has caused two people to lose their life, and she couldn't help but feel somewhat affected by it.

After pushing her feelings aside for the moment, she wondered if Lord Aidan and the king had found anything out about the men. Deciding there was only one way to find out, she stood up out of the bed and found her dress sitting on a chair. She changed and ran a comb through her hair, trying to look presentable. Looking in the mirror, she could see that she looked pale, and her eyes tried. There was nothing she could do about it, so she turned and left the room.

Walking downstairs she heard the sound of conversation coming from the large parlor. She walked in to find Lord Aidan and King Maddoc sitting close together talking. When they saw her, they both stood, King Maddoc moving towards her.

"How do you feel this morning?" he asked as they met each other in the middle of the room.

"I am a little tired but better than last night."

"You must be hungry, my dear. We saved you some breakfast and had it brought in here. Come sit down and eat," said Lord Aidan as he pointed to the tray in front of the sofa.

She walked over and sat down at the end of the sofa in front of the tray. The king sat down next to her with a small smile. She looked down at the food before her and started to eat. She swallowed a bite and asked, "Did you find out anything about the men?" King Maddoc poured her some tea and held up the sugar bowl. She nodded her head, and he put in two large spoonsful in her tea.

"Not much, they were simply dressed with no markings on where they might be from." Lord Aidan sniffed a little. "We did figure out how they knew the king was here."

She looked up at him expectantly, but it was King Maddoc who spoke next. "There was a short message on one of the men. It stated that whoever wrote it had intercepted the letter from here and knew I was residing in Lord Aidan's home. It seemed to imply it wasn't the first letter they had intercepted."

Anwen swallowed the food she had been eating. "That means whoever wrote this probably took the letter I sent from my palace."

King Maddoc nodded. "And one that the captain of my royal guard sent as well."

"We will need to leave today as soon as we can," said Anwen, thinking the king was very much in danger here as well as whoever was in this house. "Lord Aidan, you will need to shut up your home for a while. I would hate for something to happen to you or one of your servants." The king and Lord Aidan exchanged looks. "What is it?"

Lord Aidan leaned towards her. "I plan to travel back to Awbrey today with most of my servants. They are preparing my carriage now. I was hoping you would accompany me."

"But I cannot leave the king on his own. He does not know the way, and he would be unprotected." She turned to the king. "I do not mean to cause offense, your majesty."

"And you have caused none. I think we can all agree you know more about traveling safely and defense than me."

"I have a solution to our problem," said Lord Aidan. "I can send two of my men with the king who know the road very well. They are able fighters and can see him to his palace without harm coming to him."

Anwen sat back and little and looked at Lord Aidan and then the king. She wondered if the king had requested this. Perhaps he was tired of her company. She could be troublesome and hurtful. She wouldn't blame him if he wished to part from her. "Is this what you wish, your majesty?" Her voice came out petulant, and she hated herself for it.

"If it is, it is only because I want you to be safe. If you choose to go with your old friend back to your home, I will miss your company, but I will understand it." The king sounded sincere, and it caused her to look up.

"I am not sure I could settle not knowing if you were safe." She turned to Lord Aidan. "I would hate to disappoint you and leave you alone. If you really wish for me to go with you, I will leave the king in the hands of your men."

"Anwen, I do wish you to go with me for several reasons, but you must do what you believe is right. I hate to think of you in danger, but if you think you are abandoning the king, you will not be able to stand it. I know you very well, my dear. I know when you believe you have a duty, you have to do it, or you will be miserable."

She nodded. "I do not feel as though I can leave him at this point. I promised to see him safe. My Gift is unsettled when he is out of my sight. I am not sure why it has chosen to protect him, but it has." She looked over at the king. "If you do not mind me continuing on with you, I will, but I will not force the issue. If you wish to travel with Lord Aidan's servants, just tell me."

He looked at her silently for several moments. She was about to take this as his answer, believing he wanted her to go with Lord Aidan, but he finally spoke. "I would like it if you continued on with me, even though I know I should tell you to go with Lord Aidan. It would be safer."

"Not for you, your majesty," she teasingly said causing him to smile. "Lord Aidan, I hope you truly do not mind."

"I shall worry endlessly about you until I hear you are safe, but I understand it. Your mother would as well. Your aunt will be angry, but when is she not? My two servants could still attend you. It would be better for your reputation."

"It probably would, but it would slow us down and put two others in danger," said Anwen. "They would do better riding alongside you and protecting your carriage. Whoever is watching us, might believe the king is sneaking off with you and attack. I hate to say it, but I doubt two male servants attending us could save my reputation at this point."

"Well, maybe a king can," said Lord Aidan as he looked over Anwen at Maddoc. Anwen looked at Lord Aidan who only smiled and then to King Maddoc who nodded.

She finished her breakfast and went upstairs to pack up her things. She noticed the room she had originally been in had been cleaned with no traces of the gruesome deaths that had happened there the night before. She closed her eyes for a moment, still able to hear the awful sound the two men's bodies made against the wall. She could still see the blood coming from their heads. She opened her eyes and hurriedly packed her things, knowing when she stayed at Lord Aidan's house, she could never come into this room again.

When she got downstairs, King Maddoc was ready to go in the entryway. He was wearing the clothes she had given him in the palace, but they had been cleaned. There was something else different about him.

"You have shaved," she said as she walked down the last few stairs.

"Albert offered to do it before we left, and I decided to let him." King Maddoc rubbed his chin. "It will likely be a few days before I get the chance again. Hopefully, I look more presentable now."

She stood before him, noticing how much younger he looked with his freshly shaved face. "I don't know. I didn't mind your beard, your majesty. I think it suited you."

He frowned, but then gave her a grin. "It grows rather quickly, so you shouldn't have to look at my bare face for long."

She laughed a little. "On second thought, I might like you this way better. It may help me read your expressions easier. Hopefully, it will mean fewer misunderstandings between us."

"I would like that, princess. I would like if you and I are always of one accord."

Something about the way he said it made Anwen feel warm. There was a funny feeling in her stomach she could not place, but it was not unpleasant. Lord Aidan walked in and looked at them both. "Your horses are ready, and I have had my kitchens pack you enough food to last a few days." He turned to Anwen and took her hand. "I do wish you would travel with me, your highness, but I do not blame you for your decision. I know you must do what you believe is right."

"You are correct, my lord, but I will miss your company." She reached up and put her hand on his cheek. "When you see Lachlan, try to remember your love for him. He is your grandson, and he does care for you and your opinion. Do not be overly harsh with him."

Lord Aidan pulled the hand he was holding up to his lips and kissed it. "You are too good, my sweet Anwen. You have no idea how much you mean to me. I know you have a mother that loves you very much, and your father adored you, but you have always felt like a daughter to me. I always wanted one, and you filled that void in my life."

"I know my mother cares for me, and I miss my father, but there will always be a special place in my heart for you. You understand me better than anyone ever has. You have been my champion and my guide, but I am grown now. I have to make my own decisions, even if they are stupid and dangerous."

He squeezed her hand and let it go. "Dangerous maybe, but not too foolish, I don't believe. I just hope this young man is worth it. I hope he will prove a good king to Calumbria."

"I think he has much potential, my lord." Anwen glanced over at King Maddoc and gave him a wink.

Lord Aidan laughed. "Be safe, dear one. I could not bear it if something happened to you."

"I will do all I can to see the king safely to his palace, and me back to Awbrey. I hope you are still there when I arrive."

"I will not leave until I see you." Lord Aidan looked at the king. "Watch over this one if you will, your majesty. The princess is very good at seeing to everyone else's needs while ignoring her own."

"She will arrive safely back to you and her kingdom, my lord. I give you my word. I will also see she is recognized and rewarded appropriately. All will know of her deeds and bravery."

Lord Aidan held out his hand to the king. The king took it, and Lord Aidan bowed. "I'm glad to hear it, your majesty."

They walked out to their horses that were waiting out front. The king waited by Anwen's horse. "Let me help you, your highness."

She nodded, and he put his hands on her waist. He lifted her up and placed her in the saddle. She threw her leg over and nodded at him. He moved over to his own horse and hoisted himself up. Once he was settled, they both looked at Lord Aidan. Anwen smiled down at him. "I will see you soon, my lord."

"I hope so, my dear Anwen. Keep safe." He looked at the king. "Safe journey, your majesty."

"You as well, my lord," responded the king.

Anwen urged her horse forward and the king followed. They rode back towards the road and away from the manor. They were both silent as they made their way through the fields of Lord Aidan's estate. Anwen looked to her right, remembering happy days of riding over the lands with Brennan and Lachlan.

She turned her head as they passed a large tree. Lachlan had kissed her there under that tree. She remembered him pushing her up against the rough trunk as he covered her body with his own. It had excited her then, but now it made her feel violated and alone. She kept her head straight, careful to not look at anything that would bring up old memories.

They got to the main road and the king turned to look at her. "Are you truly well, princess? I think you might be regretting coming with me."

"I am not. Why would you say so?"

"You have not said one word to me since we left the manor. I am afraid you are wishing you were with your old friend."

"No, I do not," answered Anwen truthfully. "I love to visit with Lord Aidan, but I am in no hurry to return to my village. There are things there I do not wish to see or deal with at the moment."

"I understand. I know I am the cause of some of it, and I am sorry for it. I will find a way to make it right, princess. I will make sure all know of your honor and virtue."

"You are only a small part of it, your majesty. I believe you have heard and witnessed enough of my sad tale to not know what I truly wish to avoid."

Maddoc looked at her. "I know a betrayal of that magnitude must hurt you very much, but I hope you are not avoiding the young man because of shame."

"What do you mean?"

"The only person who should feel shame is that man you call Lachlan. He is the one who mistreated you. He is the one who misled you and broke his word. He must be a stupid young man, indeed."

She couldn't help a grin. "You don't know the whole tale. Perhaps he was justified in letting me go. I could have been a terror to him."

"No, I know it is not true. You could not be a terror to anyone. No one as good and lovely as you could be anything but a true delight."

Anwen felt her face grow warm. She wasn't sure she had blushed her whole life as much as she had these past few days. She sighed. "I do not wish to speak of him, not now when he is out of my sight. I would like to forget him, at least for a while."

"Then would you tell me more about your kingdom? I would like to know how you spend your time in your role as princess. Tell me how your mother rules as queen."

"That could take quite a while, your majesty. I am afraid I will bore you."

"Not at all," replied the king. "I believe what you have to say will be very beneficial to me."

She gave him a curious look.

"Princess, I'm asking you to teach me how to rule a kingdom. If you do not wish to take the time to do it, I will understand. I might be a lost cause."

She was surprised by this request, but not unwilling. "I believe I told Lord Aidan that you have much promise. As you know by now, I do not lie. I will be happy to tell you all I know, King Maddoc. I am afraid it will be a lot to take in, and I hope you will pay good attention."

"There is nothing I would like more than to hear everything you have to tell me on the matter."

She nodded and began telling him everything she could about being a ruler of a kingdom.

13

Chapter 13

Maddoc listened to the princess talk, overwhelmed, and impressed with all she had to say. She started first with what her mother did as the queen. It all sounded very much like Queen Eira was a very active ruler, but Maddoc was equally if not more impressed with the princess's knowledge and duties. She knew all of the principal lords of her courts very well. It seemed as if she was active in dealing with all of them, even the ones she found unpleasant.

She knew about most of the villages in her kingdom. She understood the needs and worries of her people. She spent time around the common folk, knowing she could never truly understand their struggles, but that did not mean she could not listen and be sympathetic.

"The common folk are the heart of a kingdom, your majesty. Your kingdom will rise or fall with the prosperity or suffering of your people. You should not dismiss their needs."

Maddoc nodded, enjoying seeing her so animated. "So, you actually go into the villages of your kingdom and speak with villagers?"

"I do try to visit villages and walk the roads at times, but mostly I check in with the leaders of our towns. The good ones know what their people need, and the bad ones are easy to pick out and replace. I also make sure and keep in contact with lesser lords. They tend to know what is going on with the land and farmers.

"I keep some correspondence with some stewards of our lords. They know how the crops and livestock are doing. They can tell me where the famine is the worst and if there is any sickness on their lands."

"Your mother trust all this to you?" ask Maddoc.

"She has little by little. I would sit with my father when he was alive and watch him work. Then Lord Aidan took over the work after my father died. He taught me everything I needed to know and saw that I learned by doing. Now, it is almost second nature."

He shook his head.

"What is it? Do you not approve of something?"

"I am just overwhelmed by what you have told me. What you manage to do amazes me."

She waved a hand at him. "It really isn't all that much. I could do more, but my mother did not want me to work constantly. She wished for me to have some carefree years."

Maddoc looked down, feeling some shame. What she called carefree years sounded like days filled with work. He looked over his short life and knew he had accomplished little. He spent his days truly carefree, drinking with younger lords of the court, flirting with their sisters, and bedding their servants, tenants, and on occasion their mothers.

He had thought his life was full and enjoyable, but now he saw how empty and dull it really was. If he kept on his present course, he would be known forever as a do-nothing king. His name would barely be mentioned in history. He would just be known as another in the line of kings. His name in the Great Book of the Calumbria library would have little more written of him than his name and dates of birth and death.

He looked over at the princess. She was the type of ruler and woman great stories were written about. He could imagine one day a book, or maybe more would be written about her. It would tell of her benevolence, her fierceness, her fairness, and her beauty. There would be great stories of battles she would fight for her kingdom, and beautiful songs written of her deeds would be sung.

"I think that is enough for today, your majesty," said the princess as she pulled her cloak tighter. "My throat is growing hoarse, and you must be tired of my prattling on."

"Not at all, but you should rest as my head is full. I need some time to think over what you have told me before I can take in any more."

She smiled, and she seemed to shudder. Maddoc realized it had gotten much colder as the sun sunk down behind them. "Are you growing cold, princess?"

She nodded. "I believe it is growing much colder as we travel. It is to be expected as fall is truly here. I am not looking forward to spending the night outdoors, but there is nothing for it."

"Any ideas where we might stop for the night?"

"The further north we get, the less familiar I am with the area, but if we follow the river, we will soon come to the base of the Ewellian mountains. There should be some alcoves or caves we can hide in for the night. It will give us some protection from the cold wind that is starting to blow."

They continued on in silence for a while as the wind picked up. Maddoc pulled his own cloak tighter to his body as he looked over at the princess. She was huddled upon herself, her cloak covering every bit she could manage. "Are you alright, princess? Perhaps we should find a place to stop and light a fire."

"No, there is some light left, and it would be too dangerous to start a fire with no cover. We need to not draw attention to ourselves."

"You seem very cold. I would not like you to fall ill."

"I will not get sick from a cold wind. I just do not like the cold. I dread winter every year. I spend time praying for warmer days during the entire season." She sat up a little straighter in her saddle. "Can you talk to me of something?"

"What would you like me to talk about?"

"Anything, really. Tell me about your mother. You must be close to her."

"I suppose I am," he said slowly. He wasn't sure what to say. After listening to Anwen talk of her mother as someone she depended on for advice, love, and direction, he was sure she would be disappointed to hear of his and his mother's cold relationship. "She has been ruling my kingdom since my father died almost ten years ago. My uncle did not like it, and I doubt he likes it now, but she has the support of the council. It was what my father wanted. He said so before he succumbed to his infection."

"What is she like?"

"She is known to be beautiful and intelligent." Maddoc searched his mind for something else to say. "She likes strawberries and apple tarts."

Anwen looked over at him as though she expected him to go on. "What else?"

Maddoc shrugged. "What else would you like to know?"

"Is she a fair ruler? Is she kind? What is your favorite memory of her? There must be more."

"I believe she has been a good ruler for Calumbria. I have not heard any complaints. She is not unnecessarily harsh. I rarely ever see her truly angry." Maddoc tried to think of ways to describe his mother. She was not kind in the way the princess was kind. She would not go out of her way to help someone or see to her people, but she was not cruel. "She would never do anything to hurt someone for no reason."

Anwen gave him a concerned look, but he wasn't sure what she meant by it. "And your favorite memory of her?"

Maddoc tried to think of a time he felt a fondness for his mother. She was never an overly affectionate parent. She always seemed to be busy, and Maddoc was always needed for a lesson or to go see some lord even before he was grown. He thought back to a time when his father was still alive. "One night when I was no more than ten there was a grand affair at the palace. It must have been some festival. I snuck out to see the festivities. I stayed hidden on the second-floor landing of the great banquet room, hiding underneath some tables. I watch the people dance. I saw my mother laugh more that night than I had ever seen before or have seen since. She even danced with my father that night."

"Was that so unusual?" asked Princess Anwen.

"Perhaps not. I suppose she was often made to dance one dance with him at each event, but that night she actually seemed to enjoy it. They even danced more than once. My parents did not choose each other for love. My father wanted a connection to my mother's kingdom, and my mother wanted only power. That night, though, it almost seemed as if they enjoyed each other's company.

"Later I noticed they had both left the banquet hall, so I went to look for them. I found them on the third floor, out on the smaller balcony that overlooks the river. I snuck out and watched them. They just stood in silence together, looking out at the river. At one point my mother put her head on my father's shoulder. I must have made a noise or breathed too loudly because my father turned a little and saw me. He did not yell at me or tell me to go to bed.

"He looked down at my mother and whispered to her. She looked behind her at me and held out her hand. I walked slowly to her and took it. She pulled me close to her. We spent several minutes together as a family just looking out over the river in the moonlight. I am sure they talked of something or asked me questions, but I don't remember it. I only remember the feeling of her soft hand in mine, and the moment my father patted my shoulder."

Maddoc shook his head and quickly wiped one of his eyes with his finger. It was probably just the wind, but he found his eyes were watering a little. "I'm sorry I don't have more to say about her or my father."

"You don't need to be sorry." She looked at him in a way he had never seen before. Her eyes were so soft, and her lips were curved down, but it did not seem as though she was frowning. "I appreciate you sharing such a personal experience with me. I am glad you have such a good memory of your parents."

"We cannot all be as fortunate as you with your loving family," said Maddoc with a small laugh.

Her lips turned a different way into a real frown. "My life has not been perfect, your majesty. My parents had their faults, the same as anyone else, and I have my own as well. I know my father loved me, and I believe my mother cares for me, but there have been many times of difficulties."

"I did not mean to dismiss your own struggles, princess. I was just thinking of how many wonderful memories you have of both your mother and father. I could only think of one."

"You should remember that as you choose your own wife and have children. Try to give the future queen and any princes and princesses you have many wonderful memories of you. Live in a way that when you are gone, your sons or daughters talk of you with fondness. Do not make them search their minds for one happy moment. Let them have plenty to choose from."

They had to ride past sundown to make it to the foothills of the mountains. The princess found a small space behind two large moss-covered boulders. It was not perfect, but it would have to do as the princess now looked as though she would fall from her mount due to weariness and being chilled through.

Maddoc hopped down off his horse and hurried over to her. She slipped from her mare and into his arms as he steadied her. She leaned into him as though trying to feel his warmth. He did not push away or hurry her. He rubbed her arms with his hands, trying to warm her, finally pulling her fully against him and holding her in his arms.

"This is not necessary, your majesty," said the princess against his chest. Despite her words, she didn't try to leave his embrace.

"We rode too long, and you are still tired from last night. It has become very cold, and there is not much to you. I can feel how chilled you are through your cloak."

"We need to find some wood for a fire if we can. We can build a very small one behind the rocks, and we should be safe."

Maddoc held her for a few more moments, not really wanting to let her go. She eventually pulled back from him on her own and stood up straight. "Why don't you go see what wood you can find, and I will grab our bags." The princess straightened her cloak and backed a few steps away from him.

He nodded and turned to search the area for large sticks. He managed to find an armful. Luckily, it had not rained recently, and the wood was dry. He brought it back behind the boulders to find the princess sitting on the ground with some food and a skin of wine in front of her. Maddoc sat down next to her and arranged the wood. The princess took off her gloves and blew on her hands before placing one over the wood. She closed her eyes, and a small spark struck the pile of stick and leaves Maddoc had arranged. A small fire burned before them.

The princess passed Maddoc some food and poured two cups of wine before putting her gloves back on. They ate together quietly before the small fire. Once the food was gone and the wine was drunk, the princess leaned towards the small fire. The wind had picked up and blew through their rocks, making the fire dance before them. The princess closed her eyes and shuddered, and Maddoc pulled his cloak tight to his body, leaning forward.

"I did not think it would get this cold this early in fall," said the princess with chattering teeth. "I am used to spending the season in Awbrey though. Maybe it is always like this here and in your kingdom."

"I am sure it is a little cooler in Quinlan compared to Awbrey, but nothing like this. I believe this is unusual for this time of year."

The princess nodded as she looked at the fire. She added another two sticks that laid close by. The small fire did not provide much warmth, and Maddoc thought it would be a long night. The princess moved closer to him and leaned against him. He looked down at her as she kept her eyes on the fire.

"I hope you will not take this as anything but me wanting to be warm and keep you warm as well, your majesty. I'm afraid the night will only get colder, and this fire will not last for long."

"Do not think you have to explain everything you chose to do to me. I hope we can move past what I said the other day. I am very ashamed of my words, and I did not mean them. You hurt my pride with your truth. I lashed out in a childish spoiled way. We will have to rely on each other if we are to make it to Quinlan." Maddoc shifted and put his arm around her, pulling her as close as he could.

She did not struggle or refuse. She seemed to snuggle against him. "You are very warm." She was quiet, and Maddoc thought perhaps she had fallen asleep before she sat up slightly and took a loud breath. "I almost forgot."

The princess stood up and walked over to their horses which stood by one of the boulders. She pulled off a bundle and brought it back over to Maddoc. "I took these from the manor. I thought we might need them."

She unfolded two small blankets and handed one to Maddoc as she sat down next to him. She draped hers around her, covering her legs as she leaned back into him. Maddoc looked at his blanket and spread it out over her other blanket pulling it up to her waist.

"What are you doing?" protested the princess. "You are cold as well."

"Not as cold as you, and I believe my cloak is thicker than yours. I think you need sleep more than me." He smiled down at her. "I would not want my great defender to be tired as we travel."

She gave one of her delighted laughs, and Maddoc believed it warmed him more than any blanket or fire. "This is very silly. No one is out here or can see us, and we both need sleep. Even if one of us kept watch, I doubt we could see anything before it was close enough to wake me up. We can share the blankets."

She moved a bit away from him and lay down. She looked over at him expectantly and he moved to lay on his back. The princess moved over to where her body was touching his and placed both blankets over them. Once she was satisfied with their positioning, she turned her back to him and placed her hands under her head.

"Try to get some sleep, King Maddoc. We will need to leave at first light."

"Good night, princess," he said as he glanced over at her.

"Sleep well, your majesty."

Maddoc lay there for what seemed like hours but was probably not even thirty minutes. The wind blew over them, circling around their space. He sat up once to throw some more sticks on the fire, but he knew it was a losing battle. Their small source of warmth would be gone soon. Every so often he could feel the princess shiver next to him, and eventually, he could take it no more.

He turned towards her and put his arms around her, pulling her against him. Either she was asleep and did not notice, or she chose the warmth over asking him to let her go. Whatever the reason, Maddoc was much happier feeling her warmth against him. She stopped shuddering, and Maddoc's eyes grew heavy. Just before sleep overtook him, he nuzzled into the princess feeling her soft hair under his chin. As he drifted off, he caught the scent of lavender, and it made him dream of warm, sunny days.

14

Chapter 14

As Anwen woke up she snuggled into the warmth next to her. She sighed as she felt arms tighten around her making her feel secure. Somewhere in her mind, she knew she needed to fully wake and start her day, but the draw of the warm and safe arms that held her was too strong. It looked to still be dark, so she saw no harm in sleeping a little longer. She had almost gone back to sleep when she felt something against her forehead. It took her a moment to realize it was a soft kiss.

Her eyes flew open, and she found herself staring up at the still sleeping King Maddoc. She must have turned towards him in the night. His lips again brushed her forehead. He gave a soft sigh and bent down to place his forehead against hers. She lay still watching him. Was he dreaming of a lost love? Perhaps there was a woman back home he was fond of but unable to be with.

Anwen knew she should push away from him and wake him up, but she found herself unable to do it. As his hands moved against her back and his forehead pressed against hers, Anwen felt something she had not in a while. She felt wanted. It was a silly thought because the king could not possibly know what he was doing in his sleep, but she did not want to push it away.

She wanted to stay in her delusion for a little while longer and let it lull her to sleep. She wanted to believe she was wanted, even needed by this man. She wasn't sure why. She didn't really want him. At least she didn't believe she did, but to imagine that a king, one as handsome as him, could be satisfied holding her and kissing her gently, was enough to make her desire to be special to someone sated for a few moments.

She let the security of the fleeting feeling draw her back to sleep. As she drifted off, he kissed her forehead again and pulled her even closer. He whispered, and she wasn't sure if it was real or just her mind letting her hear what she wanted to hear, but it sounded as if he said her name.

"Princess, princess," said a voice from somewhere far away. It felt as if someone was gently shaking her. "Princess Anwen."

Anwen forced her eyes open and looked up to see the king sitting next to her. His hand was on her upper arm, and he was slightly shaking her. She sat up as the king's hand fell off of her. She yawned and stretched before putting her hand through her hair to move it out of her face.

"I am sorry to wake you, but I believe we should be going soon," said King Maddoc softly.

He held out a cup to her, and she took it. It felt warm in her hand, and she noticed the fire in front of her.

"I found some tea in your pack, so I made some to try and warm you before we start traveling. I hope you do not mind."

"Not at all," said Anwen as she took a sip of the tea. "How did you manage the fire?"

"I found the flint and fire striker in the pack as well. It took me more tries than I would like to admit, but I managed it. I thought it was worth the effort as I am sure we could both use the warmth before braving another cold day on horseback."

She grinned at him before taking another drink. The tea felt wonderful as it moved through her body, warming her from the inside out. She looked at the king to see him watching her. "Thank you for your trouble. I can't tell you how good this tea tastes."

"I wish we had brought some sugar to put in it. I believe you prefer it sweet."

"I do, but all that matters now is the warmth it provides." The princess took another drink as the king handed her an apple. "You are very obliging this morning." She was careful to put a little playfulness in her voice so he would not be offended.

"I have finally wised up and realized how essential you are to me."

She took another sip of tea, feeling her cheeks warm a bit. "I suppose you mean that you will have to depend on me if you wish to make it home."

The smile on his face faded a bit. "Of course," he said in a voice barely above a whisper.

Anwen finished her tea as King Maddoc looked at the fire. "Have you eaten, your majesty?"

"I have. Would you like anything else before we leave? We have some bread or cheese if you are still hungry."

"No, I am ready to be on our way. If we ride hard today, I believe we can make it to a small village inside of your kingdom, and I would like to find a safe place to rest indoors. Maybe a small inn where no one would recognize you. Unless you know of a trusted lord that lies within your borders?"

"I think you know enough about me by now to know I have little knowledge of the lesser lords who live in the kingdom." Anwen looked away for a moment at the sound of shame in his voice.

She tried to put some cheer in her voice as she said, "It is no matter. I have long wanted to see the city of Quinlan and your palace. I will be very happy to ride with you the whole way. I have come this far after all."

The king nodded, and they packed up their things. They walked over to their horses, Anwen happily greeting her pretty mare. She secured her bag and looked at the king who stood next to her. He moved closer to her, and Anwen found she was more aware of his presence than ever before. She thought of earlier that morning when she had first woken and felt the soft feel of his lips upon her forehead.

She tried to keep the blush from her cheeks as she felt him put his hands on her waist. They were large and together they almost fit all the way around her slim figure.

"Are you ready?" he asked as his fingers moved against her.

She nodded, not daring to speak. He picked her up as though she were as light as a feather and placed her on her saddle. He kept his eyes on her as she gathered up her skirt so she could throw her leg over the saddle, revealing a little of the tight pants she wore underneath. Once she was settled, she looked down at him. He put his hand on her horse and stroked its side for a moment as he watched her.

"I am ready to leave when you are, your majesty," said Anwen as she picked up the reins in front of her.

He patted her horse one more time and walked to his own. After he mounted, and Anwen saw he was settled, she moved her horse forward, the king coming up to ride by her side. They rode together, side by side, at a good pace. Anwen talked again of her kingdom and the duties of her and her mother. The king asked questions when he had them. She answered all she could, being as descriptive as possible. He spoke a little of his childhood to give her a break from talking, and the way he spoke of his life made her sad.

It seemed to her that the king had been used by others most of his life. He didn't have much of a choice of how he spent his time as he grew up. She could tell he had capable teachers as he knew much of the history of his land, and he spoke well. He had little practical knowledge, and she wondered if he was kept locked up in the palace most of the time as he grew.

Knowing this, it was no wonder the king had rebelled somewhat as a young man. When he was able to have freedom of course he would want to find a way to enjoy life. She was sure he spent his days now in leisurely activities. He probably drank too much and spent too much time with loose women, but she could not look down on him because of it. It did not make her think any less of him. It only made her a little sad at what his life had been. It was a wonder he wasn't worse.

He was a little spoiled and lazy at times. He could be hurtful with his words, but she did not believe him a bad person. She thought he must have a good heart to be as caring and respectful as he was towards her and others. He had not been unkind to the servants in Lord Aidan's home. He had been very respectful to her old friend.

"Are you examining me in some way, princess?" asked the king with some amusement.

"I believe I am, your majesty," returned Anwen with playfulness.

"You find me very wanting in many areas, I am sure. Perhaps you could tell me my main deficiencies so I can begin to work on them."

"Well," she began with a teasing smile. "You are a little spoiled, but that is to be expected in a king. You have little practical knowledge, but we have already been over that. I believe you are already planning to remedy it. I think you probably spend too much time in leisure but that is just a guess."

"Your guess is correct. I defiantly drink too much with the young lords of my kingdom."

"And spend too much time with pretty young women, I imagine." The princess tried to keep her tone light.

"I suppose I do, though there have been some not so young ones as well." Anwen raised an eyebrow at him. "I'm only being honest, princess. If you want a thorough examination of me, you will need all the facts." He laughed a little. "Can you tell me anything you find positive about me?"

"You are not unintelligent. I enjoy many of our conversations. I do not believe you are unkind, though you can be a little snobbish. I think underneath all your pomp and haughty manors, your might be a good person."

The king sighed. "I hope you are right, princess, though I believe you would find many who would disagree with you."

"To be fair, you would find some in my kingdom who do not think much of me. I will not depend on the opinions of others, your majesty. I will decide for myself what I make of you."

"Then I shall have to continue to endeavor to make a good impression on you, Princess Anwen."

"Will you?"

"Yes, because I find that I care what you think of me."

She felt herself color again, wondering how this man could make her blush so often. She gathered herself and decided to be bold. "Then I should tell you ways to please me."

He blinked rapidly and then laughed. "Please do."

"I like it when you smile at me, and I enjoy it when you wake me up with a cup of tea. I believe I know for certain now that I prefer you with a beard. I would not like it to get too bushy, but I think a short, nicely kept beard would suit you very well. I shouldn't say it, but I enjoy it when you help me up on my horse, which makes me think I would like to dance with you someday."

"What does helping you upon your horse have to do with dancing?" asked the king.

"It shows me that your touch is not altogether unpleasant. How easily you lift me means you could easily correct any missteps I take. I think you would make an ideal dance partner."

"Then one day soon I will make sure I dance with you."

They rode on, spending the morning laughing together. Anwen knew she was flirting too much, but she found she could not help herself. When the king smiled at her and laughed, it made her happy. She wanted to see more of his smiles. She longed to hear his deep merry laugh. The one that sounded as if it came from deep inside of him where she thought the real, wonderful Maddoc resided.

Just before lunch, they were passed by a man on a horse that looked as though it had seen better days. They had passed a few people on their journey but unlike this gentlemen, the others had paid them no mind.

"Good day, to you," said the man as he came upon them. "Where are you headed this fine morning."

Anwen looked him over as she stopped his horse close to hers. Not wanting to be rude or draw unnecessary attention, she stopped as well. King Maddoc halted close to her side. "We have been to the village of Haverly to visit our cousin, and we are trying to make it to Winslow before sundown."

"You will have to hurry if you want to make it that far," said the man with a smile.

"Yes, so we need to be on our way," said King Maddoc with a glance at Anwen.

"Those are fine horses you have. Are you some lord and lady of a small estate outside of Winslow? Perhaps you know my brother, he is a tenant farmer on the Lord of Farley's estate."

"What is his name?" asked Anwen.

The man paused for one moment before replying, "Thomas Mitchum."

Anwen knew the Lord of Farley's steward very well. She had never heard him speak of anyone named Mitchum. "I am sorry, I do not know him. We do need to be going, sir."

"Of course, my lady. I hope you have a safe journey." The man bowed and continued on his way.

Anwen moved her horse forward feeling very anxious. King Maddoc rode beside her, glancing at her from the corner of his eyes. "Anwen, what is it?"

He had said her name again, but she had no time to examine it. "That man has no brother named Thomas Mitchum I willing to wager. No Mitchum resides on the Lord of Farley's estate."

"Do you think he knows who we are?"

"I think he might have a clue of who you are. We need to get off this road as soon as we can and take a different route."

She led him through some trees close to the river. They traveled as close to the rocky shore as they could, the area around them becoming less tree-covered as they truly entered into the mountains. They stopped only briefly a few times to rest and eat. Anwen was constantly searching around her, looking for any signs of trouble. Maddoc stayed mostly quiet, throwing concerned glances her way periodically.

As the afternoon went on, Anwen started to relax a little, thinking maybe they had been careful enough. She hoped that if the man had alerted someone or a group, perhaps they could not find them protected as they were by the river and the mountains. As the sun started to go behind the mountains, she found out her hopes were not to be.

She had just started to look for somewhere to stop for the night when she first became aware that something was very wrong. She heard the whinnies of horses, and it made her stop. They were a long way from the road, which meant whoever was up ahead could only be someone who was trying to meet them. She looked all around. To her left was the river moving swiftly along and to her right the mountains. Their horses could make it, but it wouldn't be a swift ride.

"What is it, princess?" asked the king quietly.

"We have to get out of here somehow. There is trouble up ahead. We need to try to make it up the mountains."

She turned her horse to head up the steep side of the mountain when she was met by six men on horseback coming down. She turned to head back, and three more headed their way. She looked at the way ahead and a group of at least twenty-five was coming towards them.

"What do we do?" asked the king.

"I don't know," she said trying to think.

She could feel the power of her Gift moving inside of her. There were so many men coming their way. She didn't believe even her power could take them all out. They were trapped.

"Hello there," said a man who rode ahead of the rest of the group in front. "We have been trying to catch you for some time."

"Do you know these men?" Anwen whispered to Maddoc.

He shook his head, and she turned to face the man "And what business do you have with us?"

The man smiled at her. "I have none with you, your highness. I only wish for the king to accompany us on a little journey."

"And who are you?" Anwen glanced at King Maddoc.

"It is none of your concern who we are."

"It is if you wish for my companion to journey with you. I have sworn to keep him safe. I do not believe he will be safe going with you."

"I don't believe he will have a choice." The man raised his hand all the men on horseback behind him pulled out bows. They each drew an arrow from their backs and placed them on their strings and pulled back. "Now if you wish to leave here alive, princess, the king will come with us."

Anwen felt her Gift's power grow within her. She shook as her breathing increased. Her voice came out, but she hardly knew what it was saying. "You will not have him, and you will not harm us."

"Anwen, what are you doing?" murmured the king. "I must go with them."

She ignored him and stared at the man ahead of her. She could feel her hair rise as the wind picked up around them. The man in front of her moved his horse back a little, a hint of fear showing on his face. "We tried to do this in a way to spare you, your highness, but I see you will not let it be." He turned and looked back at the men. "Try not to kill the king, but do not let the princess leave this place alive."

He put his hand down and at least twenty-five arrows flew towards Anwen and the king. The king said something, but Anwen couldn't hear it. Her mind was buzzing with her power. She held up her hand, and the arrows flew to the sides and above her. She heard them hit the men behind her and to the side. She looked over at Maddoc whose eyes were large. "Run, your majesty. Your way should be clear behind you. I will hold off those in front."

The king shook his head, but she did not hear what he head to say. She kicked her heels, and her horse jumped forward. She pulled her sword from her side and held it up, charging towards the men. The men had put down their arrows and picked up swords or spears. She pushed out her hand, and five horses on the left reared up, throwing off their riders. They continued to buck around, trampling the men who had been on their backs. She looked to the right of the group in front of her and stared. A light erupted from her and at least ten men and horses fell where they were.

She felt herself growing weak, but there were still at least ten men left to face. She was trying to concentrate when her horse screamed and reared up. Anwen fell from the saddle and rolled out of the way. Her beautiful, sweet mare had a spear in her chest. The horse struggled and walked sideways, falling right into the raging waters of the river. She moved swiftly out of sight, lost forever.

Anwen looked up to see the men riding towards her. She picked up her sword that had fallen close by and ran close to the river, the water at her back. She felt exhausted and ill. She wasn't sure what she could do with ten men coming towards her, but she would not go down without a fight. They were slow to approach her, seeming to be frightened she would do something.

She heard a horse approached and she looked to her left as King Maddoc dismounted and stood at her side.

"What are you doing?" she asked angrily. "You should be far from here by now."

"Do you think I would just leave you?" He pulled out his sword. "Anwen, I could not abandon you, and I will not so do not ask me to do it."

She huffed and turned to stare at the men in front of her. She closed her eyes to try to settle herself and regain some power. She wasn't sure what she was going to do. Eventually, those men would try something, and she had to be ready. They moved closer, and Anwen held up her sword.

She could hear the river raging behind her. The wind circled around them, lifting up her hair and cloak. This is where she would die. She would die falling short of her goal. It seemed a fitting end for a princess who never did measure up. She was too small, and her Gift stunted. She should have known she would not serve the king well by traveling with him. She had done nothing but cursed him to a horrible end.

"Maddoc, I am sorry," she whispered.

The king moved closer to her. "You do not need to be sorry, Anwen. It is I who has doomed you to this. I would do anything to spare you."

He reached out and took one hand from her sword. He threaded his fingers with hers, and Anwen looked at him. He gave her a very small smile, and she felt her power flow through her. Maddoc's eyes grew large, and he gripped her hand tighter. Something was building inside of her, and she had never felt anything like it. The power of her Gift overtook every part of her.

She dropped her sword and turned to the king. "Do not worry, your majesty. All will be well."

She squeezed his hand and then let it go, walking forward two steps and raising her hands. Her power moved through her as a light brighter than she had ever seen erupted from her. It moved over the men and horses in front of her. She barely heard their cries of anguish and fear. The light slowly faded, and Anwen could see all the men and horses lay dead in front of her. Her hands fell at her side. She stumbled backward, unaware of what she was doing. She heard Maddoc scream her name, and then she was falling. The cold, raging water of the river swallowed her.

15

◦∽

Chapter 15

Maddoc watched in horror as Anwen fell into the river. He called out her name and tried to reach her, but he was too late. He had been in too much shock after what had just happened. The things he had seen her do, and the gruesome things he had witnessed were too much. Through it all, he had been scared out of his mind. Not for himself, though he knew there was some fear there for his own life. His fear was mostly for Anwen. He could not lose her. He wasn't sure he couldn't make it, and not just because she was his guide. Her very presence felt necessary to him now. His life felt tied to hers in some way, and he could not do without her.

He ran along the banks, trying to spot her. He finally caught sight of her not too far off the bank holding on to a bolder. She was moving her hand in the water, and he saw that she was trying to control the water in some way. She was having limited success, and he could see she was losing strength. He needed to get to her, but how? If he went into the water, he would be taken by the river. He had no rope with him. He searched around for a long branch or something but saw nothing.

As he searched for something to help her, in the distance up the river, he saw a large rock that jutted out into the water. If he could get there and she let go, he could catch her as she moved down the river. As long as she could keep above the water, he would have a chance. It might be her only one.

"Anwen," he called loudly, hoping she would hear him over the water. She looked at him and he pointed to the rock. "I'm going to crawl out onto the rock. When I get there, you have to let go."

It looked to him as if she nodded so he wasted no time. He ran along the bank to the rock. He climbed up on it seeing it was wet and slick with slime and moss from the river water. He carefully and as quickly as he could crawled across the surface, looking over to see Anwen was still hanging on to the rock in the water. He finally got to the edge, and he looked over at her.

She took a large breath before she let go of the boulder. The river took her, sending her down towards Maddoc. She was able to manipulate the current a little, but she misjudged once and rammed into a jagged rock. She hit her shoulder hard and bounced off. He was afraid she would go under, but somehow, she stayed afloat.

Maddoc leaned off the edge of the rock, his arms out, knowing he had only one chance. If he did not catch her, she would be lost. She came closer and closer, and Maddoc leaned further towards the river. She came close to him, and Maddoc reached for her. He managed to grab her arm. She cried out in pain, but he did not let go. She moved her other side over through the water, and Maddoc put his other hand on her other arm. He pulled as hard as he could and heaved her out of the water onto the rock with him.

They both fell back hard against the surface, lying close together, Anwen gasping for breath and coughing. Maddoc rolled over and pushed himself up, hovering over her.

"Princess, are you alright?"

She turned and coughed a bit before turning back and looking up at him. She nodded but seemed to be having a hard time keeping her eyes open.

He sat up. "We need to get your somewhere warm and into dry clothes." He stood up carefully on the rock and bent over, scooping her up into his arms.

He walked very slowly on the slick rock, only slipping slightly. When he came to the end he gently put her down, and she leaned against the rock as he climbed down. Once his feet hit the ground, she fell back into him, and he took her into his arms. He saw his horse standing nearby and walked over to him.

Wanting to get some distance away from the carnage around them, he placed Anwen up on the saddle. She leaned into the horse as he climbed up behind her. He put one arm around her and pulled her close to him, grabbing the reins with his other hand. He rode along the shore of the river, not wanting to get lost in the mountains.

As they rode, the little light that was left was fading fast. He could feel Anwen shudder against him, and he knew he had to find somewhere quickly. He caught sight of an opening in the rocks a little ways off the shore. Moving his horse close to the opening, he stopped and hopped down. Anwen who was still somewhat awake slipped down into his arms, and he carried her into the very front of the opening.

He gently placed her down on the ground, and she leaned back against the stone.

"Anwen, do you think you can get undressed on your own? I can find you something to wear, but you must get out of these wet clothes."

She nodded and started untying her cloak. Maddoc walked out to his horse and looked through his pack until he found the shirt he had been wearing when he had first left Parvilia. They had lost the blankets with Anwen's horse, but he could give her his cloak.

He walked into the cave to find the princess trying to reach behind her to undo her dress. She was struggling, wincing at the pain from her hurt shoulder. He placed his shirt down next to her.

"Let me help you, Anwen." She looked up at him and nodded before leaning forward.

Maddoc looked at the lacing of her dress. He had undressed plenty of women and was pleased that it would finally be useful. He undid the few buttons at the top and unlaced the rest of her gown until the back hung open.

"I'm going to go find firewood. Can you manage the rest?"

She nodded again, seeming to not have enough strength to talk and do what was needed. Before he left, he untied his cloak and put it next to her. "Wear that as well when you are through."

She looked up at him. "But you will be cold," she said in a quiet voice that shook.

"I will be fine, but you will not if you don't get warm. Don't argue with me, Awen, please. I will be back in a moment."

He turned and walked out of the shallow cave. He searched until he found enough wood to last for a while. He placed it out at the mouth of the cave and walked to his horse. Luckily, the fire striker and flint had been with him because he doubted Anwen had the strength to start a fire. He had one bag of some food, a wineskin, and two full water skins. He grabbed it all and walked to the cave.

"Is it all right if I come in?" he asked.

"Yes," answered Anwen's weak voice.

He walked in and found her standing wearing his shirt which came almost to her knees. She was swallowed up in his cloak which she was fastening as he walked in. Maddoc dropped the bag on the ground and looked at her. She was an odd sight in her strange outfit, but something about it made him want to grab her and hold her close. Perhaps it was the fact she looked so vulnerable wearing clothes many sizes too big with her damp hair splayed all around her.

He forced himself to look away. He hurried outside to grab the wood. He gathered a few leaves that rested at the base of the rocks nearby and brought them inside with all the sticks he had gathered. He kneeled down and arranged the sticks as Anwen sat beside him. After seeing all was satisfactory, he went to grab the bag behind him when Anwen held out her hand.

He grabbed her wrist. It felt so small and cold wrapped up in his hand. "Please do not. You are weak from earlier, and you should not overextend yourself. I can handle starting a fire. I think it might only take a half dozen tries this time."

She looked down at where he touched her, and he let her go, thinking she did not like it. She gave him a slight grin and nodded. He grabbed his bag and found the flint and fire striker. It took him well over a dozen tries, but he did manage to get a decent fire going. Anwen reached behind her and grabbed her clothes, spreading them near the fire.

Maddoc managed to warm up some water. There was a little tea left, so he brewed some in a small stone bowl he had with him. He poured it into a cup and handed it to Anwen. She took it with a smile and drank a little. She sighed as her little hands wrapped around the cup.

After taking another drink she handed the cup to Maddoc. "You should have some as well. You must be cold."

"You should drink it all. I can't imagine how chilled you are after being in that water."

She tried to extend her arm further to put the cup closer to him when she winced and drew her arm back. He took the cup from her and looked at her with concern. "Let me look at your shoulder, princess."

"It is only a small cut and a bad bruise. There is nothing that can be done for it."

"I'd still like to look at it if you will let me."

She took a deep breath and nodded. He reached forward and unclasped the cloak that lay on her upper chest. He carefully slipped it down before pulling gently at the shoulder of his shirt she wore. It slipped right down, showing the angry wound found there. He looked over it closely.

He knew quite a bit about different kinds of wounds. It had been a nasty cut that had eventually taken his father, and Maddoc had been obsessed with finding out how to treat wounds for a while. He spent many days of his adolescence looking through books on healing and medicines. He did not like how long and red the gash on the princess's shoulder was. He could see where blood had come from it and dripped down her body. It was not bleeding heavily now, but he worried it would get infected.

He poured some more water into the bowl and cleaned it out. He put yet more water in it and let it heat up for a few moments. Hoping it was not too hot, he brought it close to the princess. "I need to wash your wound. I wish I had some ointment or bandages, but this will have to do until we can find a village tomorrow." She nodded, and he carefully poured the water on the gash. She hissed and turned away. He tore a strip of fabric from the bottom of his cloak that lay around Anwen. He wrapped it around the wound and tied it, hoping it would give some protection.

Once he was satisfied with all he could do, he carefully pulled his shirt back up over her shoulder and refastened the cloak around her. She stared at him as he did the clasp. He turned from her and brought out some dried meat, bread, and cheese. He handed them to her, but she only took the bread. They ate their meager meal side by side, not talking very much.

When they were through, Maddoc took a swig of wine and offered some to the princess, but she shook her head. "Are you sure? It might warm you and help you to sleep."

"It would take ten times the amount of wine to warm me in any way, your majesty." She pulled at the cloak and leaned towards the fire. Her eyes closed, and she swayed a bit.

Maddoc put away their things back in his bag. "Lay down, princess. You need to rest."

She opened her eyes and did as he bid. She lay on the side away from her hurt shoulder, making sure the cloak was between her and the cold ground. "I wish we hadn't lost our blankets," she said quietly. She shuddered a bit. "Poor Mystic. She was such a good horse."

Maddoc looked down at Anwen. "Did you have her long?"

"My father gave her to me for my thirteenth birthday. It was not long after that he became sick and died. She was just a foal, but Lord Aidan helped me break her in. She was always such a gentle, willing thing." She sniffled and sat up a bit, wiping at her eyes. "I'm so silly, crying over a horse."

Maddoc lay back and took her into his arms. "You are not silly. I have had Adelio not quite as long as you have had your horse, and I would miss him terribly if I lost him. Your horse was also the last gift from your beloved father. It is a lot to lose, Anwen."

She nodded against his chest, crying in earnest now. "It is not just my horse. I killed so many people, Maddoc. I have never killed anyone until the other night, and now I am truly a murderer."

He looked down at her. "You are not, Anwen. You have done nothing but defend yourself and me. All of those you killed would have killed you in a second if they had the chance. You would never hurt anyone without a just cause."

"It doesn't make it any easier to take," she gasped between sobs.

Maddoc held her close, careful to watch her shoulder. He closed his eyes and thought of all the death he had seen today. He had seen men die before, but not so many, and certainly in not such a way. "What can I do, Anwen? How can I help you?"

"Tell me I'm not awful. Tell me I don't always make things worse."

"How could you ever think you are awful? I think you might have more goodness in you than anyone I have ever met. I have never wanted to be around anyone as much as I do you. I am not sure how I will part from you once we reach Quinlan." He leaned down and kissed her forehead. "Perhaps, I'll keep you as my captive." He gave a small chuckle.

She looked up at him and smiled through her tears. "A well-treated prisoner I would hope."

He looked down at her. Her face turned serious, and he knew it reflected his own. He brought his hand to her face and caressed her cheek. "You have no idea how well I would treat you, Anwen. I would see that you had everything your heart desired."

She continued to look up at him as he looked down at her. He took his hand off of her cheek and wrapped her in his arms. "You should sleep. I will stay awake for a while and make sure all is well."

She burrowed into his embrace, and he closed his eyes wondering how he could feel so at peace and safe in such a precarious situation.

"Maddoc," she said very quietly. He pulled back a little and looked down at her. "Thank you for saving me."

He rested his forehead against hers. "It is I who should thank you. I owe you my life so many times over, I could never repay it."

"I don't ask anything of you, except that you stay safe. I cannot have you die, my king."

He smiled a little. She had called him Maddoc and now her king. He had heard his name in other's voices. Many had addressed him as my king, but nothing sounded so sweet as Anwen's soft voice when she said his name. Her calling him, 'my king' had such a different meaning to him than when others had said it.

"You cannot die either, Anwen. You cannot sacrifice yourself for me. I could not live with it." He took a breath. "I don't think I could live in this world knowing you were not in it."

"You barely know me," she said as she moved up a little. Her face was very close to his.

"I have not known you long, but I feel as though I know you better than anyone I have ever met. I think you might be the only one in this world who really knows me." He leaned down wondering what would happen if he kissed her.

He did not have to wonder long as she closed the small gap between them, her lips brushing his. He leaned down further and kissed her more firmly. Her lips were soft and surprisingly warm. He could taste a hint of tea as he daringly let his tongue run over them. She opened her mouth slightly, and he took the opportunity to deepen their kiss. She made a small noise but did not pull away. She slowly brought her hand up and put it on his cheek as she moved her lips against his.

Maddoc had kissed many women, but never like this. He had only kissed the lips of women in the past to move on to other things. As he kissed Anwen, all he wanted was to hold her, and somehow show her how much he already felt for her. As he pulled her against him, moaning against her lips, he realized that this must be a little of what love felt like. He wanted nothing from her except this, the opportunity to just be with her and hold her close.

He finally pulled back and looked down at her. She leaned up and softly kissed his lips once more before laying against his chest. He closed his eyes and whispered her name, realizing he would have given up all his nights of meaningless passion for this one moment with her.

16

≈

Chapter 16

Anwen woke up as something brushed her cheek. Her eyes opened as Maddoc leaned down and kissed her softly on her jawline.

"I'm sorry, we don't have any more tea, but I have to admit I would much rather wake you up this way," he said softly before lightly brushing his lips against hers.

She smiled up at him. She had wondered if last night had been some strange dream, but now she could see it had been very real. She wasn't sure how she felt about it all, but she found his sweet kisses did not repulse her in any way. "I think I might prefer it as well."

He smiled before kissing her tenderly again and helping her to sit up. She winced as the movement made her remember the injury on her shoulder. It felt as though the wound was pulsing.

"Let me check your wound, Anwen." Maddoc started unclasping his cloak that was around her as she looked at him.

She liked it when he said her name with no titles or formalities. As he undid her cloak and pulled down the shoulder of the shirt she wore, she breathed in deep. She looked down and watched his long fingers nimbly undo the clasp. She sighed as they gently brushed her neck before pulling her shirt down off her shoulder. Unwinding the fabric there, he leaned in closer to look at her wound, and she had a very strong urge to pull his face up and kiss him. She wasn't sure of her feelings for him, but there was definitely something physical between them.

"We need to get going now," he said as he gently pulled up her shirt. "Get dressed as soon as you can, and I will give you something to eat on the way."

"Is there something wrong?"

"Your wound looks like it is becoming infected. We will need to get some medicine in a village, and maybe a healer to look at it." He gently pulled up his cloak on her shoulder. "Do you think your clothes are dry enough to wear?"

"They will have to be," replied Anwen.

He nodded. "I will start packing things on the horse. Get dressed as well as you can, and I will help you as needed. Do not touch your wound or do anything that feels as though you are over-taxing yourself. You need to be careful with it."

She nodded as he stood up. He held out his hand to her, and she took it. He pulled her up gently. She leaned into him as she stood up, and he carefully put his arms around her. "Will you be alright to get dressed." He leaned down and kissed her forehead.

"Yes, but I might need your help to fasten the back."

"Do what you can. If you will alright for a moment, I will give you some privacy."

She looked up at him. "Thank you."

He smiled down at her and let her go before gathering a couple of bags that held what little they had with them. As soon as he left the cave, she took off his cloak and shirt. She shivered in the cold, feeling how sore her body was. She glanced down at her shoulder and wished she hadn't. It was bruised badly, and the cut was swollen and very red. She felt a little lightheaded looking at it, but she closed her eyes and took deep breaths, able to stay on her feet.

She picked up her undergarments and dress. They were still damp, but not as wet as the day before. She put them on, fighting through the pain in her shoulder and the soreness she felt all over her body. She still felt weary from her release of power from the day before, but she thought she managed to do fairly well. She could not lace up the back of her traveling dress, but she was at least fully covered.

"Maddoc?" she called towards the mouth of the cave. He came in, and she turned around. "Could you help me, please?" She moved her hair out of the way.

He walked up behind her, and she felt him tug at the back of her dress. He pulled and tied until she could feel the dress was well secured. Before he buttoned the top he leaned in and kissed the back of her neck. She felt herself shiver, and it had nothing to do with the damp dress or cold wind.

She turned around and looked at him. "I am ready to go."

He stared at her for a moment. "Am I making you uncomfortable? After last night, I thought..., but..."

She cut him off. "You are not making me uncomfortable at all." She looked down and felt her cheeks grow warm. "I find that I enjoy your attentions." She knew what she sounded like, and she wondered what he thought of her. Did he think she was the kind of woman that would give herself to him with no promises or intentions? She looked up at him. She wondered if that was exactly who she was.

"We will talk more of this later, but we need to go so we can have your shoulder treated properly." He took her hand. "I want you to know that I will do nothing to dishonor you. I know who you are, Anwen, and I will ask you to do nothing to betray it."

She nodded. The soft look he was giving her almost took her breath away. He seemed so different than the man she had first met only a week ago, but perhaps he was not so different. She thought this was the real Maddoc, and he had been hiding behind a shield of what he thought he had to be.

They walked out to his horse, and she was reminded of her lost mare. She had been such a good horse and the last thing her father had given her. It was like losing the last little bit of him she held on to. She felt tears threaten her eyes, but she did not let them fall. It would do no good to cry now. They had a long way to go, and the danger was still out there. The quicker they got to Quinlan the better. Her shoulder also ached terribly, and she would be happy to get some relief.

"You will have to ride with me," said Maddoc as he put his shirt in a bag attached to his horse. "I think the easiest and safest way would be for you to ride in front."

"Of course," she said quietly as Maddoc put his hands on her waist.

He lifted her up, and she moved as far to the front as she could, swinging her leg over. Maddoc mounted up behind her and grabbed the reins with one hand. The other he wrapped around her waist under her cloak, and she leaned back into him, his warmth a welcoming feeling in the cold morning air.

"Which way to the closest village," he asked.

"I believe that would be the town of Deryn just inside of your kingdom's border. We can follow the river for a bit further and then turn north once we clear the mountains."

Maddoc's horse moved forward towards the river. They rode along the rocky bank, Maddoc keeping a firm hold on Anwen. She felt drowsy against the warmth of him, and the way his hand would rub against her side made her eyes close. She was almost asleep when he whispered in her ear.

"How are you feeling, Anwen?"

"I am tired, and my shoulder aches, but it is not too bad."

He bent down and pressed his cheek against hers. "You do not feel feverish, which is good. Hopefully, we can take care of your cut before the infection becomes too bad."

"You seem to know a lot about wounds."

"I do. I read many books on infections and medicines when I was younger," replied Maddoc.

"Can I ask why?"

"My father died young from a gash on his leg after a hunting accident. After that, I spent many hours in the great library finding all I could on infections and how to cure them."

Anwen turned and glanced at him. "I know how hard it is to lose your father when you are young. It must have shaken you."

"I believe it did, but not in the same way as losing your father did for you. I was not very close to the previous king. He was not cruel to me, and he did try to see me several times a week to teach me about running the kingdom, but he was not an affectionate father. When he died, I realized I would have to be the king sooner than I thought.

"Besides that, it shocked me that one could die so young from a simple cut. Everything in my life and the palace changed. It struck me that one incident could change the course for so many. I suppose I was looking for some kind of control in my life, so I chose to try to see what I could have done to save my father or anyone else in my life who was in the same position."

Anwen again felt a pang for Maddoc. His life growing up sounded so sterile and cold. Her parents taught her many things, but they also made sure to include moments of merriment and care. She had many wonderful memories such as dancing with her father in the open field as her mother laughed. Her mother would disappear with her for days on end. They would do nothing but travel the kingdom, visit beautiful sights, and eat food from different villages. It sounded as if Maddoc's parents saw him as nothing but a duty they had to check off each week.

She leaned back even further into him, wishing she could put her arms around him. He tightened his arm around her waist, and she laid her hand on his.

"Are you well?" he asked. "Do we need to stop?"

"No, I am fine. I was just thinking about how wonderful you really are."

"Hardly, Anwen. You of all people know just what a worthless man I am. I have lived my life in such a way that amounts to nothing. I have used people and ignored my duty. I think we better hurry if you are so delusional to think I am anything close to wonderful."

"You are not perfect, but who is? After all your life has been, it is a wonder you are as kind as you are. You say you have used people and done awful things, and that might be true, but it is not who you truly are. The more I know of you, the more I am convinced of what a good man you are. I think you could do so many amazing things, Maddoc, if you will let yourself."

He kissed the side of her face. "I think if I try to live as a man worthy of someone like you, I might be able to do something right."

"Live your life as someone worthy to lead a large, glorious kingdom. Live your life for Calumbria and for yourself. You are worth so much more than you think."

It was a long day of riding, and Anwen dozed off more than once in the embrace of Maddoc. They stopped a few times to stretch and rest. Maddoc checked her wound each time, growing more concerned as the day went on. Just as the sun was setting a small village came into view.

"I believe we have entered your kingdom, my king," said Anwen with a glance and smile at Maddoc.

"Is that Deryn up ahead? It does not look very large."

"No, it is a small village, but it should have an apothecary and a tidy inn. What is more important, you will not be recognized. There could still be those out there who would like to see your end, your majesty."

"Don't."

"Don't what?" asked Anwen, sitting up a little and looking at him.

"Don't call me that, especially when we are alone. I like the sound of my name coming off your lips."

"You didn't protest when I called you my king."

"Did I not?" He laughed before bending down close to her ear. "I think I might like that sound of that coming from you as well."

Anwen felt herself grow so warm she wondered if she was starting to run a fever. She leaned back into him, and he gave a contented sigh loud enough she could hear it. Whatever feelings she was gaining for Maddoc, it was becoming clear they were not going to go away.

They rode on to the village. They searched until they spotted a small inn that looked as though it was in good repair. Finding the town stables not far, Maddoc stopped the horse there. He slid down from his horse before reaching up and helping Anwen to dismount. He placed her on her feet and grabbed their bags. After leaving the horse in the hands of a stable boy, he offered Anwen his arm. She took it and they walked into the inn together.

The bottom floor was one big room. There were several tables throughout, and a few men sat at a couple, drinking. It was too early for the supper crowd, which suited Anwen very well. The fewer people that saw them, the better. They found the innkeeper and inquired about a room. There was one available, and Maddoc gladly took it, placing some coins on the counter. Anwen cringed a little looking at the amount. It was probably three times what the room cost.

The man asked Maddoc's name, and he looked at Anwen before answering, "Elis Glynn."

"Where are you from?" asked the innkeeper.

"We are from Devinsville in Bellican. We are on our wedding trip actually. We visited with some of my family in Lucidala and are making our way up to Quinlan for the Harvest Celebration. You will have to excuse my husband. He knows little of coins outside of his kingdom, but it works well for merchants such as yourself." Anwen put her hand on Maddoc's arm and looked at him fondly. "Perhaps he is being so generous because of his good fortune of finding such a good wife."

"He indeed has found a lovely one, miss," said the innkeeper with a smile. "Your room is up the stairs and to the left. Supper is usually served down here until whenever people around her go home, but if I am awake, I can cook up something anytime."

"Is there an apothecary in the village?" asked Maddoc.

"There is, sir."

"Could you tell me where?"

"I could, or my son could take you there himself. We are not a large village, but spread out enough that finding certain places can be tricky."

"Very well, I will see my wife to the room and come down here directly." Maddoc started walking away with Anwen on his arm.

The man nodded, and Maddoc and Anwen walked together up the stairs. When they got to the room, Maddoc opened the door letting Anwen enter first. The room was not large, but it was pleasant. There was a small fireplace on one side with two chairs and a table. A good size bed sat in the center with a place to clean off to the side.

"Please make yourself comfortable and rest here while I get what is needed for your injury."

He turned to go when Anwen stopped him. "Try not to go broke shopping in town. It might be wise to let the young man who assists you see to your coin pouch."

He smiled sheepishly. "I know little of coins it is true, but I would pay a good amount to see you well."

She couldn't help it. She walked up to him and stood on her tiptoes to kiss him gently on his lips.

17

Chapter 17

Maddoc hurried up the stairs with the supplies he had gotten from the apothecary. He hoped he would be able to treat Anwen's infection before it spread. He did not like to think of her falling ill so far away from any reliable healers. He had found out the only thing resembling a healer in that village was the old woman who ran the apothecary. Hopefully, the balm and linen she gave him would be enough to help Anwen.

He opened the door of the room they had been given and stepped in. Anwen was sitting in front of the fireplace, not in her dress, but wearing his shirt. Her clothes were laid out in front of the fire on the floor.

She smiled at him as he walked towards her. "I hope you do not mind, but my clothes were still very damp. I could not get comfortable, so I thought it best to dry them for a while. I can put them back on if you wish."

He sat down in the chair next to her and stared at her. He wasn't sure why, but he found her very alluring curled up in the chair wearing his shirt. "I do not mind at all. It will not do for you to be sitting around in wet clothes."

She nodded and sat up straighter. "Did you find everything you needed?"

"I believe I did." He scooted his chair close to her. "I hope this will be enough to help with the infection, or at least hold it off until we can get to Quinlan." He pulled down the shirt and looked at her shoulder. He picked up a clean cloth and some medicine he had gotten.

"How far do you think we are from your palace?" She winced as he pressed the medicine soaked cloth onto her shoulder.

"I would guess about two days. Maybe a day and a half if we rode hard." Putting down the cloth he picked up the balm.

"That feels better," she sighed as he rubbed the balm on her wound very carefully.

"I will need to wrap it now, and you will need to keep it dry." He pulled down the shirt further as she held it up to cover herself.

He wrapped her wound as carefully as he could. She winced a couple of times, but she managed the pain well. Once he was done, he took her hand and kissed it. He wanted to bring her forward and kiss her lips, but he wasn't sure if it was a good idea. He had never been so drawn to a woman. Just holding her all day on his horse had been one of the most enjoyable experiences of his life. Kissing her and holding her already felt so natural. He had never had those feelings before, and it was confusing to him in every way.

He knew he felt for her in some way, but he wasn't sure what it meant. He had felt desire plenty of times, and he knew desire was a part of what he was experiencing for Anwen. There was something else to it. When he had desired women in the past, all he wished was to bed them and be done. With Anwen, he was happy to just be in her presence. He looked forward to talking with her. While he knew he would enjoy bedding her, doing so seemed out of the question. He couldn't imagine loving her so and then having to let her go. Loving her wouldn't be like with other women. He thought it might tie him to her in such a way, he could never untangle himself. He didn't think he would even want to try.

"What are you thinking, Maddoc?" she asked. "It looks to be something serious."

"I am thinking of you." He picked up her hand and held it. "Of you and me."

"Oh," she said quietly. "And what have you decided?"

"Nothing, I don't know what to think, honestly. I know I enjoy being near you. I think the more I am with you, the harder it is to imagine my life without you."

"But you will have to." She took her hand back. "Maddoc, I don't expect anything from you. I know you have expectations on you as the king, and I have my own responsibilities. Maybe I should apologize for kissing you last night and today, but I cannot. I wanted to kiss you. I want to kiss you still." She swallowed and looked up at him. "I find that I want you."

He felt his breathing increase wondering if he understood her. She couldn't mean what he thought she did.

"I have said too much." She sat back in her chair away from him. "I have scandalized you and undone all the good things you thought I was."

"No," he said quickly. "I am only surprised. I have felt my feelings grow for you for some time, but I can't imagine you would feel so strongly for me."

"I am not sure how I feel about you, to be honest. I know I enjoy your company, and I believe you are more than you think. I feel drawn to you in some way, and if I am honest, you make me feel wanted and desired. I have not felt so in a very long time. I am beginning to wonder if I have ever really felt wanted."

He smiled. "I do want you, Anwen, but I cannot have you, not in that way. I am afraid if we go that far, I will not be able to come back. I could not give you what I would want to give. I'm not sure you would even want it."

She leaned forward and took his hand. "We shouldn't complicate this. It is enough to be here with you now. I will not ask you to do anything you don't feel right about doing. I will even never kiss you again if you wish."

He shook his head and pulled her forward gently. "That is not what I wish."

She smiled and put her hand on his cheek. "Then perhaps we can just agree to enjoy the moment. What happens will happen. I am tired of trying to plan my life and trying to be what everyone wants me to be. Just this one time, I want to do what I feel like. I will not force you into anything but do not think you have to protect me. I know what I am doing."

She moved forward and placed her lips on his. He did not resist. He didn't want to. He wasn't sure he was able to. He pulled her as gently as he could until she sat in his lap. She leaned her good shoulder into him as he wrapped his hand around her waist, claiming her lips again. She moved from kissing his lips to his jaw, and he lifted his head and groaned as she shifted against him. He started moving his hand up her side. A knock at the door made his hand stop, and she pulled back from him.

"I asked that dinner be brought up to us. I didn't think you would want to go downstairs."

She kissed him quickly and stood up. He got up and walked over to the door, opening it, and taking the tray from the person who held it. He brought it over to the fireplace and placed it on the table. Anwen was already sitting back in her chair, and Maddoc sat down next to her. They ate dinner together, Maddoc trying to encourage Anwen to eat more. It bothered him how little she ate. She should be very hungry by now, but she said she had no appetite. He reached over and felt her cheek again, but it was not unusually warm.

"Will we leave for Quinlan in the morning?" Anwen asked before taking a sip of wine.

"I am not sure. We will see how you are feeling and decide. We do not seem to be in any danger here. The town was quiet when I went to the apothecary. It might be good to take a day or two of rest before we venture on."

He was in no hurry to get to the palace. He knew the sooner they were there, the sooner Anwen would go home. He was not ready to part from her. Especially not now that there was a new dynamic to their relationship. He wasn't sure what could come of it, but that didn't mean he didn't want to find out.

"I would not mind resting a bit," she said with a yawn. "I'll also admit to some trepidation to visiting your palace. I am not sure how I will be received."

"I will make sure you are treated well, Anwen. Everyone will know what you have done for me, and you will be celebrated. You can also leave as soon as you want for your own kingdom. I will see you are sent back in as much comfort as you like." He took a drink of wine. "I do hope you will not run off too quickly. Our Harvest Celebration will be soon, and I would like you to attend."

"Will there be dancing?" He nodded. "Then I shall try to stay for it. You did promise me you would dance with me."

He smiled. "I did, and I will keep my promise to you."

They finished their meal, and Maddoc gathered up their plates and put them outside the door for someone to come take. He walked back over to find Anwen leaning back in her chair watching the fire. Her eyes look tired and heavy.

"You should go to bed, Anwen. I know you must be tired."

She stood up and walked over to the bed. She looked back at him. "You must be tired as well. I doubt either of us has slept well on this journey. You should join me."

He looked at her and finished his wine. He stood up as she pulled back the covers and lay down in the bed. He walked over and sat down on the bed, pulling off his boots. She was on her back, and she turned her head to look at him. He lay down on the bed and turned towards her on his side. He looked down on her, thinking of how lovely she was. Her golden hair was all around her, and her full lips were red from the wine. Her beautiful eyes looked tired, but they gazed up at him. His shirt on her had ridden up a little, showing off her toned legs.

He leaned down and kissed her gently on her lips. She put her uninjured arm around him and pulled him down over her. Their kissed deepened as he moved his hand down her body. He could feel her trim waist under his shirt. She ran her hand down his back as he moved to kiss her neck. He could feel his body start to react to the desire that was building inside of him. His hand moved down to the hem of the shirt she wore, and he slid it under the shirt, his hand working its way up her thigh.

He was in danger of losing himself in his need for her, and it seemed as if she was not going to stop him. He shifted and accidentally hit her sore shoulder causing her to cry out in pain. He pulled back and moved his hands off of her. Rolling away from her, he lay on his back, trying to settle himself.

"You didn't have to stop," she said after a moment. "The pain is not bad."

He rolled over and looked at her. "Anwen, if I am going to love you, I am going to do it at a time and place, I can do it right. We shouldn't be doing any of this."

"I told you this is what I want," she said with a little pout. "Do you not want me? Is that it."

He laughed a little before kissing her cheek. "My princess, I don't think I have ever wanted anyone the way I want you, but I will not let my desire for you overcome me in a place like this. You deserve better than some awkward tumble in a strange bed while you are injured."

She sighed and pulled up the covers.

"You are also tired and need to sleep."

She rolled over on her good shoulder to face him, and he put his arms around her. She nuzzled into him, resting her head against his chest. She was quiet for some time, and he thought she had gone to sleep. Just as he thought he should blow out the candles she said sleepily, "I am not some innocent maiden you have to protect, Maddoc. I know what I am doing, and what I want."

He kissed the top of her head and held her close. "I know you do, but I will not have you think you are just some woman I can spend a night with and forget." He paused, wondering if he should say what he was thinking. "Anwen, I do not want to frighten you, and I am not even sure I know what love is, but I believe I could easily fall in love with you."

She did not respond, and Maddoc looked down to find her eyes were closed. He could feel her soft steady breaths against him.

"Good night, princess," he whispered with a grin. He leaned behind him and blew out the candle on the table, before pulling her as close as possible and closing his eyes.

He awoke as Anwen fidgeted against him. There was a pale light coming through the window showing the sun was just rising. Maddoc opened his eyes and looked down at Anwen in his arms. He bent down to kiss her forehead to find it hot and sweaty. He swore quietly and pulled away from her. Gently he pulled down her shirt on her shoulder and unraveled the wrapping around it. Her eyes blinked open as he looked over the obviously infected wound.

"Maddoc," she whispered. "I am so thirsty."

"You have a fever, Anwen," he said sitting up in bed. "I will get you some water, but then I must run and fetch someone to see to you."

He got up out of the bed and poured a cup of water from a pitcher on a nearby table. He brought it over to her and helped her to drink. Once she had finished the cup she lay back in the bed, and Maddoc took some of the leftover linen and dunked it in some water.

He placed the wet cloth on her forehead. "You should try to sleep. I am going to go visit the apothecary and see if the woman who works there will come to see you."

She nodded slightly with her eyes closed. Maddoc sat on the bed and put on his boots. He grabbed his cloak and fastened it around his neck. He walked over to the bed and made sure Anwen was well covered up, bending down to adjust her wet cloth. She seemed to be back asleep, but she was moving around. He was afraid her fever was very high.

"I will be back as soon as I can," he whispered before kissing her hot cheek.

He did not want to leave her, but he saw no choice. He hurried from the room, and down the stairs. He walked quickly through the town, trying to find the place the innkeeper's boy had taken him the day before. He finally found it and pounded on the door until a servant answered. He eventually convinced the old woman who owned the shop to accompany him. Too much time had passed, and the old woman was much too slow walking with him to the inn. He almost picked her up and carried her.

Once they got to the inn, the innkeeper behind the bar looked up at them curiously as they both went for the stairs. They entered the room to find Anwen still in bed. She was awake and breathing very hard. The old woman sat down her bag on the table by the bed and looked at Anwen.

"Take off her wrapping so I can see the wound," directed the old woman.

Maddoc did as she asked, and the old woman bent over very close to Anwen's shoulder to look at the cut. She prodded it a little with her fingers, causing Anwen to cry out. Maddoc took her hand, scared at how hot it felt. The old woman took something out of her bag and placed it on the wound. She shook her head and sighed, wrapping up Anwen's shoulder in fresh linen.

She looked down at Anwen and then up at Maddoc before she walked towards the fireplace. Maddoc kissed Anwen's hand before letting it go. He walked over to join the old woman.

"I am afraid she has a very severe infection that has spread through her body," said the old woman. "I do not have the skill or supplies to treat it here."

"Who does? Where could I take her?" asked Maddoc desperately.

"For something like that, you would probably need the healers in a large village, maybe even the ones in Quinlan themselves. She is very ill."

"How far is Quinlan?" asked Maddoc.

"From here? If you go by horseback you could make it in less than two days. It would be a hard journey for someone as sick as she is."

Maddoc paced a little. "Is there something you could give her for her fever and pain? I can take her on horseback. I can make it."

The woman looked at him closely. "She is wearing an interesting standard on her shirt, I see."

He stopped pacing. He had forgotten what Anwen was wearing. Even here at the edge of the kingdom, his family standard would be recognized.

The woman took a deep breath. "It might be better for you if you left her here to her fate, sir. I am sure you would not like to get caught up in the trouble of seeing her back to the gods. You would probably like to avoid anything having to do with a lady such as she."

Maddoc closed his eyes. "You have no idea who she is," he snarled. "You don't know what she means to me."

"I did not mean to offend. I was only giving you an option."

"It is not an option so do not mention it again. Now, can you give her some medicine to help with her fever and pain?"

"I can."

"Do it. Give me as much as you think she would need to get her to Quinlan. I will pay you well for your trouble and your discretion." Maddock pulled out his coin pouch.

"Very well, sir."

Less than an hour later, Maddoc rode along the main road that ran north through his kingdom. Anwen lay in front of him, bundled up in her cloak. The old woman had given her some medicine which had temporarily dropped her fever. The pain medicine Anwen had taken left her tired and confused. After helping her to dress, Maddoc had run to get his horse. Now Anwen lay against him asleep as he held her as tight as he could with one arm.

They were riding much too fast, but he didn't dare slow down. He would ride with little rest and few stops. They would make it to Quinlan in time to save her. There could be no alternative. It was a day and a half of hard riding. He stopped only a few times to rest and take care of what needs he had. He slept little, his desire to see Anwen well keeping him awake. She slept most of the way. When she was awake, she seemed confused, not knowing where she was. She asked for her mother once. She whispered his name many times, and it broke his heart to hear the pain in her voice.

As the sunset on the second day, he almost cried in relief to see Quinlan before him. His horse made a noise, and Maddoc almost thought the poor animal was celebrating the chance to rest. He rode through the village paying no mind to those around him, and none seem to care about him. He made it to the palace gates and stopped, looking up at the guards in the tower. It took them a few minutes to recognize him, but when they did, they opened the gates with no questions.

Maddoc rode straight to the front door. He jumped from his horse, and gently slid Anwen off the saddle. Two guards and several servants met him, and he trusted someone would see to his horse without asking. He walked up the steps to the front door with Anwen in his arms, and a servant opened it. Maddoc walked in and was met by his own servant, Evan.

"Your majesty," gasped Evan. "Thank the three gods you are here. We haven't heard anything since Matthias returned confused. We had feared the worst." Evan shook his head a little and looked at Maddoc. "Who is..."

"This is Princess Anwen Claran of Lucidala. I owe her my life many times over. She was injured and is very ill. I need to find her a room and have a healer see to her."

"Of course, your majesty," said Evan. "She can stay on the third floor in one of the guest quarters."

"No, she will stay on the second," said Maddoc as he made for the stairs.

"That is where the family rooms are," said Evan following him.

"I am well aware of it. I do not want her far away from me. Is the yellow room prepared?"

"All the rooms are always prepared, your majesty. You know that, but are you sure it is appropriate she stay there?"

"I don't care what is appropriate at the moment. The princess will stay in that room. I need you to alert the palace healer this very moment. Have him come to the yellow room as quickly as he can. Tell him he needs to treat an infected wound."

"Yes, your majesty," said Evan as they reached the second floor. Evan turned and hurried back down the stairs as Maddoc turned to the left.

He walked a few doors down and opened the third one he found. Inside he found a dark, but clean suite of rooms. He walked through the sitting room and placed Anwen on the bed. She made a slight noise and moved over on her injured side before crying out and laying on her back. Maddoc sat down next to her and took her hand. He watched as Anwen seem to settle, her breaths coming quick. He closed his eyes and prayed the healer could help her.

18

❦

Chapter 18

Time passed strangely for Anwen. At one point she knew she was on a horse. She could feel the wind whip all around her as Maddoc held her close. She was aware of being on the cold ground a few times. Maddoc made her drink some water and other foul-tasting things. Her shoulder hurt horribly at times, and at others, she felt nothing at all.

Eventually, it became clear to her she was on a very soft bed. She would open her eyes occasionally and see faces she did not recognize. An older man looked closely at her shoulder. A young woman who cleaned her and combed her hair, braiding it. A beautiful woman with dark curls looked at her curiously. A man that looked almost like Maddoc, but not as handsome.

At almost all times she was aware of Maddoc's presence. She didn't know if he was always near, or if she dreamed of him sometimes. She could feel his hand cover hers. His lips would graze her forehead, cheek, and sometimes lips. A few times he caressed her face. She thought she whispered his name many times, but she wasn't sure. She had no idea how long she existed in this strange daze where time had no meaning, but eventually, she woke up and everything seemed much more real and clear.

"Good morning, princess," said a woman's voice next to her.

Anwen turned her head to see the dark-haired woman she had seen occasionally in her hazy state. "Is it morning?"

"It is. Though not early morning. You have been asleep for some time."

Anwen moved up in the bed a little, trying to sit up. Her body ached and her shoulder felt stiff. "How long have I been asleep?"

"You were brought here to the palace over three days ago. You were in and out the first two days. Our healer didn't know if you would live. You slipped into a deep sleep yesterday mid-morning and have slept soundly since then. I believe your fever broke last night. It was the only way I could convince my son to finally sleep. When he hasn't been in here, I am sure he has been pacing his room. He looked half-dead last I saw him."

"Your son?"

"Yes, the king says you saved his life more than once on your little journey."

Anwen sat up a little further. "You are the queen mother."

"I am Queen Evalin Cadden, and you are Princess Anwen Claran."

Anwen nodded.

"It sounds as if you have had quite an adventure these past few days."

Anwen blinked her eyes wondering how to respond. Her head still felt fuzzy, and her body ached terribly. "Your majesty, I am not sure what you want me to say or what you are trying to say."

"It does not matter, not at this moment. You are tired, and I should wait to hear your tale of your journey. My son has given me his account, but I would like to have yours as well."

"I am sure King Maddoc told you the truth, your majesty. He would have no reason to lie."

The queen stood up. "I have no doubt he told me the truth of the parts he told me, but I am not sure he gave me the whole story. Also, I think I will benefit from hearing what you have to say. I believe I have many questions for you."

Anwen worried with her covers a little. The queen did not sound threatening, but there was definitely a hint of mistrust and worry in the way she spoke.

"But it is no matter. I will see to a servant bringing you something to eat. Perhaps you would like to bathe, your highness?"

"I would like to, but I hate to be so much trouble."

"My dear princess if we won't go to the trouble of seeing to the needs of the person who saved our king, what could we possibly be troubled with? I will have someone in to serve you soon."

The queen swept from the room and closed the door. Anwen turned carefully adjusted her pillows. She sat back into them and glanced down at her shoulder. She could see it was wrapped under the nightgown she wore. The gown was a little too big and had slipped off her shoulder. She carefully touched the wrappings when she heard something coming from the side of the room. She looked over but couldn't see anything.

"Your majesty?" called Anwen. She thought she had misheard, and the noise had come from the front of the room. Perhaps the queen had forgotten something.

Anwen blinked as part of the wall opened up, and Maddoc entered the room. "I thought I asked you not to call me that. At least not when we are alone." He walked over to her side and sat next to her on the bed. He picked up her hand and brought it to his lips.

"Where did you come from?" she asked as he kissed her hand tenderly.

"There is a reason I chose this room for you. I wanted a way for you to be close to me, and this room is connected to mine through a secret passageway. Very few know about it as it is a secret passed down by kings. I don't think even my mother knows."

"Why is this room connected to yours?" Maddoc kept a hold of her hand.

He shrugged a little. "No one really knows, but the rumor has always been a king some time ago would keep visiting women in here if he wished to bed them."

Anwen snatched her hand away. "I know I have been rather forward with you, Maddoc, but this might be going too far. What if people found out why you put me here?"

He took her hand again. "Anwen, I only brought you here so I could keep watch over you. I was scared you were going to die. You have no idea what the past few nights have been like. I was forced to leave you by my mother and others, but at least this way I could check on you anytime."

She sighed. "Your mother mentioned your healer wasn't sure if I would live."

"You've been very ill. You must still be tired."

"I am and sore, but it is manageable. Your mother went to send a servant to come prepare me a bath, so you will have to leave soon."

"The servants will knock before they enter. I can be gone before they come into the room. I'd like to sit with you for a while longer."

She looked down half feeling like smiling, and half feeling as if she should demand to leave his palace this instant. Him becoming more attached to her, and her to him could not be a good idea. She couldn't understand his feelings for her, and she certainly didn't feel like examining her feelings for him at the moment.

She did feel at ease in his presence, and the way he was holding her hand and looking at her was not objectionable at all. She could not leave now even if she wanted to. She was tired and still did not feel well. She would enjoy his company now and, in a few days, when she was recovered, she would revisit what this was between them.

"What have I missed while I've been ill? Did your guards make it back here?"

"They did. They said they arrived back outside of Quinlan with no memory of traveling here. Once it became known I was not with them, a few different parties were sent out to look for me. They looked on the road through Lucidala but not on the side paths you took us."

"I suppose I should have listened to you and stayed on the main road. They could have found you quicker than we made it here," said Anwen.

"Or I could have been killed within the first day. Perhaps a larger group than we faced was stalking the main roads watching for me? Maybe large enough that even you could not have saved me, Anwen." He paused and held her hand tighter. "Besides your injury and a few ridiculous things I said, I do not regret our journey. I could never regret spending time with you."

"There is much I enjoyed about our time together, Maddoc. It will be strange not seeing you after I leave soon."

He swallowed. "But you cannot leave too soon. You will need to recover, and then our Harvest Celebration is coming up. You told me you would stay for it."

She hesitated to answer. She did tell him she would dance with him at the festival, but she made that promise when they were far from his palace. Now here, amongst his people, she was sure she would feel like the outsider she was. She would remember the gulf between their two kingdoms. She was fond of Maddoc now and very attracted to him, but if she pulled away now, she could manage the separation. If she let herself linger close to him, her fondness for him could grow.

She should tell him her staying was not a good idea, but when she opened her mouth, she could not do it. "It seems I have become your captive, after all, my king. After I am well, I will stay for your celebration with hopes of winning my freedom."

He laughed a little. "Maybe by then, you will not desire your freedom, princess."

He left when the servants knocked, giving her assurances he would see her later. She spent a luxuriously long time in the large bath of her washroom, basking in the lavender-scented water. She thought it was good luck the servants knew her favorite scent. After her bath, she was given a clean nightgown and robe that were both a little too large, but they were comfortable and finely made.

She walked into the sitting room of the suite she was in and sat down in front of the large fireplace. Running her fingers through her hair to dry it, she watched as some servants sat some food and wine in front of her. She dismissed them and poured a cup of wine. She ate a bit of the food in front of her, though her appetite wasn't great. If she wanted to grow stronger, she knew she would have to force some food.

Once she was done, there was a knock at the door. She stood up and adjusted her robe, tying it tight around her middle. "Please enter," she said, not sure what else she could do.

An older woman dressed like an upper servant walked into a room followed by a man who looked to be almost middle age. He was tall and thin. His hair was dark brown, and his eyes gray. She realized she had seen him at some point during her sickness. He did look a little like Maddoc. While not a bad-looking man, he was not as handsome as the king. His eyes were dull instead of deep blue, and his chin somewhat weak.

He bowed to the princess as Anwen folded her arms in front of her. "Your highness, I do not wish to make you uncomfortable. I only wanted to check for myself that you are well. My dear sister had said as much, but after all, you have done for my nephew and our kingdom, I could not be settled until I saw you were truly on the mend."

Anwen kept her arms over her, not liking being so vulnerably dressed in front of this man. His words were kind and appreciative, but his tone was haughty. She might have been imaging it, but it felt as if his eyes were looking over her thinly dressed figure. They seemed to settle somewhere along her neckline.

"I am doing much better. May I have the honor of an introduction?"

"Oh, yes, of course. I am Prince Korben Cadden. I am our king's uncle. My brother was the king before King Maddoc."

"Princess Anwen Claran. I am pleased to meet you." Anwen gave a small curtsy, feeling her legs shake.

"Please sit down, your highness. I know you must be tired. I will not trouble you long." Prince Korben nodded to the servant who sat down in a corner chair as he sat in the chair facing Anwen.

"Would you like some wine, your highness?" asked Anwen as she picked up the pitcher to pour a little more into her cup.

"No, but thank you. I had my mid-day meal not too long ago. It looks like you haven't eaten much, so please continue with your own meal if you wish."

"I am not very hungry. I am sure my appetite will return as I continue to feel better."

"I can only hope, Princess Anwen." He gave her a small smile as she took a sip of her wine. "My nephew seems to hold you in high regard. I have never seen him take such care of anything or anyone as he has of you the past few days."

"We have experienced much together over the past week or so. I am sure he is only anxious after such a perilous time." Anwen took another sip of wine. She had a feeling she needed to be careful during this conversation.

"Perhaps," said the prince. "The king tells me you saved him multiple times during your journey. He mentioned your Gift. I have heard tales of your people and your powers, but I have not witnessed any for myself. Yours sound very impressive."

"They can be, but I am not in good control over them. They tend to do as they like, and lately, they seem to want to keep your king safe."

"Curious," said the prince. "Is this why you agreed to accompany the king? Because your Gift wished you to do it?"

"Maybe in some part, but the main reason was that it was the right thing to do. My aunt shamed me and my family by not letting your king stay at the palace in Awbrey. She wouldn't even give him a properly guarded escort to his home. I felt I had no choice but to see to his safety. Our gods believe every life is precious. I could not let the king's life be thrown away."

"And gaining aid for your kingdom must have entered your mind."

Anwen put down her cup. She knew she should watch her tongue. She was in a strange palace with a man who held much influence and power. She took a deep breath. "You know our kingdom needs aid?"

"I believe you know I do, princess. I can tell you are not a simpleton, and my nephew has babbled on about your little adventure. He told me of all the things you do for your kingdom. Your mother sent us letters in the past telling of your kingdom's troubles."

"And you ignored them."

The prince nodded. "I did, though it wasn't out of malice. Our kingdom has many demands on its resources. Our own people must come first. I and the council have longed to discuss seeking to aid Lucidala." He crossed his legs and said in a quiet tone. "Our queen has been less enthusiastic about the idea."

"Could you tell me why?"

"You should probably ask her yourself, but I think it has much to do with where she grew up. She grew up in the kingdom of Arvelia. They are very devout to their simple gods and mistrust any unnatural powers. They think your kingdom cursed."

"I have heard there are some there and throughout the land who believe we are unnatural, but I thought it was simpler folk. Not ones who would marry into such a great family and kingdom." Anwen leaned back in her chair, feeling her exhaustion start to take its toll.

"Perhaps not in practice, but there is still a general prejudice against your kingdom and people in certain areas of the land. The queen mother may be affected by it, but you would have to find out from her. Now, back to my original question. Were you hoping at least a little to gain aid for your people?"

"It was in the back of my mind, but not my main motive," said Anwen truthfully. "I told King Maddoc as much."

"I do not fault you, Princess Anwen. You are a great leader of your people. You must seize opportunities for them when you can. I believe some recognition is in order for your safe escort of our king. As soon as you are well, you will want to travel back to Lucidala. I will make sure you are well guarded and supplied with medicine and food for your people. I will continue to make sure carts and carts of supplies are sent all over your kingdom during the harsh winter months."

"That is kind and would be appreciated."

"It is earned by you. Of course, you will want to head back to your people as soon as can be. I have spoken to our healer, and he thinks in a week you shall be ready to travel."

"Which is what you want, your highness? You wish me out of your palace and away from your king as soon as can be."

"I don't know what you mean, princess," said Prince Korben with a smile. "I am only thinking you will want to return to your people with needed aid very quickly. Your family must be worried about you. We have sent a message, but they will want you home with them as soon as can be, I am sure."

"I will travel home as soon as I am able, and as soon as the king wishes me to go, your highness. It is his palace, isn't it? I would not like to insult his hospitality with a hasty exit. We had some talk of your Harvest Celebration on our journey, and he mentioned he would like me to see it." Anwen crossed her arms in front of her.

"Did he?" He does like a good festival and pretty young women. He often entertains young women, your highness." He paused and glanced over to the servant in the corner of the room. "If you are planning on spending time with the king you should know you likely won't have his undivided attention."

Anwen almost laughed. She had no doubt Maddoc had a very long list of women, young and old he had entertained. He had told her himself, but at the moment she had no doubt she held almost all his attention. "I understand where I stand with the king, your highness. I also know who I am and what I owe my people. While I appreciate your veiled advice, I can handle my own affairs."

"Very well, your highness. I will leave you now as you must be tired." The prince stood and Anwen stood with him. "I hope you will take what I have said with the kindness and goodwill it was said with. You seem a very intelligent woman with many worthy attributes, and I am sure you will be a good queen to your people someday." He moved a little closer to Anwen and looked down at her. "A good relationship with Calumbria could go a long way to securing your kingdom's future. I would like to help you with it."

Anwen wanted to close her robe further and back away, but she held her ground under his provocative gaze. "I will remember all you have said, your highness. I thank you for any help you can give my people. Please excuse me as I wish to lie down."

He picked up Anwen's hand and brought it to his lips. She almost shivered, feeling the way he slowly kissed her hand, letting his lips linger too long. "Good day, your highness."

"Goodbye, Prince Korben."

He left the room, and the servant in the corner stood up. She came before Anwen and gave a deep curtsy. When she stood up straight, she gave Anwen a kind smile before walking to the door and leaving. Anwen walked to her bedroom, wiping her hand on her robe. She fell down in the bed, half wanting to be alone and half wanting the wall to open so Maddoc would come in and hold her.

19

‿‿

Chapter 19

Maddoc walked back towards the side door of the place. He had taken a short walk around the palace grounds to give Anwen time to clean and rest. He hoped she would be awake and feeling better by now, and he could spend some time speaking with her. It seemed strange, but he missed being constantly around her. As he walked outside and observed things, he would find himself wanting to talk about them with the princess.

He saw an old lord who bowed with a sour look on his face. He wondered if the old man was mad at his king or bitter because he had never had an heir to his estate, and now his stupid great-nephew would inherit. He observed a large wagon of supplies being made ready towards the front of the palace. He inquired and found out it was headed to the southwest part of the kingdom. When he asked why the servants did not know. He wished Anwen had been by his side so he could hear her thoughts on both matters.

He almost reached the door when a familiar voice stopped him.

"Your majesty, I can't tell you how good it is to actually see you."

Maddoc smiled and turned. "I never thought I would hear you say that, Lord Elias."

Lord Elias Bennington was the highest lord in their land. He had come into his title young like Maddoc. He had grown up close to the palace, and the two had been lifelong friends and adversaries. They enjoyed each other's company, but also constantly competed with each other. They sparred with swords and shot arrows side by side, seeing who could hit the target the most. They raced horses, always trying to acquire the fastest animal with the surest feet. They vied for the attention of ladies, to see who could bed who the quickest. Their lifelong friendship had been tumultuous, full of argument and hurt feelings, but there were few Maddoc trusted as much as Elias.

"There was talk you were dead, my friend. I might wish you disfigured in some way at times, but I never would want you to die." Elias walked forward and took Maddoc's hand, giving it a good shake.

"As you can see, I am well, and unfortunately for you just as handsome as always."

Elias laughed. "I hear there is a certain person to account for your safe return. I understand she is a princess and a very pretty one at that."

Maddoc stepped back a little and crossed his arms. "Princess Anwen of Lucidala was my guide on my journey. She saw me safely back to my home. She has suffered for it."

"I heard she was injured. How is she? Will she be well?"

"I believe she will. I have heard from the servants that she is without fever and up moving around her room."

Elias smiled. "I hope she will not runoff. My mother is particularly interested in meeting this princess."

"Whatever for?"

"She is young and unmarried, is she not?" Maddoc nodded. "And she is to be the queen of her kingdom?" Again, Maddoc gave a short nod. "You must see that many mothers and some fathers will want at least their younger sons to meet this princess. My mother is thinking of Avery."

"Avery is barely sixteen," said Maddoc shaking his head.

Elias shrugged. "He won't be sixteen forever, and to be a king would be something. Though I would hate for my younger brother to best me.

Perhaps I will charm this princess and run away with her to Lucidala. My brother can keep the lands, manor, and position."

Maddoc closed his eyes for a moment. He should have seen this coming. Bringing her here in the midst of the court was not a good idea. She would of course be a curiosity. Once her beauty and position were known, young sons of lords would come to pay court to her. The thought made Maddoc's head hurt, and his chest feel strange.

"She did not come here looking for a husband," said Maddoc.

"Perhaps not, but it might benefit her to find one. She has been on the road with a king who has a certain reputation. I do not mind a woman with some experience, but there are those who will look down on her."

"The princess is everything good and worthy of respect, Elias. She has acted with nothing but the utmost honor." Maddoc tried to keep the edge out of his voice as thoughts of kisses he had shared with Anwen and the feel of her soft body in his arms filled his head.

Elias leaned back with a wicked smile on his lips. "You like this woman, your majesty."

"I'm not sure what you mean, my lord."

"Yes, you do. You like the princess, and I don't mean in the way you usually like a woman. You care about this one."

"She is owed my respect and my protection, and that is it, Elias. She has done much for me, and I am appreciative. There is nothing more." Maddoc hopped his cheeks weren't as red as they felt.

Elias smiled wide as he ran a hand through his light brown hair. "If that is the case, you won't mind if I do try to court her then."

"I most certainly will mind it. I know how you are with women. She doesn't need some cad like you trying to dishonor her with false promises."

"Who says they would be false? She has much to offer, and if she is as pretty as I hear she is, she could be worth looking at as a wife."

Maddoc shook his head. "What of Lady Alys? Weren't you just paying court to her last week?"

Elias waved his hand away. "She couldn't care less if I back off. She has two other suitors already. Besides, I find her dull and dispassionate. I bet she would be as quiet as a mouse, and still as a rock in bed. What is this princess like? She must be something if she was able to protect you in some way."

Maddoc took a deep breath. "You will have to meet her for yourself, Elias, and take your own measure of her. I warn you, she will not fall for any of your usual tricks."

"We will see, my king." Elias smiled and rocked back slightly on his heels. "Now, you should come spend some time at the manor and dine with me. My mother would love the honor, and my aunt will be joining us. Though I don't like to think of it, I believe you two have a very special relationship."

Maddoc blew out a puff of air thinking of Lady Phaedra. They had spent some time together over the past few years. She had taught him many things in a few different areas. He found her a woman easy to talk to, and a very experienced lover. While he wouldn't mind spending an evening talking with the lady, anything else strangely did not appeal to him.

"I am not sure. I have been away from the place for too long. I am sure my uncle and mother would rather I eat with them."

Elias shook his head. "But what would you rather do, your majesty? The palace is yours. All in it should serve you. If you wish to come to my house and enjoy good companionship, you better do it."

Most nights, Maddoc would much rather spend a comfortable evening around Elias's table over his own quiet, tense one, but he was hoping to spend some time with Anwen. She was better, but he would like to be sure she was truly well. If he could just sneak in and perhaps spend an hour speaking with her, or maybe she would be as bold as she was on their journey and let him lie next to her. He would not push her for anything more, not when she was sick, but an evening holding Anwen sounded better than a night basking in the light of Lady Phaedra or any other woman.

"I will make plans to join you soon, Lord Elias, but not tonight."

"Plans for what your majesty?" said Prince Korben as he walked up to Maddoc and Elias. "Have you been offered an invitation from the lord?"

"He has, your highness. I thought he might like to come eat with me and my family tonight. We have all been worried about him, and it would do him good to visit with old friends."

"I believe you are right, my lord." Maddoc's uncle turned to him. "You should go to the lord's manor tonight. I believe your mother talked of turning in early and taking dinner in her room. She has not slept well with your fate being up in the air. I might see whose table I could take advantage of or maybe even check in with our guest. If she is up to it, I could eat with her."

"I should be the one to entertain our guest, uncle. She is here because of me. I cannot leave the princess alone in a strange place."

"But she will not be alone, King Maddoc," said Elias with a sly smile. "The prince has declared he shall check in with her, leaving you free to do as you please. Unless you would rather spend time with the princess?"

Maddoc most certainly would, but he could not say so in front of Elias and most definitely not in front of his uncle. He sighed. He could go with Elias now and spend some time speaking with him, his mother, and his aunt before supper. He could then leave directly after the meal and go to Anwen. He did not like the idea of his uncle bothering her, but what could the prince really do to her? He had no doubt, Anwen could hold her own against anyone.

"Very well, Lord Elias, I will come with you, though you will have to excuse my casual attire. I have no wish to change."

"You are our king and are always dressed accordingly. It is us who must meet your desires, your majesty," said Lord Elias with a laugh.

The late afternoon into the evening passed pleasantly enough. For a few hours, Maddoc and Elias drank in Elias's study, speaking over Maddoc's journey. Elias shook his head and laughed as Maddoc recalled some of the things the princess had said to him. He looked in wonder as Maddoc tried to describe what Anwen had done with her powers. Elias asked a few questions, and Maddoc was afraid the young lord would believe his king had lost his senses, but Elias seemed to take what Maddoc said as truth.

Maddoc did not include some aspects of their journey. There were some things he did not want anyone knowing, the least of all Elias. In the past, they had both enjoyed sharing their conquest of women, but what Maddoc had shared with Anwen was off-limits. It would feel wrong to explain to anyone how kissing Anwen was unlike anything he had ever experienced. He didn't want any other man to know what holding her felt like. He wanted it to be only for his ears how she whispered his name against his lips.

"And that was it, was it?" asked Elias when Maddoc had finished speaking.

"That was it?" asked Maddoc incredulously. "Did you not just hear my tale? I was almost killed at least four times. The princess's powers alone should be enough to entertain you. What else would you have liked to hear about?"

"You were on the road alone with a beautiful young woman. Are you telling me nothing happened?"

"I have already told you the princess is honorable in every way. Do not question it again, or you will not like my answer."

"I hope you defend me as well as you do this new friend of yours, your majesty. Are you sure you do not have plans for the princess?"

"What plans could I have, Elias?

"I suppose you could plan to make her your wife? She is a princess of an old kingdom. She would be acceptable, wouldn't she?"

"She is the princess of an old kingdom, but one many look on with mistrust and fear. I know that is all superstition and old tales, but it is what it is. Besides, she will be the queen of her kingdom someday. How could I convince her to give that up to be my consort here?"

Elias gave his wicked smile again. "So, you have thought about it?"

Of course, he had thought about it. The more he got to know Anwen, the more he knew he would never find another woman like her. He wasn't sure he would call his feelings for her love at this point. He wasn't even really sure what love felt like, but whatever was building in him for the princess was something he wished he could experience more and more.

"It may have crossed my mind as it does whenever I interact with any high-born lady, but it is nothing more than that. I respect Princess Anwen and hold her in high regard, but there is nothing more between us."

"Well, if you have nothing more to say, then I think we should join the ladies and see if my brother has gotten himself home."

Maddoc found himself relating his story again over supper. He had a feeling he would be telling his story a few times or at least answering questions about it. Avery found it exciting, and Elias's mother found it hard to believe.

"Do you think our king would lie, sister?" asked Lady Phaedra. She looked at Maddoc who sat next to her. "I believe you, your majesty. I should like to meet your princess. She sounds very interesting."

"She is Lucidala's princess, my lady. I merely borrowed her for my journey."

"With all that happened, it sounds like any trouble you went through to have her guide you was worth it," said Elias with a laugh.

"I am afraid all the trouble was on her side. I doubt I would be here without her. I know for a fact I would not be. All the while she lies injured in my palace."

"But she will recover," smiled Lady Phaedra. "She will leave here hopefully better than she came, and maybe with more than she thought."

"Ah, sister, now you come to the point," said Lady Rowena, Elias's mother. "We know that the princess is brave and intelligent from your story, your majesty, but what does she look like. I hear she is very lovely, but that is just servant talk."

Maddoc took a drink from his cup and set it down. "She is very lovely, my lady, though perhaps not what you are used to seeing as beautiful. She is small for what one usually describes as a beautiful woman, but she is not oddly formed. Her hair is golden and long. Her complexion is very clear and fair. I believe her eyes are her best feature. I am sure you will see her soon, and you can judge for yourself."

"Will she be staying long in Quinlan?" asked Lady Rowena.

"I have asked her to stay for our Harvest Celebration. I would like to honor her properly, and what better time to do it than during a festival?"

"And that will give plenty of time for her to meet the higher lords of the kingdom and their younger sons and brothers. Very good idea, your majesty." Lady Rowena smiled before eating a small bite of food.

"To be honest I had not thought to introduce her in such a way, my lady. I am not sure the princess would like it."

"You don't think she would like to be courted by handsome and eligible lords? I am sure the princess would like nothing more. She could make a very good connection here in Calumbria for her and her kingdom. I am sure it has entered her mind." Lady Rowena smiled knowingly at her sister.

Maddoc was sure Anwen had not thought of it at all, but he paused to consider. Perhaps Anwen would meet a lord or lord's son she liked. What could he really do about it? The thought made him unsettled, a little angry, and something else, but he couldn't state what it was. He took another drink of wine to try and settle his feelings.

"I am sure the princess can handle whatever our young men throw at her, your majesty," said Lady Phaedra as she patted his hand. "As I said before, she sounds like quite a woman."

The meal passed with the ladies sharing other local gossip, but Maddoc barely listened. He could only imagine someone like Elias charming Anwen. He could see his friend kissing her hand and making her laugh. He closed his eyes and saw Anwen on Elias's arm. She turned, and Elias took her hand. He brought her close. Maddoc's eyes flew open, and he abruptly stood up.

"My king, is something wrong?" asked Lady Rowena.

Maddoc looked around the table to see all looking at him. "Not at all, my lady, but I think I must go. It is getting late, and I am still tired from my journey."

"I didn't not realize how late it had gotten," said Elias as he stood as well. "Let me see you out."

"Actually, I will walk with the king. I need to leave as well, and I am sure he would not mind seeing me to my door before he walks on to the palace," said Lady Phaedra as she smiled at Maddoc.

"Of course, my lady," said Maddoc, not seeing how he could refuse.

They both bid goodnight to their hosts and walked out the door, Maddoc offering his arm to Lady Phaedra.

"It is a nice night for being so close to the cold season," remarked the lady. "Before you know it, the snows will come."

Maddoc nodded as they walked.

"I am very glad you came back safe. I did worry for you. I would not like anything to happen to you, my king."

"I am glad to be home. While my journey was not what I anticipated, it was not altogether terrible."

"No, I don't believe it was, your majesty. You seem to have made a new friend at least. I have never heard you talk so much about one person, let alone a young woman." Lady Phaedra glanced at him out of the corner of her eyes.

"I suppose I have not met anyone like the princess. She impressed me in many ways."

The lady sighed. They arrived at the front of her manor, and she turned to the king. She was very lovely even though she was at least a decade older than Maddoc. Her light brown hair was swept over to the side in a becoming way. Her red lips were full, and her blue eyes clear. Maddoc looked at her, noticing her eyes did not sparkle like Anwen's. Her lips did not curve down in a subtle way as Anwen's did. They always made it look as though the princess was thinking things over in her mind. The lady before him was lovely, but she was not as captivating as Anwen. He didn't believe anyone could be.

"You can come in for a bit if you would like. The young lord will be in bed by now," said Lady Phaedra as she moved close to Maddoc.

Her husband had died not long after the birth of his son. Now Phaedra lived in the manor seeing over the lands until the boy was of age. Maddoc often wondered why she didn't marry again, but perhaps she was happy as she was. He doubted he was the only man she entertained. He really did not mind.

She stared up at him, and he looked down at her. Usually, he would agree instantly to accompany her for a night of pleasure, but that night he did not have the desire. He had no ill feelings towards her, but the thought of holding her and kissing her made him step back.

"I believe I am too tired for any conversation tonight, my lady. I need to get back to the palace."

She smiled. "You want to check on your friend, no doubt. I suppose I always knew this time was coming, but I had hoped it might be a few more years."

"What time is that, my lady?"

"I have gotten to know you, your majesty. You are not cold like your mother or calculating like your uncle. You have a good and passionate heart. You were made to love, and I knew one day a young lady would finally catch your eye and find her way into your heart." She leaned forward and kissed him on the cheek. "I would like to meet your princess soon. I hope to find her all I expect her to be."

"My lady..." started Maddoc.

"Do not worry, your majesty. I will not speak of it to a single person. Good night." She swept into her house, leaving Maddoc thoughtful and in a hurry to return to the palace.

He entered his room to find his servant, Evan waiting for him.

"How is the princess?" asked Maddoc as soon as he stepped into the room.

"Mrs. Owens says she is well but tired. Your uncle asked to dine with her, but Mrs. Owens told him the princess was already asleep for the night."

Maddoc grew concerned. "You don't think she is feeling unwell again, do you?"

Evan smiled a little. "I think it has more to do with the wish to avoid your uncle's company. Mrs. Owens said he was a little rude to the princess this afternoon."

Maddoc sighed. "Not surprising. I can see to myself for the night, Evan. You can go."

"I have left you some more comfortable clothes for the evening on the bed, your majesty." Evan turned to go. He got the door and turned back around. "Mrs. Owens mentioned she would check in with the princess just before breakfast time. I believe your mother wishes to eat with the princess tomorrow morning if she is up to it."

"Thank you, Evan. That will be all."

Evan bowed and left the room. Maddoc walked into his bedroom and changed quickly, pulling on a simple shirt and pants. He walked to a certain place on his left wall and pushed. It opened, and Maddoc grabbed a nearby candle. He slipped into the passageway, closing the wall behind him. He moved along the short dark hallway until he came to the end. He pushed the wall opened slightly and peered into the princess's room. All seemed dark and quiet.

Maddoc pushed the wall open a bit more and moved through the opening. He placed his candle on a small table and walked to the bed. The princess was lying on her back, her face turned towards Maddoc. The moonlight from the nearby window fell across her lovely features, illuminating them in a strange light. He stood next to the princess and looked down at her. A bit of her hair had fallen in her face, and Maddoc carefully moved it, his hand brushing her cheek. She sighed and turned towards his hand. He didn't want to wake her, but he couldn't help but bend down and gently kiss her forehead. He turned to go.

"Maddoc?" she said quietly. "Are you leaving?"

He turned back to her. "I was trying not to wake you. I know you need to sleep."

"It is hard to sleep well in a strange place surrounded by people I don't know or trust."

He sat down next to her on the bed. "I heard my uncle wasn't very welcoming. I hate that I have to leave you alone so much." He picked up her hand and held it.

She looked down at their hands and then up at him. "Will you stay with me for a while. Just until I fall back asleep?"

He nodded and brought her hand up to kiss it before he let it go. She moved over in the bed, and Maddoc lay down next to her, placing his arms around her. He was careful to avoid her wrapped shoulder as she snuggled close to him. He looked down at her, and she gave him a small smile. He felt that feeling in his chest again. It was warm and spread throughout his body. She moved up a little until her face was close to his.

"I have missed you today," she said softly. "I shouldn't say it, and I shouldn't ask you to be here with me now, but the truth is I like being here with you."

He bent down and brushed her lips with his own. "I like being with you, Anwen. I am not sure what this is, but I find that I don't like being away from you."

She leaned in and kissed him. She pulled away, but Maddoc moved his hand up to her head and gently pulled her back in. He kissed her, not worrying about what it meant or where it was leading. All he cared was she was in his arms, and her soft lips were on his. He pulled back and looked down at her. She was looking at him, but her eyes looked heavy. He kissed her forehead and pulled her close to him.

"You need to sleep, Anwen. You will not get any better unless you rest."

"You won't leave me until I fall asleep, will you?"

"I will not," he said as he pressed his lips against her forehead. As comfortable and relaxed as he felt with her in his arms, he found he did not have the will to rise from her bed even if he wanted to.

"Good night, my king," she said quietly.

As he closed his eyes, he murmured, "Sleep well, my princess."

20

~

Chapter 20

Anwen woke up as she felt Maddoc's lips against her own. She leaned in and kissed him gently before opening her eyes and seeing Maddoc looking at her. She noticed the light shining from the window behind them.

"Shouldn't you be in your room at this time of the morning?" asked Anwen as she pushed away from him, wincing at the pain it caused in her shoulder.

"There is still time before Mrs. Owens wakes you up." He pushed down the shoulder of her gown and looked at her wrapped shoulder. "The healer will need to check on your wound today and rewrap it."

"How do you know what time Mrs. Owens will wake me up?"

"She let my servant, Evan, know. I asked her to let me know your schedule." Maddock leaned over and kissed her shoulder close to her neck before pulling her gown back up.

"You mean your servants know about this?" she asked with a hiss.

"They know I wish to check on you and spend time with you." He gave her a very small smile. "It isn't like that, Anwen. They do not question your honor. How could they judge you knowing what king they serve? You think Evan doesn't know everything I have done? Mrs. Owens has kept watch over me since I was born. She knows every mistake I have made and is still fond of me. They will not think less of you for any time you spend with me. I think Mrs. Owens hopes you will redeem me in some way."

Anwen sighed and sat up. "I don't know how I will look that kind old woman in the face after knowing this. She must think I am some sort of trollop laying here in this room waiting for the king to come take his pleasure."

Maddoc laughed. "I assure you, she does not. You have barely been conscious your time here in the palace, and you still aren't well. When would we have had time?"

"Perhaps I should change rooms."

"There is no reason to," said Maddoc as he brought his hand up to her face. He stroked her cheek. "I would rather you didn't. I like being able to visit you whenever I want."

"What am I doing?" asked Anwen as Maddoc leaned into her.

"What you want, I hope," he said before he kissed her.

After Maddoc left her, Anwen lay back in bed thought over her relationship with Maddoc. He was right in she was doing what she wanted. She had spent most of her life trying to do what was asked of her. She spent hours and hours trying to release her Gift. She spent days visiting people of her kingdom, trying to understand their needs. She studied and studied to learn more and more about what it meant to lead a kingdom, wanting to be a truly worthy queen someday.

It wasn't that she didn't enjoy her life. There were many things she did that she found enjoyment in. She liked learning new things. She enjoyed learning how to fight and defend herself. She had met many interesting people in her kingdom. Her life was full in many ways, but when it came down to it, her time was rarely her own. What little she had spent of her free time had largely been with Lachlan, and now those memories seemed tainted and empty.

Here away from the responsibilities of her kingdom she found herself spending time with a man she was increasingly attracted to. She felt drawn to him. The more he kissed her, the more she wanted his kisses. His touch sent a flame through her body, and it made her want him to explore more and more of her. She wanted the king. She knew she did. She just needed to know if it was safe for her to have him.

She wasn't overly concerned with her virtue no matter how much she blushed at the idea of the servants knowing her business. She had given up what virtue she had to a very unworthy man, and most people knew it. She knew the king had been very open with his own promiscuous ways. Why could she not find pleasure where she could? The real reason she wondered if she should push things further with Maddoc was the fear of falling in love with him.

She did not want to fall in love with the king. There would be nothing for it. She couldn't spend her life loving him. He had other responsibilities that would come before her, and she had her own as well. She was already fond of Maddoc, and the more she got to know him the more she liked him. If she gave herself to him and connected with him in an intimate way, she was afraid he would tear down every barrier she had put up around her heart since Lachlan.

She did not have to decide that day. She could go on with the way things were and see how they played out. If it became too much, she could drawback. Soon, when she was well, she could leave. He would not force her to stay. Satisfied with her decision, she got out of the bed just as there was a knock at the door.

Anwen put on her robe and asked whoever it was to enter. Mrs. Owens walked into the room carrying a blue dress. She curtsied and smiled at Anwen.

"How are you feeling, your highness?"

"Better than yesterday," said Anwen. "Not quite like myself, but not so tired and sore. My shoulder does hurt a bit."

"Yes, I was told to fetch the healer for you later today so he could see to your shoulder. He will come before lunch." Mrs. Owens put the dress down over a chair. "The queen was wondering if you were well enough to eat breakfast with her downstairs."

Anwen nodded. "I believe I am. I should like to get out of this room. At least for a little bit. I am sure I will have to rest later this afternoon, but breakfast and a short stroll sound nice."

"I have brought you a dress. I believe it is close to your size. Once I see how it fits, I have several others I can have altered to fit you. If you are up to it tomorrow, I will see that a dressmaker comes to see you to make you a gown for the Harvest ball."

"This sounds like a lot of trouble for one person, especially for you. You must have better things to do with your time than see to me."

The old woman smiled. "My king asked that I assist you, and I like to see him happy. I have also dressed woman much lower stationed than you, your highness. Many of them not so lovely or so kind."

"You think me kind?"

"Yes, very much. I have seen how you interact with the servants as they attend you. Only one who is kind would be so pleasant with those stationed below you." Mrs. Owens gave a quick smile. "I believe you are strong too after seeing how you dealt with the prince. He was rather rude, and you handled yourself well even though you were still feeling ill."

"You get used to rude men in my position," said Anwen. "I am a woman and a small one at that. Men tend to think they can dismiss me or overpower me. They soon see how wrong they are."

"I have no doubt of it. Now let's get you dressed. You will have to go back into battle right away. The queen mother is suspicious of your relationship with the king. She has plans for King Maddoc making a certain match, and she is worried you will interfere with those plans."

"It is not my intention," said Anwen as she took off her robe.

"I do not believe it is, but I don't think I would mind if you did."

Once Anwen was dressed, she walked out of her room, wondering if she could follow the directions Mrs. Owens gave her to the dining hall. It turned out it did not matter as Maddoc was waiting for her, leaning against the wall across from her room. He pushed off of the wall and raised an eyebrow as he looked her over.

"Is something amiss? I know this dress isn't a perfect fit, but Mrs. Owens did her best. I don't think it looks too terrible."

He walked close to her. "It does not look terrible at all. I am not used to seeing you dressed as a proper princess. I am used to seeing you as a fellow traveler with twigs in your hair."

"And you prefer me this way?" asked Anwen with a grin.

Maddoc offered her his arm, and she took it. He leaned in and whispered. "I rather like you dressed in nothing but my shirt, but I doubt that would be appropriate for any place in the palace."

"Perhaps my room," said Anwen, trying to not blush.

"Or mine," suggested the king making Anwen's cheeks flush fully.

He took her downstairs into a grand dining hall. The table found there was very long. Anwen guessed it could easily hold fifty people. The queen was seated at one end with a plate holding little food though many different dishes surrounded her. Maddoc brought Anwen over to stand close to his mother as the queen rose.

"My dear king, I did not expect you to join us. You rarely rise so early," said the queen as Anwen let go of Maddoc's arm.

"I slept rather well last night and got up early. I was about to come downstairs to find some food when the princess exited her room. She told me where she was headed so I offered to accompany her. Now that she is here, I can leave if you wish, mother."

"Of course not," said the queen as she sat back down. "There is plenty of food and space."

"There is plenty of that, your majesty," said Anwen as she sat down. "Do you always eat in this large room?"

"Not always," said the queen as she grabbed her teacup. "I often take breakfast in my rooms, but when I am entertaining such an important guest, I like to show them every courtesy."

"You need not take such steps to impress me." Anwen poured some tea into her cup. *Or intimidate me*, she thought.

"It is no bother really." The queen turned to her son. "So, you slept well last night?"

"Yes, I suppose it was the company I experienced last night."

Anwen coughed a little, choking on her tea. The queen looked at her before turning back to the king. "Oh?"

"I dined with Lord Elias Bennington last night," said Maddoc with a smile in Awen's direction. "He is an old friend of mine. I am sure you will meet him soon. His mother and aunt are particularly interested in meeting you."

"Lady Phaedra was there, was she? I suppose that means you came in quite late," said the queen taking a sip of her tea. "If you came in at all."

Anwen quickly took the queen's meaning and looked at Maddoc with a raised eyebrow. He seemed non bothered. "I actually came home early in the night. I saw Lady Phaedra to her door and continued on here. I was anxious to be in bed."

"I suppose your journey tired you out. You do seem subdued since you came back. Maybe even a little more settled, I dare say," said the queen.

"I believe the journey did change me in many ways, mother. Having your life threatened constantly will do that to you."

"What has been found out about the threats on the king's life?" asked Anwen. "I should like to know all is being done to keep him safe."

The queen put down her cup. "We have sent out inquires all over the land, trying to gain information. Several of our guards have ridden off to sniff out what they can. Do not worry, princess, we will find out who is threatening my son."

"I would like to know more before Princess Anwen ventures back to her own kingdom," said Maddoc. "I would not like her out on the road if there is still an unknown threat. She was seen with me by many different people. I would hate for something to happen to her because of me."

"I am sure we will hear something soon," said the queen. "When the princess leaves, we will make sure she is well guarded. We will show her every courtesy that she deserves. Which is more than I can say for her own kingdom."

"You are correct, your majesty," said Anwen as she put down the bowl of potatoes she was holding. "My own aunt did very wrong to your king, and I am ashamed. It is why I am here now. I have tried to do everything I can to see that any wrong done to King Maddoc is made right."

"I am sure you have," said the queen. "He is here safe now, and that must be enough. I do not blame you, princess, but it does not surprise me of the cold reception my son received in your kingdom. Lucidala is not known for its hospitality."

"If my mother was not away trying to help her kingdom, then the king's reception would have been much different. She would never have sent him out as my aunt did. I don't know what you think you know of my kingdom, but it is full of generous and hospitable people."

'It is indeed," asserted Maddoc. "Mother, I told you about Lord Aidan and his kindness. I believe Lucidala's people must be worthy if they are half as good as their princess."

The queen sniffed a bit before taking a small bite. "My son has spoken of your travels and your powers. Perhaps you could explain them to me. I should like to know how you kept our king safe."

Anwen took a breath. "I am not sure what explanation I could give you that would be satisfactory. I was born with the Gift of life-saving, but it has never fully developed no matter how hard I try. I can usually only manage to protect life, and I do not have good control over it. My Gift does not like the king's life in danger, and I am not sure why. It seems determined to protect him. The power from my Gift did away with those who would harm the king."

"Just as I told you, mother, Lucidala and its gods hold much regard for life. Princess Anwen was just doing her duty as the leader of her people and a follower of her gods."

"She must feel very strongly about it to go on the road by herself with a single young man," said the queen. "Unless she had other motives."

"Mother," said Maddoc harshly. "The princess has been nothing but upstanding and honorable. How can you say such things with all she has done for me? She has suffered due to her actions."

"What things have I said? I was merely referring to the fact that she must want something for her kingdom." The queen sighed. "Besides, if she was trying to find a way to be your queen, who could blame her? Many women would have done much to be in the situation she was in. She had your undivided attention for over a week. Your very life was in her hands. It would be a very good position to find a way to entrap you in some way."

"But that was not my motive, your majesty. I had no idea to try to gain the king's favor in any way. I have my own kingdom and will wear its crown someday. I have no need to marry for position."

The queen said nothing as she finished her tea. "When do you think you will return to your kingdom. I know my son would like to keep you here until he deems it is safe, but you are not his prisoner."

Anwen almost laughed, and she did glance at Maddoc as he gave her a small smile. "I told the king I would stay for your Harvest Celebrations, so that is my plan."

"For almost three weeks then?" asked the queen.

"I hope that is not a problem," said Anwen as she took a bite of her food.

"It is no problem, princess. I would like it if you would stay twice as long," said the king. "You could stay through the Winter Festival if you like. You did promise you would attend that as well."

The queen looked at her son and then turned to Anwen. "It seems you have made many promises to the king, your highness."

"Only ones he asked me to make himself," said Anwen with a grin at Maddoc.

The queen stood up. "I need to get on with my day. I am sure you are still tired, Princess Anwen, and would like to return to your rooms."

"I actually thought to take a short walk outdoors. I am not one who does well sitting in a room all day. I will just walk around the palace grounds if you don't mind."

"Of course, you can walk, princess," said Maddoc standing up. "Let me escort you to a nearby courtyard. You will not be bothered there as you would out in the more public areas."

Anwen stood and nodded as the queen turned to her son. "I am sure a servant could show the princess to a courtyard, my king. You need not be bothered."

"It is no bother, mother. It is what I want to do." Maddoc walked over to Anwen and offered her his arm. "I am sure I will see you later, mother."

"You most certainly will, my king," said Queen Evalin. "Princess Anwen, I hope to have more conversations with you as you stay in the palace."

"I look forward to them, your majesty," said Anwen as she took Maddoc's arm.

Maddoc led her away from the dining room and to the left side of the palace. He took her out a door at the end of the hallway. They exited into a large courtyard that had two trees that were losing their leaves, a few stone benches, and some rose bushes that still held some blooms.

"This is a lovely place," said Anwen as she let go of Maddoc's arm and looked around.

"It is my favorite courtyard we have, though most prefer the one with the full rose garden. Very few come here, so I can usually have some peace and quiet when I need it."

"There are times you crave peace and quiet?" she asked.

"Of course. Are you surprised I like to sit and think quietly about life and my place in it?"

"I would have been when I first met you, but not now," replied Anwen as she walked around.

She moved close to the rose bushes, letting her hand brush the soft petals.

"Do you like roses?" asked Maddoc as he came to stand close to her.

"They are very lovely, but they bring up some rather bad memories," said Anwen as she looked down at an almost perfect flower. "When I was younger some clerics would take me to the rose bushes close to the forest at the back of the palace. They would make me try to open blooms for hours, trying to unlock my gift. When I couldn't do it, they would become angry. A few times, one grew so angry she raised her hand at me. I suppose she was hoping a good beating would be enough to release my gift. All it did was scare me from even trying for a few months."

Maddoc took her hand and pulled it to his lips. "I would have every rose bush in this village destroyed if you asked it of me."

She smiled. "No, many are cheered by their blooms, and they are lovely. It is not their fault I have bad memories." She took her hand back from him and walked a few steps away. "You do realize you bringing me out here and acting this way will only make your mother question our relationship more?"

Maddoc shrugged. "What if I don't care what she thinks of my feelings for you, Anwen? I can act as I see fit as king."

"You know that isn't true, Maddoc. You have to act as the king of this kingdom and do what is best for it. Aggravating your mother, and dare I say, uncle, by showing me attentions cannot help you or Calumbria."

"You will not run away, will you?" he asked as he moved closer to her. "You will stay at least through the Harvest Celebrations?"

"I promised you I would, my king. I will not break a promise to you."

"And the Winter Festival, you will come?"

"If I can get away, I will keep that promise as well."

"You have made me several promises, Anwen." Maddoc took her hand and pulled her close. "Are there none you want from me?"

"What promise could you make me, Maddoc?" she asked as she looked up at him.

"A few that I would very much like to make if I could. I believe it is coming to the point, where I will have to make them if I am to be true to myself."

"You cannot make them, and you know it. I don't want your promises, Maddoc. I won't ask any of you." She reached up and placed her arms around his neck.

"What do you want, Anwen?" he asked quietly.

"Just this time with you for as long as it can last," she replied as she pulled him down into a kiss.

He wrapped her in his arms as he kissed her, pulling her to him. After a few moments, she pulled back and out of his embrace. "This is foolish. Anyone could see us."

"I already told you I don't care," he said as he reached for her.

He caught her and pulled her back to him. As he leaned down and kissed her, her hand moved from her side to his shoulder. As it passed through the air, it grazed the rose bush next to her. Anwen felt the slightest release of her power as her hand made contact with the bush. She tried to turn to look down at the flowers when Maddoc deepened their kiss, making her forget anything but him.

21

⌒

Chapter 21

The first few days spent with Anwen in his home were some of the happiest Maddoc could remember. He would find ways to walk by her side in the courtyard. They would talk of their lives. She told him even more about her kingdom, and some of her adventures when she was younger. He spoke to her about growing up with Elias, always in constant competition. She laughed at some of their antics and shook her head at others.

"I wonder how many hearts you and the lord have broken in your pursuit to best each other?" she said with a sigh one afternoon as they sat together on a bench.

"Most of the ladies we spent time with knew what was really happening, Anwen. I doubt any of them felt more for me than a general attraction and the want to increase their station."

"I can't imagine being so intimate with a man and not feeling at least something for him."

"And yet here we are, princess," said Maddoc with a smile.

"A few kisses and touches do not equal what I am sure you have done with many young women. Besides, who says I feel nothing for you, my king?"

"But you keep a guard up against me, Anwen. I have noticed. You are charming and warm, but I sense you are keeping some of yourself from me."

She nodded. "I have to protect myself, Maddoc. I don't think I could take another heartbreak."

"Could you tell me about him?" asked Maddoc.

Anwen closed her eyes for a moment. When she opened them, she stood up and walked over to a nearby rose bush. She looked down at the flowers and then back to Maddoc. "I have known Lachlan my whole life. As you can probably guess, his family grew up close to the palace much like your friend and lord, Elias.

"He was a few years older than me, so he ignored me when we were younger. I spent my days with his younger brother, Brennan. We ran through the forest together and learned how to ride and fight. He was and is still my best friend. It wasn't until after my father died that Lachlan started showing me any interest. I think at first, he was under orders from his grandfather to be kind to me, but after a while, I truly believe he spent time with me because he wanted to.

"We went on long rides together. We would walk through the village trying to find something interesting to do. Sometimes we would visit his family's country estate and spend our days running through the fields or reading in the library. It was on one of those trips when he first kissed me.

"It was early fall, and we were out walking amongst the large, old trees. He talked a little of his future as the lord and worried if he would be worthy. I assured him he would, and it was I who could never be the queen Lucidala needed. He stopped me and told me how wonderful I was. He took my hands and said he had never met anyone as intelligent, brave, and good as me.

"He pushed me against a nearby tree and kissed me thoroughly. It was a little shocking for a first kiss, but I attributed it to young passion. After that, we became inseparable. We spent every moment we could together. The night after my eighteenth birthday, he snuck into my room. We stayed up late talking about our future. He said his greatest wish was to spend his life loving me. I let him love me that night, though I had no idea what I was doing." She laughed a little. "I can scarcely remember it beyond being frightened and feeling awkward, but after that our times together became more enjoyable.

"I thought it was all settled. He never officially asked me to be his wife, but it was assumed we would marry. Everyone knew just how close we were. Then late last year after my mother left to go help our kingdom, he started pulling away. I tried to talk about it with him, but he assured me all was fine. His kisses became infrequent and short. He stopped coming to me at night. He would barely speak to me. Then one night at our spring banquet, he announced his betrothal to Gwendolyn."

Maddoc got up and walked over to her. She looked up at him with tears in her eyes. "Every eye in the banquet hall was on me. I had to sit there and put a false smile on my face to not make a scene, but everyone knew. Later, I tried to make him tell me why, but he never would. He ignored me. I heard rumors that he never intended to marry me. He was only taking his pleasure where he could. He used me and then threw me away. They said he told his friends I was nothing but a stunted princess who could never be queen."

Maddoc could not stop himself. He pulled her into him and held her. He could feel her shake slightly, and he knew she was crying. He kissed the top of her head. "He is not worth your tears, princess. Any man who would treat you as such is not worth any thought from you."

She nodded a little. "I think I should feel lucky I did not tie myself to such a man, but it still hurts to remember how he betrayed me. I loved not only him but his whole family. I love them still. To know I will always be separated from them in some way is hard. They may talk of their loyalty to me, but in the end, they will have to choose him."

As Maddoc thought about the care Lord Aidan showed Anwen, he wasn't sure he agreed with her, but he understood her thoughts. It would be hard to throw off the oldest son who stood to inherit everything. One who was still marrying a princess, even if it wasn't the one the family wanted.

"You could leave them all, Anwen," said Maddoc quietly. "You could let your cousin rule someday, and you could find a new future somewhere else." He wanted to say with me, but he could not do it. She had told him she didn't want promises from him. He would not trouble her with them that day no matter how badly he wanted to make them.

She pulled back from him. "I would be lying if I said I haven't thought of it. My mother may even have to make me if the talk doesn't die down. Everyone knows I gave myself to Lachlan. Many still support me, but there are enough in power who look down on me and question my ability to lead. My mother might have to marry me off to some foreign prince or lord."

Maddoc looked down at her. She looked up at him and smiled. "But I would like to lead my kingdom. I don't think I could abandon my people unless I am forced to."

"I am sure Lucidala could not find a more worthy ruler, Anwen, though they might not deserve you."

She shook her head and laughed a little, wiping her eyes. "I have plenty of faults I will have to overcome. You have witnessed at least one of them yourself. I tend to say things without thinking."

"What you say is always the truth. It is up to the listener how they will take it. I am ashamed of how I reacted to your truths at times, but I believe I needed to hear them. I think they will help me become a better man and king."

"You will be a good king, Maddoc. You just need to start trying." She sighed. "See, once again I have said something that will anger you."

"No, you have not. You are right, and I do plan to start trying. I have been a little distracted lately." He smiled at her as she laughed and threaded her arm with his.

"Come, I wish to walk somewhere besides this courtyard. I should like to see the grounds of your palace and maybe a few of your people if they are about. If you are not ashamed of me that is."

"I could never be ashamed of you, Anwen. I have been trying to keep you to myself. Once I let others see you, I am afraid I will lose your time to young lords trying to win your favor."

She laughed. "Then you will have time to reign over your kingdom. A little harmless flirtation might be good for me. Now, let us go beyond the palace walls."

He did not like the idea of her flirting with anyone, but he could not deny her. Besides, he would have her nights no matter what lord tried to fill her head with pretty words during the day. They walked back into the palace to head to the front door when they were met by his mother and uncle.

"King Maddoc and Princess Anwen," said Prince Korben with a bow. "Where have you two been this afternoon?"

"Just exploring the west courtyard," said Maddoc. "The princess has decided she is well enough to go out onto the palace grounds and see who we might meet. I was just escorting her now."

"I am sure you will find many about on a fine day such as this," said Prince Korben. "The queen and I were just on our way to a council meeting."

"A meeting of the king's council?" asked Anwen as she looked up at Maddoc. "Shouldn't the king be going to this meeting?"

Maddoc's uncle smiled. "We do not like to trouble the young king with routine meetings. I am sure nothing of importance will come up."

"I find that even the most mundane news can have a great effect on a kingdom," said Anwen. "Your majesty, you should go to this meeting. I can walk outside another day."

Maddoc was about to protest when his mother interrupted him. "I could walk with the princess, my king. She is right. You should attend these meetings. It is your council."

"I know I have distracted you of late due to your appreciation of the duty I performed for you, but I am well now. I am sure I will have a pleasant afternoon with the queen. You should go to your meeting, King Maddoc."

She took her arm off of his and went to stand next to his mother. Maddoc wasn't sure what to do. He wanted to walk with the princess, but she had spent time talking to him about being responsible for his kingdom. He wanted to please her and make her think well of him.

"If you are sure, Princess Anwen, I will accompany my uncle to the meeting."

"I am very sure, your majesty."

"And you, mother? You are alright missing this meeting?"

"If it means you starting to take responsibility for your title, I shall be very happy to miss any number of meetings. I have been wanting to speak more with the princess anyway."

Maddoc nodded as the princess smiled at him. He watched her walk away with his mother. She turned at looked at him one more time before she disappeared down a hallway.

"Come on, King Maddoc, your council awaits," said Prince Korben sounding very irate.

Maddoc went with the prince to the council hall. At first, he sat and listened as his uncle ran the meeting. He noticed that the lords on the council kept looking at him as though waiting for their king to say something. Maddoc realized he really didn't know these older lords. He wished the council was full of lords he knew and trusted. His friend, Elias, should at least be on the council as the highest lord in the kingdom. Maddoc would have to mention to his uncle.

"And Lord Heartly request food and medicine be sent to his lands at the very north of the kingdom," said a lord at the end of the long table. Maddoc believed his name was Jeremiah Mavens.

"Unlikely," said Prince Korben with a small laugh. "Tell Lord Heartly it is not our fault he cannot produce enough food for his own people or lure a competent healer to his lands."

"Your highness, I don't believe this is the lord's fault. They haven't had much rain this past year. The drought has caused problems with the food production, and their healer was called here by you to see to our village's people." Lord Mavens glanced at Maddoc.

The prince rolled his eyes. "I am sure Lord Heartly is just being greedy. There should be plenty of food for the people in his lands. If not, perhaps a few dying off wouldn't be the worst thing. They have become too populated and unmanageable up north as of late."

"Uncle, what a horrid thing to say," said Maddoc with disgust. He turned to the council. "Do we have extra food and supplies here in Quinlan?"

"We do," said Lord Mavens. "The southern lands also have an abundance of food. The harvest has been very good to my lands and Lord Davin's."

A man, Maddoc supposed was Lord Davins nodded. "Then we should send what is needed to Lord Heartly. I am sure we will still have plenty here and to the south. If our people are suffering, we should do something about it," said Maddoc.

"Very true, your majesty," said Lord Mavens with a smile.

His uncle huffed. "I suppose a little food and medicine wouldn't hurt. Perhaps it will stop Lord Heartly from asking for anything for a while. Send three wagons worth and see if that is enough to stop his complaining."

The rest of the meeting passed without further incident. Maddoc's uncle didn't wait for him. He left promptly, and Maddoc got the impression the prince was not happy with his king.

"Your majesty, if you don't mind me saying it, I am pleased you have decided to join the council meetings," said Lord Mavens as he walked up to Maddoc.

"I do not mind it at all, my lord. I have ignored my duty to my people for too long."

"You lost your father at too young of an age. You only needed time and someone to push you along, I think. Your mother has coddled you too long, and your uncle does not wish you to take his power. It seems someone has pushed you in the right direction, and you would do well to keep them close," said Lord Mavens.

Maddoc nodded. "I think you are right, my lord. If you hear of any more suffering in the kingdom due to shortages, please let me know. Come straight to me."

"Yes, your majesty," said Lord Mavens. "Good day to you."

Maddoc left the meeting room and walked towards the front door. He hoped to find his mother and Anwen still walking outside. He met his mother close to the door.

"Are you done with your walk already, mother?" asked Maddoc.

"I am. The sun is bright today, and I found myself tired after walking in it," replied his mother.

"And has the princess gone to her room to rest?"

"No, Lord Elias found us walking and struck up a conversation with the princess. They seem to get on well, so I left her to him. She didn't seem to mind." The queen smiled. "I think the young lord might already be smitten with her. He was very flirtatious with her, and the princess seemed to enjoy his attentions."

Maddoc didn't say another word. He left his mother standing there and walked out the front door. He looked around the palace grounds, wondering where Anwen could be walking with Elias. As he turned to the side of the palace, he was met with the lord himself.

"Your majesty," said Elias with a bow. "Where are you rushing off to?"

"I was looking for you actually. I heard you were walking with Princess Anwen." Maddoc looked around, trying to see if the princess was close.

"Yes, I just left her with Lord Elliot. The poor fellow seemed desperate to talk to her, though I doubt he will be able to keep up with her. He is so dull, and she seems very sharp."

Maddoc nodded. "Do you know where they are walking?"

"Oh, he mentioned taking her to the old well. What for, I do not know. I shouldn't have given up my place by her side, but I told my mother I would be home in time to receive Lady Alys and her mother." He rolled his eyes. "Who could think of the boring Lady Alys after spending almost an hour talking with Princess Anwen. You should have warned me about her, old friend. I think I'm half in love with her already."

Maddoc gave a short laugh. "You say that about any halfway interesting and beautiful woman."

"But I think I mean it this time. Never has a woman spoken to me so. I asked her what her first impression of me was, and she told me I seemed pompous." Elias laughed.

"You are pompous," pointed out Maddoc.

"I know, but never has a young woman told me so. She said it so charmingly too. I half thought she might be giving me a compliment even with her harsh words. She is very lovely. A little small to be certain, but her figure is definitely womanly. I let her know I was quite serious in my intentions towards her."

"You what?" asked Maddoc. "You aren't serious."

"That is what she said as well, but I assured her I was. I said, of course, I would not be so if you had any plans for her, but I told her you had assured me you had nothing in mind but friendship for her."

"You told her that?" asked the Maddoc. He felt a dropping feeling in his stomach.

Elias shrugged. "It just came out. She didn't seem surprised or unhappy about it. I should probably be going. My mother and our company will be expecting me. I will have to tell her how I found the princess. She wants her for Avery, but why waste such a woman on him. Good day, your majesty." Elias patted his shoulder and walked away as Maddoc moved forward, finding himself desperate to see Anwen.

He had to let her know he did not mean what he had said. He felt much more for her than simple friendship. He was quickly beginning to understand that he could not do without her in his life. He had already in the back of his mind been trying to find a way for them to work. He could spend half the year in Lucidala if he had to. She could travel back and forth. Of course, he wouldn't want to be apart from her for long. They would have to have at least two children. One to see to the future of Calumbria and one for Lucidala. He had thought at some point close to the Harvest Celebration he could declare himself to her, and she would listen. Now it could all be ruined.

"Where are you going, my king?" said his uncle's voice to his left.

Maddoc stopped and turned to see the prince walking up to him. "I was trying to find the princess. She has been walking out in this sun for too long. I would like to see her back to the palace."

"She is a grown woman and very able to take care of herself. You will walk with me so we can talk about that meeting," said his Uncle as he grabbed Maddoc's arm.

Maddoc looked down. "You are angry with me."

"It is not my place to be angry with the king, but I do think you could use a lesson. If you want to make decisions in the meetings, you need to know all the powers that are at play. Now come on, we will walk and then go back to the palace study."

Maddoc looked ahead, seeing a group of people walking about. He wondered if Anwen was amongst them. He glanced at his uncle who looked expectant. "Very well, uncle."

He was not able to get away from his uncle until it was already past supper time. He walked into the dining parlor to find only his mother. She informed him the princess was tried and had taken a tray in her room. Maddoc sat through a long, unnecessarily formal meal with his mother. He was already in a bad mood, having to listen to his uncle talk all afternoon about how Maddoc knew nothing of what the kingdom needed. When Maddoc pointed out that the prince should tell him, his uncle grew angry.

Now he had to listen as his mother related the town rumors and news. She had a visitor before supper who was all a buzz about the princess and the number of suitors she already had. Of course, everyone noticed Elias's attention to her, and this seemed to please the queen. Maddoc only nodded his head, wanting nothing more than for time to speed up so he could go to the princess's rooms.

Supper finally ended, and he went straight to his rooms. Maddoc only paused in his doorway to wave Evan away before walking straight to the wall at the side of his bedroom. He opened it and hurried through. He opened the wall that led to Anwen's bedroom and walked in without checking. She was not in her bed as was usual. She sat in a chair with her robe tied tight around her.

"Anwen," said Maddoc walking towards her. "I've been trying to find a way to talk to you for hours."

"I imagine your time is very busy, your majesty," said Anwen with a tight smile.

"Don't call me that, Anwen," said Maddoc as he walked closer to her.

She stood up and adjusted her robe. "It is the proper way to speak to you even if we are friends. I do hope that we are."

"Please don't listen to Elias. You know you are more to me than just my friend."

"Oh?" asked Anwen as she hugged her arms around herself. "Was the lord lying then?"

Maddoc closed his eyes and then looked down. "No, he was not. I did tell him I had no interest in you beyond friendship and appreciation."

"King Maddoc, you do not need to look so miserable. I am not angry with you. How could I be? I knew all along we could be nothing more than friendly acquaintances. I let my attraction to a very good-looking man cloud my better judgment. I hope you do not think ill of me for it."

She sounded so formal. Her voice was tight. It had lost the merriment and lightness he was used to hearing. He did not want it to be like this. "Anwen, please don't be like this with me. After all, we have shared, how can you act so?"

She sighed and dropped her arms. "Because it is the way it has to be. I knew it all along, and yet I let myself get too close to you. I have begun to feel too much for you. It will do no good. It will only lead to heartache for both of us."

He moved forward and took her hand. "I don't know if I can stop whatever this is between us, Anwen. I don't want to."

She squeezed his hand and looked up at him. He could see tears on the surface of her eyes. "You will have to. I cannot bear to love again and have it taken from me."

He pulled her hand to his lips and kissed it. "I will figure out a way. I promise you."

She pulled her hand back. "No, please do not make me any promises. You may wish to keep them, but I know you will not be able to. Let us stop now and acknowledge what we must be. I will always think well of you, King Maddoc. I hope we will be allies when I take my throne."

He took a breath, feeling as though he could cry himself. "Do you plan to leave the palace soon?"

She smiled a little. "I told you I would stay for your Harvest celebrations, and I will keep my word. Mrs. Owens is already having a dress made for me, and I won't let it go to waste."

He nodded, feeling as though he should sink to the floor and beg her to listen to his declaration of love, but instead he gave her a small smile. "I shall say goodnight then. I hope you will not shy away from me or avoid me in the week to come."

"No, indeed, your majesty. In fact, I believe your friend, Lord Elias, is going to have a small party in a few days. He mentioned he would like me to come and you."

"Good, I would like you to enjoy yourself while you are here. I will let you get some rest. You must be tired."

She nodded. "Good night, your majesty."

"Good night, princess."

He walked back to the wall and put his hand on it. He wanted to turn and look at her, but he was afraid of what he would see if he did. He pushed the wall and somehow walked back to his room. He fell on his bed fully clothed and lay on his back looking up at the canopy that covered his bed. His eyes felt full of tears, and his stomach sick. How could he get through the next days without holding her and kissing her? How could he watch her flirt with the lords of his kingdom? How would he let the woman he loved just walk out of his life for good when she returned to her kingdom?'

He closed his eyes knowing for sure he loved Anwen. He could try to tell himself he barely knew her. He could spend hours reasoning with himself that they could never be, but the truth was he loved her.

22

Chapter 22

The days following the night she dismissed the king were not the happiest for Anwen. There were times of some enjoyment as she walked the palace grounds getting to know the local lords and ladies. The more she talked with Lord Elias Bennington, the more she liked him. He would never do as a husband for her, but she enjoyed his company. He was smart and humorous. They walked around the grounds together as he talked about everyone they would meet, joking about how none of them would make her a good husband.

"Ah, there is Lord Lyle Greenish. He is a handsome devil, but so very dull, princess. You might think his pretty face would make up for his deficiencies but think of spending nights with him. He would rather gaze at himself than you."

Anwen laughed. "But a distracted husband has its merits, my lord. I could do as I pleased with a husband like that."

"We can do much better than poor Lyle for you, my dear. Any man worth anything would never keep you from doing anything you wish, as lovely as you are," said Elias fondly as he covered her hand that lay on his arm.

"You are taking your flirting too far, my lord. I think you wish for me to fall in love with you so you can break my heart."

"I would not wish to break your heart, princess. I don't think anything good could come of me causing any harm to you. I am sure my gods would punish anyone who would hurt one as good as you, and I am sure I would meet them swiftly if the king thought I had done anything to upset you."

Anwen frowned and looked down. She did not like thinking of Maddoc, though she spent much time doing it. The more she thought of him, the more she missed him. She still saw him many times a day for brief moments. They were polite to each other, but any familiarity between them was gone. She missed her conversations with him. She wanted to feel his arms around her. She missed the way his kiss made her feel wanted and desired.

"I doubt he would notice much. He seems to have other concerns at the moment, and those who can distract him." Anwen looked over to see King Maddoc standing with Elias's, Aunt, Lady Phaedra.

"I would usually agree with you. My aunt has been known to turn the king's head, but right now he only follows your movements. I do not think he likes you on my arm, princess."

"He has told you he has no plans for me, has he not?"

"Princess..." started Elias.

"We must take your king at his word, my lord," interrupted Anwen. "What good is a king if he doesn't mean what he says?"

Elias shook his head and walked Anwen closer to some rose bushes away from others. He pulled her close. "Look, I have played games with our king for years. I have tried to best him in everything from sword fighting to women, but this feels too far. I never should have said he had no plans for you beyond friendship when I knew he was lying. He likes you, princess. I think he more than likes you to be honest."

Anwen shook her head. "Even if he does, Elias, how could anything come of it? I will have to go back and prepare to rule my kingdom someday, and he will have to stay here. I also think his mother and uncle have plans for him. I have heard them speaking with him of a princess from Parvilia."

"I do not think any gulf between you cannot be overcome. Call me a romantic, princess, but I do believe in love. My own father and mother were very fond of each other. I am sure you have had experience with it as well."

"I have, and I am not sure I wish to repeat it. I could not trust any promises from the king. Even if I believe he would want to keep them, I know he would have to choose his kingdom and family over me."

Elias sighed. "I don't believe it is as hopeless as you say, but I do not like to see you looking so forlorn. I will try to keep you cheered until you realize the truth, and that is you are in love with our king, and the feeling is mutual."

"I would appreciate you keeping me amused, my lord, but do not hope for such impossible things."

Each night, the princess would eat overly elaborate and awkward suppers with the royal family. Prince Korben would always manage to sit next to her. He would ask her of her kingdom and find reasons to brush his hand against hers as he reached for his cup or utensils. She had a feeling the man had someone watching her room because most times when she walked the halls, the prince would find her. He would walk with her, sometimes stopping her to speak with her.

Two nights before she was engaged at a party in Lord Elias manor, she was walking to her room after selecting a book from the palace library. She hoped some reading would help her sleep as she had not slept well since the king had stopped coming to see her. She had just made it up the stairs and turned towards her room when the prince called her name. She turned, and he caught up to her, walking by her side.

"Good evening, princess. I thought you would have retired by now," said Prince Korben as they walked slowly down the hall.

"I wanted to find something to read to ease my mind before I slept, your highness."

"Have you been having trouble sleeping? If so, I could have the healer give you something. I would not like you to suffer unnecessarily."

"No, it is no big thing. I am sure it is just the thought of traveling to my kingdom soon. I am anxious to be home, but not looking forward to the long journey."

The prince smiled at her. "Perhaps you should delay it then."

Anwen stopped and turned to look at him. "Forgive me, your highness, but I thought you were in a hurry to get rid of me?"

"At first, I was anxious to get you out of this palace it is true, but I find my reasons for having you leave are not valid anymore. I find that for me, I would rather you stay. I have barely gotten to know you." He moved towards her, and Anwen backed away.

"We have eaten almost every meal together, and shared many conversations, your highness. I don't know how else you would like to get to know me."

A grin that did not make Anwen feel comfortable came upon the prince's face. He kept walking towards her, and Anwen kept backing away until she felt the wall behind her. "I think you do know a few certain ways, I would be very happy to know you better, princess."

Prince Korben reached forward and picked up a lock of her golden hair. He held it between his fingers and then let it run between them. "You are very lovely and lively, dear princess. I have never taken a wife, but that does not mean it does not appeal to me. Having an heir is something I should see to."

"Prince Korben, this is highly improper," said Anwen looking for a way around the prince.

"I am merely stating my attentions, princess. After all, wouldn't be a fine thing to connect our two kingdoms? Do you know what an alliance with me could do for Lucidala and your people? It is something you should think about. I would treat you very well."

He leaned in and Anwen felt panicked. She felt she should push him away or step on his foot, but instead, she stood against the wall paralyzed in fear. His hand reached for her face, but just before he touched her cheek there were footsteps nearby. The prince backed away, and Anwen moved towards her room.

"Princess Anwen, is there a problem?" asked Maddoc as he walked towards her.

Anwen turned and looked at the prince. She tried to look at Maddoc but could not meet his eyes. She shook her head.

"I was merely wishing the princess a good night, your majesty. She was showing me what books he had picked to read."

Maddoc walked closer to Anwen. She slowly looked up at him to see his eyes staring at her in concern. "Is that all, princess?" he asked softly.

"Yes, of course, your majesty. If you will excuse me, I find that I am more tired than I thought." She hurried to her room and closed the door. She leaned against it and saw Mrs. Owens looking at her.

The old lady held out her arms, and Anwen walked into them, crying against the woman. She held Anwen, making soothing sounds. "It is alright, princess. Whatever it is, can't be that bad."

"It is though," said Anwen miserably.

Mrs. Owens pulled her back to look at her. "I am sure it is not. Why don't you sit here and tell me about it? I have some tea that is still hot. You can drink some and talk to me. I know it will make you feel better."

Anwen nodded and sat down in front of the fire as Mrs. Owens fixed her some tea. Once Anwen had a cup and regained some of her composure, she told the old woman about the prince.

"I knew he watched you too closely. You should tell the king what is happening, your highness. He would not like you being made uncomfortable by the prince."

"I cannot tell Maddoc, not after I pushed him away." Anwen didn't even care that she had used the king's name. She was beyond caring about such formalities.

"There has been some awkwardness between you. I thought perhaps he had pushed you too far, and I had half a mind to tell him off. He may be the king, but that does not excuse his bad behavior over the years."

Anwen managed a small grin. "I don't know what he has done wrong in the past, but he has done nothing with me that I did not want. It is only, I know he and I can have no future. I believe he knows it as well though he won't admit it. Why else would he tell Lord Elias as much?"

"What did he say to Lord Bennington?" asked Mrs. Owens.

Anwen found herself telling Mrs. Owens much of her and Maddoc's history. She skipped over some of the more intimate details, but the woman seemed to understand most of it anyway. She explained how Maddoc had told Elias he felt nothing for Anwen but friendship and gratitude. Anwen told Mrs. Owens a little of her own history with Lachlan. When she was done, Mrs. Owens sat back and shook her head.

"Oh, my poor stupid boy. He has really made a mess of things," said Mrs. Owens.

"I have blame in this as well," said Anwen.

"Perhaps a little, but the king has not been truthful with you it seems. If he would just tell you how he feels, all would be well."

"I have not let him. I have asked him for no promises."

"He can say he loves you without giving your promises," cried Mrs. Owens.

"You don't know that he loves me," said Anwen. "I am also not sure how I feel for him."

Mrs. Owens smiled. "I will not tell you how you feel, princess, but it is as clear as day that the king loves you. I have seen the way he acts around you. I have seen how tender he is with you, and how his eyes follow you wherever you go. He always talked as if he would never fall in love, but I knew better. I have known him since he was born, and he has such an affectionate heart. I knew a woman would find her way in there someday. I only hoped she would be worthy."

"If it is truly me, I am afraid you are disappointed."

"Oh, for our gods sakes no, my dear. I could not have asked for a better woman to catch his eye and win his heart. You are just the woman who can maneuver all it will take to stay by his side."

"But how can I? I have my own kingdom, and I doubt I am who his uncle or mother want him to marry. They want him to make another connection."

"They can want it all day, but it will do no good if the king loves you as I think he does. Do not give up on love just because it seems hard, princess. I know you have had your heart broken before, but don't let that one bad experience make you miss the real love you have been waiting for."

"I don't know," said Anwen softly.

"You will," said Mrs. Owens. "Give it time and keep your heart open. Do not worry about the future. Live in the present and listen to your heart. I think you will find all will be well if you do it."

Anwen smiled a little. "You make it sound so simple."

"It is really. It is very simple. It is just not easy."

A few nights later Anwen found herself at the manor of Lord Elias. She was dressed very fine in a dark green gown that Mrs. Owens had altered for her. Her hair was pulled up with a few curls falling down her neck. The queen had given her a tiara to wear, stating that a princess should dress for her station. Anwen walked around the parlor with Elias at her side. They viewed a few of the large portraits in the room, Elias telling her what he knew of the subjects.

They were not a large party. It was just the family of the manor, two other young lords, a young lady and her mother, and the royal family. As she made her way around the room, Anwen was aware of three sets of eyes on her. One was the prince, and she had been trying to avoid his notice since the incident a few nights ago. The prince had not sought her out as much since the time in the hallway, but he did always brush against her as he passed her in the palace.

Another set of eyes belonged to a young lady. She did not look angry but curious as her eyes followed Anwen who had spent much of the evening on Lord Elia's arm.

"Have you been courting that young lady, Elias?" asked Anwen as he handed her a drink.

Elias took a drink from his own glass. "Somewhat. My mother would like me to make a match. I suppose it wouldn't be so bad. She is not altogether objectionable."

"She is very beautiful."

"She is, but she is so dull. She hardly says three words unless it is about fashion or flowers. It has been hard to get to know her at all."

"Perhaps she is shy," remarked Anwen. "She might fall back on the things she knows best. You should not just dismiss her. She has an intelligent look about her and a very pretty smile. I think there is something about her that makes me believe she is kind."

"Well, I suppose I could try harder with Lady Alys." He took another drink and looked at her. "I would rather have a fiery princess, but I believe you might already be taken." He nodded his head towards Maddoc who was staring at her as he had been most of the night.

Anwen looked at him, and he did not look away. She had been trying to work up the nerve to speak with him. She wasn't sure why she hadn't done it yet. She thought maybe it was due to fear. She wondered if his feelings had changed for her. Maybe with time to think about it and separation from her, he had decided his feeling for her had been fleeting. With the way he was staring at her, she thought she didn't need to fear, but maybe he was just angry his friend seemed to be winning her in some way. She didn't like to think Maddoc would think that way, but she couldn't completely dismiss his past.

"Princess Anwen, I believe it is time for dinner. Might I escort you into the dining room?" asked Lord Asher. A kind-looking young man with blonde hair.

"I thought to escort the princess, Asher," said Elias stepping forward.

"I believe there is another young lady who requires your attention for the rest of the night. She deserves at least that," said Anwen glancing at Lady Alys.

Elias looked in the same direction and nodded. Anwen turned to Lord Asher. "I will be happy to walk with you to supper, my lord."

Lord Asher looked pleased as Anwen took the arm he offered. As she walked by Maddoc she glanced at him. She gave him a small smile, and he grinned at her. At supper, Anwen found herself between Lord Asher and Lady Phaedra. Lord Asher seemed a very nice man, but his conversation was not very interesting. Lady Phaedra proved to be a much more entraining supper partner. By the time the ladies stood up to leave the table, Lady Phaedra hooked arms with Anwen and turned to her.

"It is rather hot in this house, is it not? Would you walk with me out onto the back lawn, your highness?"

"I would be glad to, my lady," said Anwen. She walked with Lady Phaedra out the back door of the parlor and onto the moonlit lawn. "This is a very handsome space."

"It is. This manor is very lovely. The wife of my nephew will be a fortunate woman. Unless of course that wife has a palace of her own," said Lady Phaedra giving Anwen a significant look.

"If you are asking, my lady, I will tell you the truth. I will not be marrying Lord Elias. He is a good and entertaining man, but he would not make me a good husband. I would not make him a good wife. I believe we are best as friends."

Lady Phaedra smiled. "I agree. You would get bored of him after a time. He is not altogether stupid, but he is not as intelligent as you." She paused for a moment. "Or the king."

"Do you know King Maddoc well?" asked Anwen.

"I do. I know him very well. People dismiss him too easily. He has hidden his true self behind his shield of indifference and indulgence, but I know he is actually a very thoughtful, intelligent young man. I think with the right partner for life, he could do very well as the king."

Anwen looked at Lady Phaedra. She imagined this woman did know Maddoc most intimately. Anwen found she could not be angry about it. There might be a bit of jealousy, but she tried to push it away. "I agree with you, my lady. The more I have gotten to know the king, the more I do like him."

"I think you are just the woman to bring out the better side of him. You would not let him get away with doing anything but his best, but you would care for him even when he failed. I don't know you well, but I think he would suit you as well."

"I won't say I disagree, but I don't know if it can ever be. We both seem to have different callings in this world, and I am not sure those who advise and care for him would approve."

"Many of those who advise him do not care for him at all. They would rather see him fail or continue to sit out of the way. His mother may care for him, but she does not know what is best for him. I have to believe, though, that if she saw him happy, she would relent." Lady Phaedra took Anwen's hand. "As for callings, what good is doing your

duties without someone you love by your side. It might be challenging and take some time to figure it out, but do not dismiss the king just because you cannot see how it can work. Trust in what you know is true, princess, not what you think might be true."

"You are the second person to give me advice like that in the past few days."

"Perhaps you better follow it then."

Anwen spent the rest of the evening in quiet contemplation on the sofa in the parlor. She tried to attend to conversations around her, but her mind kept wandering to the king. She watched him as he spoke with others and laughed with Lady Phaedra. The woman put her hand on his arm like she had done it hundreds of times. Anwen liked the woman, but she thought she was much too familiar with the king.

The more she thought of Maddoc, the more it became clear to Anwen that she felt like he should belong to her. Her heart told her he should be hers, and she should be his. No matter how he really felt, she thought perhaps she already belonged to him. If she was forced to let him go forever, she knew she would be changed.

She believed she really did love Lachlan, but it had been a young, first love that never really ran very deep. He had touched her heart for the first time, and though hurt by his betrayal, she knew with time she would truly recover. What she was experiencing with Maddoc was completely different. It was still new, but it already ran deep within her. She found herself becoming bound with him in a way she never was with Lachlan. She had been holding herself back from Maddoc, but she didn't want to. She wanted him to know every part of her, and she wanted to know every part of him.

As they walked back to the palace after the evening was over, Anwen fell into stride with Maddoc. He looked over at her, and she glanced at him. She wished she could convey her feelings with a simple look, but there was no way. As they entered the palace, the queen said good night and walked up the stairs. The prince walked to the study, leaving Maddoc and Anwen standing together in the entry hall.

"You must be tired, princess," said Maddoc. "You had plenty of conversation tonight."

"I did, your majesty, and some of it not very thrilling." She moved a little closer to him, and he did not back away. "I had a very interesting conversation with Lady Phaedra."

He looked down with a frown. "She is an interesting lady."

"She is and seems very intelligent as well. She gave me some advice tonight, and it made me realize how much I have missed our conversations, my king."

He looked up at her, his lips curving up a little. "I have missed them as well."

"I have especially missed our evening meetings," she said quietly. "I find that I have not slept well since they ceased."

"I have suffered the same, princess," he said quietly as he took her hand. "Would you be open to me visiting again soon?"

"I would, very soon, actually."

"You are free tonight, then?" asked Maddoc as he held her hand.

"I am free any night for you," she whispered.

"Anwen," he began when a door opened loudly, and they split apart.

"King Maddoc, you are still here, good. Come into the study. There has been news on your attackers, and we need to see to it tonight."

"Surely it can wait, uncle," said Maddoc.

"No, it cannot. You want to be king, don't you? Then you will need to learn to take care of things when it is necessary."

Maddoc sighed. "I will come, uncle." He turned to Anwen. "I hope to continue our conversation soon, princess. I am very interested in all you have to say."

"I am available anytime, my king," she said with a curtsy. She looked at the prince and nodded, before walking up the stairs.

23

Chapter 23

Maddoc walked up the stairs, exhausted by all the information he had been given well into the night. The message that came from one of their contacts implied that someone in the palace was feeding information to those who would hurt the king. Maddoc and his uncle met with Matthias and Evan trying to go over every guard or servant who could be a suspect. It was finally decided that Matthias would investigate every guard while Evan would check on the servants with Mrs. Owens.

Maddoc would have to be cautious, and some very trusted guards would be close by when he was out of the palace. Preparations for the Harvest ball to be held the next night would now include a bevy of guards watching over the festivities. Maddoc supposed he should feel unsettled by it all, and he was in a way. He cared more that he wasn't able to go to Anwen earlier.

He smiled a little as he entered his room. She wanted to see him at night again. She missed their conversations. She seemed ready to pick up where they left off. He hoped that meant she was open to their relationship growing into something. He knew he loved her. He would make sure she knew it, not just with words and promises, but with his actions. She had been hurt in the past and leery of letting herself be loved. He would have to gain her trust. He would show her a future they could both share.

Maddoc took off his clothes and boots, putting on a comfortable shirt and pants. He had told Evan to go to bed. He left his clothes and boots to be collected in the morning and walked over to the wall and pushed. He knew Anwen would be asleep, but he had to see her. He just wanted to see her for a moment, then he would leave her alone.

He opened her wall carefully and stepped in trying not to make any noise. She was lying in the middle of the bed, curled up on her side. Her arm was extended out towards the edge of the bed. Maddoc carefully sat on the bed and took her hand. She was so very beautiful. He was sure there were other women in his kingdom some men would think more attractive than Anwen, but to Maddoc there could be none so lovely.

He reached out to touch the soft skin of her cheek when her eyes opened slowly. She seemed to study him for a moment before she quietly said his name. She pulled on his hand, and Maddoc lay down on her bed. She moved over a little to give him room. He pulled her into his arms and kissed her forehead. She moved her head up, and he leaned down and softly kissed her lips.

She gave a contented sigh, and whispered, "My king."

She snuggled into him and Maddoc closed his eyes. Before he fell asleep he quietly said. "Good night, my love."

Maddoc awoke alone in Anwen's bed. He looked around the room and spotted her in her simple traveling dress pulling on a cloak.

She fastened her cloak and walked over to sit on the bed next to him. "You will need to rise soon and get back to your own room."

Maddoc took her hand and kissed it. "Why are you dressed as you are so early?"

"I need to run into the village for a few things. I thought I would go early so I am not missed at breakfast."

"If you need anything a servant can fetch it for you. I do not like the idea of you running around the village unprotected. I know you did it back home, but Quinlan is not Awbrey. It is at least twice as large."

"I need to go get these things myself. I will not be long, and Mrs.

Owens has a male servant who will walk with me. I will be back before you are even dressed."

"Anwen, you need to be careful. We found out last night that it is possible someone in the palace is feeding information to those who tried to kill me. They could try to get to me through you. I don't think I could take it."

She smiled and leaned up to kiss his cheek. "You know I am perfectly capable of taking care of myself. I will not be gone long, and I know where I am going. All will be well, my king."

"You may be capable, but you aren't always sure of looking out for yourself over others. I need you to remember how important you are to me."

"I will. I can guarantee nothing bad will happen from a simple stroll through town. Now, I have to go, and you need to get to your own room. It will be a long day with the celebration tonight."

"You will dance with me, won't you?" asked the king.

"Of course, any dance you should like, I will stand up with you."

"I would like to dance them all with you, but I will let you know soon when I think of which I want to claim," said Maddoc.

Anwen kissed him. "I will see you soon."

"There is something I need to see to this morning as well, but I will find you later," said Maddoc.

"How will you spend your morning?"

Maddoc grinned. "You will have to wait and find out later."

"Very mysterious," said Anwen standing up. "I hope I will like what I find out later."

"I believe you will. Will you not tell me why you are headed into the village?"

"No, not now, but if all goes as I believe it will, I will let you know later."

He looked at her confused, but she only smiled and walked from the room. Maddoc went to his own room to change. He walked downstairs for an early breakfast. As he was finishing his meal, his mother walked in.

"Good morning, mother. This is early for you," said Maddoc.

"There is much to oversee for tonight's preparations. I look forward to when you have a queen to be over it all," said his mother as she sat down.

"I hope to provide the kingdom with a queen in the near future," said Maddoc with a smile.

"Yes, I hope you do as well. I understand the Parvilian princess has written you. You have written back, haven't you?"

Maddoc took a sip of tea. "No, I have not had the time to even look at the message."

"If you wish to court the woman, you will need to put in some effort, my king," said his mother with a sigh.

"I don't believe I wish to court her. I will read her letter when I get to it," said Maddoc.

Queen Evalin shook her head. "You should not dismiss her so easily."

"What are we speaking of?" asked Prince Korben as he walked into the room and took a seat.

"The king's choice of a bride. I was telling him to not overlook the Parvilian princess," said the queen as she spread some jam on a piece of toast.

"No, indeed. She is a fine choice for our queen. She is well position to help the kingdom gain more power. Her father has no real heir. I suppose one of his cousins will be king, but his daughter will still hold much sway with the lords of the land. If you marry her, Calumbria's influence over Parvilia will grow."

"Why does our influence over Parvilia need to grow? We have always had good relations with that kingdom, and I don't think it will change," said Maddoc.

"Your only duty as king is to see to growing the kingdom in power and influence. You will need to make an alliance that secures our kingdom's future." The prince poured some tea while he looked at Maddoc.

"I believe my duty as king is to my people. I want to see them safe and prosperous. I can let the Parvilian royalty look out for their own people. If we force our ways on them, I don't think we will gain favor with the people of Parvilia even if I do marry their princess."

"You will have the powerful lords on your side, and that is all that matters," said the prince.

"You shouldn't dismiss the common folk, uncle. They are the lifeline of any kingdom. If they are unhappy and revolt, it can destroy the land. I will pick a queen that understands the full responsibility of a kingdom includes those who many of our station overlook," said Maddoc as he stood up.

"I hope you aren't thinking of Princess Anwen as a real choice, Maddoc," said his mother. "I know she is very pretty and vivacious. I even like her, but she will not do at all as your wife."

"No, indeed," said his uncle. "I have my own thoughts on how we can handle the princess and create a bond with her kingdom. You do not need to worry about it, my king. I know you are fond of her, but once you are settled with a proper queen, her influence over you will lessen."

Maddoc took a deep breath. "As I will have to live and love my wife, I will be the one to choose who serves as my queen. I believe I know better than either of you who I need by my side. I will not have some loveless marriage full of nothing but duty. I want to not only secure the future of my kingdom but also create happy memories for myself.

"As I look back on my life so far, I realize how lonely I have been, and how I have wasted my time. No longer will I sit aside and let either of you tell me how to rule my kingdom or live my life. I appreciate both of you as members of my family and leaders of Calumbria but from now on, I will see to my own duties and decisions.

"Now, I have much to do today, so I need to get on. Good day to both of you."

As Maddoc walked out of the room, his mother only stared at him, holding her toast halfway to her mouth. His uncle looked like he wanted to rage at Maddoc, but he kept in his seat. It did not matter what either of them had to say further on the subject. He would not marry the Parvilian princess they wanted him to. He only wanted one woman by his side, and he would find a way to have her.

Maddoc walked outside and behind the palace to the royal stables. He searched until he found the stable master, asking him to bring a certain horse out front. Once the horse was in front of him, Maddoc looked it over.

"She is dependable and safe, isn't she?" asked Maddoc looking over the mare.

"She is as gentle as I have ever seen but still spirited. Although young, she is well trained and listens," said the stable master.

Maddoc walked around the dapple gray mare. She was large, but not so big as to be intimidating. "How quick is she?"

"She is a fine runner, your majesty, and very sure-footed. I would trust my own young daughter on her."

"And her lineage is good?"

"She comes from stock right here in our stables. You know how pure our bloodlines are yourself. She is as fine of a mare as you can find, your majesty. She is a horse fit for a queen."

"That is all I needed to hear," said Maddoc with a smile. "I will want her saddled tomorrow mid-morning along with my own horse. Have them brought to the front of the palace."

"Yes, your majesty," said the stable master as he took the mare by the bridle and started walking her off.

"Wait, what is the name of the horse."

"Allinar, your majesty," said the man.

Maddoc raised his eyebrows. "As in the mythical first ruler of our land?"

"I told you she was a horse fit for a queen," laughed the man.

"Indeed," said Maddoc with a nod.

The horse was perfect. He could just imagine Princess Anwen atop the mare. He knew the horse would never replace the precious gift of her father, but he hoped she would like Allinar. Even when she had to go home to her kingdom, she would have something with her that would remind her of him.

Maddoc walked into the stables and checked on his own stallion. He rubbed his nose before going down the rows of stalls and looking in at all the royal horses. He took his time, checking over each one, trying to waste the entire morning. Once it was well past time for the mid-day meal, Maddoc walked back to the palace. He asked for food to be brought to his room as he did not want to eat with his uncle or mother at the moment.

As he entered his room, he was greeted by Evan who was putting up some of his washed clothing.

"Good day, your majesty. I take it you had a full morning as I have not seen you."

"I had a very satisfying morning, Evan." Maddoc sat down as the door opened and a tray of food was brought in. He nodded to the servant as she curtsied and walked out. He took the plate and started eating. "Do you know if the princess made it in from her own morning outing?"

"She did, your majesty. I spoke to her myself." Evan finished putting something away and turned to him. "I believe she is in her room now."

Maddoc took a drink of wine and raised his eyebrows. "Do you know if she has any company?"

"I do not believe so as Mrs. Owens was just downstairs. She said the princess wished to rest before preparing for the evening in a bit."

Maddoc nodded. "I believe I would like to rest as well, Evan. You can go do as you please until later this afternoon."

"Very well, your majesty. Ring if you need anything before then," said Evan as he bowed and left.

Maddoc finished the food in front of him and drank his wine. He quickly cleaned up a bit and changed his shirt, trying to get the smell of the stable off of him. Once he believed he was ready, he grabbed a candle and lit it from the fire that burned in his rooms. He walked to the wall in his bedroom and pushed it open. He hurried down the passageway to the end, pushing it open a bit and looking out.

He couldn't hear anything or see anyone, so he pushed it completely open and stepped out. As he blew out his candle, the princess walked in still wearing her traveling dress. She stopped a few feet from him with her hands on her hips and a lopsided smile on her face.

"If you wanted to visit me, you could just knock on my door like everyone else," said Anwen.

Maddoc put his candle on a nearby table. "This is much more fun and surprising, I think." He walked forward and put his hands on her hips, pulling her to him. "Besides, this way I don't have to find some servant woman to chaperone. I can have you all to myself."

"Oh, do you have plans for us this afternoon?"

"I always have plans for us, Anwen," said the king as he bent down and kissed her.

She pulled back and took a step away from him. "You will have to go soon so I can get ready for tonight. I believe I have a crowd of suitors to face and dance with, so I need to look presentable."

Maddoc huffed and reached out for her. "I don't like to think of any young men paying you attention, Anwen. I especially don't want to think of you dancing with any of them."

"You will have to think of it because it will happen. Your friend, Lord Elias, has already asked me for my first dance," she said, raising her head.

"You are cruel, teasing me so. You don't know how horrible it has been watching you walk around on his arm."

"Probably as bad as me having to watch you laugh and smile with Lady Phaedra," retorted Anwen.

Maddoc gave one short chuckle. "You have no reason to have any worry about Lady Phaedra, Anwen. She is nothing, especially compared to you. I don't think anyone is."

"And you have no reason to worry about Elias or any of the other young or old man I dance with tonight."

"Let's forget the whole thing," said Maddoc as he pulled her to him. She placed her hands on his chest.

"You know we cannot," said Anwen.

Maddoc bent down, his face very close to hers. "I am sure I could convince you."

"You are free to try."

Maddoc closed the small gap between them, kissing her in a way he had been thinking about for a while. She made a small noise and moved against him a little, her hands roaming down his chest. Maddoc's hands started their own journey. One moving from her waist up her side until he slowed it as it grazed her breast. She pulled back for a moment and stared at him while breathing hard. She pulled him closer to her bed, and he kissed her, laying her down as he hovered over her.

She whispered his name against his lips as he moved his hand up her leg, bringing her dress up with it. Her hands had found their way under his shirt, and he moved to kiss her neck as his hand grazed her inner thigh. She made a wonderful noise that made Maddoc groan. He kissed down her throat as one of his hands lay underneath her, trying to undo the back of her dress. She arched up a little after realizing what he was doing, and he managed to untie enough of her dress to pull down the neckline a little. His kisses went lower as his hand on her leg went slowly higher.

She was so lovely and soft. The smell of lavender surrounded him as he found pleasure in making her shiver with his touch and kiss. Her own hands had moved lower, and Maddoc's desire grew. It wasn't just the idea of the pleasure of love-making that urged him on. It was the need to connect with her in an intimate way. He wanted to experience all of life with this woman and share everything with her.

His mind barely registered there was a knock at the door.

"Maddoc," breathed Anwen as she raised up from the bed a little.

"Ignore it and they will go away," said Maddoc as he moved from her chest to kiss her lips.

She pushed him away from her a bit. "It is Mrs. Owens and the servants to draw my bath. I will have to get it."

There was another knock at the door.

Maddoc gave a heavy sigh. He kissed her one more time before standing up and offering her his hand. She took it and stood up before turning around and holding up her hair. "You will have to undo the damage you did, my king."

He tied her dress back up and dropped a kiss on her neck. Before she could pull away, he put his arms around her and held her against him. "Tonight," he breathed into her ear. "You will come to me tonight."

"To you?" she asked looking over her shoulder at him. "How would I even do it? I do not know how to open the wall."

"No sneaking in. Come to my door, and I will let you in. I want you in my bed, Anwen. It is where you belong." He felt her shiver as he kissed her neck.

There was another loud knock. "I really must get that, and you must go." Anwen walked out of his embrace and towards the front of her rooms.

"Anwen," he said stopping her. "I know what dance I want to claim from you."

"Oh?"

"The last one. You will dance the last dance of the evening with me."

"The last one; are you sure?"

He nodded. "It will have to be the last one because once I hold you in my arms, I will not want to even touch anyone else."

She laughed a little. "Very well, I shall dance with you the last dance of the evening as you wish my king." She walked over and picked up his candle, touching the wick with her finger. It lit, and she handed it to him.

He let his finger graze her hand as he took it from her. He gave her one more smile before he opened the wall and walked back to his room.

24

Chapter 24

Anwen walked down the stairs, following a couple of guards that were showing her to the largest courtyard in the palace. It was there the celebration for the Harvest was set up. She saw that there were guards all around the palace as she walked. She supposed it was due to the information they had learned about someone within their ranks being aligned with those who would kill the king. She shivered a little thinking about it. The thought that someone could still be trying to kill Maddoc even here in Quinlan made her stomach hurt with worry.

She could not lose him now. She wasn't sure what their future held. She has some hope they could be together somehow, but even if they weren't, she could survive if she knew he was well. Above all she wanted him to be happy and to grow into who she knew he could be. She knew he was capable of much more than what he had been doing with his life, and she hoped he would continue on the path to becoming the king Calumbria needed.

The guards led her to a hall that had several torches lit. They bowed and moved out of the way. Anwen saw that a few people were moving down the hall towards the open doors at the end. She stayed still for a moment and looked down at her dress. It really was beautiful. It was dark red with a neckline that came off her shoulders. The sleeves ended at her elbows. The bodice had gold threads sewn across it, making a diamond pattern. It fit her trim waist better than any she had ever worn and finished in a full skirt that barely covered her slippers.

She wore a simple gold necklace with one red jewel that hung off of it. Her golden hair was half pulled up in a simple bun with the rest flowing down one shoulder in curls. She wore the tiara the queen had loaned her. She thought she looked quite well and would fit in even with the finest lords and ladies of Calumbria. She took a deep breath and walked down the hallway, exiting into the candle-lit courtyard.

The space was magnificent and was filled with beautiful people. The festivals back home were very well done, but nothing like this. It seemed as if no expense had been spared. There were several lit torches all along the walls of the courtyard. Tables were scattered about with fall flower arrangements. An area had been left clear towards the front of the space with some musicians sitting on a raised platform.

Anwen walked around slowly, taking it all in. She noticed Lord Elias coming towards her with a large smile on his face. He met her and bowed as she curtsied.

"You look very lovely tonight, princess. I know of none among us who look so well as you," said Elias.

She rolled her eyes a little. "You flatter me too much, my lord. What of the young lady you are supposed to be courting? Is she not here?"

He rocked back on his heels slightly. "She is, though I am still not sure I have any serious intentions with her. I feel as though I barely know her. She is so guarded."

"You will have to try harder. Perhaps you should have given her your first dance instead of me. You still could."

"She is opening the ball with her cousin it seems, so you will have to endure me for the first dance, princess. Unless the king comes and sweeps you away." He laughed a little.

"I have a dance planned with your king, but it is much later in the evening. If you are sure, you better offer me your arm, as it looks like the dancing is about to begin."

He stuck out his arm, and she took it. Together they walked towards the dancing space where Maddoc stood with his mother on his arm. The prince was next to them ready to dance with Elias's mother. He turned and looked at the princess as she walked up to stand just behind him with Elias. She looked to Maddoc and saw him glance back at her over his shoulder. She detected a small smile on his lips before he turned to escort his mother to dance.

Anwen enjoyed her dance with Elias. He was very graceful and as always, a good conversation partner. They both laughed their way through their dance, and at the end, Elias escorted her to the edge of the dancing space.

"Now, I will make sure you only have the best dance partners, princess. I can scare away any I or you don't think are acceptable."

"You think you can frighten any man here?" she asked.

"Most of them. I am the highest lord in the land. Besides the king and prince, I outrank everyone. Some of the older lords might think they can withstand my glares and biting tongue, but they will soon find out how wrong they are."

Anwen laughed a little as Elias handed her a drink he grabbed from a nearby table. "I hope you will be too busy finding your own partners. I think you better go ask Lady Alys now. If nothing else, it will please your mother."

"So, it shall," said Elias before draining his glass. "Here comes Lord Timbley. He will do fine for you, though you might be a little bored. I expect one more dance tonight, princess."

"Any dance, but the last, Elias. It has already been taken," replied Anwen taking a sip of her drink.

Anwen was partnered for almost every dance. She talked to many young lords and a few older gentlemen as well. She found something amusing about all of them and was having a better time than she expected. She had drunk enough wine to make her feel somewhat giggly, but not enough to where she was unaware of what she was doing.

Many times, throughout the celebration she would glance at Maddoc to see him watching her. The look in his eyes had the curious ability to make her feel warm and shiver at the same time. It was a look of longing and love. She could tell he would like nothing more than to walk over to her and kiss her. He might want to pick her up and carry her out of the courtyard. She hoped she conveyed back to him how much she wouldn't mind if he did.

She was being particularly careful to avoid the prince. He walked towards her several times, but she was able to procure a dance partner before he was able to speak to her. It was one of the times she was distracted staring at Maddoc when the prince finally was able to ask her to dance. She could not refuse him, so she nodded and took his hand.

"You seem to be enjoying yourself tonight, Princess Anwen," said the prince as they began to dance.

"I am. I like to dance very much, and I have had more than enough partners."

"Yes, it seems as if you have caused quite a ruckus amongst our lords. Have any of them caught your eye particularly?"

"There are many who are very pleasant, and I think I have made a friend out of Lord Elias."

"Yes, the young lord is very friendly with the young women. I would say only the king is more insatiable in the pursuit of young women than Lord Elias. They are both known for enjoying familiarity with many young ladies." He paused for a moment as they danced. "I would hate for you to get caught up in one of their games."

"I know my business, your highness. I am not some helpless maiden who does not know what men may want. I also know how to take care of myself." She smiled up at him. "No man would take something I didn't want to give. I am very good at defending myself."

The prince raised his eyebrows. "I am glad to hear it. It does not surprise me. You are very spirited." He leaned down closer to her. "I like a spirited woman. There are too few in our lands."

Anwen leaned back a bit. "I am sure there are plenty if you take time to look. Perhaps if you found the right one, you would have a wife. Unless of course, you aren't interested in such things."

"I am very interested in such things, especially recently," said Prince

Korben. "I am hoping to find a pleasing woman who comes with the right connection."

"I wish you luck then."

They danced in silence for a few moments before the prince spoke again. "When will you go back to Lucidala?"

"In less than a week. I need to get back to Awbrey and the palace. I will need to see how the harvest is going in all areas of my kingdom. I am hoping my mother will be returning soon."

He nodded. "I will have the wagons ready to leave tomorrow. They will be loaded with supplies and make stops in different areas of Lucidala."

"That is much appreciated. I know it will do much good."

"I would like to be able to help your kingdom more, princess. I believe it could be a worthy endeavor if I had the proper inducement. You and I should talk more fully about it before you leave."

"I am sure if I need help from Calumbria, I should speak with the king," said Anwen.

"King Maddoc knows nothing of our supplies. He has little power when it comes to where they go. If you want help for your kingdom, you should go through me."

"I believe the king is taking more of an interest in all areas of his kingdom. I believe he is already learning more than you realize about Calumbria and its villages."

"Maybe so, but he will be distracted soon. His future bride will come for the Winter Festival in a few months, and he will have much to do to prepare for the wedding. She is a beautiful princess from Parvilia. Have you spent much time in that kingdom?"

"Some, as it does share a border with us. I believe I have met the princess when I was younger, but I do not remember much about her."

"She is known as one of the greatest beauties in the land. King Maddoc had longed to meet her for some time. He spent almost a month paying court to her before he was attacked outside your village on his way back home."

"He mentioned her on our journey here. He said you and the queen wanted the match, but that was all. If he does find himself wanting to marry her, I hope they are very happy."

"It does not much matter what he wants. It is what must be. Assurances have been made to the King of Parvilia. They are as good as betrothed."

Anwen glanced over at Maddoc who was not dancing. He was drinking a glass of wine and watching her dance with his uncle. She would not be agitated by the man in front of her. Maddoc had made her no promises, but she knew he cared for her deeply. She even believed he loved her in some way. It might have been a new love, but it was not shallow. She would not worry about any arrangements made by others. She would follow what her heart said. At the moment, her heart beat for Maddoc. Tonight, she would focus on that and worry about the future at another time.

The dance finally ended, and the prince walked with the princess to the side of the space.

"I hope you do return for our Winter Festival, Princess Anwen. I would enjoy getting to know you better. I think your opinion of me might approve if you will allow it. You seem like a rational person, so I expect soon you will see how things have to be."

Before she could respond he picked up her hand and kissed it before walking away.

"Princess, are you well?" asked Maddoc as he came over and stood by her.

She nodded. "I am. I just had an interesting dance with your uncle. He had much to say about you and your upcoming marriage to the Parvilian princess, your majesty."

"Anwen," he said quietly. "You must not listen to him."

She leaned in closely and whispered to Maddoc. "I paid him no mind, my king. Whoever you have courted in the past or will in the future has nothing to do with us tonight. I am living in the moment, and right now I only want you. I am not concerned with what the future holds. It is enough to be with you now."

He looked as if he would say more to her, but his mother walked up.

"Your majesty, it is almost the last dance, and you must bless the harvest with the priests."

He nodded and held out his hand to Anwen. "Come, princess, I have a duty to do, and then you owe me our dance."

She took his hand and walked with him to the platform in front of the dancing space. She waited at the edge as he joined a priest upon the raised surface. The priest prayed for their harvest, and then looked at Maddoc. Anwen took the opportunity to study the king. He was wearing a dark blue shirt with his family's fox standard on the front. His hair was combed back behind his ears, and he wore an impressive gold crown on his head. She glanced at the crowd and could see many women had come forward to look at the king. She could understand why. She wasn't sure she had seen a more handsome man before.

She looked down at her dress. A finely made as it was and how well it fit, it still did not disguise her small figure. She could see many beautiful, tall, curvy women in the crowd before the king. They were attired in dresses that did not hide their many assets. She wondered why he should want her. It had been a while since she had felt truly beautiful. She had never thought much about her looks. Lachlan had always assured her she was beautiful, but how could she trust his word now?

She sighed. It was not a night she should second guess herself. The king had shown and told her he wanted her. Even if it was just for a short time, she would enjoy what it was. She would listen to what she truly knew, and not what others would say. She would not give in to her self-doubts that evening.

"I am grateful for our bountiful harvest this year," said King Maddoc looking out over the crowd. "All of your lands have done well. We have all your lords to thank for keeping watch over Calumbria's fields, but more so we should toast the people who work those lands. I hope this year and, in the years to come, you will treat them all fairly. We can only be a successful kingdom by caring for all of our people whether high or low born. May we all look to the future of Calumbria together."

Many in the crowd raised their glasses and took a drink. Anwen noticed the prince did not look happy.

"There is one more toast I would like to make tonight. As most of you know, I was recently attacked and thought lost. I would have been lost had it not been for a kind and impressive person who took pity on me. I would like to recognize Princess Anwen Claran of Lucidala. She saved my life multiple times, and I owe her a debt I could never repay." He looked down at her with a small smile. "To Princess Anwen."

The crowd raised their glasses and drank again. Anwen felt herself color a bit as the king hopped down from the platform. He took Anwen's hand and led her to the dancing space.

"You will dance with me, won't you princess?" he asked.

"I promised I would, my king," she said quietly as she moved into his arms.

They danced in silence for a long while. The king holding her very close.

"Anwen," he finally said. "I don't want you to feel as if you have to come to me tonight. I know what you heard from others tonight may make you think differently of me."

"I have learned nothing I didn't already know. I understand your responsibilities to your kingdom, and I know that Calumbria must come first in all you do. It will affect who you choose for your wife. I have duties as well. I am not concerned with the future tonight. I still want to come to you, but if you have changed your mind, I will understand."

"No," said Maddoc. "I want you, Anwen, and not just tonight. You say you are not concerned with the future, but I am. The only future I see worth anything includes you. I believe I can only be the king I need to be with you by my side. I know you have your own kingdom and cares, and I will not dismiss them. I will find a way for us. I have to."

She shook her head. "You are coming too close to making promises. I do not want that from you. I believe you would want to keep them, but I am not sure you could. There are things you and I can't control. We have tonight, and that is enough for now."

"I will show you, Anwen," he softly. "I will not just make you promises. I will show you how I will keep them."

Anwen wanted to kiss him so badly. She might have done it had not the music ended, and she moved away from him. He took her hand and kissed it softly before pulling her closer. "Come to me as soon as you can. I will dismiss Evan quickly."

She nodded, and he turned away. Anwen made her way through the crowd, saying good night to many people including Lord Elias.

"I hope I will see you again before you leave for your home," he said as he walked a little with her.

"I believe you will. I will not leave for a few days yet. I also plan to come back for the Winter Festival. I will probably bring my family and some of my court. You will have new women to charm unless you are a betrothed man by then."

Elias looked over toward Lady Alys who was getting ready to leave with her mother. "You never know, princess. Good night."

"Good night, Lord Elias."

Anwen walked into the palace to go to her room. She stopped and thanked the queen for a pleasant evening. The queen only gave her a tired smile before turning to speak with a servant. Anwen walked on to her room. She found Mrs. Owens waiting for her in front of the fire.

"Do you have a pleasant night, princess?" asked the old woman.

"I did, but I am exhausted from it. I will want to change quickly so I can go to bed."

The old woman nodded and followed Anwen into the bedroom. After helping her with her gown and seeing Anwen dressed for bed, Mrs. Owens wished her a good night and left the room. Anwen walked and stood before her long mirror. She had on a simple white nightgown and robe. Her hair was completely down, falling in curls and waves over her shoulders. She thought she looked a little pale and nervous. She wasn't sure why she should be nervous. She wanted to go to him. It wasn't like she was some untouched maiden. She had been with a man before. She took a deep breath and walked to her door before she lost her nerve.

She opened her door and peeked her head out. Seeing no one, she snuck out of her door, her slippers making little noise on the stone floor. She carefully closed her door behind her and walked down to the double doors on the end. She stood before them with her hand up ready to knock. She paused, hoping the king was truly alone. She took a deep breath and worked up her nerve. She wanted this. She wanted him.

Before she could knock, one door opened. Anwen's heart dropped before she realized it was Maddoc peering out from the door. He gave her a small smile before moving out of the way so she could enter. She walked into the large set of rooms. The front room was a good-sized sitting area with a grand fireplace. Anwen walked closer to look at it. In front of it were two chairs and a comfy-looking sofa. There was a low table with a pitcher of wine and some cups sitting on it.

"Would you like to sit and have a glass of wine? We could talk for a while." Maddoc walked over and stood behind her. He put one arm around her waist and moved her hair out of the way with his hand. He dropped a kiss on her neck.

"I have already drunk more than enough wine tonight," she said as she leaned into him. "I am not in the mood for talking."

He kissed just below her ear. "We can do whatever you like, my princess. Do not feel you have to do anything you don't want or are uncomfortable with."

She turned in his arms and stared up at him. "You know what I want, Maddoc. It may make me wicked to admit it, but I want to be truthful with you. I just want you tonight. Whatever happens tomorrow is no matter to me at the moment."

"I will give you tonight, Anwen, and everything else I have. There will be a future for us, and I will show it to you."

She leaned up and kissed him. It was not a timid kiss or a gentle kiss, but one that was full of need and desire. She did not want his reassurances or a promise that night. His hands went to the tie on her robe as they kissed. He slowly undid the knot and slipped it off of her. He stepped back a bit and stared at her, standing in front of the fire. It made her unsure and nervous. She worried with her hands in front of her and looked away.

Maddoc took her hands and caught her eye. "You are beautiful, Anwen. I am not sure I've ever seen anything more lovely than you."

She shook her head. "You do not need to flatter me unnecessarily, Maddoc. I am already in your bedroom half-dressed."

"I say it because it's true. I will never lie to you, Anwen. You have always been so truthful with me, and I will never be false with you." He pulled her to him and kissed her.

She didn't care if she knew what he said wasn't really the full truth because at that moment it felt true. As he kissed her, she let herself believe this king really thought she was the most beautiful, important thing to him. In the morning, she might feel different, but for one night she would let herself believe.

He picked her up at some point and took her into his bedroom. She barely registered what was around her as he laid her down on his large bed. Before she had a chance to fully breathe, he was upon her, kissing her, his hands sliding up under her nightgown. Her own hands found their way under his shirt, and he lost it sometime soon after.

Anwen always thought it was interesting she could barely remember her first night with Lachlan. Her memory had always been excellent. Perhaps she had blocked much of it out due to pain, awkwardness, and if she was honest, a little disappointment. She had built it up in her mind so much, for it to be over so quickly. A few kisses, a touch here or there, some pain and noises, and then it was over. Her first night with Maddoc was so different. No matter how old she lived to be, she knew she would never forget almost every detail of when she first loved the king.

As anxious as he seemed to have her, he was slow with his kisses and attention. He took his time as he raised her nightgown over her head. He stared down at her with a look that made Anwen audibly sigh. Then she believed he kissed almost every inch of her body, including some places that caused her to have pleasure she could hardly believe. She eventually rolled him over to show him attention as well. She knew she wasn't as skilled as him, but he seemed to enjoy all she did.

She lay back on the bed, and he hovered over her. She was beyond ready to be with him fully. He whispered her name and kissed her lips gently. As he loved her, she became overcome with sensations and emotions. It wasn't just the pleasure for Anwen, even though there was plenty of it, it was the way he loved her. He seemed to want to savor every moment. He said her name more times than she could count. His hands seemed to know just where to go. He kissed her at the perfect times and in the perfect way.

When she could take no more, she said his name loudly and arched up against him. He wrapped her in his arms and lifted her off the bed. Time lost all of its meaning, and the world around her disappeared for a few moments. He leaned down and grasped her name next to her ear as she shuddered against him. He laid her back down gently, and time started again. He rolled over bringing her into his arms. She could feel how fast he was breathing by the rapid rise and fall of his chest. He kissed the top of her head and groaned her name.

Anwen blinked feeling her own body come down from its high. She looked up at him to find him staring down at her. She said it without thinking. It came so natural and easy that she immediately knew it was true. "I love you, Maddoc."

His eyes closed for a second and he held her tighter. "You have no idea how much I love you, Anwen. I don't think I could ever let you go."

"I don't want you to," she said in a whisper, her eyes feeling heavy.

He kissed her forehead, and she burrowed into him. Exhausted and feeling more peace, safety, and even joy than she could ever remember, she quickly fell asleep in his embrace.

25

Chapter 25

Maddoc slept soundly at first. He was exhausted from the act of their lovemaking and the emotions it stirred up in him. He had bedded more women than he wanted to admit, but he knew they would all fade from his memory after his night with Anwen. He had been with more skilled women, and some most people would say were more beautiful, though he would disagree. There was much more than just passion and lust with Anwen.

To be with her in that way brought forth something within him he had never felt before. It was hard to describe, but it was almost as if she was tied to him in some permanent way. He needed her, and to lose her would cause him to lose himself. He would never want to be with anyone but her.

He awoke sometime in the night, feeling the cool air of the room. He opened his eyes and looked to see the fire had burned down very low. It took him a minute to realize Anwen was not in his arms. He felt panicked, reaching over in the bed. His hand landed on her arm, and he gave a sigh of relief. He moved over closer to her and pulled her back to him wrapping his arm around her.

He didn't want to wake her, but he could not resist the urge to move her hair so he could kiss her neck. His hand slid up to caress her breast, and she stirred slightly against him. It was enough to ignite his desire for her. She turned her head and looked at him, her eyes opening slowly. Though he probably should have felt like a beast, he took her again as soon as she was fully awake. In the end, he didn't think she minded. She seemed to him very enthusiastic with it all.

When he awoke again, light poured in from the windows of his bedroom. This time she was still in his arms. He kissed her shoulder as she stretched next to him.

"Maddoc?" she said softly. "What time is it?"

"I am not sure," he answered, kissing her shoulder again. "Early, I think. No one has come in to see to the fire, and Evan hasn't entered to wake me for breakfast."

"I need to be going to my own room," said Anwen with a sigh as he continued to place kisses on her shoulder and neck.

"Why?" he asked.

She let out a breath. "Maddoc."

"Seriously, Anwen, why does it matter? I love you, and now I am certain you love me as well. Why would it matter if my servants found us in bed together?"

"It would cause talk in the palace and beyond. Your mother and uncle would not be pleased. Though I don't care as much about mine as yours, my reputation would be unrepairable."

"Not if you married me," said Maddoc quietly into her ear before he kissed her again.

"You aren't serious."

"I am. You could marry me and become my queen. No one would dare say a word against you after that."

She was quiet and still.

"You think I am too hasty in wanting to marry you. I have rushed you," he said moving his head away from her a bit.

"That is not it at all, Maddoc. I suppose people would say it is rushed, but people marry all the time with only barely knowing each other." She turned around in the bed to face him. "I was only a little surprised to find how much I liked the sound of being your wife."

"Then what is stopping us. I want no one but you, Anwen. I don't believe I deserve you, but I will do everything I can to become a man worthy of being your husband."

She shook her head. "There is plenty stopping us. Your own family would not allow it. I am sure some of your lords would be furious, you marrying a princess from Lucidala. And what of my kingdom? How could I just abandon it to come here? I do love you, Maddoc, but I have a responsibility."

"I would never ask you to throw off Lucidala or your duty. We could work something out. We could half our time between Awbrey and here. There might be times we would have to be a part for a bit, but not for long. I was already thinking I wanted to rearrange my council. I will fill it with lords I know and trust. They can rule my kingdom while I am with you so you can see to yours. I am sure you could do the same one day when you are queen."

"And what of your family? What will you do when your mother and uncle forbid it?"

"They cannot forbid me to do anything. I am a grown man, and I am the king," said Maddoc.

"You would cause such a rift in your family?"

"For you, I would. I would hope eventually they would see how I could choose no one but you. I would hope for reconciliation at some point."

"I don't know, Maddoc."

"You don't have to decide now, Anwen, but do not give up hope if it is what you really want. Know that there is nothing I want more, and I will do all I can to make it happen." Maddoc pulled her close and held her.

"I will think it over. I really do love you, Maddoc. I don't think that will go away. I think it will just grow."

He held her, happy with the thought she did not totally dismiss the idea of them marrying. He would still have to convince her somehow. He would try to make his mother and uncle understand, but in the end, all that really mattered was making Anwen see there was no other way.

"Of course, you could end up carrying my child, I suppose," he said as he pulled back from her a little to look down at her.

"You do not need to worry about that, my king. I know enough about things to ensure there will be no child in my life until the time is right."

"I was not worried about it. I was merely stating that it was a possibility, but I guess it is not. You were prepared for this?"

She blushed a little. "Not until yesterday morning after I walked into the village."

"Oh."

"Are you shocked I was so bold as to assume last night would happen?" asked Anwen.

"No, of course not. I am just impressed with how prepared you were."

"You would be surprised how prepared many of the women you bedded have been, I imagine."

"Usually I take my own precautions," he said with a small laugh. "With you, I didn't even think of it. I'm not sure it would have been possible even if I tried."

Anwen looked at him with a confused look for a moment, but then seemed to understand what he was saying. She looked away for a moment her cheeks reddening again. Then she turned to him and boldly said, "I suppose I shall take that as a compliment."

He laughed and kissed her quickly.

"I will have to get up soon. I can't lay here in your bed all day," said Anwen.

"But I would like nothing more than for you to be in my bed much of the day," said Maddoc.

She smirked a little. "If you brought food in, perhaps. I am rather hungry."

"Then I suppose you should rise, and let Mrs. Owens bring you something to eat. Tell her to dress you in something you can ride in. You could even wear your pants if you like."

"Am I going riding this morning?"

"You are if you are willing. I would very much like to spend most of the day riding with you. My council will not meet as most of my lords in the kingdom will rest after last night. I am not in the mood to meet with my uncle so I would like to avoid him for as much of the day as I can."

"I would like to be outside. If you will loan me a horse, I will be happy to ride with you," said Anwen.

Maddoc couldn't help a cryptic smile. "You will have a horse; do not worry about that."

"Why do I feel like you aren't telling me something? Does this have something to do with what you secretly did yesterday morning?"

"It might. You will have to wait to find out."

She shook her head with a laugh before looking around for her gown. After finding it she put it on and moved to the sitting area to find her robe. Once she was dressed, Maddoc showed her how to open the wall and walked with her down the short passageway to her room. He opened the wall and checked that the room was empty. Once he saw all was still, they walked out. He kissed her a few times, not really wanting to leave her, but she eventually shooed him away. He asked her to meet him out in front of the palace in a few hours.

He went back to his own rooms, and Evan came in with breakfast. Once he ate and was dressed, he walked downstairs to be outside and make sure the horses were ready as he asked before Anwen came downstairs. He greeted the second in command of his royal guard, Bram, who was patrolling the halls on the second floor. Unfortunately, he ran into his uncle as he made it to the entry hall.

"We need to talk, your majesty," said his uncle with a scowl on his face.

"Not today, uncle. I have plans that I cannot delay."

"Do they involve the princess?" His uncle stood in front of him to block his way.

"They do. I told her I would take her riding outside of the village for a bit." Maddoc looked up the stairs to make sure Anwen wasn't coming down.,

"She will be leaving soon, won't she? I believe she wanted to get back to her kingdom."

"I am sure she will leave when she feels she needs to. I am in no hurry to see her go, so she may stay in my palace for as long as she likes." Maddoc hoped one day she would know the palace as her home.

"You can enjoy her smiles and company for a time, my king. You can even get what favors you can from her, but all your delights in her must be short-term. Whatever you might have said during your immature tantrum yesterday, I trust you actually know better."

"What I said yesterday was not some immature tantrum; it was the truth. I plan to include the princess in my future if she will allow it. As much as I respect both of you, I will not allow you and mother to decide my future. I know what I require to be a good king to this kingdom, and much of it is tied to Princess Anwen."

"I will not argue with you about this today and out in public, but you need to think very hard about what you are saying. If you are serious about running the kingdom, there is much I will have to teach you quickly. You will find out just how important it is to make the right alliances and choose your queen with more than just your own lust and desires in mind."

Maddoc shook his head and pushed by his uncle.

"If you are going to be out riding, you will need to take some guards with you. I will go find Matthias and let him know."

Maddoc stopped and thought to tell him he did not want guards accompanying him and Anwen, but he knew it would do no good. He only nodded and walked on through the front door. His horse and the one he was giving to Anwen stood out front, ready to go for a ride. The stable master was checking over the bridle on Maddoc's horse so Maddoc went over to Anwen's and made sure all was secure.

As he stepped back, content that all was as it should be, the door opened and Anwen stepped out of the palace. Maddoc turned and looked at her. She had on a long dark blue dress with a matching cloak. Her hair was braided and pulled to the side. The wind blew as she walked towards him, causing a few tendrils of her hair that had come loose from her braid to blow around her face. He thought she looked enchanting that morning. He wished there would be no guards on their ride so he could be with her alone. It was not very cold today, and there were some very secluded areas he could think of in the forest that could work very well for what he had in mind.

He shook his head a bit and tried to clear it. They could still have a very enjoyable time together. He liked his conversations with her, and he had a servant bringing some food they could take with them. That, combined with the delight he hoped she would express when she received her gift, would make for a very nice day. Perhaps later this evening he could express his love for her in other ways.

"Good morning, princess," said Maddoc as she came to stand next to him. "Are you ready?"

"I am. Do you have a horse for me?"

He nodded and took her hand. He brought her over to stand in front of the dapple gray mare. She walked forward and stroked the horse's neck.

"She is very lovely. What is her name?"

"Allinar," replied Maddoc.

"That is quite a grand name, but I think she might be grand enough to live up to it."

"So, you like her?" asked Maddoc as he too patted the mare, putting his hand next to Anwen's.

She gave the mare one last pet and walked over to stand in front of the horse. She rubbed Allinar's nose. "I like her very much. I am looking forward to spending the day on her."

"You can look forward to riding her for many years, princess. She is yours."

Anwen stopped petting the horse's nose and looked at Maddoc. "What are you talking about?"

"Allinar is yours. I would like you to have her."

"I couldn't possibly accept something so grand as this," she said her voice rising. "It is too much."

Maddoc moved very close to her and took her hand. "It is not too much. You lost your beloved horse because of me. I know this one could never take her place. I don't want her to, but I hope you will accept this gift. I would have given her to you earlier, but I wanted to make sure I picked the right one. I've been trying to decide almost since we got here."

"You really wish to give her to me? I know what a precious gift this is."

"I do wish to give her to you, Anwen," he said softly. "I know you will have to return home soon, at least for a while, and it will please me to think you will have something that will cause you to remember me from time to time."

"I will think of you almost constantly without any reminders, my king. You should have no doubt of that."

"Even so, will you please accept this gift? I already think of her as yours. It would seem strange now for you to not be her mistress."

"I do need a way to travel home," said Anwen with a grin. "I will take her, but if you change your mind, I will bring her back when I come for the winter festival."

He raised her hand and kissed it tenderly. "I will not change my mind, Anwen. She is yours."

"I wish I could kiss you," she said in a voice barely above a whisper. "I will have to show you my appreciation later."

"Your majesty, are you ready to go?" asked the guard named Bram as he walked towards them with another guard.

"You will be joining us, Bram? There is no need for someone of your status to follow me around on a simple ride."

"I received word that Matthias wished me to accompany you. I am at your service, my king."

Maddoc gave a small shrug. He thought it was a waste of the second in command of his guard's day, but if it was what Matthias wanted there was no use to argue.

"We are almost ready. I am expecting some things from the kitchen."

A young boy appeared holding a basket. He brought it close to the king, and the guard with Bram took it. He fixed it to the king's horse.

"Are you ready, princess?" asked Maddoc.

"I am if someone will help me up on my horse," replied Anwen.

Bram moved forward, but Maddoc put his arm out. He put his hands on Anwen's waist and carefully lifted her up on the back of Allinar. She gave him a smug smile as she lifted her leg over the saddle, her pants under her dress showing a bit.

Maddoc gave a quick chuckle before he walked over to his own horse and mounted. He rode side by side with Anwen through the gates of the palace. They went to the left and made it through that side of the village quickly to enter the forest that was there. The guards kept behind them, giving them enough space so Maddoc felt free to speak openly with Anwen.

"How do you find your new horse?" he asked. "You look very fetching on her."

"She is lovely. I can't wait to actually be able to gallop over an open space and see what she can do," said Anwen.

Maddoc smiled. "Come with me, my princess. I will see that you get what you wish this very moment."

He rode to the right, and Anwen went with him. After a few minutes, they cleared some trees and entered into a large open field that ran flat all the way to the river. Maddoc looked at her, and she grinned before taking off. Maddoc watched her for a moment, her braid blowing behind her as her horse raced across the field. He moved his own horse forward and urged him into a gallop, eventually catching up with the princess.

They rode along the field, running parallel with the river that was beyond them to the right. They finally both pulled up as they reached an interesting and small building on the edge of where the forest began. Anwen circled her horse around and looked at Maddoc.

"What is this place?" asked Anwen.

"It is our forest temple in this part of the kingdom. It is where we worship the goddess Alyvian. She is over natural forces. We pray to her for rain and sun for our crops, and for our winters to be short and not severe."

"It is a very interesting building. It almost looks like it sprung up from the ground."

Maddoc agreed. The walls were made of moss-covered stone, stacked together in an almost haphazard way. The roof was wood with sun-baked mud covering it. There were plenty of windows to let in light, and the door was large, made of dark wood.

"Would you like to see inside? It is normal for people of my kingdom to stop and pray to the goddess to thank her for the good harvest this time of year."

"Will anyone else be inside?" asked Anwen.

"It doesn't seem like there is. It would be a long walk from the village, and I know of no one who lives in this area."

"Then I would very much like to see it."

Maddoc got down from his horse and walked over to Anwen's. She slid down off her saddle and into Maddoc's waiting arms. He steadied her by putting his arms around her for a moment. He held her wanting very much to steal a quick kiss when he heard his two guards riding up to them.

"We are going to go into the temple to pray for a bit," said Maddoc as Bram rode up to him. "You are free to stay out here or ride around for a moment. "We will be several minutes at least."

"Very well, your majesty," said Bram with a nod.

Maddoc offered Anwen his arm, and she took it. They walked up to the temple, and Maddoc opened the door. He escorted her inside, and she let his arm go as she slowly walked towards the front, looking around. The room was bright as the windows let in ample light. The floor was many different colors of stone. There were rough wooden benches placed throughout the room for people to sit and reflect.

At the front was a small wooden table with three unlit candles. Above it, on the back wall, was a portrait of a dark-haired woman wearing a green dress. She had olive skin and black eyes. One of her hands was open holding a flame. Her other hand held a sheaf of wheat close to her body. A river ran behind her, and the sun blazed over her head.

"Is this Alyvian?" asked Anwen as she looked up at the portrait.

"It is one depiction of her. We don't really know what she looks like of course." Maddoc stood next to Anwen and looked up at the portrait.

"She reminds me of one of our goddesses, Nysal," said Anwen.

"What is she the goddess of?"

"Life, death, nature, everything. We have three gods, and we believe they all work together to watch over us and the world they created. Nysal is often depicted as holding some wheat and near a fire." Anwen turned to look at Maddoc. "How many gods do you have?"

"Three main ones, though each god has many different helpers who are also worshipped at times. They watch over different aspects of the land and our lives."

"Interesting. I don't know much about your gods, but I think I might want to find out more."

"I think it would be good if you did, Anwen. I will have to study about Lucidala's gods as well." Maddoc took her hand.

She turned towards him. "I believe we will both find many similarities in the gods we serve. I have found it is the case with a few other kingdom's gods with which I am familiar. I am growing to think we all worship the same gods but give them different names, and worship in different ways. I would like to believe it is true anyway."

"Why?" asked Maddoc as he brought her closer.

"It would mean the land is more connected than we realize. I believe we are all dependent on each other in this land. We may stand as separate kingdoms, but if one kingdom suffers, we all do in some way. You may not realize it, now, but if Lucidala was to fall, it would change your kingdom."

"You think we should all be one kingdom?" asked Maddoc.

"No, not at all. Each kingdom has its own traditions and ways. I think that is important, but we all have some common ground somewhere. We can be connected and support each other without pressing our own agendas. We worry too much about power, and who has it. Instead, we should see that all have enough and support each other."

"Is that how the people in your kingdom feel?"

"Many do. My mother certainly does. A few of our lords would like to increase their land, but the highest ones do not. I do not pretend to know my aunt's thoughts on anything."

"Would you do away with kings and lords if you could?"

"I don't believe that would be possible. There will always be those who have more than others, but it does not make them any better. A lord's life is not worth more than a farmer's life. We all have roles to play, Maddoc, and I do not pretend to even know how to change those. All I can do is try to do is use my position to make sure all are provided for as can be."

"I do wonder what it would have been like to not have been born a king. I know I should be grateful for the position I am in, and I am. I will never have to worry about hunger or no shelter, but ..."

"There are other burdens you must carry," Anwen finished for him. "You may be in a position that many would envy, but it does not mean you are not without troubles."

"If I weren't king, I could have already convinced you to marry me," said Maddoc with a small smile.

"You are very sure of yourself," said Anwen with a laugh. "I am still a princess, you know."

"Yes, but then I could come and be your consort someday. We both know you are already a better ruler than me. I would do better to support you than try to run my own kingdom."

Anwen took his other hand. "You are very capable of being a wonderful king, Maddoc. You are intelligent and even more important, you are kind. You have been a little irresponsible with your life so far, but you are very young. If you take the right steps now and listen to the right advice, I think you will do much for your kingdom and people. You could even change the whole land for the better."

"Not without you," said Maddoc as he pulled her into his arms. "Anwen, for me to be the king you think I can be, I must have you by my side."

She leaned up and softly kissed his lips. "You are capable of so much, Maddoc, even without me, but I would love to be by your side. I don't know how I will leave you in a few days."

He brought his hands up to her face and kissed her. As he pulled back, he held her face in his hands. "I don't want to be without you, Anwen. I know I can't ask you to stay here and never go back, but I wish so much you could just be here with me."

"I wish you could come with me, but you need to be here. I will come back to you. I will think of little else but you while I am gone. I will speak to my mother about you, and I will tell her what I want. When I return for the Winter Festival, I hope we can both figure out a way for this to work."

He spent a good amount of time kissing her. As his lips roamed down her neck, he wondered how awful it would be to take her in the temple. Surely the goddess would not be offended by two people so in love showing their affection for one another.

"Maddoc, we need to go. Your guards are outside, and it will be lunch soon. I would like to eat."

Maddoc kissed her one more time and nodded. They spent the rest of the day pleasantly. They ate lunch under a few trees and rode close to the river. Anwen tried out her new horse by jumping some logs. By the time they returned to the palace stables, it was almost time to change for supper. As Maddoc helped Anwen dismount, he noticed three small wagons were being loaded with some supplies.

"Where are these headed?" asked Maddoc to a servant who was overseeing the wagons being loaded.

"To Lucidala tomorrow. The prince has ordered they leave at first light."

"Are these the only wagons going?" asked Maddoc.

"I believe so, your majesty," said the servant.

Maddoc turned to look at Anwen before looking back at the servant. "I thought it would be twice as much. Are you sure this is what my uncle ordered?"

"It is fine, my king," said Anwen placing her hand on his arm. "Any amount will help my people."

"Double this. I would like three more wagons to go to Lucidala, stacked with food and medicine," ordered Maddoc.

"It is not necessary," said Anwen.

"It is," said Maddoc. "I owe you my life many times over. I want your kingdom to know just how much you are appreciated. Besides, I hope to better my relationship with your kingdom very soon. I would like to impress the queen if I can."

Anwen grinned a little as the servant spoke. "Where would you like the wagons to go?"

"Wherever the princess thinks they are needed."

"Send them to Awbrey. Leave word that if Queen Eira is present, she should see to the distributing of the supplies. If she is not present, the supplies should wait until I return. I will be leaving for Lucidala in two days."

"Very good, your highness," said the servant.

Maddoc offered Anwen his arm, and she took it. They walked back to the palace together. "I do not like to think of you leaving so soon, Anwen. It won't seem right, you leaving me."

"I have to get back to Lucidala. I am surprised I have received no word from them. I suppose my aunt does not mind me being gone. She probably prefers it. I did hope my mother would be back by now, but perhaps her letter has not come yet."

They walked into the palace and towards the stairs. As they started to climb, Maddoc's mother called out to him.

"I will go change. You should go see what your mother needs," said Anwen as she let go of Maddoc's arm.

He took her hand and kissed it. "I will see you at supper."

As Anwen walked up the stairs, Maddoc turned to greet his mother.

"You have been gone for some time," said his mother.

"I went out riding with the princess. We had a very pleasant day," said Maddoc.

"Well, there is no time to speak of it. Something has happened while you were gone. Each bedroom of the palace and guards' quarters have been searched, and something was found."

"What was it?" asked Maddoc as the queen took something out of her pocket.

She handed Maddoc a bundle of what looked like letters. He started opening them, finding the first one to be Anwen's letter to the palace in

Quinlan, stating Maddoc was injured in her palace. He opened another to find the one he wrote at Lord Aiden's.

"Where were these found?" asked Maddoc as he looked up.

"In Matthias bed-chamber," said his mother darkly. "You know what this means, my king."

"I do," said Maddoc with a heavy sigh. "Where is he now?"

"Being held in the cells under the palace. I believe the princes is speaking with him at the moment."

"I will go now as well." He turned from his mother and walked towards the stairs that would take him to the calls. His heart was heavy that one he trusted so much would turn on him.

26

~

Chapter 26

Anwen sat in her bedroom wearing her nightgown and robe. After a tense dinner in which she learned of the captain of Maddoc's guard betraying him, Anwen went to her room and fretted by the fire for a while. Maddoc had come into the dining room to eat but left soon after. She could tell how unsettled and unhappy he was. She wished she could comfort him somehow or at least talk to him about it, but she wasn't sure where he was. She didn't know when or if he would come to his room that night. So, she sat and waited in her own room, wondering when she should give up and go to bed.

She hated to lose a night with him. She would leave in two days meaning after that night, they would have only one more. Still, what was going on was bigger than her concern to spend time with the king. He needed to find out what he could to ensure his own safety. She would feel better leaving him, if she knew it was assured, he would be safe.

She was about to go to bed when the wall opened. She stood up as Maddoc walked into the room. He hurried to her and took her into his arms, kissing her without saying a word. She threw her arms around him as he continued to kiss her. He finally pulled back and rested his forehead against hers, both of them breathing hard.

"Why didn't you come to me, Anwen? I thought you would come," he said as he held her close.

"I wasn't sure you would be in our room or even if you would want to see me tonight. With everything that is happening, I thought you might have other things to do or want to be alone."

"I will always want to see you, my love. Especially when things like this happen. You don't know how your presence alone soothes me." He bent down and started kissing her neck.

"Would you like to talk about it? Maybe it would help?"

He looked up at her. "I might want to tomorrow morning, but right now there is something I would much rather do with you."

Anwen kissed him and started to pull him towards her bed when he stopped her. "Not here, Anwen. You know where you belong, and it is not some guest bed in my palace."

"You may take me wherever you wish, my king," she said with a small smile as she moved into his embrace and kissed his jaw.

He made a noise halfway between a groan and growl before pulling her towards the wall and to his room. After a late-night, Anwen slept soundly until she heard a door open somewhere in the king's rooms. She opened her eyes and looked at Maddoc who held her close. She moved to leave his bed when his grip on her became tighter. She slinked down into the bed covers as his servant, Evan, came into the room.

Evan walked into the bedroom and stopped as soon as he came close to the bed. He took a couple of steps backward and looked to the side. "I am so sorry to disturb you so early your majesty, but Prince Korben is requesting your presence as soon as possible."

"He will wait until I am ready to start my day, Evan. It will not matter if we speak now or in a couple of hours. Nothing will change in the meantime."

"Is that what you would like me to tell him?" asked Evan.

"Tell him, I will start my day soon, and I will see him at the normal time for breakfast in the dining hall."

'What if he will not take that answer, your majesty?" asked Evan still looking away.

"Am I the king, Evan?"

"Of course, King Maddoc."

"Then remind him of that if he does not like my answer. He lives and serves in the palace under my pleasure. When I am ready to speak with him, I shall."

Evan bowed. "Yes, your majesty." He turned to go, but then stopped and turned around. "Is there anything you or the princess need before I go?"

Maddoc looked down at Anwen with a smile. "No, I believe we are very well, Evan. I will not need your services at all this morning. Let Mrs. Owens know she should let the princess sleep a little longer as she had a late night."

"Very good, your majesty," said Evan as he left the room.

As soon as he left, Anwen pushed out of Maddoc's embrace. "What must he think of me, Maddoc, finding me in here like one of your other conquests."

Maddoc pulled her back to him. "He has never found me in here with any woman, Anwen. Do you think I bring just any woman here into my bed?"

"I assumed you preferred your own room for such activities," said Anwen as she looked down.

"I have bed too many women, it is true," said Maddoc as he tried to get her to look at him. "But only you have ever been in my bed. I only want you in here, Anwen. In fact, I never want anyone but you, anywhere."

"Still, he must think I am some kind of loose woman," said Anwen shaking her head. "I suppose I am."

"He will not think that at all because you are not a loose woman. I imagine he will think that he will have to prepare for my wedding soon. I believe he has already picked up on how important you are to me, he and Mrs. Owens."

Anwen wasn't sure what to say as Maddoc kissed her shoulder. She was still feeling a little embarrassed at Evan seeing her in the king's bed. She closed her eyes for a moment. Why should she feel embarrassed? She was where she wanted to be. She loved Maddoc, and she would not stop coming to him while she was there. Once she got away to her own kingdom, she planned to think the matter over. She knew she would not stop loving him, but she had to decide if she could really believe marrying him to be a possibility.

She thought that she would like to be his wife. She felt very strongly for him. She had not known him long, but she was very sure in her love for him. She was also becoming sure of his love for her. It was a little hard to believe at first. He was the king of the most powerful kingdom in their land. He was extremely handsome. He could have just about any woman he wanted. To think that he wanted her was almost too much to believe, yet with his actions and words towards her, Anwen was starting to think it was true.

"What are you thinking, my love?" he asked as he kissed further up her shoulder.

"I am thinking about my love for you. I do love you, Maddoc."

He propped himself up a bit and smiled down at her. "I love you as well, Anwen. Tell me you know it is true."

She looked up at him and raised her hand to caress his cheek. "I do believe it, though I hardly know why. I am not sure how I could ever capture your attention for long, let alone gain your love."

He moved the covers away from her, letting his hand run down the side of her body. He leaned in and kissed her gently. "Because you are wonderful in every way, my princess." He kissed her again. "You are kind, brave, and one of the smartest people I have ever met." His hand roamed up and down her body as he gazed down at her. "And my gods, you are beautiful. It is I who must wonder how you could love me."

She put her arms around him and pulled him down on top of her. "Perhaps neither of us should question it then. We should just be satisfied to be together."

"I do want you to be satisfied, Anwen," said Maddoc with a small laugh before he started kissing down her body.

"So far I have been, my king," sighed Anwen as she forgot her embarrassment from earlier and let him love her."

She worried how Mrs. Owens would act around her, but the old woman seemed to be in a pleasant mood as she dressed Anwen.

"Will you still be leaving tomorrow, your highness?"

"Yes, I plan to leave very early. I know I don't have much to pack, but I hope to have it all ready tonight. I will wear the dress I came with."

"I will have everything you need packed to go with you. Does the king plan to send you in a carriage?"

"We haven't really spoken of it, but I plan to go on horseback. He has given me the most beautiful mare, though I hardly think I deserve it."

"I am sure you do, princess. The king thinks you do, and that is all that matters," said Mrs. Owens with a smile. "If you are going on horseback, I am sure he will send some guards with you. He could not have you go unprotected. I am surprised he has not offered to go himself."

"I would not let him," said Anwen. "There could still be those out there who would try to hurt him. I do not want him to leave the safety of Quinlan until we know all is well."

"You shall have to be careful as well. Excuse me for saying it, but our king does not hide his fondness for you, and there could be those who would use you to get to him."

"I know how to take care of myself, and I am sure you are correct in that he will send guards with me. I will be on the lookout continually."

Anwen went down to breakfast where she found an empty dining room. She ate by herself, figuring that Maddoc must be with his uncle. Once she was done, she thought to go take a walk and maybe visit Lord Elias to say goodbye, when the queen walked into the room.

"Your highness, I am so sorry you had to eat alone this morning. I should have sent word to have food brought to your room," said the queen.

"It is no matter, your majesty. Have you eaten?"

"I have. I was actually looking for you. Do you have plans this morning?"

"I was going to take a walk and make some calls, but I can change that if you need something," said Anwen.

"Will you let me walk with you this morning? Perhaps we could walk to the side of the palace. There is a pretty pond there, and not many will be about this time of the morning."

Anwen agreed, and the queen called for their cloaks. They walked out of the palace with two guards at their back. When they got to the side-walls of the palace, the queen dismissed the guards and walked on with Anwen.

"Princess Anwen, I am a woman who likes to get to the point, and I believe you value truth," said the queen after they arrived at the pond.

"I am, your majesty, so whatever it is you would like to speak to me about, please do it."

"I know my son is fond of you. He does not hide it. I do not believe you are indifferent to him."

"I am not indifferent to the king at all," said Anwen as she made sure to stand straight, her arms at her side. "I believe the exact opposite is true."

The queen sighed a little and looked out over the pond. "Princess, before we continue, I would like you to know I do respect you. In a different world, perhaps you would be a good wife for my son. I have never been a very involved mother to our king, but I would like for him to be happy."

Anwen stood by the queen and looked out over the water. "You wish for me to leave and never come back here."

"I would not say that. As I said, I respect you and dare I say, even like you. I have never cared for Lucidala and avoided people from it. You may have heard that my home kingdom does not look on yours with favor."

"I have been told, though I don't understand why. I don't believe we have ever done anything to Arvelia."

"It is an old mistrust that runs deep in my people. I am not sure most even know why anymore, only that those from Lucidala cannot be trusted."

"You know, though, don't you?" asked Anwen.

"I know some of it, but I will not spend time speaking of it today as it has nothing to do with you and the king. The bottom line is he cannot have you, and you cannot have him. It may sound cruel, and perhaps it is, but it is what it is." The queen turned to look at Anwen.

Anwen felt her cheeks color a little. "Can you tell me more? If it has nothing to do with my kingdom, why wouldn't I be able to marry your son?"

"How could you be a good consort to him? You will have your own crown someday, or are you prepared to give up that crown for him?"

Anwen closed her eyes for a moment. She had thought of this a little. Sometimes she thought she would give up being queen for Maddoc. He felt worth it to her, but he had said he didn't want her to. Lucidala was a part of who she was. She was meant to be the queen someday. "I have no plans to give up my duties to my kingdom."

"I do not blame you. You have a responsibility to your people. You will need to focus on your own duties. You cannot possibly support my son as a queen consort should."

"Maddoc thinks I can," said Anwen quickly. The queen raised her eyebrow at the use of the king's name. "He thinks he can figure it out; that we can together."

The queen waved her hand and shook her head. "My son has no idea what it really means to rule. He has done little of it in his short life. He does seem to want to learn recently which I suppose I should attribute to you."

"So, you admit I have already had a good influence on the king's life?" asked Anwen.

"You have. Whatever happened on your journey seems to have changed him and for the better, but it does not change the fact he will have to marry a certain type of woman. That type of woman is not you."

"Who will he have to marry then?" asked Anwen feeling the fury grow within her.

"A woman who is well connected to a powerful kingdom. One that will grow the influence of Calumbria. He will need a woman will support him and help him rule as he needs to rule. You may have brought out some qualities in Maddoc that are helpful, but you lack some things he will have to be in order to be successful."

Such as?" asked Anwen.

"Making hard decisions that can make it feel as though you have done wrong. Playing power games that make you feel dirty, even a little ruthlessness. Maddoc is not good at any of it, and I don't think you are either. You are too caught up in the idea of goodness and fairness. I think if you did half the things I have had to, you wouldn't be able to take it."

Anwen took a step back. "This is who you want Maddoc to be? A ruthless king who only cares about power?"

"No, but I need him to have the ability to act as one on occasion. He needs a queen who understands this as well. I believe his very life will depend upon it."

"I feel like there is more that you are not telling me, your majesty."

"Perhaps there is, princess, but this is all I will tell you. You leave tomorrow. You will go home to your kingdom, and you will endeavor to think of my son no more. He may write you, but you will ignore every letter. He wants you to come to the Winter Festival, and you should come. Bring your mother as well. While you are here, you will meet the woman who will be his bride and see why I have picked her myself."

Anwen huffed. "You cannot command me in what to do, Queen Evalin. You most certainly cannot command my heart. I could no more not think of your son than breath. Maddoc has told me he loves me and wants me to be his wife. I care only for what he wants."

"My son has told you he loves you?" asked the queen with some surprise.

"He has, and I love him."

"Then you will want him to be safe and successful. Love sometimes means making a great sacrifice, Princess Anwen. Trust me, no one knows that more than me. If you love Maddoc, you will let him go."

"I am not sure I could let him go even if I tried," said Anwen. "And I don't want to try."

"You should. Go home, and spend time in your kingdom. I believe you will be a good ruler someday, and I would like to think you will improve your relationship not only with Calumbria but many other kingdoms as well. Maybe even my home. Then think about what pressures are on my son. Think about the power he wields as the King of Calumbria.

Think of what he will have to do to keep that power, because the moment some of these lords smell weakness, they will destroy him."

"I don't believe you and I define weakness the same way, your majesty," said Anwen.

"No, I don't believe we would, but what is important is in this instance my definition is the correct one. I will let you go about your day, princess, and I wish you a safe journey back to Awbrey. If you do decide to come to our Winter Festival, I hope it will be with open eyes."

"If nothing else, I appreciate your honesty, your majesty, but I do believe you are wrong. I hope to show you just how wrong you are one day," said Anwen as she turned from the queen.

"If I had any hope of that, things would be much different, your highness," said the queen before she walked away.

Anwen spent some time thinking by the pond. She would not believe that Maddoc needed the ability to be ruthless and harsh. There were times any ruler must make difficult decisions, but not with the malice the queen was implying. She did not believe Maddoc craved power. His kingdom was already powerful. If he could see to his people being happy and the land being prosperous, he would rule well.

She didn't know what her or Maddoc's future held, but she knew she could not give up hope they could be together. The more time she spent with him, the more she grew to love him. She would be leaving the next day, but she didn't believe distance would stop her feelings from growing.

She had told herself she would not fall in love with the king. More heartache was not something she believed she could handle, but now it was too late. She was thoroughly in love with Maddoc, and it could very well end in heartbreak. She would not think of it. Even if it all ended with nothing but memories, she didn't believe she would ever regret her time with him.

She walked on towards Elias's manor when she met the very man on the path. He happily greeted her and offered her his arm.

"I hear you are leaving very soon," said Lord Elias as they walked towards the palace.

"Yes, tomorrow, actually. I will leave at first light," said Anwen.

"So soon? I thought we might have a few days left to delight in your company."

"I need to get back to Awbrey. I have stayed away too long. I am hoping my mother will be returning soon, and I would not like her to worry about me."

"You will come back for the Winter Festival, won't you?"

"I plan on it," answered Anwen. "The king has insisted I come, and I would hate to disappoint him."

Elias smiled. "I think you better come, or our king may leave in the middle of all his guest and go to you. I am surprised he is letting you leave now."

Anwen laughed a little. "No one can truly tell me what to do. The sooner your king learns it, the better."

"I believe you are sadder to leave him than you let on, princess. I have a feeling our king will be in quite a mood for at least a few weeks. I shall have to cheer him somehow."

Anwen stopped him and took his hand, turning him towards her. "I hope you will watch out for him, Elias. I know he depends on you for many things despite your rivalry. I hope you will help him where you can."

"I am always ready to serve my king, princess, but you sound rather serious."

"I am serious. King Maddoc is going to take more effort in ruling his kingdom, and I believe he will need your help. You are the highest lord of Calumbria. It is time you step up into your position as well. You need to join his council and support the king."

Elias sighed and looked aside for a moment. "I know I need to act like the lord I am at some point, but I hoped to have a few more years of being a useless cad."

Anwen smiled a little. "I am sure you will still find times where you can get into mischief, but you are a grown man and the head of a great family. It is time you act like it. I think you will find more enjoyment in your responsibilities than you think."

"I am not sure you are correct about my enjoyment, but I know you are right about me needing to take on more responsibilities."

Anwen turned and took his arm again. They started walking. "I am, Elias. Your kingdom and your king need you. Promise me you will at least try."

He looked at her. "It is almost impossible to say no to you, princess. I am not sure why that is, but when you put on that lovely smile and turn those eyes on me, I find all I can do is agree with you."

She laughed fully. "You are ridiculous sometimes, but I hope you do as I ask."

"I will at least try, princess."

"Will you write me, Elias. I won't expect a letter often, but if there is something you think I need to know about King Maddoc, will you send me a message?"

He nodded. "I shall write you even if it is only to raise your spirits, and I hope you will write me something amusing back."

"Of course, I will. I think you will find I am a very reliable correspondent."

"I have no doubt about it, princess." He smiled down at her and then looked up. "I think we will have to part ways here."

"Why?" she asked as she looked at him.

"Because I believe your king is coming to claim you," replied Elias with a smile.

She could see Maddoc walking towards them. He did not look very pleased with a scowl on his face, but when he spotted Anwen looking at him, his expression softened.

"Lord Elias," said Maddoc as they met. "I see you have been entertaining the princess."

"She was saying farewell to me since she is leaving tomorrow," replied Elias as he moved his arm away from Anwen to take her hand. "I am not sure how we will deal with losing her company."

Maddoc closed his eyes for a moment before he opened them and stared at Anwen. "She has promised to come to the Winter Festival, so I have great hopes to see her again soon. Perhaps by then, someone can convince her to stay longer."

Elias looked at Anwen with a raised eyebrow. "I hope that is the case. I wouldn't mind being able to flirt with her whenever I like."

Anwen laughed again and shook her head. She leaned up and kissed Elias on his cheek. "I will miss you even though you are ridiculous."

Elias raised her hand and kissed it slowly. "If I am ridiculous around you, it is only because I am overcome by all your loveliness."

"That is quite enough, my lord," said Maddoc impatiently. "I plan to walk with the princess so you will have to give her up. Your king commands it."

"Very well, your majesty." Elias let go of Anwen's hand. "I will miss you, princess, but hope to see you again soon."

"I have had great pleasure it getting to know you, my lord. I am sure we will meet again at some point. Perhaps, you will even be betrothed by then."

"If only," muttered Maddoc.

Anwen rolled her eyes a little but took the arm he offered her. They walked on towards the palace.

"How have you spent your morning?"

"Besides my quick walk with Elias and a lonely breakfast, I had a conversation with your mother."

"I was afraid of that," sighed Maddoc. "My uncle cornered me for one as well. I had hoped to finally talk to Matthias myself since I was not allowed last night, but my uncle had other plans. He spent all morning trying to convince me to think of you no more."

"Your mother did the same with me. She gave me reasons why I should never think of marrying you."

Maddoc looked to their right and took Anwen off the path into a small gathering of trees. Whatever guards he had that were probably following him did not join them.

As soon as they were in the covering of the trees, Maddoc pulled her close. "Tell me you won't listen to her. Tell me you won't give up on us."

Anwen leaned up and kissed him. "You know by now that I make up my own mind. Your mother could never convince me not to love you; no one could. All she did was make me worried for you. The things she wants you to be are not you, Maddoc. You must be careful when I am gone. I am afraid they will try to change you into the creature they want."

He looked down at her, pulling his hand gently through her hair. "I only have to think of what is waiting for me if I stay on my present course. I will never do anything to become someone you couldn't love, Anwen. You have shown me how a ruler truly should be. I know what I need to do. My mother and uncle may be obsessed with power in some way, but I will not become so."

She leaned into him. She knew she had to go home tomorrow. She had been gone too long, but it felt so wrong to be leaving him. She felt a few tears come to her eyes thinking of it. "I don't want to leave you, Maddoc. I know I must, but it is not what I want."

He leaned down and softly kissed her forehead. "I am not sure how I will do without you, Anwen. How shall I sleep without you next to me? Who can I talk with as I do you? I am afraid I will be a horrible mess by the time you see me next."

She reached up and wiped a tear from her eye. "No, you will be the strong king I love because I refuse to believe anything else." She pulled away a little. "I am just being silly. I will see you again within a few months. We will both be busy with our duties. You will write to me, won't you? Your mother said I should ignore every letter from you, but you know I will not."

"I will write you almost every day, Anwen. Even if it is just to say how much I love you. You must write me back and tell me everything you are doing. I won't rest unless I hear from you very often and know you are safe and happy."

She nodded. He gave her a very small smile. "When will you leave to-morrow?"

"Very early. I told the stable master to have Allinar ready at first light."

"Will you not go in a carriage, Anwen? I can spare one to take you. I can send as many guards as we can spare to accompany you. I have already spoken to Bram about it since he is captain now."

"I will not take a carriage. I will ride. If I stay on the main roads, I can be home in less than three days, and I know of good inns on the way. I will take some guards, but not too many. I do not require them."

"You admonish me for thinking as you do. I had five guards with me."

"But I know the roads well unlike you. Once I am in my kingdom, I know of many places I could find safe refuge." She put her arms around his neck and smiled playfully at him. "I am not as helpless a traveler as you."

He smiled a little before he kissed her. "I would like you to be well protected. I cannot bear to think of anything happening to you."

"I am not hunted as you were. I will be home quickly. I will write you as soon as I walk into my palace." She kissed his jawline, moving her hands down to his chest.

He groaned. "And what shall I do if I do not hear from you promptly? Do you expect me to wait a few more days because you know I won't be able to? I will bring every guard I have and find you myself."

"No matter what happens you will stay in Quinlan." She kissed his jaw one more time and moved away from him. "What have you found out about the plot to kill you?"

He let out a groan of frustration. Whether it was due to her moving away from him or the answer he was about to give, she did not know. "Nothing yet. My uncle says Matthias will not speak to him, but I have not been permitted to talk with him yet."

"No permitted?" asked Anwen. "You are the king, Maddoc. If you want to speak to your guard, you should do it."

"It got too late last night, and I wanted to see you. My uncle detained me this morning, and now I only have a few precious hours left with you. I will speak to him once you are gone. All I care about now is how you would like to spend the rest of this day."

Anwen thought she should press him to go speak with Matthias, but she did want to spend time with him. What could a few more hours hurt before he spoke with the man. "I should like to spend as much of it alone with you as I can. Perhaps there is a private place we could eat lunch either in the palace or on the grounds?"

Maddoc smiled. "I know of several places we could be alone. I do have a council meeting late this afternoon, but I could skip it."

"No, you should go to it." Anwen moved back close to him and ran her hands down his arms. "Afterwards perhaps you could be too tired to take supper anywhere but your rooms. I will be preparing for my journey and planned to eat in my own room to go to bed early. Perhaps you might want an early night as well?"

He grinned down at her. "I believe I might."

27

⌇⌇

Chapter 27

Maddoc walked up the stairs towards his room at a quick place. He wasn't sure how to feel. He was anxious to spend time with Anwen but wanted time to slow down in the worst way. In just a few hours he would have to say goodbye to her. He had gotten so used to being able to speak with her whenever he wanted. He wasn't sure how he would sleep without her curled up at his side. The thought of watching her ride off tomorrow made his stomach clench and his chest hurt.

He got to his door, hoping to dismiss Evan as soon as he could. Before he could open it, his servant stepped out.

"Evan," said Maddoc as he took a step back. "Are you going somewhere?"

Evan had a very slight smile on his face. "I was informed by a reliable source that you would not require my services tonight, your majesty. I was going to spend my evening as I choose unless I was misinformed?"

"No, you are very correct. You may go spend your evening as you wish, I will have no need for you until almost breakfast tomorrow."

"Have a good evening, your majesty."

"You as well, Evan," said Maddoc as he opened the door to his room.

He walked into the sitting area just as Anwen walked in from his bedroom. She was wearing a robe tied tight across her waist. He walked up to her and took her hands as she leaned up to give him a quick kiss.

"Good evening, your majesty," said she with a smile as she let his hands go.

"You address me so formal, do you?" asked Maddoc. "I would think someone who just acted as my queen by dismissing my servant would greet me in more intimate terms."

"I did not dismiss your servant, my king. I only relayed a message from you. You did say you wanted an early night, and I know for certain you will not require any help from your servant to undress."

Maddoc gave a low chuckle as he reached for her. She moved away from his hand and walked towards the sofa. "Come and eat with me first. I would like to hear about your council meeting and anything you have found out about the captain of your guards."

She sat down on the sofa, and Maddoc came to sit next to her. She poured him a glass of wine before pouring herself one as well. As they ate together, he talked over the meeting with her. He had listened to the lords complain about the lack of healers and other skilled workers in the kingdom. When Maddoc pushed further it turned out there was little opportunity for young people to learn a trade in many parts of the kingdom. There was only one place someone could study to be a healer and that was in Quinlan.

He had an idea to set up new places of learning in different parts of Calumbria. He wanted many different young people to have the opportunity to learn if they wished. His uncle laughed at his idea as did a few of the older lords. Many, though, did not dismiss it including Anwen. She shared the ways her own kingdom trained healers. She too hoped to make learning available to more people, not just those with means.

They moved on to talking about Matthias, and Maddoc felt his mood change. He did not like thinking of his trusted guard betraying him. He needed to talk to Matthias. He had put it off partly because he didn't want to waste time away from Anwen, and partly because he wasn't ready to face the man yet.

"And did your uncle not wish to speak with you tonight over supper?" asked Anwen as she leaned back into the couch.

"I am sure he did, but I let him know I had a headache and wished an early night. He might guess the real reason why, but I don't care."

Anwen finished her wine and put her glass down. She looked at Maddoc with a serious look on her face. "I want you to know I will spend much time thinking about our future together, Maddoc. I do want to be with you, but it may not be possible."

"Anwen, I hope you will not listen to my mother or uncle. They do not speak for me, and I will not let them be the reason we aren't together."

"I am not interested in what your mother had to say. I refuse to believe you could ever be ruthless or heartless or would need to be. I am only stating the truth that a relationship between us would be difficult. We both have a lot of responsibility in our lives, you especially. I am not sure I could give you the support you need."

Maddoc put his own glass down and took Anwen's hand. "Anwen, I think you are the only one who can give me what I need. I know what you owe Lucidala, and I respect it. It will not be the reason we aren't together. I can accept that there are times we would have to be apart, but I could bear it as long as I knew you were mine."

She looked down for a moment before looking up at him with teary eyes. "No matter what happens, I am afraid I will always be yours, Maddoc."

He leaned down and kissed her before letting go of her hand. "Wait here a moment."

She gave him a curious look as he got up off the couch. He walked into his bedroom and picked up something he had left on a small table by his mirror. He hurried back to the sofa and sat down next to Anwen.

"I know you said you never wanted any promises from me, but I can't help but make you one, Anwen. You say you are mine, but I believe I have been yours for longer. I think I started to fall in love with you on our journey. I didn't know what it was at first. You brought up such intense feelings in me that I was very out of sorts for much of our trip. They made me lash out in ways I cringe to think of now.

"I can't begin to tell you of the dreams I had of you starting that first night in that small house."

"Surely not, Maddoc, you barely knew me," said Anwen with a laugh.

"I may not have known you, but I could see you. You are so very beautiful, Anwen. I think I could stare into your eyes all day and not grow tired." She shook her head as he took her hand. "My feelings for you have grown with each day that I have known you to where I know now there is no one I shall ever love as I do you."

He opened his hand and held out a necklace with a pendant on it to her. "This has been in my family for generations. Many queens have worn it. My mother never cared for it, but I think it is beautiful. I want to give it you, and I want you to wear it. Let it remind you that I am always yours. I give it to you with a promise that one day I will marry you if it is what you want."

She looked down at the pendant. It was an oval made of some sort of dark stone, almost black. On top of It in gold and red jewels was his family standard of a fox.

"Maddoc, you cannot give me something so precious," she said in almost a whisper.

"It is meant for my future wife. Who else could I give it to?" He took the chain into his hands. "Turn around, Anwen."

She hesitated for a moment but eventually turned on the sofa. He slipped the chain over her head. Her hand went to the pendant that rested over her chest. Maddoc moved her hair and kissed the back of her neck.

"I have nothing for you, my king," said Anwen as she looked down.

Maddoc rested his head on her shoulder. "I want nothing from you except for you to say you will keep my gift and wear it. It could be helpful on your journey in my kingdom. If you need any kind of help, people will know you are connected with the king."

She turned around and kissed him. "I will wear it. I will keep it as long as you wish for me to have it."

"Why do you always think I will ask for the gifts I give you back?" he asked as he kissed her forehead. "I give them to your freely. I want to give you everything I have, Anwen."

She stood up slowly and held out her hand. "I have an early morning coming, and I would like to go to bed. I hope you will join me."

He smiled up at her and nodded as he took her hand. As soon as he stood, he took her into his arms, kissing her in a way he hoped showed her just what she meant to him. She was eager with her kisses back, her hands moving under his shirt. His own went to the tie on her robe, but she stepped back before he could make any progress.

He looked up at her with a frown, but she gave him a playful grin before turning and walking into his bedroom. A moment later, Maddoc followed her. He walked in as she was undoing her robe. She slipped it off and looked at him. His eyes grew wide as he walked towards her.

"I hope you don't mind me borrowing it. You did say it was the thing you had seen me wear that you liked the most."

He stopped when he was right in front of her. He looked down at her wearing his shirt as she did on their journey. He felt his desire for her grow in such a way he needed a moment to compose himself.

"Perhaps I have misjudged," she said as she looked away.

In response he put his arms around her and kissed her, almost lifting her off the ground in his eagerness. She stumbled backward as he moved her towards the bed. By the time they fell down on it, his hands were already under her shirt, examining every inch of her body that he could. She had managed to almost pull his shirt completely off, and he finished the job for her. With more strength than he thought could come from someone so small, she managed to roll him over. She straddled him, her hands working to undo his pants.

"You know, I am not sure I ever properly thanked you for my beautiful mare, and now I have two precious gifts from you in which I much show my gratitude."

Maddoc raised up a little and looked at her. "I would normally say you owe me nothing, but I believe I will allow you to show me how thankful you are just this once."

She only laughed as she bent down and kissed her way down his chest.

The rest of the night was sweet agony for Maddoc. He experienced more pleasure than he thought possible as he and Anwen loved each other, but in the back of his mind, he knew her time with him was growing short. It came to the point where they needed to sleep, especially Anwen before her long journey, but neither seemed to be able to get enough of each other.

Sometime late in the night or very early in the morning, he finally rolled off of her exhausted. He reached for her and brought her to him, feeling her quiver against him. He bent down to look at her to find her eyes were closed. Himself too exhausted for words, he kissed her gently and held her close to him as he drifted off to sleep.

They both awoke a few hours later. He didn't want to let her go so she could leave his bed, but he knew he had to. He kissed her soundly before she rolled out of his embrace. Once she was gone, he threw on some comfortable clothes. He stood still for a moment trying to grasp what was happening. She was actually leaving. He would not sleep with her later that night. He would not be able to speak with her or hear her laugh. He shook his head. She would come back in a few months. By then he would have everything figured out, and he would convince her to stay with him.

He walked out of his room and leaned against the wall in the dim hallway waiting for Anwen to come out of her room. He did not have to wait long as she walked out dressed in her traveling dress with her cloak fastened at her neck. Mrs. Owens came out behind her. Anwen turned around and hugged the old woman. When Mrs. Owens pulled away, she smiled at Maddoc before turning and walking away from them.

"Are you ready, princess?" asked Maddoc as he offered her his arm.

"As much as I can be, my king," said Anwen. She took his arm as he grabbed the bag she was carrying.

They walked down the stairs of the quiet and dark palace. When they got to the front doors, Anwen stopped them. "Should we say goodbye here? Your guards and a few of your servants will be outside."

"I do not care what they see, Anwen. Let them all know who you are to me. I do not mind if the whole village, even the whole kingdom, knows, but if you wish me to stop here I will."

"No, I should like to see you as much as I can before I ride away," replied Anwen.

They walked out of the door and down the stairs of the palace to find Anwen's horse ready. A servant took her bag from Maddoc and worked to fasten it to her horse. Maddoc looked at Bram who was already on his horse.

"Keep close watch over the princess, Bram. If anything seems out of sorts, do what you must to keep her safe even if it means bringing her back here. You must make sure nothing happens to her."

"I will keep a close watch over her, your majesty," said Bram with a nod.

"You are sending the new captain of your guards with me?" asked Anwen. "Can he be spared?"

"I will have him watch over what is precious to me, and there is nothing dearer to me than you, Anwen. He will not be gone long."

She nodded, and they moved over closer to her horse. "I need to be going," she said as she reached out and patted her horse. She turned to look at him. "I will write you as soon as I arrive."

"And every day after that if you can," said Maddoc as he took her hands.

"Will you be such a reliable correspondent?" asked Anwen.

"I will for you. I am sure I will have a hundred things to tell you each day. I have gotten used to talking over things with you. I will need your opinion and your support, so you must write me often."

"I will, I promise," she said.

Maddoc didn't care that his guards were watching. He paid his servants no mind. He pulled Anwen into his arms and kissed her. Her arms went around his neck, and he pulled her even closer. Eventually, he pulled back placing kisses on her cheeks.

"I have to go, Maddoc."

"I know, but it is hard to let you," he said as he kissed her forehead.

"I will be back," she said before she kissed him gently.

"Do you promise?" he asked

"I do. I promise, my king. I will come back to you."

He let her go and took her hands. "I will hold you to it. If you don't come for my Winter Festival, I will ride directly to Awbrey and fetch you."

She smiled a little. "Will you help me on my horse?"

He nodded and moved closer to the animal with her. He placed his hands on her waist and slowly hoisted her up onto her saddle. She adjusted herself, swinging her leg over. "I will see you in a few months, my king." She said as she looked down at him.

He nodded, and she moved her horse forward. He watched her ride away with two guards moving to her front, and Bram with two others at her back. Before she got too far away, she looked back at him one more time, and Maddoc felt his breath catch in his chest. He had the strongest urge to call for his horse and go after her, but he knew he could not. Instead, he walked back into the palace.

He went to his room to find Evan gathering his clothes from the night before off the floor.

"Not that one," said Maddoc as Evan picked up the shirt Anwen had worn to bed. She must have just put her robe back on to walk to her room.

"What, your majesty?" asked Evan confused.

"Do not wash that one. Leave it there on the bed."

Evan looked even more confused, but he laid the shirt on the freshly made bed and looked at Maddoc. "I have laid some clothes out for you. I can have a bath drawn for you if you like. You might want to shave as well?"

Maddoc ran his hand over his chin, feeling the short beard that was starting to grow in. He was not interested in bathing at the moment. The thought of washing away Anwen's touches, and kisses were too much. "No, I shall do without a bath today, maybe tonight. I think I will let my beard go for a few more days. I might prefer to wear one."

Evan nodded. "As you wish, your majesty."

Evan left the room, and Maddoc walked over to sit on the bed. He picked up his shirt that Anwen had worn. He held it up to his nose and took a deep breath. He could smell lavender with a unique, wonderful scent mixed with it that was Anwen. He held it for a moment, thinking of the night before. He smiled a little as he remembered her bold kisses and touch. He closed his eyes and held on to the memory of holding her. He would not forget how she felt in his arms.

He sat there on his bed in his memories until the light outside told him it was time for breakfast. He put the shirt away in the drawer of the table close to his bed. It would not be washed as long as her scent lingered on it. He dressed in the clothes Evan had left him and walked downstairs to the dining hall.

He found only his mother sitting at the table. Maddoc sat down next to her and started to fill his plate.

"Where is the prince this morning?" asked Maddoc.

The queen shrugged. "I was told he would be eating on his own and spending the day outside of the palace. I wonder if he slept here at all last night." She grinned a little and shook her head. "I suppose he is where you get your promiscuous ways."

"There will be no more of that for me."

The queen kind of moved her head around. "We will see." She continued to eat. "I suppose the princess got off alright."

"She did," replied Maddoc. "I saw her off myself as the sun rose. She should be well on her way now."

The queen sighed a little. "I do hope she makes it back to her kingdom safely."

"Do you?" asked Maddoc as he looked up.

The queen stopped eating and stared at her son. "Do you think me so heartless that I would wish ill on someone like her, Maddoc?"

Maddoc shrugged. "It might fit your plans if something were to happen to her."

The queen huffed. "I might not believe she would make you a good queen, but it does not mean I do not like her or wish anything bad should happen to her. I have hopes you will come to your senses."

Maddoc made a noise but decided not to argue with his mother. He did not have the will at the moment. In the days to come, he would make sure she knew how he felt about Anwen. He would have no other for his queen than the princess, and his mother would have to accept it.

"So, uncle will be gone most of the day?"

"That is what I understood," said the queen as Maddoc stood. "Where are you going, Maddoc?"

"There is something I have been putting off that I must do now."

Maddoc didn't wait for his mother's response. He walked from the dining room out into the entry hall, down a long hall to an old, heavy wooden door. There was a guard there who bowed and took a key from his belt. He opened the door and moved out of the way so Maddoc could enter.

Maddoc walked down the stairs he found there. They spiraled around, deep into the grounds of the palace. He finally came to the bottom where he found another old wooden door. He opened it to find a guard waiting behind it. The guard looked at him.

"No one is to see the prisoner on the prince's orders, your majesty."

"Except me, I am sure. Now move out of the way."

"Prince Korben said only he should speak with the prisoner." The guard did not move.

"Am I your king?"

The guard nodded.

"Then you should move now. I am not in the mood to argue with you. I really do not wish for another prisoner in these cells, but if you do not move, I will call every guard in the palace and have you locked away for good."

The guard hesitated but moved out of the way. Maddoc walked down the long room until he found the cell that held Matthias.

Matthias was sitting on the floor with his back against the wall. He was wearing a thin, filthy shirt and a pair of pants. He glanced over when he heard footsteps. He moved his hair out of his eyes and stared up at Maddoc. A moment later he put his hands on the bars in front of him and stood up.

"Your majesty," he said in a hoarse whisper. "You have finally come."

"Yes, I should have come earlier, but I had other matters to see to. I am here now, and I want to hear why you betrayed me. Was I so awful? I know I was a useless king, but I don't believe I did anything to you to deserve to die."

"You did nothing to me, your majesty. Just as I did nothing to you." Matthias leaned on the bars. "I would never betray you or my kingdom. You must know it, my king."

"But the letters were found in your room, Matthias. You had them intercepted to track my whereabouts. What letter did you really send before we entered the forest of Lucidala? Was it to alert the others you knew to attack me?"

"No," said Matthias vehemently. "I sent a letter to the palace to let them know which way we went. Everything I have done has been to protect you."

"How did the letters end up in your room then?"

"I have already tried to tell the prince what I believe, but he refused to listen."

"Tell me then," said Maddoc shaking his head. "I will listen, but I don't know if I will believe it."

"My king, I grew up in Calumbria, in Quinlan. I was the youngest son of an impoverished lord. I may have had it better than many, but I didn't have much. All I ever wanted was to serve as a guard of the royal palace. I trained my whole life. My father could not afford me a regular teacher, so I read books and practiced on my own. I worked to make myself strong. When I finally was accepted to train as a guard, it was the happiest day of my life until the day came you named me as your captain.

"You were only nineteen, but I heard you speak with the prince. You insisted that I be chosen though I was so young. You said you had observed my hard work and dedication. You raised me up, and from that day on I swore an oath not just aloud to you, but silently to myself to protect you. I serve you, your majesty, you and Calumbria."

"What about the letters?"

"There is one amongst us that I should have known was up to something. He grew up in Parvilia with his mother's family. They were even poorer than me, but he always seemed very attached to his homeland. He said he came here to make a name for himself, and I trusted his word. I was a fool.

"I wanted him to be truthful because I liked him. He seemed driven just like me. It seems he was driven but not by devotion to you or our kingdom. I started noticing he was watching you closely in Parvilia. I didn't think much of it. It is our job to keep you in our watch, but then when you came back to Quinlan, he was always slinking around your quarters. I would find him in the oddest places, wondering why he was there, and then I would see you come by a few moments later, usually with the princess.

"He started watching her too. I heard him making comments to a few other guards about her and you. I approached him about it and told him to keep his comments to himself. He laughed it off. I kept a closer eye on him. I never caught him doing anything that I could say was completely improper or extremely suspicious until the night before the letters were found in my room.

"I heard him speaking to one of the fellow guards late that night in the hall. I didn't hear their whole conversation, but I heard enough to want to find out more. I cornered the other guard after they separated. After many hours, I finally got him to admit he was involved in helping him to find a way to get you out of the palace grounds so they could trap you. They believed they had to separate you from the princess after what happened on the road. They were prepared to kill her if it came to it.

"It was morning by the time I had it figured out. I tried to find you, but by then the letters had been found in my room, and the prince had me arrested. He would not listen to my pleas. I not only wanted my freedom, but I worried about what was happening to you and the princess. No one would listen to me or let me speak with you."

"Who was this guard you speak of, Matthias?" asked Maddoc, feeling sick. He believed he already knew the answer.

"It was Bram, your majesty. I am ashamed to say I ever made him second in command."

Maddoc walked away for a moment and paced a bit. Was Matthias telling the truth? If he was there wasn't much time. If Bram really was wanting to get to him, he had the perfect way by threatening Anwen somehow. He turned and looked at Matthias.

"You swear this is the truth?"

"I do, your majesty. I swear by my own life. You may kill me yourself if you find I have spoken false."

Maddoc sighed. He had to make a decision. He called over for the guard at the end of the hall before he turned back to Matthias. "Do you think you are able to ride with me, Matthias? Do you think you can fight?"

"Yes, your majesty. I am more than able and willing."

28

༄

Chapter 28

The sun was high in the sky and the wind not too bad. Though it was a chilly day, Anwen could bear it. Normally the sun would make her feel cheery. She was on a beautiful horse that she owned, and the road was good and smooth. The guards who accompanied her seemed like decent men. Bram was particularly chatty with her, but she didn't mind. She liked talking to pass the time on a journey. Everything about her travel should make her mood good, but instead, she felt unsettled and miserable.

Every step her horse took was another step away from Maddoc. Every hour she rode on was another hour between them. Soon she would be days from him, and it seemed all wrong. She had known him barely over a month, but now he seemed so much a part of her that it physically hurt to be away from him.

She would focus on what was ahead. Hopefully, her mother would be home soon. Anwen was anxious to see her and speak with her. She would get to meet Brennan's future wife. Anwen smiled a little. She felt she could finally look at Lachlan and Gwendolyn and not feel intense grief. She still felt betrayed, but she could see now that Lachlan was not worth her tears. She had experienced more love and pleasure from Maddoc in the past few weeks than she had over many years with Lachlan. There were many ways the man did not measure up to the king.

"Are you well, your highness?" asked Bram as they approached a pretty forest.

She smiled a little at him, trying to shake herself out of her thoughts. "I am just a little tired. I did not sleep much last night. I suppose I was anxious about the journey."

Bram nodded and gave her a commiserating smile. "Perhaps you will have a good bed somewhere tonight. For now, I think we should stop and have our mid-day meal. I am sure it will revive you."

Anwen agreed, and they turned to the side of the road into a small clearing in the trees. After securing their horses they all sat down amongst the shade against the thick trunks. Anwen pulled some bread and cheese out of her pack while Bram poured some wine into cups.

"You are fond of your kingdom, your highness?" asked Bram as he passed her a cup.

"Yes, very. It has its problems, but the people are wonderful and so resilient. I have missed much of Lucidala while I have been away."

Bram smiled as she took a drink. "You seem like a very kind person. You do not always find that amongst royalty."

"Perhaps not, but I have met a few rulers who possess much goodness. My own mother is an excellent queen who cares about her people." Anwen took another drink of her wine.

"It is a shame then that you should be caught in the middle of all of this. You seem a decent woman even if you did murder all of those men."

Anwen stopped mid-drink and looked at Bram. "Excuse me?"

"I am not saying that makes you an evil person, really. I am sure you only did what you thought was right. It turns out you were just very wrong. You wasted yourself on that king. I guess we all have our weaknesses."

"What are you saying?" asked Anwen. She put down her cup as her head started to spin slightly.

Bram sighed. "Yes, I think you might be a very decent woman, but you are still a princess. What he has planned for you shouldn't be all that bad. It is something you should expect with your position."

"What do you mean what he has planned for me? Who are you speaking of?" Her words seemed to come out slow, and she was having a hard time seeing.

"Don't fight it, princess. There is no use. You said you were tired, and I am sure you are after entertaining that king well into the night. You can have a nice long sleep and not have to worry about a thing. When you finally wake up, it will all be over."

Anwen shook her head not comprehending fully what was happening. She felt herself slump down into the grass.

"I will get the princess and take care of her. One of you mind her horse. He may want her to keep the animal. If not, we can sell it."

Anwen tried to open her eyes, but she could not do it. She started feeling herself fade away. She felt arms pick her up. She thought she was placed on a horse. Before the darkness fully took her, she pulled at the chain around her neck. She let it fall from her chest, hoping maybe someone would find it and have a clue of where she was being taken.

****

Maddoc rode hard down the road with his guards around him. Matthias, looking rough and thin, rode next to him. Maddoc's mother was furious with him letting Matthias go and leaving the palace to go after Anwen, but it was the only thing he could do. He found he did believe Matthias, and it meant Anwen was in trouble. He tried not to think what Bram and the other guards he had chosen to go with him could be doing to her.

"You must not think dark thoughts, your majesty," said Matthias as he turned to look at Maddoc.

"Am I so readable?"

"At the moment, yes. You look like you have lost all hope, but you must remember they will keep her alive to bait you to them. I suppose we are falling right into their trap."

"It does not matter. They may keep her alive, but it does not mean they will not hurt her in some way."

"You care very much for her?" asked Matthias.

"I do, and you probably already know it. I have not hidden my feelings for the princess. I did not see a need for it. I suppose I should have been more careful."

"You could not have known this would happen. How could you know you had such a viper so close to you?"

"I have plenty of vipers besides Bram all around me Matthias, and I should have protected her better from all of them. I let my uncle try to intimidate her, and my mother tell her she wasn't good enough. I doubt she will even want to see me again after this."

"I don't know the princess well, but from what I have observed, she is not intimidated easily."

Maddoc gave a half-smile to Matthias as they heard a new sound of hurried hoof beats coming up behind them. They both looked behind them to see Lord Elias with several of his own men coming towards them. His men fell in with the rest of the guards as Elias rode up alongside Maddoc.

"What on earth are you doing here, Elias?"

"You caused quite a stir leaving your palace, and rumors spread that the princess might be in danger. I saw you ride out and knew whatever the reason was, I could not let you go alone. I gathered what I could of my own personal guard and rode quickly."

"I appreciate the support, but I would hate to put you in danger. I am sure Princess Anwen would as well."

"So, she is in trouble, is she? I cannot let you get all the glory by saving the princess," said Elias with a grin. Maddoc shook his head. "My king, I promised her I would watch over you, and what is more we have been friends for as long as I can remember. I cannot let you ride out into unknown danger alone. Now tell me what is happening."

Maddoc relented. He and Matthias let Elias know all that had happened. Elias looked thoughtful for several minutes and opened his mouth as though he might say something, but in the end, he only nodded. "Then we should hurry on our way. Hopefully, they did not travel too fast."

They didn't talk much after that conversation. They rode on down the road the way Anwen would have traveled. Maddoc was worried they would take her off the path at some point. He only hoped they could tell where. He mentioned to the other men to keep a sharp eye out. It was a shame that she was the one they were looking for. The princess was probably a better tracker than any of them.

He was lost in his thoughts again hoping Bram did not harm Anwen in an attempt to subdue her. He knew if Bram tried to take her where she didn't want to go, she would not go willingly. He was praying for the first time in a while to the gods when Elias caught his attention.

"King Maddoc, up ahead. Those men don't look like regular travelers on this road."

Maddoc looked up to see two men on handsome horses. He slowed down the pace of his own horse causing those around him to slow down as well. As they came close to the men who were very familiar to Maddoc, they could hear their conversation.

"I don't understand why you made me ride ahead with you, Brennan."

"And I don't understand why you are here at all. You must see how the queen does not desire your presence, Lachlan. How could she after what you have done to her daughter?'

Lachlan looked at Brennan. "You think I don't still care for her? You know nothing of my feelings, brother. I could not stay behind wondering what was happening, wondering what the king might have done to her."

Brennan looked up and hushed his brother as Maddoc rode up to them with Matthias and Elias at his side.

"Good day," said Brennan as he rode forward a little. "King Maddoc, I don't believe you remember me as you were unconscious when we met, but I am Brennan Dunne the son of the highest lord of Lucidala. You might remember my grandfather Lord Aidan. I suppose you also remember my brother, Lachlan." Brennan looked over at Lachlan.

Maddoc stared at Lachlan for a moment before turning his gaze on Brennan. "I do remember your grandfather. I owe him quite a bit. I do not remember you, but I have heard the princess talk about your fondly." He gave a nod before he said dismissively. "I do remember your brother."

Lachlan moved forward. "We have ridden ahead of our queen's party. We were coming to Quinlan to claim our princess. We have had no word from her for too long."

"I know that cannot be true. I saw that a letter was sent when we first arrived. She wrote another a few days later to her aunt. Are you telling me you received no word?"

"We have heard nothing about Anwen since my grandfather came to Awbrey," said Brennan. "When the queen came home a week ago, she was concerned about her daughter. We left three days ago to come inquire about her at your palace. Can you tell us if she is well?"

Maddoc glanced at Elias and then Matthias. They were wasting time. "She was well when she left my palace this morning to return home, but unfortunately I believe she was inadvertently sent with some untrustworthy men as guards. I have come to try to find her."

"Inadvertently?" asked Lachlan with disbelief. "You sent our princess with some guards you didn't know well enough to trust?"

"I thought I knew them," said Maddoc. "I can assure you I would never do anything to put the princess's life in danger."

"And we should just believe that?" asked Lachlan.

"You doubt our king's word?" asked Elias as he moved his horse forward.

Maddoc shook his head as Elias continued to trade words with Lachlan while Brennan tried to calm them both down. Maddoc looked around the area they were in. They were just on the edge of a forest. He was looking at the side of the road when something caught his eye in the sun that was slowly sinking in the west. He hopped down off his horse with no mind to the men around him. He hurried to the object and crouched down. There on the ground just off the road was the necklace he had given Anwen the night before. He picked up the necklace and looked at the jeweled fox in the sunlight. The chain was broken as though it had been torn off her neck.

He looked at the area next to them, to see it looked like a good place to stop and rest. He walked over the grass, trying to remember what Anwen had told him about tracking. He looked up to see Brennan next to him.

"Some horses were here," said Brennan as he looked down at the ground. He moved forward, following some unseeable trail. "These horses did not go back out onto the road. They moved through the forest."

"Do you think you could track them further into the trees?" asked Maddoc.

"I can try, why?"

"I believe whoever has Anwen went this way." He held up a necklace in his hand. "I gave her this. Either it was ripped off of her in a struggle, or she did it herself to leave a clue."

"What are you two doing?" asked Lachlan as he rode over next to them.

"I think we might know where Anwen is headed," said Brennan. "Lachlan, you should go back and alert the queen what is happening. Tell her to travel on to Quinlan, and we will meet all of you when we have Anwen."

"You think I am going to leave knowing she could be in trouble or hurt?" asked Lachlan. "You go back and tell the queen, brother."

"She will not want to see you no matter what condition she is in, Lachlan," said Brennan angrily. "You shouldn't even be here."

"Well, I am, and I will not run away to leave her safety in the hands of you and some foreign king."

Maddoc looked at Elias who had ridden over with Maddoc's horse. Elias shook his head. "I will go find your queen with two of my men. I will let her know what is going on and escort her to the palace. I am sure our queen mother will see to your queen's hospitality. If not, she will be welcomed in my home."

"Are you sure, Elias?" asked Maddoc.

"You don't have time to argue about this any longer. If you want to see the princess is safe, you will need to hurry. You will need at least one of them to help you track, and it doesn't seem as if they will come to an agreement anytime soon."

Maddoc nodded. "Thank you."

"Saving your princess will be thanks enough, my king," said Elias before he moved over to talk to his men. Two accompanied him as he rode on down the road.

Maddoc remounted his horse. "Brennan, you should lead the way. Tell us to stop when you need us to."

Brennan got on his horse and rode towards the trees, Maddoc and the rest following him. There wasn't much conversation as all watched Brennan while he looked around constantly. He stopped a few times to check something on the ground or a tree before remounting and changing their direction. Lachlan tried to speak a few times and give his brother some advice, but Brennan only threw a scathing look at him before going back to his tracking.

Maddoc looked over at Lachlan as they rode wondering why the man was here at all. He had broken Anwen's heart and cast her aside like she was nothing. He had no right to be there, and he doubted Anwen would want to see him. Maddoc may have been curious, but he was not curious enough to start a conversation with the man.

The day was growing long, and Maddoc was afraid they would not locate her before dark. He knew if night fell, they would have a hard time recovering her at all. He was growing impatient and irritable. Worry filled him, making him feel sick and weary.

"Do you have any idea if we are close?" asked Maddoc looking at Brennan.

Brennan turned around and hushed him. He hopped down off his horse and looked at Maddoc and the others. "I will sneak ahead and see what I can. I believe they are close. Perhaps most of you should circle around and see if you can surprise them from the other way."

"I will come with you," said Maddoc as he started to get off his horse.

"Are you sure that is a good idea, your majesty?" asked Matthias.

"Good idea or not, I am going," replied Maddoc as his feet hit the ground.

"I will come too," said Lachlan.

"No," said Brennan in a harsh whisper. "You ride around with the others."

"Brennan..."

"There is no time for arguing. If you want our princess back safely to us before night falls you will go now." Brennan turned away and looked ahead.

"I will go with you," said Matthias who climbed down off his horse. "I will stay by the side of my king."

Brennan looked back and nodded. He then turned to Lachlan who shook his head but turned to look at the men behind him. He snapped his reins and the group started to the left. Brennan tied up his horse while Matthias saw to his and Maddoc's horses.

"They aren't too far ahead. We should try to see what we can before we approach them."

They all three hurried together as quietly as they could through the trees. Brennan finally stopped them by holding up his arm. He moved very quietly between two trees and made a small noise. Maddoc crouched next to him and looked. The traitor palace guards were all circled up, drinking from a few wineskins. Their horses were tied up with Anwen's behind them near some trees. They were not alone.

There were several rough-looking men sitting around the clearing. Some were near their own horses, others were cleaning swords or sharpening knives. Maddoc scanned until he found Anwen lying on the ground not too far from the guards. Her hands were bound, and her hair covered most of her face. It scared Maddoc how still she was.

All he wanted was to go to her and hold her. He wanted to see that she was breathing. He wanted to wake her up so he could see her bright eyes looking at him. He started moving forward without realizing it.

"Your majesty, wait," said Matthias as he grabbed Maddoc's arm. "You will not help her by rushing in and getting killed."

Before Maddoc could respond, the men in the clearing all looked behind them.

"What was that?" asked one of them as Bram got up.

"I don't know, but we have rested long enough. We can still get a ways into the forest before dark. Let's leave now." He walked over and picked up Anwen.

"We have to go," said Maddoc urgently.

Brennan nodded pulling a sword that was sheathed at his side. Maddoc and Matthias did the same and walked into the clearing.

"I don't think you will be going anywhere, Bram," said Maddoc as he entered the space.

Bram seemed started, and Anwen slipped in his arms. He caught her halfway, letting her dangle in his arms. "Your majesty, this is rather sooner than we expected. I don't think you've even been invited to come get your princess yet." He looked at Matthias. "I see you managed to convince him to let you out. Took long enough it looks like. I suppose your king is not as loyal to you as you thought."

"Silence, Bram. I have made my peace with Matthias, and I will continue to do so. I may have not received word of you ruthlessly abducting an innocent woman, but I will be leaving with her all the same. You need to decide if you would like me to leave you alive or do away with you like the traitor you are."

Bram pulled a knife from his belt and held it up to an unconscious Anwen. "I am no traitor. I am loyal to the people I came from. I have to protect them from power-hungry rulers like you. You will not take over my people and destroy my kingdom."

"I have no idea what you are talking about, and I'd rather not get into your delusions at the moment. All I want is to keep the princess safe with as little bloodshed as possible." Maddoc took a step towards Bram. He had to get close enough to the man so when the others got to the clearing, he could hopefully get Anwen out of danger before Bram could hurt her.

"Then you will come with us."

Maddoc took one small step forward. "I will come with you if you leave the princess here with these two men."

"No, the princess will come with us. She is needed somewhere, but if you come now, I will not harm her in any way."

"Where is she needed?" asked Maddoc as he stepped a little closer. "For that matter, what have you done to her?"

"It is not your concern where she is needed. Indeed, you might be beyond such concerns soon. Right now, all you need to know is she is fine.

She will sleep for a good long while, but there shouldn't be too many bad effects, not if I gave her the right amount."

Maddoc glanced over at Brennan who was looking into the forest behind Bram. He gave a very slight nod that Maddoc just caught. Before Bram could react, Maddoc reached forward and grabbed Anwen as men on horses burst through the back tree line. Bram turned for one second, allowing Maddoc to wrench Anwen free. Bram moved forward with his knife out striking Maddoc in the side. Maddoc stumbled, and Anwen fell to the ground.

Maddoc did not stop to see how deep or serious his wound was. He could barely feel it. He held up his sword just as Bram pulled out his. Their swords met as men all around jumped own off their horses to fight. Maddoc had trained many years, but he had never been in a real fight. Bram was a well-trained palace guard. It took Maddoc a few moments to get his bearings, but when he did, he found his instincts took over.

He blocked Bram's strikes and then made his own moves. Their swords met, and they stared at each other for a moment before they broke apart and circled around. Maddoc's hand went to his side as he felt the first pains from his wound. He shook it off and went to face the man again when Matthias appeared at his side.

"You can't finish me yourself, your majesty?" laughed Bram. "You have to call in your pet here."

"He could, and I should let him," said Matthias as he held up his sword. "But I have sworn my life in protection of the king so you will have to deal with both of us."

Bram moved towards Maddoc as Matthias moved towards Bram. Maddoc blocked Bram's move. Bram pushed off sending Maddoc falling on the ground. Maddoc felt another sharp pain from the wound at his side. He put his hand on it and pulled away to find a good amount of blood. He paid it no mind and stood back up. He watched for a moment as Matthias and Bram fought, looking for his opportunity to help. He finally found it when Bram slipped very slightly on an uneven part of the ground.

Maddoc lunged and hit Bram's arm. Bram turned in surprise, and

Matthias was able to take advantage and plunge his sword into Bram's chest. He let it sit there a moment before pulling it out, letting Bram fall to the ground dead. Maddoc's hand went back to his wound, feeling how wet it had become with blood.

"Your majesty, you are hurt," said Matthias in alarm.

Maddoc looked down at his hand and took a deep breath. It did appear as though he was bleeding a fair amount. "It is nothing. I will be fine." He wiped his hand on his shirt and looked around. He spotted Anwen still laying on the ground. Lachlan was hurrying towards her as all the rival men seemed to be dead or subdued.

Maddoc could not let Lachlan be the first face Anwen saw if she woke up. He would not have it. He pushed past Matthias who was standing in front of him. He jogged over to Anwen and knelt down pushing Lachlan away who had gotten there at the same time. He gathered Anwen into his arms and carefully pushed her hair away from her face. He could feel her breathing, and he gave a sigh of relief.

She stirred a little, and he put his hand up to her cheek. Her hand slowly came up and held his as her eyes blinked open. "Maddoc?" she asked quietly.

"Yes, my love. I am here. You are safe."

She sat up a little very slowly as she continued to blink her eyes. She finally opened them fully and stared at him. Looking down, she saw the bloodstain on his hand. "Are you injured?" she asked.

"Yes, but it is nothing. All that matters is that you are here with me."

"Where are you injured?" she asked looking him over.

"It is my side, but it will be well. You do not need to worry."

She paid him no mind and looked down to where his shirt was torn and wet. She raised it as he hissed a bit. She gasped as she looked at it. "This is not nothing."

"Your majesty, we need to get you help," said Matthias who was now standing over him.

"There is no time," said Anwen as she raised his shirt further. She placed her hand over his bleeding wound and closed her eyes.

"Anwen, what are you doing?" asked Brennan who was standing next to Matthias.

She said nothing. She kept her hand on Maddoc's wound and her eyes closed. Maddoc stared at her. He didn't know if it was her presence or if he had lost too much blood, but his pain seemed to be lessening. All that mattered to him at that moment was her. He placed his hand over hers that was on his wound. It felt warm, and he could almost feel something running through it.

She opened her eyes and stared at him. He gave her a smile which she returned. She lifted her hand and though it was covered in blood, his side was as if nothing had happened. He looked down at it and ran his hand over it. There was no pain, no wound, just pink skin.

"Anwen," said Brennan as he crouched down. "Your Gift, it is fully released."

"I am tired," she said quietly in response. She closed her eyes and fell against Maddoc.

"Anwen," said Lachlan in a worried tone as he reached out for her.

Maddoc encircled her in his arms, blocking his touch. He stood up slowly, picking Anwen up. "We need to get her back to the palace so she can rest."

"Let me get your horse, your majesty," said Matthias. He walked away.

Brennan stood close to Maddoc and looked down at Anwen. "She healed you. She used her Gift. She hasn't been able to fully use it before."

"I know," said Maddoc. He was not concerned about her Gift or any injuries he had suffered. All he wanted was to get her somewhere she could rest.

"This will change everything," said Brennan excitedly. "She could save our kingdom."

Maddoc looked up at this. He knew she was already important to Lucidala. Now she would become completely essential. He tried not to think of what that would mean for their future. It did not matter now. He wanted to brush it aside as Matthias brought over his horse. He wanted to believe it would not matter. Anwen was his future. He was sure of it. As he rode towards his palace with Anwen in his arms, he told himself over and over, they would figure it out. No matter what he had to do, he would have Anwen as his wife.

29

Chapter 29

As Anwen woke up she felt a soft hand grip hers. Her eyes opened to see familiar deep brown eyes looking at her. She smiled up and tried to sit up a little.

"No, my darling, you must not rush yourself. The healer said you will be groggy for some time."

"Where am I?"

"In the Grand Palace in Quinlan. The king brought you here to this room. He said you would be comfortable here as this is where you stayed before."

Anwen nodded. "And Maddoc, is he alright?"

Her mother sat up a bit, but kept a hold of her hand. "King Maddoc is very well. I hear it is thanks to you. Brennan told me what happened. You do remember, don't you?"

"A bit, I think. I remember waking up and seeing Maddoc's face. He was injured, and it was bad." Anwen looked down for a moment. "I healed him, didn't I?"

"Yes, you used your Gift fully. Brennan told me he believes it was the first time."

"It was. I don't know why I knew I could do it, but I did. I had to save him," said Anwen.

"I think you and I will need to have a longer discussion about the king when you are feeling better, my lovely one. Right now, you just need to rest and get better," said her mother as she let go of Anwen's hand fussed with her blankets.

Anwen grabbed her mother's hand. "I am just so happy to see you, mother." Anwen felt a small tear escape her eye. She had wanted her mother so many times over the past year. Having her near now was overwhelming.

"My poor, sweet daughter, you have been through too much this past year. I never would have left you alone had I know all that would happen. I am so sorry, Anwen. I have failed you as your mother."

"No, you did what you had to for our kingdom. You could not know all that would happen." She licked her dry lips. "You must have been very angry with me when you heard I left with the king."

"I was angry, but not with you. Especially not after speaking with Brennan and Lord Aidan. Of course, you could not leave the king to fend for himself, but you never should have been put in that position. I am very angry with my sister. I had no idea she would be so cruel and unfeeling. She did not represent us well in that. I have apologized to the queen mother already. I believe she accepted. It helps that you have saved her son multiple times."

Anwen glanced over at the pitcher of water on a table near the bed. Her mother poured a cup of water and helped Anwen to drink. "He saved me too, mother."

Her mother smiled a little. "He does seem fond of you. He carried you in here himself."

"Mother, I...," started Anwen but her mother cut her off.

"I told you we would speak of the king later. You do not need to worry about it now."

"I am not worried about it, but I do not want to hide anything from you," said Anwen.

"You cannot hide anything from me, Anwen, even if you tried. I know what you are going to say. Your feelings are written on your face, but we will speak of it later when you are stronger." She sighed a little. "You've had so much heartbreak already. I can't bear to think of you going through anymore."

"I suppose we all have to go through it at some point, but I don't believe Maddoc will cause any for me, mother."

Her mother only smiled down at her and kissed her cheek. "Rest now. Unless you are hungry? I could have some food brought into you."

Anwen shook her head. "I only want to sleep." She saw a little movement behind her mother close to the wall. "Mother, you should go to your own room. You must be tired from your travels. I am well. I just need to rest."

"Are you sure, Anwen? I would hate to leave you."

"I am very sure. I will do nothing but sleep. You would do no good to sit here next to me and be restless all night. If I need anything I know how to summon a servant."

Her mother stood. "You are sure?"

"I will rest better knowing you are comfortable. You can come here and eat breakfast with me. I am sure I will be hungry by then."

"Alright. If you awaken in the night and need me for anything, please have me summoned. I will come the moment you send for me. I will not leave you so alone again, Anwen."

"I love you, mother."

"I love you, my daughter," replied her mother before bending down and kissing her cheek.

She walked slowly from the bedroom. Before she left through the door, she turned and looked at Anwen. Once Anwen heard the door to the front room open and close she whispered into the night. "She is gone."

Maddoc opened the wall fully and walked out. He hurried to Anwen's side and sat on the bed, taking her hand and kissing it. "My love, I am so sorry."

"What are you apologizing for?"

"I sent you off with a traitor. If I had spoken to Matthias earlier as I should have, this never would have happened. I don't know what I would have done had they harmed you, Anwen."

"They didn't. All they did was give me something to make me sleep. You are truly well, aren't you?"

"Yes, thanks to you. You saved me again," said Maddoc as he held her hand. He was quiet for a moment. "You used your Gift fully."

"I know. I don't know why, but I knew I could for you. I was afraid you wouldn't make it somewhere to get help. I can't lose you, Maddoc."

"I can't lose you either, Anwen. We will figure everything out later, but for now, you should sleep."

She blinked her eyes and looked up at him. "I wish I could sleep in your bed. I have gotten used to it, and this one feels strange."

He stood up and pulled her covers down. Putting his arms under her, he picked her up.

"What are you doing?" asked Anwen as he moved towards the wall.

"I shall always give you whatever you want if it is within my power. This request is rather easy. He shifted her a little as he opened the wall before picking up a candle while keeping a hold of her. He walked through the open wall, holding the candle carefully away from her. After shutting the wall, he took her to his bed-chamber. He carefully put down the candle before laying her on his bed.

He put out all the candles in the room and threw a log on the fire while Anwen got under the covers. He crawled into bed next to her and took her into his arms. She snuggled down into him and looked up at him.

He bent down and kissed her lips gently. "Sleep now, my princess. I will make sure you are up in time to get back into your room before anyone notices."

"I am beginning not to care if they find me right here," said Anwen sleepily.

She felt Maddoc laugh quietly. "I am glad to hear it."

She spent the next two days quietly. She would eat in her rooms with her mother and sometimes Brennan. Maddoc would come to see her officially in the afternoon, but he would sneak in at different times. She received Maddoc's mother a few times, though not for long. She was very formal but friendly with both Anwen and her mother. Anwen took at least two naps a day, still feeling groggy from whatever was given to her. At night, Anwen slept in Maddoc's arms in his bed.

As she grew stronger, a date to travel was set. Three nights before she would leave, Anwen laid in Maddoc's arms. It had been the first night they had done anything but sleep in his bed, and while she was feeling content at the moment, she worried about being apart from him.

"I thought last time was bad when I had to leave you, but now I believe it will be worse," she said as he held her close.

"I don't even want to think of it, but I know I must. I'm scared to let you go, even more so than last time."

"I will be safe this time. We know now who was after you, and from what your mother says, the group is being subdued in their own kingdom."

"I still wonder where the group in Parvilia got the idea I had any designs to invade their kingdom. I did consider their princess as my bride, but I had no thoughts to rule over them," said Maddoc.

"They have no direct heir to their throne. For some reason, their law forbids the princess to rule. I guess when you came to pay court to her, they thought you had your eye on combining the Parvilian crown with their own."

"It was not in my head at all. I was only following my mother's and uncle's wishes. I know they would like to spread the influence of Calumbria, but neither talked to me of taking over that kingdom."

"Whatever the reason, I hope the Parvilian king is able to stop those rumors and those who would harm you. You will still have to be careful, my king," said Anwen.

"Matthias barely lets me out of his sight if I am out of my room, and I understand you commanded Elias to watch over me. I am well looked after. I only worry for you. You must watch out for yourself. I know you are not good at it."

"I will have many traveling with me, and now it seems as I am more precious than before. With my Gift fully awakened, I will be needed in much of my kingdom."

"You are precious to me Gift or no Gift, Anwen," He held her even tighter. "I do know that this new development must make it harder for you to choose to be with me."

"Why?" asked Anwen.

"You will be even more needed in Lucidala than before. You will want to spend all your time there to help your people. I cannot stand in the way of you doing what you know is right."

Anwen pulled away from him a bit so she could look at him better. "Maddoc, I have always felt a large responsibility for my kingdom, and I always will. I will want to do what is right for Lucidala, but when you talk about knowing what is right only one thing comes to my mind. It is you. Being with you like this is what feels right. I know I said I would go home and think it over, but I don't believe I have to. There are things I need to work out and time I will need to see to my kingdom, but the only future I see for myself includes you."

Maddoc smiled down at her. "I feel the same way. I will do anything to be with you, Anwen. I will travel with you to your kingdom as often as needed. I will endure times we have to be apart, but you must be my wife. It must be soon."

She kissed him. "Let me go back to Lucidala and see what I can do for the people and the land for the rest of the season. You can work on ruling here and setting up your council. You can talk with your mother and even uncle, and try to get them to support you in your decisions. When I come for the Winter Festival, if you still want me, we will figure out the way together."

"And you will not leave me again after you come back? You will stay here until we wed, or I will travel with you back to Lucidala. We will do whatever you want," said Maddoc.

"I don't think I will be able to leave you again after this time. Not if you truly want me."

"I will always want you, Anwen. Do not forget it."

****

Maddoc walked down the hall after lunch, heading to his study. He wanted to write some thoughts down before his next council meeting.

"King Maddoc," said Queen Eira from behind him.

Maddoc turned around and looked at the woman. She was giving him a kind smile that seemed to make her already lovely face impossibly beautiful. As she walked towards him, he studied her. Her hair was much like Anwen's, golden, full, and wavy. Anwen had inherited her mother's mouth as well. They both had full pink lips. There was something about the shape of the queen's eyes that reminded him of Anwen as well, but that is where the similarities ended.

Queen Eira was a commanding presence. She was tall for a woman with a graceful figure. She moved as though she was almost floating, and every gesture she made seemed to be done to captivate. She was a beautiful woman, but Maddoc thought he preferred the daughter in looks. He liked Anwen's trim and small figure. Anwen smiled easier and wider. Above all, while the queen's eyes were a lovely dark brown, they were nothing compared to the bright honey-colored eyes of Anwen.

"Can I do something for you, Queen Eira?"

"I was hoping you and I could speak for a moment. If you are busy, we can find another time before I leave."

Maddoc needed to impress the queen somehow. He wanted Queen Eira to approve of him as a husband for her daughter. "I have nothing so important that I cannot speak with you. Will you come into my study?"

She nodded and walked forward with him. He opened the door of his study, and she glided ahead of him into the room. She waited for him to pick a place for them to sit, and he chose the area in front of the fireplace instead of his desk. He offered her a large chair next to the fireplace and she took it. He sat down close to her and waited for her to speak.

"King Maddoc, you can probably guess why I wish to speak with you," said the queen.

"I can think of a couple of reasons why, Queen Eira," replied Maddoc.

"True, and to be honest there are at least two things I would wish to speak with you about, but one is forefront on my mind. It has to do with the most precious thing to me in this land."

Maddoc smiled a little. "I believe I know to what or who you are referring. She is very precious to me as well."

The queen folded her hands in her lap. "I have guessed that you might have grown attached to my daughter, and from what I have seen, I believe she has feelings for you as well."

Maddoc decided being completely honest and open was the best course with this woman. "Attached doesn't even begin to describe it, your majesty. I believe Anwen has become quite necessary to me."

"Can you tell me why?"

Maddoc sat back a little. "Surely you know how wonderful your own daughter is?"

"I do, but I would like to hear why you think so," replied Queen Eira.

Maddoc looked down and thought about Anwen. "Well, she is beautiful. I think she is the most beautiful woman I have ever met. I mean no slight to you, of course, but there is no more pleasing sight to me in this land than Anwen. She is intelligent, kind, and charming. She tells me the truth when I need to hear it no matter how hard it might be."

Maddoc paused for a moment and stared at the queen. "I have not been a very good king in my short life. I have done things I am not proud of. I have wasted my time and used people. I have always felt some shame in it, but before I met Anwen, I could easily brush aside that shame. She made me want to confront it. She made me see how truly unhappy I was in my present course. She inspires me to be a better man and king."

Queen Eira nodded. "That was a very good answer, King Maddoc. I was not expecting such an answer. It makes it harder for me to do what I came in here to do."

"And what is that?"

"To tell you to let Anwen go," said Queen Eira as she unfolded her hands and put them on the armrests. "It is not that I did not think your feelings for my daughter were not real, but I believed they might have been shallow. She is a beautiful woman, though she doesn't believe it, and I know how charming she is. She has left many men a little heartsick for her though I believe she is mostly unaware of it." The queen took a deep breath. "Now I see that I was wrong. I think you might see my daughter better than most people."

"You can tell me to let your daughter go, but I don't believe I can do it. I also know Anwen feels the same way. As much as I respect you, if the princess says she will have me, that is all I need. I will find a way to be with her. I would much rather have your support, but I will marry your daughter even without it."

The queen laughed a little. "You may be young and inexperienced, but you are still a king I suppose, and a powerful one at that." The queen's smile faded. "I am sure you know that my daughter has been through much heartbreak in her life. I know she loves me, but the bond she had with her father was beyond anything. When he died, she was devastated. Then there is this business with Lachlan." The queen paused and closed her eyes for a moment to compose herself. "It hardly seems fair all that has happened to her. She deserves none of it."

"I agree. She deserves everything that is good, and I will see that she gets it."

"She will be the next Queen of Lucidala, you know. Others may talk of Gwendolyn taking the throne, but I will only leave it to my daughter. She has the support of all the highest lords in Lucidala including the highest of them all no matter what his son might have done. With her unlocked Gift, the love for her will only grow. Will you want her to give up her crown?"

"No," said Maddoc adamantly. "A big part of who she is, is tied to Lucidala. I would never want to sever that tie. I know our life together will have some difficulties, but I am willing to do anything to make it work. If she is by my side and I by hers, I think the rest will work itself out."

"Your mother has other plans for you, I believe?"

Maddoc nodded with a sigh. "She and my uncle."

"She has spoken to me of these plans, and warned me to tell my daughter to leave and forget you." She shook her head. "As if I could tell Anwen what to do."

Maddoc chuckled. "So, what will you try to tell your daughter to do?"

The queen stared at him for a moment. "Your mother mentioned who she has in mind for you, and I believe the young woman is coming to your Winter Festival. You have invited Anwen and my whole court as well. We will come if you still wish it."

"I do," said Maddoc.

"Here is what I ask you, King Maddoc. At the Winter Festival, do not show Anwen too much favor out in the open. You do not need to be cold or cruel, but do not let your true feelings for my daughter be known too early. I would not like her to become a target from the other ladies who will be visiting.

"Spend time with the Parvilian princess and the other high-born young ladies that will come. Make sure a life with Anwen is what you really want. I will ask Anwen to do the same with you. I will tell her to meet other men during your festival. You both could make matches that would fit your lives much easier. You could find a queen who could be at your beck and call and increase your influence. Anwen could find a consort who would be able to live full time in Lucidala and give her all his attention.

"Towards the end of our time here, if you both feel as though you would rather do the hard work of being together then I will support you."

Maddoc smiled widely. "I know my feelings for your daughter will not change, Queen Eira. I also trust in Anwen's love for me, but if Anwen agrees to this, I shall do as you ask."

"Good. Anwen will agree. She is a sensible woman,\ and does like to please me when possible. You should tell your mother about your plans as well. It might help smooth things over with her when the time comes."

The day came for the group from Lucidala to return home. Maddoc spent the early morning hour in his bed with Anwen, wishing he could keep her with him somehow. It felt even more wrong than the first time to let her go.

"These few months will be too long, Anwen," he said as he rubbed his hand down her bare side.

"They will go by faster than you think. You will have much to keep you busy."

"And then when I finally do see you again, how will I keep myself from not staying by your side constantly?"

"It will not be easy, but it is for the best. My mother is right in that we both need to be sure."

"But I am very sure, Anwen. I don't need to spend time around selfish, boring women to know you are preferable in every way." He kissed her forehead as he ran his hand through her hair.

"Still, if we do this, we will gain my mother's support which will mean much to me. It might even help with your mother. We may never convince your uncle, but everything will never be perfect."

"It will be close enough if I always have you," said Maddoc with a grin as Anwen moved up a little so she was face to face with him.

"Besides, we will still have this at night. I am sure you will put me in my preferred room when I visit. We might have to hide some of our feelings during the day, but in here all that will matter is you and me."

She kissed him. When they finally broke apart Maddoc said, "I will find other ways we can sneak off and spend time together. I will need it after trying to be pleasant with some of those women."

"I am sure I will bear my own trials speaking with some men who are in attendance."

"You will be charming and easy with all of them, and I will have to watch it," said Maddoc with annoyance. "How I shall not grab you and pull you away, I do not know."

"You will just remember that I am yours already," said Anwen as she touched the pendant on the necklace she wore. Maddoc had it fixed as soon as he could.

"And I belong to you, my love. Don't ever doubt it."

The morning was cold, gray, and windy as Maddoc stood outside by his mother and uncle to see the Lucidalans off. Anwen stood next to her mother. Maddoc took Queen Eira's hand and kissed it, wishing her a good journey. As he did, his uncle gave his own farewell to Anwen. Maddoc glanced over and did not like the way his uncle's lips lingered on her hand or the smile on the prince's face as he looked up at Anwen.

When Prince Korben finally moved, Maddoc took his place in front of Anwen. As he did, Lachlan moved closer to her causing her to look at the man with a grimace. She moved up a little, closer to Maddoc.

"Thank you for your hospitality, your majesty. I have enjoyed much of my time in your palace."

"All thanks should be to you, princess. I owe you my life many times over. I shall see that you are rewarded for it continually," he said with a small smile.

She gave him a playful smirk. "I look forward to continuing to improve the relationship between our two kingdoms"

"I as well," said Maddoc as he kissed her hand. He held it for as long as he thought possible before he let it go. He straightened up and stepped back to look at Anwen and the queen. "More supplies will continue to come to your kingdom from Calumbria through the winter. Let me know where they are most needed."

"We will, your majesty. You are very kind," said the queen.

"All I want is for all to know that they are due to the bravery and goodness of their Princess Anwen. Calumbria and I could never thank her enough."

"I shall see it is known," said Queen Eira. "Now I believe we must be going."

She turned and a guard helped her to mount her horse. Maddoc automatically moved towards Anwen, but it was Lachlan who put his hands around her waist to lift her up in her saddle. Maddoc felt a small bolt of rage and jealously move through him, watching the worthless man put his hands on Anwen.

Anwen looked down at Maddoc from atop her horse. "Thank you again for this lovely creature, King Maddoc. I look forward to seeing you at your Winter Festival."

"I will count the days, princess," said Maddoc as he stared at her, wanting nothing more than to pull her down from her horse and kiss her.

She nodded at him as Queen Eira moved her horse forward. Anwen followed with the rest of their group, and Maddoc stood still watching her go until she was out of sight.

CPSIA information can be obtained
at www.ICGtesting.com
Printed in the USA
LVHW022034240521
688343LV00011B/1834

9 781087 880341